Ne

We Live

ISBN-13: 978-1530320783
ISBN-10: 153032078X
Gappa and Kragt Publishing © 2016
gappaandkragtpublishing@gmail.com

To all the Storytellers
Who let us live in their worlds,
While helping us learn
How to navigate our own.

The two children were so fond of each other that they always held each other by the hand when they went out together, and when Snow-white said, "We will not leave each other," Rose-red answered,
"Never so long as we live,"
-The Brothers Grimm

Prologue

Sweat beaded on his forehead as he leaned closer, concentrating on his work. This story had been hard earned, and difficult to execute. But he had loved every second of it.

All good things must come to an end, and it was almost finished now. He stood, knees cracking, walked over to the river, bent down, and let the cool water take the red off of his gloves. This was it, the deepest place in the river. The final setting of his story.

He straightened again and looked back at his masterpiece. She glowed a little bit, the dawn light illuminating and drenching her ebony skin with gold. He walked over to her and ran his fingertips over her eyelids, closing them into peaceful sleep before touching the salt that had spilled over and dribbled down the corner of her mouth.

The body of April Marsden was rolled into the water and the story came to a close.

Chapter One

The orange morning sun glinted off the smoky gray hood of the 1967 Chevelle. Coby Anderson sat on the edge of the driver's seat, one boot planted on the floorboard, the other on the asphalt of the motel parking lot. She glanced over the open door of the car toward the old gas station that was conveniently located right next to the motel. She'd bought breakfast there, and it now sat in a paper bag on the roof of the car, next to one of two coffee cups. Coby held the other.

The door to last night's motel room swung open, and a dark-haired young woman stepped out, hauling a duffel bag and a laptop case.

Coby stood, grabbed the other coffee cup off the car, and opened her mouth to speak.

"Amboy, Indiana," the woman said, jutting her chin toward the trunk as Coby rounded the car, keys in hand. "That's where we're going."

Coby smirked. "Okay then, Professor X. What am I thinking now?"

"You'd better be thinking that you're happy you got me good coffee."

Coby rolled her eyes and held out the cup. "It tastes like the inside of an old soup can, but you can't blame me for that."

LJ slammed the stuffed trunk closed and reached for the cup in Coby's outstretched hand. She pulled her dark Aviator sunglasses down to her eyes from their perch on her head and wrinkled her nose as she sipped from the Styrofoam. "Next time we find a joint with decent coffee."

"We can't afford your standards for decent coffee." Coby snatched the white bag off the roof, slid into the driver's seat, and shut her door with a creak and a slam. "Now, what's in Amboy?"

LJ joined her on the passenger side, set her cup on the dashboard and shimmied out a rolled up newspaper from the back of her jeans. "Apparently there's an annual go kart race through the town square, a brat eating contest, and a cemetery called 'Friends.' Get on 72 and head east." She picked up her coffee again as Coby started the engine and the Chevelle snarled to life.

"'Friends Cemetery'?" Coby cranked her window down and rested her elbow on the door, adjusting her glasses with her fingertips. She switched her hands on the wheel and grabbed her cup, sipping it with a grimace.

"Technically that's in Jackson. But you should see the town limits of this place, they're ridiculous. Anyway, Ron gave us our usual deadline, so we need a piece by Monday."

Coby nodded distractedly. "When was the last time you talked to our editor-in-chief?"

LJ slammed her head against the headrest. "That's your job. Officially. I'm officially making it your job."

Coby laughed and let the radio's low volume fill the car.

The landscape gradually began to turn from skyscrapers and office buildings to shopping centers and home improvement stores to housing developments and school buildings. Inside of an hour, Springfield, Illinois faded in the rearview mirror, traffic scattered, and the highway stretched out before them.

The coffee turned cold long before either of them worked up the stomach to finish it. Greasy breakfast burritos were eaten from the convenience store paper bag, which ended up in a wad on the backseat. LJ reclined her seat and crossed her cowboy boots on the dashboard, eyes closed behind her sunglasses, hair fluttering in the wind from the open windows. Coby changed the radio station when it turned to white noise, settling back once she found a Bob Seger song playing.

When they cruised past a blue and red "Welcome to Indiana" sign, LJ adjusted her seat and sat up. "I think you should take the piece on the go kart race. I've got too many ideas for the brat eating contest."

Coby rolled her eyes. "Do you ever *not* think about work?"

LJ slid her sunglasses off and rubbed the bridge of her nose. "We spend half our lives driving around the country *for* work. Personally, I find it the best time to plan out my writing." She replaced the glasses and turned them toward Coby. "What were you thinking about?"

Coby hunched her shoulders to her ears, then rolled her neck to relieve the tension. "We should get a dog."

"What?"

"Maybe some kind of hound. They like laying around a lot, right? We'd need one that doesn't need to run around all the time."

LJ snorted. "There's no way we're getting a dog."

"Who died and made you queen? It's my car."

***

"I'm just saying, cuddly cuteness, endless love and affection –" Coby waggled her eyebrows at LJ as she pulled the keys out of the ignition and threw open her car door, stepping out into the parking lot of a small, old-fashioned diner.

"Endless hair and drool, vet bills, bags of poop –" LJ rolled her eyes, yanking her boots back on and unfolding herself from the car.

Coby arched her back until it popped and slid a hairband off of her wrist, throwing her hair up in a fast ponytail. "I have never heard so many pathetic attempts at excuses in my life," she said over the roof of the car. "Methinks the Lady doth protest too m –"

"Can you just lay off the dog thing Coby, please?" LJ said, slipping her sunglasses on top of her head and stretching as she surveyed the local diner. "This place looks old... I bet you everyone inside knows what's worth knowing and a whole lot more about this town," she said, leaning back in the car and rummaging for a pen and note pad.

Coby sighed dramatically, planting her hands on her hips. "LJ! Can we please just get some food and save the interview?" They had been driving in the car for about four hours and the only thing Coby wanted to focus on was supper. Actual supper that wasn't beef jerky or apples or the bag of tootsie rolls that they had grabbed at their last pit stop.

LJ narrowed her eyes at her. "My mind needs something to focus on other than your five-year-old begging," she said, sticking her tongue out at her.

Coby blinked at her and a grin broke across her face as she shook her head. "Oh, *I'm* the five-year-old?"

"Yes," LJ said, with an exaggerated snooty expression before closing her car door and sliding the notepad and pen into her bag. "You are."

Coby chuckled and led the way up to the restaurant, swinging open the door and holding it open for LJ. "M'lady."

LJ shook her head and strode past her. "Dope."

Chapter Two

Clyde Burkiss slumped behind the wheel of his car and stared blearily at the red light. Seven a.m. was too early to go into work, and despite his usual enthusiasm for all things by the book, he planned to make that very clear the second he walked into the building.

He rubbed his bloodshot eyes and ran the hand across the rest of his face, a jolt of panic spiking his pulse as he suddenly realized he'd forgotten to shave. As if breaking regulation wasn't bad enough, he was sure to look sixty-seven with the day old beard, undoubtedly streaked with more gray than his hair. He was only thirty-five, but his hair had been convinced he was well over forty since he'd hit drinking age.

At least it wasn't falling out. Yet.

Burkiss pulled into the police department parking lot and parked in the back, stuffing his keys in his pocket as he headed around the building to the front door. He gave his parked cruiser a glance, making sure the vehicle hadn't been bothered since he'd left it the night before.

The night before being a mere four hours ago, he might add. He really wasn't sure why he'd bothered going home.

"Morning, Clyde." Julia, the receptionist, winked at him from her desk. She was nearing sixty and wore red, large-framed glasses, currently perched atop her head. Julia was affectionately considered the mother of everyone in the police department, and Clyde was unsurprised but still touched when she waved toward the coffee percolators in the corner. "Hot water, fresh pot as of ten minutes ago. Just for you."

"Thanks, Jules." Burkiss managed a smile before aiming for his desk, pulling a tea bag from the top drawer. He had issues with anxiety and sweating as it was, so he tended to stay away from coffee, and Julia knew his affection for tea. She was one of the few people who didn't poke fun at him for being a Southern Good Ol' Boy from Alabama and also a tea purist. Even his mom shook her head at him when he turned down her sweet tea.

"Late night?"

"You can say that again." He settled the tea bag into a Styrofoam cup and filled it with steaming water, a sense of calm already washing over his senses. "For a small-town, farming community, there sure is a lot of overtime to put in."

Julia shook her head fondly at him. "You work too hard, Clyde."

"Grizzly in yet?" Clyde lifted the cup to his nose and inhaled the warm scent.

Julia laughed. "Oh, you're funny, dear."

Clyde moved back to his desk and powered up the computer. He hadn't really been kidding around, but, he surmised as he took a seat, if he'd had more sleep, he probably wouldn't have asked that question seriously. He sipped carefully at the tea as he watched his computer screen come to life, his brain already picking up where he left off the night before.

It was two and a half hours before the door was flung open with a bang, sending Clyde a foot and a half out of his chair, empty tea cup bouncing to the floor.

Police Chief Gregory "Grizzly" Adams filled the doorway, lidless paper coffee cup steaming in hand. As usual, he looked like the mountain man he'd been nicknamed after, hair all wet and wild, eyes squinted and face puffy from the morning, a tiny trace of a scowl everywhere. He let out a sigh, which reverberated around the room, placed his hand on his hip, and took a long, slow swig of coffee.

Clyde stared up at him, eyes still widened from nearly flipping out of his chair, and waited.

"Well, ain't it a beautiful morning!" the big man boomed, filling his lungs with oxygen and letting it out in a contented manner. He strode across the station, door swinging shut behind him.

Clyde shook his head, a small smile on his face thanks to the four cups of tea he'd consumed. Grizzly was a hulking man with tattoos, and an intimidating manner, but the man loved life and always had a sense of peace about him. Nothing could fluster him, and while he looked like he could kill you with his bare hands, he was a kind and patient man.

"I made coffee for you, Gregory," Julia tsked. "If you'd been here on time it would have been hot."

Adams held up his cup in a toast. "I appreciate the thought, darlin'."

"Some police chief you are," she snickered.

"What, you don't think I'm setting a fine example for my officers?"

"Bending the grooming standards and showing up for work two hours late? You're an upstanding officer of the law."

He chuckled, absentmindedly brushing at the rule-breaking hair on his face before taking another sip of coffee. "I'm doing you all a favor by keeping the beard, trust me, babe."

Julia just laughed at him.

Grizzly approached Clyde's desk. "Good morning, Clyde."

"It might have been," Clyde scrolled through reports on his screen, sending a desperate glance toward the folders beside him. "If I had finished all of last week's paperwork last night."

"Oh, you're always worrying about the paperwork – the world isn't gonna end because the paperwork got filed late." Grizzly perched on the corner of Clyde's desk, scoffing.

Clyde narrowed his eyes good-naturedly at the big man and just shook his head. "Why in the hell did y'all vote him in as the chief?" he asked Julia, accidentally drawling as he leaned back in his chair to see her around Grizzly. He couldn't.

"Why in the hell did you ever leave Alabama?" Grizzly kicked the base of Clyde's chair, nearly flipping it backwards and sending Clyde into a flailing panic of overcorrection. Grizzly smirked obnoxiously as he stood. "And don't you have anything better to do than show me up and get to work early?"

Clyde straightened himself in the chair and smoothed his hair back into place. "I didn't get here early, I got here when I was supposed to be here."

Grizzly rolled his eyes. "Whatever, Buttkiss."

Clyde scowled.

"You could have at least brought in doughnuts."

Clyde flushed at the concept. "You want someone to bring doughnuts, you ask Julia. I'm never doing that again."

"I still can't believe you fell for that one, Burkiss." Grizzly drained his cup and slapped Clyde on the back, nearly sending the smaller man's face through his computer screen. "You gotta stop worrying so much about what other people think."

Clyde huffed as Grizzly disappeared down the hall toward his office. It was true though, he knew it. He did worry. Too much. About everything. But as the first officer, there was a lot to worry about. There were protocols to follow, responsibility to be upheld. He loved his job, he just loved to do it right.

Chapter Three

The Festival was not a disappointment. The unpredictable Midwestern weather cooperated, allowing children to run around in t-shirts across the park's fresh spring grass. Booths were spread across the closed road through the park, where local vendors sold everything from alligator jerky and Norwegian chocolate to Hoosier themed throw blankets and kitchen utensils.

LJ had an interview with the local events coordinator, right there in the middle of the festival. LJ suspected the woman may have been hoping she was bringing a film crew. After a brief introduction they sat down at a picnic table, surrounded by families enjoying large amounts of fried food.

"What would you say is the best part of living in Amboy?" LJ asked as she dug around for a new pen when hers died. The tape recorder she generally used in sit-down interviews was useless, as the sound system boomed over their table every five minutes.

Miranda Miller sat across from her at the picnic table, blue pantsuit outdated and out of place in the nearly-summer weather. Her too-red perm frizzed around her made up face; the only thing actually fitting about the woman was the genuine smile on her lips. She wore large pearl earrings with a pearl necklace, but they didn't match. "Well, the community, of course!" she beamed like LJ actually had brought a video camera. "All the Michiganders who visit us say we have that Southern charm, you know? We just laugh about that – everybody knows the south doesn't start until you hit Kentucky – but I think we have a certain level of southern hospitality.

And everybody looks out for everybody, you know what I mean?"

LJ nodded and scribbled, flinching when an announcement started up, louder than she'd expected. "My understanding is that the population here is under four hundred people, is that correct?"

Miranda shrugged modestly. "That it is. We're a small town, for sure. But as you can see, we do know how to draw a crowd." She motioned at the turnout for the festival. "We usually bring out close to a thousand people from surrounding communities with most of our summer events!"

LJ smiled and turned back to the notebook. Her brow furrowed as she scribbled harder, knowing full well that trying to organize these notes tomorrow would be a nightmare. She scrambled to come up with questions she hadn't written down – she knew those were always the ones that made the articles. "Okay, I think that's about it. Is there anything you'd like to add? Anything I missed? What do you think Amboy should be represented by?"

Miranda leaned forward, looking thoughtful. Finally, she shrugged and gave LJ another smile. "Well I suppose I could tell you all about Crazy Earl, or the triple bacon burger Tuesdays... but really? It's just that its home. It has its quirks – but that's what makes it special."

LJ chuckled with her, scribbling Miranda's words down as she mentally cursed herself for not coming on a Tuesday. "Perfect. Thank you so much for your time, Mrs. Miller. Your hometown is fantastic, and I only hope we do it justice."

"Oh it's so exciting! I can't believe little Amboy is going to be in a magazine!"

"You'll receive a free issue in the mail as soon as it's –"

"*LJ*!"

LJ flinched as Coby ran to the table and slapped a hand down on top of it, the other hand holding her camera firmly, strap taught around the back of her neck. "Mrs. Miller, have you met my cohort, Coby Anderson?"

Coby noticed the redhead and flashed a smile. "Whoops, sorry – good to meet you. Thanks for having us – this place is great!"

Miranda shook her hand and basked in the compliment as though it reflected her personally. "We're all very honored to be featured in your article."

"Well it's a pleasure to feature you." Coby all but winked at the woman.

LJ shook her head and cleared her throat. "We were just finishing up. Thank you again, Mrs. Miller, and as I was saying, you'll receive a free issue hot off the presses."

"Wonderful!" Miranda stood, reaching for LJ. "Thanks for shining the light on us."

LJ gathered her notes and stuffed them into her bag as they walked away, waiting for either the sound system or Coby to explode, unsure which one would go first.

"You have *got* to see the shots I got of the contests. I went to three of them and holy crow – who knew brat eating could be so *exciting?*" Coby started pressing buttons on her Nikon, pulling the strap over her head to show LJ the screen. "It's not as disgusting as it sounds, I promise. These are the best ones. I feel like they really capture an element of competitiveness without losing the fun, you know?"

LJ stood, slinging her bag over her shoulder as she leaned toward the camera. "Kind of…classic in a mildly disturbing sort of way."

"Right?" Coby slid the camera case off her shoulder and started to pack the Nikon away safely. "How was the interview?"

"Useful, I think." LJ headed in the general direction of the concession stands. "I have another interview after the race, and between the insights and the pictures, we should be able to piece enough together for a four or five page story."

"Perfect." Coby trailed after her. "We've got twenty minutes until the race… I've been smelling this melted cheese thing for the last hour, and if I don't try it, I might have a breakdown."

LJ's stomach had been growling since the mentioning of the triple bacon burger. The familiar headache that liked to follow the growling was beginning to set in, and the general din of the festival wasn't helping. "I'm not going to turn down food."

They wandered with the crowd through the maze that served as a walkway through the concession stands. Cotton candy hung from nearly every window, and there was a delicious haze of fried grease in the air. Coby led the way past a stand dedicated solely to lemonade, paused at an Italian one boasting the best pizza in three counties, and then charged onward to an "All-American" stand with a large pink pig painted on the side and stood in line.

Tracy Byrd played through the speakers on the pig stand, adding to the din that included shrieking children, laughing drunk people, and the festival's own choice of music. LJ squinted at the menu from behind

Coby, immediately torn between onion rings drizzled with some sorry excuse for cheese and the elephant ear coated in cinnamon sugar, even though neither really counted as food.

Coby stepped up to the window as the man in front of her strode away with a paper container of nachos. LJ wondered what was "All-American" about nachos. "I'll have the cheese fries and a water bottle, please." Coby monkeyed with her wallet in the camera case, eyes still on the menu. "And... maybe a side of cheese curds."

A snort sounded behind LJ. She turned slightly, spying a massive tree of a man, wearing mismatched denim shirt and denim pants. His white fumanchu was thick and fluffy. "Those aren't cheese curds, darlin'."

Coby slid a ten across the counter as she looked up at the man from over her shoulder. "Sorry?"

"Those are miniature mozzarella sticks, minus the mozzarella."

LJ started to get irritated, but kept it to herself. At least the guy wasn't in line in front of her.

"Really? What's a cheese curd then?" Coby asked, genuinely interested. LJ thought she might throw up, but that could have been the level of hunger she was reaching.

"They're cold, for one. And flavored. And they're only good if they squeak when you chew 'em." The man tucked his thumbs into his belt loops, located somewhere beneath his protruding gut.

"Fascinating." Coby turned back to the window to get her food and thank the young woman behind the counter. She stepped out of LJ's way and faced the man again. "Where might one find such a thing?"

"Not here, I can tell you that much."

LJ settled on the onion rings and placed her order.

"Wisconsin's the only place worth getting them at." The man nodded in what must have been the general direction of Wisconsin. "And that's *Wis*consin, not *Wes*consin, as you Hoosiers like to call it."

"We're from Michigan, as a matter of fact." LJ turned down the bite on her tone before finishing the sentence. "Just passing through Indiana."

"I think she's trying to say that she knows how to pronounce Wisconsin." Coby did that thing again where she wasn't winking but gave the illusion that she could be. "I take it you're from the dairyland?"

"Born and raised."

LJ took her food and got out of the man's way, but he didn't move.

"Saputo Dairy. That's where I worked for years. Started up my own trucking company a few years back – still do some work for them on occasion, whenever we get out to Alto."

"Where's Alto?"

"Just northwest of Waupun." The man seemed oblivious to the impatient family standing behind him. "Not much to Waupun, unless you're counting the prisons."

Coby's face lit up like a Christmas tree. "Prisons? Plural?"

"Town of ten thousand, and the damned place has two maximum security prisons. Go figure." The big man finally stepped up to the window and ordered a snow cone.

Coby's gaze slid to LJ, who was already staring at her with a bored expression. "Sounds promising, don't you think?"

"Sounds like a disaster."

Coby glanced at the man, who was wandering off with his blue snow cone. "What's disastrous about maximum security prisons in small towns?"

LJ scowled, biting into an onion ring as she started for a nearby picnic table. "Okay, slow down 'true crime' junkie. For one thing, we write for a travel magazine. We literally get paid to make people *want* to visit the places we write about. What would we title it? 'Waupun: Great Place to Raise Families, Despite the Convicts'? Are you going to pitch that idea to Ron?"

Coby shrugged as she plopped down at the table with her food. "I don't know. We should at least Google it. Maybe it's nothing – maybe it's everything."

Chapter Four

With a contented sigh he closed his eyes and leaned back in the purple, overstuffed chair. It was done. Months and months of work and planning, and it was done.

A broad smile played across his features. There was nothing, nothing quite as satisfying as finishing a story. This was the golden hour. This was when he could bask in his accomplishment. When he could relax, step back and enjoy his handiwork, before the itch set in again. That's the thing with authors. They can't turn their brains off. The thing that compels them is always there, always working, even when they'd rather it wouldn't be.

Because no matter how much he may want to dive into the next story, there was always clean up to be done first. No matter how glorious a story may be, when you finish you're always left with a bit of a mess to clean up, loose ends to tie… So much, and it took so long…

He shook his head, pushing away the nagging thoughts. No. He wouldn't worry about any of that just now. He let out a slow sigh. He had finished a masterpiece, one that would be appreciated, and talked about for years. He would savor that and hold onto it.

***

"Did you know the iconic 'End of the Trail' statue is located in Waupun? It was created in 1915 by James Earle Fraser, as a tribute to the Native Americans. In fact, Waupun itself is known as 'The City of Sculpture.'"

LJ nodded absentmindedly, not bothering to look up from the map she had spread across the table of the

Amboy Public Library. Coby sat four feet away, using a dinosaur of a computer that was connected to the internet with dial up due to the irritating lack of WiFi. She scrolled through random webpages with the speed of a snail trudging through molasses. LJ knew every time Coby got a page to load successfully, because when it finally did she piped up with a new fact about Waupun.

"Ooh. There's also a candy shop named after the statue. They sell gourmet popcorn, specialty candy and ice cream, and coffee." Coby twisted in the chair and shot LJ an impressed look. "That's something we could feature."

LJ straightened and squinted toward the computer screen, nodded and shrugged a shoulder. "Could be."

Coby snickered and rolled her eyes. "Don't sound so excited."

"Well, I'm just not sold on this place yet." LJ shrugged again and went back to the map. "It looks like I-94 would take us the whole way. Shouldn't be more than six hours or so."

"It's a perfect next step." Coby turned to the screen again. "I won't make you admit that I'm right."

LJ sneered at the back of Coby's head.

"Here we go. Summer events include: Celebrate Waupun, Firecracker Fun Run, Waupun Truck 'n' Show…"

"What the hell is that?"

"Umm… hold on it's loading." Coby leaned forward. "Okay, truck drivers from all over the country come and decorate their trucks and drive through town. It looks like quite the event." She turned to LJ again. "See? It really is a great place for families."

"Despite the convicts." LJ shook her head and started to fold up the map.

Coby closed the browser windows and twisted to cross her arms over the back of the chair. "I wanted to talk to you about that."

LJ stopped her movements and narrowed her eyes. "You're not talking to convicts, Coby."

"No, I don't want to talk to convicts." Coby paused. "Well, maybe. That's not what I wanted to mention." She eyed LJ. "I think we should write a piece on the prisons."

LJ sighed. "Coby, we can't feature high security correctional facilities in our magazine. The whole point is to sell copies because they promote travel destinations in backroad America. If we write a piece promoting a prison…"

"No, no, I know that. You're right about that part." Coby straightened up and got out of the chair. "This doesn't have to be a piece for the magazine. I just think it would be fun to branch out a little bit. And you don't have to be involved, if you really don't want to be."

LJ scowled for a long moment, trying to read Coby's expression. "What are you saying?"

Coby slid the chair into place under the desk. "Nothing. Just that I really want to research this and work on something. It doesn't have to be for the magazine, and it doesn't have to cut into the time we put into the magazine."

LJ crossed her arms. "Are you planning on going solo on me, Anderson?"

Coby burst out laughing. "No, Reed, I just have some interests outside of *work*."

LJ studied her for a moment longer before dropping it and shrugging yet again. "Well, I don't care about the prison. And it better not drag down our process because, and I'll admit it, I think you're right about the potential of this place. It's worth driving up there."

Coby beamed and fist pumped the air. "Yes!"

LJ scoffed at her giddiness. "Don't get so excited, or I won't ever give you credit again."

Chapter Five

The sirens blared. Lights flashed. Wind poured through the open windows, carrying scents of fresh cut grass, sunshine, and the ever present odor of the dairy farms.

The cruiser hit a bump in the road and Grizzly burst out laughing as Clyde scrambled to grab onto something before he sprawled across the dash despite the seat belt's best efforts to keep him in place. "Grizzly. What the hell?"

"What's the matter, Buttkiss?" Grizzly sent a sideways grin to the passenger seat. "Can't handle a little adrenaline rush?"

Clyde's hand shot out to motion at the open road in front of them. "You're not even chasing anyone!"

Grizzly leaned back against the driver's seat, resting an elbow on the open window like they were out for a casual Sunday drive instead of tearing around with the speedometer settled at ninety. "We've gotta give the townspeople something new to talk about. Remember the last time they got bored? Big showdown at the bowling alley."

"What exactly are you giving them to talk about? 'Oh look, there goes the local law. Off their damn rockers, those guys.'"

Grizzly pressed the accelerator down harder and the car caught six inches of air as they bounced over a set of railroad tracks. A strangled shriek clawed out of Clyde's throat. Grizzly chortled again. "They love us, Clyde. Even you, with that stick up your ass and everything."

Clyde shot him a pained look that Grizzly had seen a million times. They'd ridden together since the academy, which wasn't what either of them had planned. But that was a long time ago, before they'd decided being partners wasn't as terrible as they'd thought, and long before Grizzly had been sworn in as chief. Before the unsolved cases.

Grizzly killed the sirens and slowed the cruiser to an acceptable speed as they neared their destination. A cloud of dread seemed to fill the car as they turned onto the dirt two track off the highway and bounced across the cornfield, aiming for a plot of trees near the back of the property.

Kacey Schelling had been found there three months before. It was Grizzly's first active murder case as Waupun's police chief, and the place still haunted him.

They weren't going back to the crime scene for any official reason – in fact, Clyde had balked at the idea and told Grizzly flat out exactly what they would find if they went back there. Nothing. And Grizzly knew he was probably right. But he was out of ideas, and he hoped reliving walking onto that scene would kick start him back into overdrive.

He stopped the car and they both got out wordlessly. The patch of woods was small, and Grizzly thought yet again that Kacey's body should have been discovered sooner. Especially during the winter, when the trees and brush were scarce. But she'd spent the entire season solidified in the snow, until the farmer was finally out plowing the field for spring and spotted the body at the edge of the trees.

Clyde strode over to the tree line and paused. Grizzly thought he was going to say something, but

Clyde just placed his hands on his hips and stared at the ground. The move inexplicably irritated Grizzly, and he bit back an uncharacteristically nasty comment and moved into the woods to look around.

He hated this place.

When he joined the police academy, he'd been looking to escape the chaos that had been following him his entire life. He never signed up for finding dead little girls in the woods. Grizzly wasn't cut out for being chief of police. Never had been, and as far as he could tell, never would be. When it came to faith in Grizzly's abilities, former Chief Walter DeJager was full of shit, as far as Grizzly was concerned.

"Clyde would be better for the job," he had said, standing in Walt's office, feeling entirely too large to be even standing in there, much less be sitting at that desk.

The old man smiled at Grizzly. "Clyde would be good for the job, but it wouldn't be good for him..." he folded his hands and leaned forward, looking up at him seriously. "It would be good for you, Greg."

Grizzly shifted awkwardly. He owed a lot to the chief, too much. And the man's unwavering faith in Grizzly was enough to make him want to run away, but was also enough to make him try to rise to any height Walt told him he could reach.

"I'm not... I'm not like you. The town will be disappointed... I can't fill your shoes," Grizzly said, shaking his head and crossing his arms with a frown on his face.

Walt took off his glasses and pinched the bridge of his nose. He looked older than Grizzly had ever noticed before. "It's not that hard to do Greg. I'm not perfect, I've let this town down... so many times," he said with a faraway look in his eyes. "You know I never found one of those girls, not one, in all my years here."

Grizzly's frown deepened and he took a step forward. "That doesn't mean anything. You're a great chief, and you've done everything you could for this town," he said, feeling annoyance rise within him. He owed everything to this man. Walt wasn't allowed to look so broken.

Walt looked up at him and smiled. "And you will too." He stood abruptly and held out his hand. "Congratulations, Chief Adams."

"Grizz?"

Grizzly snapped out of his daze and looked up at Clyde. "What?"

Clyde ignored his bark. "What do you think we're gonna find out here?"

Grizzly paused in his surveillance, wondering the same thing himself. He tried to lose the chip on his shoulder; Clyde hadn't done anything wrong and Grizzly didn't need to punish him. "It's all part of the job description, Burkiss."

"You're obsessing."

Grizzly didn't meet his gaze. He stared at the place Kacey's body had been. It seemed to be glowing. "It's worth obsessing over.

"We got another call about her."

He snapped to attention. "What? Why the hell didn't you –"

"No information. Just a… critical review of our work. There was a vague threat so I figured you should know about it. It kind of shook Jules up." Grizzly let out a low growl. He could feel Clyde casting side glances at him. "Don't take it personal Grizz, people lose it when it comes to this stuff."

Grizzly let out a bitter laugh. "Why do you think Walter stepped down when he did? It's crap. The girl shows up dead and everyone pins the blame on the only people trying to help." He shook his head and ran his hands through his hair, the tension creeping up his neck to the base of his skull.

"People know it's not our fault." Clyde frowned.

"The murder, maybe, but just watch Clyde, they don't have someone to string up in the town square soon and it's going to be us."

"Oh?" Clyde smirked. "What happened to 'they love us, Clyde'?"

Grizzly shook his head, pulling himself away from the scene still vivid in his mind from March. He forced a smile and winked at Clyde as he headed back for the cruiser. "They love us as long as we do our jobs… and keep looking so damn pretty."

Chapter Six

Nothing. Not that he should be surprised, if he was being honest. The river ran straight through town, but he'd be lucky if they ever found her, the way this police department was run. Maybe archaeologists of the future would unearth her there. That was the best shot she'd have at getting found.

He shook his head. What was wrong with him? This was a good thing. If the body wasn't found it couldn't be traced to him.

But what good was a story if no one ever read it?

Chapter Seven

The rain started outside of Brownsville, Wisconsin. Coby couldn't read the welcome sign until they were passing it, and the speed limit posting just beyond it made her slam on the brakes. LJ kept an eye on the map as they crawled through the town, rain pattering deafeningly on the roof and windows. The wipers hummed and sloshed across the windshield in vain, barely clearing the glass long enough to catch a glimpse of the few taillights in front of them.

It didn't take long for Brownsville to fade in the rearview. The speed limit went back up to fifty-five, and farmland spread out on both sides of the two-lane asphalt. They passed the Horicon Marsh, and LJ looked at the map once more as they cruised under the 151 overpass and eased into the town limits.

"'Welcome to Waupun.'" LJ set the map across her lap and glanced past the raindrops on the passenger window.

"'City of Sculpture.'" Coby shook her head and turned down the wipers as the rain began to let up. "We know they have statues... do they have a motel?"

LJ pointed with her coffee cup in hand, then took a sip of the long-cold liquid. "There's that one."

"Ha." Coby let out a wry laugh. "I said motel. Not hotel."

"You mean our lovely employers haven't given us enough in the budget to afford a decent place to stay? I'm shocked." LJ settled her sunglasses back on her nose despite the still darkened sky. "Google said the Van Camp Inn is straight ahead."

Coby guided the Chevelle through town, past locally owned businesses and the city hall, complete with bronze statue. They cruised into the motel parking lot with unamused expressions and Coby killed the engine.

"Seriously?" LJ stated eyeing the sign, with the flashing neon tent. "'Van Camp Inn.' Like, camping?"

Coby unbuckled her seatbelt and opened the door. "Too bad we don't have a van to camp in." She grinned at LJ expectantly.

LJ narrowed her eyes.

"Come on. It can't be worse than that motel in Phoenix." Coby stretched, then leaned back into the car for her bag.

"I'm kind of afraid it could be." LJ reluctantly climbed out of the car.

***

Robert S. Van Camp looked up from his Stephen King paperback at the old car that pulled into the parking lot of his motel. Old Chevelle; you didn't see too many of those. To his surprise, two women stepped out, younger than the car itself.

One was blonde, one brunette, both pretty. He sucked the chaw out of his teeth and straightened, closing his book. There was no way they were both going to stay here. He and his old lady didn't get many customers period, and young beautiful women who weren't traveling with a man probably came in last place on their frequent customer list.

The doors of the car slammed closed and they both made their way towards the office. Robert ran a hand over his greasy, thinning hair and tucked his gray t-shirt into his jeans. The jeans were probably older than the ladies approaching the door.

They stepped in and the small bell behind the door let out a jingle. Robert looked the blonde up and down and smiled to himself, flipping the paperback onto the countertop as he leaned forward eagerly. "Well, good afternoon ladies," he said, trying to sound charming past the wad of tobacco in his cheek.

The shorter, blonde one smiled and walked up to the desk, while the brunette trailed after her, looking around the lobby with a critical gaze. "Hello, we'd like to get a room," she said, holding out a credit card. "Two queens."

He tried to look down her shirt as he smoothed his hair back again, then glanced the brunette over. They looked interesting, like they stepped out of an Eagles' song. They intrigued him, and he wondered what their story was. "Well, look at that, we have one open."

"It's our lucky day," the brunette mumbled. Robert found himself scowling at her.

"Awesome!" the blonde before him smiled, looking genuine.

"All righty then..." He swiped her card and pulled up a log sheet on the old beige computer to his left. "Name?" he asked, already looking at the card in his hand.

"Coby Anderson," the blonde replied, glancing around the place curiously.

"Well, Miss Anderson, how many nights will you be staying with us?" he asked, looking at the large duffle bag the brunette had slung over her shoulder, like it was a constant extension of her arm.

"Well, probably five or six... I'm not completely sure. We work for a magazine out of Michigan," she offered. "We're writing a piece about the prison, and-"

"About Waupun," the brunette spoke up from the back, frowning at the blonde.

"About Waupun, and all the things it's known for. A travel piece," Coby finished, and he figured she'd probably offered that explanation a couple hundred times before.

"Well, isn't that something." He shifted his gaze between the two of them. "About this little old place. I trust you'll put a good word about me. I'd be happy to give you girls a private interview." He winked, then grabbed the empty beer can next to the keyboard and spit a stream of brown into it. He didn't miss the disgusted grimace from the brunette. He chose to ignore it.

"Of course," the blonde laughed.

He slid a key across the counter toward her. "Room four. Have a nice stay, ladies!"

Coby smiled and took the key, following the brunette who was already striding out of the lobby.

***

Room 4 was accommodated with a set of double beds and a television set that hadn't seen a good day since 1993. LJ wordlessly took the bed closest to the air conditioner despite its less-than-stellar condition, which suggested it could set the nearby drapes on fire if it wanted. Coby thought about heading for the bathroom, decided she was better off not yet seeing the state it was in, and tossed her bag on the other mattress.

LJ took out her laptop and a notepad she'd been writing in during the car ride. "I'm planning on calling city hall tomorrow and setting up interviews with some of the town officials to talk more about local attractions and stories and events. Did you want to get pictures of the statues first, or wait to see if there's something more interesting to focus on?"

Coby pulled the drapes back and looked out the window at their fantastic view of a back alley. "Let's eat before we talk about work."

LJ nodded, not bothering to look up from her screen. "I could eat." Her fingers clacked on the keyboard. "Pizza? Ooh. Wings." She glanced at Coby. "Pizza Hut has both."

"Works for me." Coby turned from the window.

"The search won't load," LJ grumbled, inspecting her screen. "I'm connected to the motel internet, too. That's going to be a pain in the ass." She sighed and gave up, pulling out her cell phone. "There's a Pizza Hut in Beaver Dam. It's a twenty minute drive."

"Let's do it." Coby snatched up her purse from the bedspread as LJ closed the laptop. They filed out the door and back to the car.

***

"I *told* you to take a *left,*" LJ snarled from the darkness of the passenger seat.

Coby rolled her eyes and gripped the steering wheel. "I *did* take a left!"

"The first time! I said left the second time too."

"Why don't you have the map?"

"Because the map doesn't have Pizza Hut locations helpfully laid out for the world to see."

"Why didn't you write down the address?"

"Because I knew where you needed to turn *left.*"

Coby let out an audible sigh and picked up her cell from the console cup holder to check the time. It was closing in on eight pm and neither of them had eaten for hours. She dropped the phone back into her lap and focused on the ten feet of illuminated road in front of them. "Why don't we just go back to Waupun and eat at McDonalds?"

LJ didn't respond, but didn't object when Coby slowed and maneuvered the car through a K-turn in the middle of the road to head back the way they'd come.

"We turned here."

"No, we didn't." Coby scowled as she paused at the stop sign, leaning forward to find the street signs. "It was the next one. The one before we came through this intersection."

"I'm pretty sure it was this one."

"I'm driving. I remember." Coby accelerated straight.

After two miles of unfamiliar territory and silence, LJ opened her mouth. "I told you it was that one."

Coby ground her teeth together and slouched in the seat, then straightened as she spotted the next intersection. "I'll just turn here instead."

"It's not Michigan. The roads don't run in a checkerboard pattern."

"Well, I'm *turning anyway,*" Coby grumbled. Her stomach echoed the growl. Streetlights shined up ahead and she felt a brief flicker of hope. "See? We're back in

Waupun already." A small green sign confirmed her statement.

"I think Main Street is that way." LJ pointed out Coby's window.

Coby scowled and glanced out the passenger side. "Isn't that way north?"

LJ slammed her head back against her headrest and sighed heavily. "Why do I let you drive anywhere?"

Coby squinted to the right. "Beaver Dam was south, right? We headed that way, so that has to be-"

"Stop trying to navigate and just listen to me, will you?" LJ grumbled. "If you just – *whoa, stop sign, STOP SIGN!*"

Coby whirled forward and slammed on the brake as a blur of headlights and blue and white paint swept in from the left. A crunching sound punctuated the abrupt jolt that sent both passengers slamming against their seat belts.

Coby gripped the steering wheel with white knuckles, mouth hanging open, face pale as she stared blindly at the vehicle sitting cockeyed in the intersection before her.

"Oh, you've gotta be kidding me." LJ gaped beside her.

The driver's side headlight of the Chevelle was dead, leaving the passenger one to shine like a spotlight across the dented side of the car they'd victimized. The scratched words "Waupun Police" glowed in the night.

Chapter Eight

Clyde's eyes were so wide open he couldn't figure out how to get them to shut again. He briefly wondered if he was dead on impact, but his racing pulse and rushing adrenaline were proof of life despite his brain's insistence of death.

"What in the damn *hell* were they *doing?*" Grizzly snarled from the driver's seat. He stabbed at his seat belt until it freed him and allowed him to roar out of the car.

Clyde looked down at his hands, pale and shaking as he held them out. He turned to look out his open window at the bent grill of the old car that had nearly ended his life. "Grizz?" He squeaked.

Grizzly stormed around the front of the cruiser and approached the assaulting vehicle. "Can you read? That big red sign right there? It says *stop.*"

The passenger door of the old car opened and a tall brunette stepped out. "She *tapped* you."

Grizzly flailed an arm back at the passenger door of the cruiser. "Does that look like a *tap* to you?"

"*Grizzly?*"

"*What?!*"

"I can't breathe!"

"You're *fine,* Clyde."

"I'm gonna pass out." Dots swirled in his vision, but he managed to distinguish a blonde figure climbing out of the driver's seat.

"I'm so sorry! I don't know what happened –"

"You blew the stop sign and hit my cruiser. That's what happened." Grizzly moved to inspect the damage.

"*Greg.*" Clyde hiccupped.

Grizzly leaned against the open window. "You're not even bleeding, Burkiss." He yanked on the handle but the inverted door didn't budge.

"I could have *died.*"

He saw Grizzly's eyes roll before the big man turned back toward the women from the car. "Look ladies, we're gonna have to write this up."

"I'm so sorry, we're not from around here – wait – is he okay?!" The blonde driver asked, tripping over her own feet as she walked closer to inspect the damage, face paling as she peered in at Clyde.

Grizzly let out a snort. "He's fine," he said, waving a hand.

"I can't move my neck – I think I have whiplash–"

"Clyde just – CLIMB OUT OF THE DRIVER'S SIDE!" Grizzly bellowed at him.

The blonde winced. "If he's hurt he shouldn't –"

"JUST – SHHHH –" Grizzly sputtered at her, holding up a hand and glancing at Clyde who was finally shifting himself over to the driver's side of the vehicle.

The brunette rolled her eyes and folded her arms. "So how is this gonna work? I would call the cops but, you know."

Clyde stumbled out of the car, moaning and grabbing his side. The blonde woman was watching him with a horrified look on her face. "Are you okay?"

Grizzly ignored him as he shuffled over to them. "Well, first thing is, I hope you ladies have insurance."

"Grizz, I think I might have a broken rib." Clyde said, wincing as he touched his side gingerly.

Grizzly let out a long-suffering sigh and looked over at Clyde. "Clyde, they were going fifteen miles an hour."

The blonde's eyes darted between them and looked back at her passenger. "Should I call the hospital?" she whispered.

"Nah, he's a scrappy little guy," Grizzly said, whapping Clyde on the back and forcing a whimper out of him. Grizzly squatted down between the cars. "Now let's take a look at this damage, seeing as I'm going to have to file the damn report."

The brunette woman moved out of the beam of the remaining headlight on the Chevelle, shaking her head. "I can't believe this."

Clyde sat on the curb and put his head between his knees.

Grizzly ran his hand along the dented side of the cruiser and shook his head as he straightened and turned toward the blonde. "Have you been drinking?"

She shook her head, eyes still focused on Clyde, expression concerned. "No, Officer, I swear – we were just trying to find Pizza Hut…"

"Oh, for the love of Pete." The dark-haired passenger ran her hands over her face. "Just ticket us for blowing the stop sign or put her down for a misdemeanor or whatever it is that you do."

"Are you going to take my license?" The blonde looked panicked.

Grizzly planted his hands on his hips and growled out a sigh. "No, ma'am, I'm not going to take your license."

"I really didn't mean to hurt anyone –" she rushed.

Grizzly stared up at the streetlight. "I'm sure you didn't. But I'm still going to have to take your statement and write a report."

"Great," the brunette muttered.

Grizzly motioned at Clyde. "Pull up the system. I'll get their licenses."

"I think I'm in shock." Clyde's voice was muffled from his ducked head.

"You're not in shock."

"I could be in shock. People *die* from shock."

"Clyde, she *tapped* us. Now get your butt to the car and punch them into the system!"

Clyde hauled to his feet and wobbled over to the banged up cruiser. He leaned into the passenger window and reached for the computer on the center console.

Grizzly approached the assaulter. "I'm going to need your license and proof of insurance."

The woman nodded and climbed into the car to obey.

"Um. Grizz?" Clyde called, upper half still inside the cruiser.

"What?"

Clyde backed up and looked at Grizzly in horror. He held up an empty travel mug, minus its lid.

"What is that?"

"I may have spilled my tea."

Grizzly stared at him blankly.

"All over the computer."

Grizzly let out a long sigh. "Dammit, Burkiss..."

The blonde girl straightened and handed Grizzly the small pile of information. Grizzly eyed it for a moment and shook his head. "All right, here's what's going to happen. You're going to follow us back to the station, and we'll figure this mess out. You keep that until we get there," he said, turning and motioning for Clyde to get in the car.

Clyde gave him a pained expression before sliding in through the driver's seat. The brunette woman let out an annoyed snort and flung herself back into the car, muttering about wings.

Grizzly felt the blonde's eyes on him as he sauntered over and turned the engine over a few times before finally getting the car to start. He watched her heave a sigh of relief and climb in her vehicle, trailing behind as Grizzly pulled onto the road.

Chapter Nine

LJ stormed after Coby as she traipsed into the police station. There was a single light on in the office, giving the room an eerie glow and casting shadows across the desks. LJ eyeballed a chair next to the door and claimed it as her own, plopping down with a huff. Her stomach growled.

Coby trailed after the chief and the first officer like a forlorn puppy.

Officer Burkiss disappeared into a small kitchenette. Police Chief Gregory Adams whistled as he swung himself down in front of a computer, launching a program while Coby hovered awkwardly at his shoulder.

LJ crossed her arms impatiently, annoyed that the chief seemed to think he had all the time in the world. After a few very long minutes, the chief glanced up at Coby, who was holding all her documents tightly in her hands and looking smaller than usual, though whether that was because she was upset or because the chief was a giant, LJ wasn't sure. "I'm going to need your full name."

"Coby Renee Anderson," she recited like she was in the military and LJ could see the tension in her shoulders.

"Oh… kay..." the big man said, typing the information in the appropriate fields. "And what about your friend?"

"La- uh..." she glanced back at LJ apologetically, and LJ scowled. Like this day could get any worse. "...Laverne Jeanette Reed," Coby said under her breath.

LJ saw the chief's mouth twitch and she briefly considered running over his car again. Or his stupid face. But before she could take action on either, a short, grey-haired, middle-aged woman in a big sweater and red glasses bustled into the room from a side office. "What happened to the cruiser, are you boys alright?" she fussed.

"We're fine, Julia," Grizzly called from his computer. "Clyde got a little bruise, don't let him tell you otherwise. What are you doing here at this hour, anyway?"

Julia had a hand to her heart. "I just stopped in to drop off –" Clyde emerged from the kitchen holding a bag of ice in one hand and a cup of tea in the other. "Oh you poor thing, are you okay?" Julia exclaimed, walking over to him and examining his face.

Clyde flushed slightly and smiled at the older woman, though it came out more like a grimace. "Ah yeah, just a bump."

LJ rolled her eyes so hard it made her lack-of-food headache pound harder.

The chief let out a loud snort. "So you're sure you're going to make it now, Clyde?" he asked sarcastically, before turning to Coby. "Here darlin', let me see those," he said, holding a hand out for her proof of insurance, license, and vehicle registration. His tone was a lot softer to her than it had been right after the crash, and LJ was ninety-nine percent sure it was because Coby looked so pathetically sorry.

Or maybe it was because they were physically wasting away before the cops very eyes from lack of food. It really wouldn't surprise LJ at all.

The short woman, who LJ could only assume was a receptionist of sorts frowned sympathetically before her gaze fell upon Coby and LJ, as if she just realized they were also in the room. "And who are these lovely ladies?" she asked.

There was an awkward moment of silence before LJ shrugged. "We hit them," she said shortly and Coby looked down in shame.

"Oh." Julia blinked and paused, pursing her lips in thought. "Well, I have some cookies out in the car, I'm sure that will help to calm everyone's nerves," she said, and LJ snapped to attention. Maybe she wouldn't wither and die here in this police department surrounded by idiots and cornfields.

"Sounds good, Julia!" the chief boomed as the older lady patted Clyde's cheek and exited. "We're just about done here," he added to Coby as he typed in some more information. Clyde stepped closer to them, peering at the screen. The chief clicked a few times and a sheet started to print out. "Just need you to fill –" he paused and glanced at Clyde, then slowly pushed his hand holding the mug of tea away from the keyboard. Grizzly grabbed the paper off of the printer and handed a pen to Coby. "Fill out a brief report of what happened."

Coby looked at the paper and hesitated. "Can't I just plead guilty?"

"It's not a trial."

"No, I know, I just… I know I made a mistake and we all know I hit your car."

"Then write it down." Grizzly winked at her. "It's just red tape. Trust me, babe, I hate it too."

LJ shot him a dark look at the word "babe."

Coby sighed and moved to an empty desk.

The door opened again and Julia reappeared, Tupperware container in hand. LJ nearly launched to her feet and snatched it away from her, but she restrained herself.

Julia was opening the container and must have noticed the look of crazed animal hunger in LJ's eyes because she brought them straight over to her. "Thank you," LJ said, attempting to smile at the woman but she was pretty sure her face muscles were on lockdown until she had food in her system. She held herself back and took two, trying to appear less like a wild boar.

Julia gave her an encouraging smile. "I hope you like chocolate chip."

"I love it," she muffled past a mouthful of cookie, not even caring that she was spewing crumbs in front of strangers in uniform and actually managing a small smile at Julia.

The police chief stood and moved towards them, coming to a looming stop behind the small, older woman. "Julia, you are a shining light of beauty and grace and all womanly virtues," he said, helping himself to the cookies.

Julia smiled at him and blushed a little. "Oh, stop it you." She chuckled before looking over at Clyde. "Come on dear, you're skin and bones and some sugar will make you feel better." The tips of the officer's ears were red as he stepped forward and took a cookie with a quiet thank you. Julia stuffed the whole container in his hands and started to take off her jacket. "Go take some to that pretty girl over there," she said, waving a hand at Coby and shoving Clyde in her direction as she made her way over to the small desk.

Clyde did as he was told, but tripped over his own feet on the way. LJ shook her head at the Andy Griffith spectacle she was witnessing. She had finished her two cookies and was staring absentmindedly at the small pile the police chief had in his hand, still starving but feeling one hundred and seventy five percent better now that she had something in her system.

"You feeling all right?" The deep voice startled her out of her reverie.

"Uh, yeah. Fine. We didn't hit you guys hard at all," she said, peering up at him suspiciously. He was huge. And hairy. And tattooed. But she wasn't going to be intimidated by him.

"Well, I'm glad no one's hurt," he said, pointedly ignoring Clyde's injured shuffling back towards them before setting the rest of the cookies on the desk in front of LJ. The chief was eating what must have been his fifth cookie, as she wondered if the Tupperware would fit inside of her purse and if she could get away with stealing when there were two cops in the room.

"Done!" Coby finally announced, setting her pen down and scooting the chair back, skimming over what she had just written.

"Great!" Grizzly boomed, turning towards her. He took the paper from her, glancing at it briefly before smiling at her. "Looks good. Well ladies, I think we're about done here." He set the report down on the nearest desk, then started rifling through papers. "I have a card for a mechanic around here somewhere…"

Clyde appeared, shooing him out of the way and reaching into a drawer. He came up with a business card and shoved it at Grizzly.

"Aha, there it is." Grizzly passed the card to Coby, who took it from him with a full mouthed smile. "You ladies can go! I hope you enjoy the rest of your stay here in the lovely city of Waupun." He winked at them. "Drive safe."

LJ bolted to her feet, overjoyed at the prospect of getting out of here and finding real food.

"Thanks so much sir, and again… sorry," Coby said, holding out her hand.

Grizzly grinned at her and shook her hand. "Grizzly. And don't worry about it. And don't hesitate to give us a call if you need anything."

Chapter Ten

The old diner was filled with the morning crowd, consisting mostly of Waupun's senior citizens. The room smelled faintly of mildew and old people, but the fresh scents of breakfast feasts overpowered anything unpleasant. Coby took in the dark interior with eager eyes, wishing she could capture every face in the room. Each one told a story in its own voice.

"Where do you want to sit?" LJ asked, nodding toward the "seat yourself" sign inside the doorway.

"Over here?" Coby motioned toward the right side of the restaurant, motioning to a table in the center with a view of everyone and everything. LJ nodded and moved toward it.

"Good morning, ladies, and welcome to Helen's." An elderly waitress greeted them as soon as they were seated. "Can I start you off with anything special? Coffee? Orange juice?"

"Ooh. Both, please." Coby smiled at the woman, again wishing her camera could capture the interaction.

The waitress set a pair of menus on the table for them. "Absolutely. And for you?"

"Just the coffee, please." LJ reached for a menu.

"Sure. I'll be back in a flash." She ambled off.

Coby opened her menu but didn't look at it. She scanned the room, carefully inspecting each occupant. But with skill – she never stared at anyone long enough for them to feel uneasy. And she had an eye for approachable people – she could always tell with one glance who would appreciate being asked an out of the blue question, and who would rather take a sharp stick to the eye. "Did you get a hold of anyone at City Hall?"

LJ mulled over the menu. "Yeah, they just got back to me this morning. We're meeting there today, around four, unless you have other plans."

Coby eyed another waitress, also an older woman, sitting at an empty table across from them, wrapping silverware in paper napkins. "Works for me."

"Don't you have a court hearing this afternoon?" LJ didn't bother looking up at Coby, though the baiting tone of her voice suggested she wanted to see the reaction she got.

Coby stopped looking around the restaurant and narrowed her eyes at LJ. "Don't even start."

"I mean, I get why you hit them. I kind of wanted to put the little awkward one out of his misery, too."

Humiliation, guilt, and worry washed over Coby all over again as she relived that horrifying moment of impact from the night before. "You don't think he's actually hurt, do you? He seemed okay last night when we left…"

LJ finally looked up and rolled her eyes. "I'm just messing with you, Anderson. He's fine. The only thing you managed to injure was the door on that cop car and their computer system, and that part wasn't even your fault. I'm still driving the next time we want to find a Pizza Hut, but you can let yourself off the hook."

Coby bit her lip. "Poor guy."

"Stop feeling sorry for him. The rest of the world probably already does that enough." LJ flipped the page on her menu.

"That's mean, LJ, and you know it."

"What? The guy isn't exactly Mr. Confidence."

"You don't need to make fun of him for that. He was really nice."

"He tripped over his own boots and blushed when he tried to hand you a cookie."

"I thought it was sweet."

"You think everything is sweet."

Coby scowled. "That's not true. I think you're a human adaptation of Grumpy Cat." She kicked LJ's foot under the table.

LJ glared at her for good measure. She looked down at her menu. "We should stop at that mechanic after we eat and get the car taken care of. We've got enough time before we have to be at City Hall."

Coby nodded. "Sure." She glanced down, finally looking closely at her open menu. "So what are you getting?"

LJ reached across the table and pointed at a line. "That, probably."

Coby nodded as she skimmed the description of eggs and toast with a side of hash browns. "Mmm…"

"You should really try the pancakes, dears." The woman wrapping silverware spoke up. She smiled as both the girls looked over at her. "They're bigger than your head. Heaven knows I can't eat them anymore – got enough love handles for four husbands – but you two look like you could use some extra pounds."

Coby scanned the menu. "Where are those?"

"Second page, halfway down. Got waffles, too."

"Even better." Coby beamed.

"Are you two new around here? Just passing through?" The nametag on her uniform shirt said "Louise."

"We're writers for a travel magazine, and we're featuring Waupun in our next piece," Coby explained with a smile. Friendly and chatty waitresses were often where they got their best information. "We just got in yesterday."

"Well, welcome. I've lived here seventy-one years, and it hasn't changed." Louise straightened her stack of silverware. "Anything you need to know, come to me. I've got more facts packed away than everyone in this town put together."

LJ closed her menu and sat back. "Thanks. Maybe we could set up an interview with you this week? We wouldn't want to take up your time at work."

"Honey, like I said. Seventy-one years. What are they gonna do, fire me? They'd be doing me a favor." Louise winked and folded her hands on the tabletop. "Ask me anything you'd like."

Coby chuckled. "What do you like about living in Waupun?"

Louise smoothed back a lock of short, gray hair, gazing across the restaurant as she thought. "I like that the community is just like it was in 1950. Little boys still ride their bikes down to the river with their fishing poles and don't come home 'til supper. Not many towns are like that anymore."

LJ was already pulling her notepad out. "So it's a safe community?"

"It's our own little Mayberry." Louise nodded, then hesitated. "But then again, I guess times *are* changing a bit."

Coby felt the woman shut down a little, and tried to pose her question without prying. "What do you mean?"

"Well, there have been some unpleasant things these recent years, missing people, and some deaths… but we don't like to talk about that," Louise sputtered, waving her hand as if to gloss past it all. "That's just the way things are these days, I suppose. Even little Waupun can't stay away from it forever."

"Deaths?" LJ tapped her pen on the pad. Coby cocked an eyebrow at her friend, hoping she was witnessing a spark of interest, but knowing LJ was probably functioning on autopilot.

"A few girls, here and there. I don't really remember the details… " Louise sighed, looking upset before moving back toward her silverware. "But you don't want to write about that for your article anyway."

Coby could tell she didn't want to talk about it anymore. Coby thought she heard LJ mutter "True" under her breath and didn't miss the glance LJ sent her way. She chose to ignore it and leaned her elbows on the table. "What about the prison?"

"Which one? There are two within walking distance." Louise shrugged a shoulder. "As long as the prisoners stay where they are... though I guess they probably wouldn't stick around if they got out." She chuckled.

"*Have* any of the prisoners ever escaped?" Coby asked.

Louise closed her eyes and shook her head. "Not since 1918, I think."

"What do you know about the prisoners held there, recently and in years past? Anyone… noteworthy?"

LJ sighed. It was quiet, but Coby noticed it.

Louise tapped her lips with her forefinger. "I'm not really sure. The library would be a good place to check. We have a wonderful library. There's a whole section on the town and I'm sure there are books about the prisons. In fact, the library is right next door to Waupun Correctional."

Coby nodded. "Perfect. How do we get there?"

She didn't need to ask. She knew LJ could search the address on the internet in half the time it took Louise to give them detailed directions. But these were the conversations they wrote about. And getting the statements like "If you pass the sculpture of the promiscuous woman, you've gone too far" was always what made their articles.

***

Jimmy leaned back on the rolling stool he was perched on and tilted the water bottle to his lips, wishing it was something stronger. But it wasn't even noon yet.

He surveyed the garage, purposely skipping over the cluttered desk next to the door to the front waiting area. One of these days he'd get around to hiring a receptionist who could deal with that crap. He was a mechanic, and this lousy shop only had two of them. It didn't matter if he was young and hadn't "done his time" yet. He didn't have time to deal with deskwork.

The bell on the front door jingled, muffled and distant from the next room. Jimmy sighed and got to his feet, leaving the water bottle on the concrete floor beside the motorcycle he'd been working on. Another thing a receptionist would be good for – dealing with the customers.

"Wow. This place is legit." The voice was dripping with sarcasm.

"Jeez, somebody really needs a good dose of happy pills." The second voice was lighter, both in pitch and in emotion.

"Are you sure about this place? There's a Chevy dealer on the other end of town –"

"It's my car, and this place was highly rated online."

"By what, the three people who come here?"

Jimmy rolled his eyes as he pushed open the door to his waiting room and put on a smile. "Hey, how's it going?" He took in the two women before him, trying to bite back the "are you lost" comment that immediately came to mind.

"Just fine – except we kind of have a car problem." The blonde one smiled warmly at him and stepped forward. "I'm Coby. This is my co-worker, LJ. We had a little fender bender last night and need to have my car looked at."

Of course they had. If Jimmy had a dollar for every car accident, serious or otherwise, that was caused by a completely sober female, he'd be rich. "You're in the right place. I'm Jimmy Washburn." He shook the little woman's outstretched hand reluctantly, much more interested in the brunette. "That your ride outside?"

The brunette, LJ, who was taller, sulkier, and exactly Jimmy's type, nodded and sighed. "It's just the driver side headlight, really. There's a little damage to the hood, but the thing is ancient."

The blonde laughed again. "Yeah, what's one more ding?"

Jimmy pushed the door open and the bell jangled again. He stepped out onto the small lot, surprised at the car they'd driven in. It was a 1967 Chevelle, smoky gray with impressively clean chrome bumpers and side mirrors. He'd expected a Vibe or a PT Cruiser, if he was being honest, and the car impressed him mildly, until he got to the other side and saw the smashed headlight. "You hit a deer?"

"Cop car, actually."

Jimmy shook his head. "Too bad. This thing is a babe."

"You mean you can't fix it?" Coby asked, worried.

"I didn't say that. It's just a shame to see her banged up like this." Jimmy crouched, inspecting the grill but keeping an eye on the brunette. "It'll run around two hundred, give or take."

LJ twitched, but the blonde piped up first. "Sounds good. When can you get started?"

Jimmy stood. "Next week."

"What?" LJ croaked.

Jimmy shrugged and put his hands on his hips. "It's almost sixty years old. I don't just have these parts lying around – it's gonna take a while to get them in."

Coby raised her eyebrows at LJ. "We're gonna be here most of the week for the article anyway."

LJ sighed. "How long will it take you to fix once you get the part?"

Jimmy shrugged again. "Hour or two." He glanced at LJ, hoping she'd be impressed. She barely lifted an eyebrow. Jimmy rubbed a hand through his wiry, red hair. "The paint job's gonna be longer. Stuff's gotta set for a couple days."

LJ tapped her boot on the pavement. "That's too long. We can get it repainted when we're home and have some time off." She shot Coby a look, and the blonde responded with a nod. LJ looked back to Jimmy. "Can we drive it until then?"

"Hey, you can do whatever you want, sweetheart." Jimmy sent her a wink. "You look like an independent woman. Just don't sue me when you get ticketed."

LJ narrowed her eyes and Coby chuckled out, "I think we'll be okay on that end."

Jimmy wasn't sure what that was supposed to mean, but it probably had something to do with them batting their eyelashes to get out of speeding tickets. Truth be told, if he were a cop and he pulled over a babe like LJ, he wouldn't be writing anything up either. "Well, let me take your information and I'll give you a call when my order comes in. Usually takes five to seven days."

"Works for us."

Chapter Eleven

Grizzly pulled into the police station, balling up a paper McDonald's bag in one hand, and taking a swig of Cola. He glanced around for Clyde before stepping out of his car. He had been to the golden arches twice that week already and he didn't relish the idea of getting a lecture on his eating habits from the mother he never wanted, his first officer Clyde Burkiss.

As he darted for the garbage can, looking around furtively, he slowed to a stop at the sight of a familiar looking Chevelle that was pulling into the parking lot. The car parked in the slot next to his cruiser and the small blonde, Coby, gave him a wave before killing the engine and hopping out. "Hello!" she called to Grizzly, smiling wide and making a beeline for him.

Grizzly raised his hand in greeting. "Hey there, Miss Anderson, what can I do you for?" he asked.

"Ugh, Coby, please," she said, coming to a stop in front of him. "I was hoping I could maybe get a few shots? Add them to an article of the local police department?" she asked, grinning and holding up the large black camera that was hanging around her neck.

"OH, uh, sure!" Grizzly said, with a shrug. "Do you want to come in, or...?"

"Sure!" Coby said brightly. "But first, how about I get one right here, in front of the building," she said, backing up and raising the camera to her face.

"Okay," Grizzly said, attempting to move out of her way.

"Oh no, stay there," Coby said, lowering the camera a bit. "Pictures tell a much better story with people in them." She smiled. "That is, if you don't mind."

"Naw, I don't mind," Grizzly said, moving back towards the doorway, before realizing he was still holding the McDonald's bag. He pitched it quickly.

"All right." She adjusted the lens a bit as he positioned himself in the doorway. "Great!" she said as she clicked the picture and lowered the camera.

Grizzly smiled at her and shrugged his shoulders. "You still want to come inside?" he asked.

"I'd love to," she said, walking through the door as he opened it for her.

Coby waved at Julia and thanked her for the cookies from the night before. Grizzly smiled to himself and shook his head. She seemed more than happy to be there this time, the nerves of that night totally gone. Julia waved them on and they made their way down the hall toward the back room containing the officers' desks.

Clyde looked up at Grizzly as he rounded the corner. His eyes narrowed. Grizzly could feel the scolding coming on. "You didn't go out to –" But his words died on his lips as Coby stepped into the room behind Grizzly and smiled at him.

"Hi again!" she said brightly. Grizzly watched as Clyde stood, nervously rubbing the palms of his hands on his slacks, a red flush creeping up his neck. "Miss –"

"Coby," she finished for him, coming to a stop in front of his desk. "How are you feeling today?" she asked, looking genuinely concerned.

Grizzly fought the urge to roll his eyes at Clyde.

"F-Fine, I'm fine… thanks…" he said, shifting awkwardly, unable to hold her gaze.

Grizzly raised his eyebrows at him and shook his head. "Well, look around, darlin'," he said motioning to the room. "Take as many pictures as you need."

"Thanks," Coby said. She held up her camera, pointed it at Clyde and smiled. "Do you mind?"

"I- uh …" Clyde sputtered.

"It's for the article we're writing," she said.

"Well I-I…guess –" He was starting to blush and Coby snapped the picture.

She winked at him. "Perfect."

His mouth snapped shut and his whole face turned beet red.

Grizzly chuckled as Coby ambled around taking a few shots. He whapped Clyde on the back, who gave him a glare before sitting back at his desk, attempting to get back to work. After a few moments she walked back towards them, looking pleased. "Thanks guys, these will be great."

"No problem." Grizzly smiled at her.

"Hey, I was wondering..." she hesitated. "Is there any chance we could interview you guys sometime? For the article? Some evening or something, you know, whatever works best for you…"

Grizzly shrugged. "Sure, that would be fun. Whaddya say, Burkiss?"

"Well, I –"

Grizzly interrupted. "There's this great Mexican place on Main Street. Best burritos in the world… tomorrow night?"

Coby's face lit up with excitement. "Sounds perfect!"

They both looked at Clyde who seemed to melt a bit at her hopeful expression. "I-I don't think I have plans."

"Great! It's a date! See you ladies tomorrow." Grizzly grinned.

Coby waved, thanked them for their time, and headed out.

***

Shaun Pritchard leaned against the break room door frame and watched the blonde as she walked down the hall. She was looking at the camera in her hands, flipping through the pictures on the screen. He'd never seen her before, but the camera and the purposeful walk implied she belonged there. "You with the coroner's unit?"

She paused, looking up in confusion. "What?"

Pritchard took a sip of his coffee, nodding toward her camera. "Crime scene photos?"

"Oh! No." She laughed. "I'm just getting some shots for a magazine article." She let the camera hang from the strap on her neck and extended her hand. "Coby Anderson."

Pritchard straightened, tossed the empty Styrofoam cup into the trash, and stepped forward to shake her hand. "Officer Shaun Pritchard."

Coby lifted the camera again, raising an eyebrow. "Could I get a shot of you?"

"What magazine do you work for?"

"It's *Pure Travel*, out of Grand Rapids, Michigan. My partner and I write travel articles about small towns. We're featuring Waupun in the next issue and we've decided to do a section on the local police force." She motioned toward his uniform. "A picture of Officer Shaun Pritchard looking all official would certainly add some detail."

"I don't mind," Pritchard replied, amused.

She snapped a picture, inspected it on the screen, and nodded. "Perfect. Thanks. I'd better get going. I'll be back though, so I'll probably see you around."

He gave her a nod, and she continued down the hallway with a wave. Pritchard watched her walk out the station door, intrigued, wondering what her story in Waupun would be.

***

LJ stormed out of city hall feeling flustered and annoyed. She couldn't believe Coby had just blown her off. Unless she'd had another accident… LJ *hoped* Coby had been in another accident.

LJ ground her teeth and glared at her cell phone as she searched for Coby's number. She stood outside of city hall while the line rang, hand on her hip.

No answer. She let out a growl and ended the call with force. She shouldn't be mad. Maybe Coby really had gotten into another accident. But… well honestly, if that was the case she was still mad. She shoved her phone into her pocket and crossed her arms, rocking back on her heels.

The interview went well despite Coby's absence. LJ obtained some town history, some information on their events, and good leads on people to talk to. But it would have gone better with Coby there. They were a good team, especially thinking up questions on the fly. However, Coby had been distracted ever since they arrived, completely obsessed with the prison.

She strode down the sidewalk back towards the motel room.

It didn't totally surprise LJ. Coby was often sidetracked by her weird interests. She had dragged LJ through the woods in Wexford County, Michigan the year before, looking for the Michigan Dogman. While that was annoying, it was part of what made their writing interesting. But not showing up for things that were paid assignments was not cool.

Her phone rang from her pocket. She seized it and answered. "What the crap, man?!" she asked as she plowed forward, ignoring the people who paused and looked at her. "Where were you?" she hissed into the phone.

There was a moment of confused silence and LJ could almost hear the dawning realization on Coby's face through the phone. "OHHHH… Oh LJ, I'm so sorry, I stopped somewhere to get some pictures and then I got distracted and I just totally spaced."

LJ clamped her mouth closed in a sharp frown before letting out a sigh. "Come on Coby, I really could have used you here!"

"I know, I'm sorry, I just got caught up and wasn't thinking."

"Obviously," LJ said, still annoyed.

Coby let out a sigh on the other end of the phone and there was a few moments of silence. "Did you get anything?"

LJ hesitated, feeling resentful enough to withhold information, but she gave in. "Yeah, I'll be back to the motel soon," she muttered.

"Awesome, see you in a few!" Coby said brightly and hung up.

LJ let out a huff and tucked her phone back in her pocket, shaking her head as she stalked down the sidewalk towards the motel.

Chapter Twelve

Neal Murphy grabbed the final stack of books and placed them on the cart before pushing it towards the rack of New Releases. It had been a quiet day, but he didn't mind really. He enjoyed being alone. It allowed him time to think.

Straightening his blue dress shirt, he traced his fingers against the spines of the books on the shelf, looking for where he needed to place *Suspect,* even though he didn't really need to look. He knew the library backwards, forwards and inside out.

He heard loud chattering seconds before the door swung open. Neal looked up, straightening his glasses as he saw two women enter and head for the front desk. Neal knew most people in town and he remembered people's faces well. He hadn't seen these women before.

He narrowed his eyes thoughtfully and turned back to the task at hand, keeping an ear open to their conversation.

"LJ, come on. No one cares about statues. Statues are everywhere. But the *prison*. Do you see this place?" The blonde girl motioned to her right, in the general direction of the prison across the street. "It looks like a castle. Can you imagine the shots I could get?"

"Let's just focus on the task at hand, okay? It's called the City of Sculpture, not the City of Psychopaths. I kind of doubt they want to be remembered that way, *Coby*." The taller one with the dark hair tied back in a ponytail sighed, striding in behind the blonde.

"Well... maybe we can do both. Come on LJ, this would be a great story. Something different. Something new." The blonde was all but bounding across the room.

The dark haired one, LJ, came to a stop and planted her hands on her hips, looking at the blonde, eyebrows furrowed. "Something *'new'*? What is up with you? Why would we want to write something *'new'*?"

Her comrade, Coby – Neal was pretty sure was her name – turned toward her but didn't meet her eyes. She shrugged. "I just think it would be a good story. Don't you ever get tired of the same old thing?"

"You mean our job? That we both love?" LJ asked, lifting her sunglasses to the top of her head.

"Well, yeah. But, I mean, you don't really think we're going to do this forever, do you?" Coby said lightly, rolling her eyes with a chuckle.

LJ's eyes widened. "What *else* would we be doing?" she said, looking appalled at her friend.

Coby blinked, her grin faltering. "Well… I just meant…" LJ just stood there, waiting for an answer. Coby glanced around the library, her eyes locking onto Neal. "Oh, hey!" she said, turning and striding toward him, a wide smile on her face as LJ glared at her retreating form.

Neal set the books he was organizing back down on the cart and gave the girl a polite smile, hoping they wouldn't realize he had heard their entire conversation. That would make things awkward, and he wasn't very good with awkward. He cleared his throat and raised his eyebrows at her. "Hello, can I help you?"

The blonde girl smiled up at him. "Yeah, hi, my name is Coby Anderson." She stuck her hand out.

Neal saw the tall girl purse her lips and begrudgingly walk towards them out of the corner of his eye. He took Coby's hand and shook it, blue eyes crinkling behind his glasses. "Neal Byron Murphy," he said. "I'm the head librarian here. Estelle and Justine shelve books on the weekends."

Coby grinned at him when he introduced himself, and her eyes widened as she looked around the sizable library. "Wow, this place is impressive."

Neal shrugged, adjusting the front of his shirt. "It's a pretty good-sized library. How can I help you ladies?" he asked, looking up and offering LJ a smile as well. LJ gave him a tight smile and nodded in greeting but didn't introduce herself.

"We're writing a piece on the town for a magazine out of Grand Rapids," Coby explained. "And we were wondering if you have a section on Waupun's local history?"

Neal's eyes widened. "A piece on Waupun? How exciting, and yes, we do, follow me."

***

Coby tossed a nervous look back at LJ before following after the librarian. He was fairly tall with dark hair and pretty blue eyes, and he seemed very nice, even though LJ was being rude to him.

He led them to the back and up the stairs to the second floor. Coby trotted to keep up with his long strides, refusing to look back at LJ. Coby loved working with her, but she never really thought they would spend their whole lives driving across the country. She had some idea of what she wanted to do, like focusing on her photography and writing more than just magazine articles. LJ might be able to see that, under normal circumstances, but she really hadn't been the same since Colin.

LJ had thought Colin was the one. He'd thought he would play the field some more. Since then, she'd stopped looking at the future and thrown herself into their work. Coby knew it had been beneficial for their careers, and LJ's dedication secured their place with the magazine. But months had passed and Coby felt like LJ needed to move on for her own sake.

Coby quickly shook her head, clearing the thoughts away. She was here for a reason and she could deal with emotions later. Way later. Or never, that might be nice.

Neal walked past a few tables and shelves that contained magazines before stopping at a row of large filing cabinets. He pulled a drawer out and ran his finger along some plastic covered newspapers. "Any particular subject you're looking for?" he asked with a small smile.

Coby smiled back. "Uh, if we could just look through some of it, that would be great. We're kind of looking for ideas...a place to start..." she said with a shrug.

He stepped back and adjusted his glasses, studying her for a moment before smiling again. "Of course, if you need anything don't hesitate to ask," he said, eyes twinkling. He nodded to LJ who came to a stop behind Coby and folded her arms.

Coby grinned and then went for the cabinet, ignoring LJ's obvious disapproval behind her. "Well, I guess I'll start here," she said lightly, rifling through some of the papers and pulling out a stack dated forty years ago.

LJ let out a huff but strode forward and took one of the papers, turning her attention to it, dropping their former conversation for now.

Coby felt her shoulders drop a little as tension she didn't know she was carrying released.

She sighed and pulled out her phone as LJ sat down with the papers. Coby frowned, googling facts. "Did you know Waupun was originally called Waubun, which means 'Dawn of Day' until some goof made a typo and they never changed it?" She snickered.

LJ looked up at her and shook her head. "Classy."

"There's also a museum we could stop by," Coby said, scrolling through pictures.

"We'll have to set up some more interviews."

Coby flinched and put down the phone. She eyed LJ and opened her mouth to try and explain the meeting she had already set up with the chief of police.

"Maybe some you can actually show up for," LJ muttered, not bothering to honor Coby with so much as a glance. "See if you can find any phone numbers."

Coby snapped her mouth shut and rolled her eyes, immediately deciding LJ didn't need to know about the interview she was attending tonight if she was going to have *that* attitude. "Well, we already have Chief Grizzly's…" Coby taunted, holding up her phone and waving it side to side.

"Yeah, preferably someone we haven't hit with the car," LJ said with a snort.

Chapter Thirteen

"Why are you dragging me here?" LJ stood stubbornly on the sidewalk.

Coby smoothed her ponytail and pressed her lips together as she sighed through her nose. "I'm not dragging you anywhere. This is where we're meeting the guys for an interview, and you want to be here."

"Pretty sure I don't."

"What's the problem? This is how we do our job – we meet people who can give us information on our topic of choice. We ask them for an interview, we pick a place to meet with them, and we take notes for the article. This is not a new thing."

"This is dinner."

"So?"

"So it feels like a date."

"Pffft," Coby scoffed and waved a hand toward the sign hanging above them. "Your idea of a date is hitting up 'Cuco's' for margaritas?"

LJ's eyes narrowed. Even further than they'd already been, if that were possible. "You know what I mean."

"If you mean we're about to sit down to have drinks with a couple of fortunate-looking gentlemen, then you're right." Coby stepped behind LJ and pushed her toward the door. "This is a rare perk of the job so let's get on with this before they get sick of waiting for you."

***

"You're kidding!"

"I'm not."

"Ed Gein. Ed Gein was incarcerated at Dodge Correctional. Not two miles from where we're sitting?"

"Swear on my life."

LJ's eyes rolled so far back in her head they were practically backwards. "Would you two like to get a room for your incessant geeking?"

Coby looked over at her without the slightest waver of excitement. "*Ed Gein*. He's the one whose house was filled with –"

"Body parts. I know. You've only told me eight times today." LJ tilted her head toward the pair of officers sitting across from them. "As if your obsession isn't hard enough to understand, why are you being so giddy about serial killers and murder in front of these *cops*?"

"She's passionate about the notoriety, that's all." Grizzly reached for the tortilla chips and slid his salsa bowl closer. "I've spent some time with serial killers and other criminals – convicted and otherwise – she's not the type. It's the quiet, somber ones you gotta watch out for." He winked at LJ.

She stared back, unamused.

"Do you want some salsa?" Coby slid the bowl resting between her and LJ toward Clyde, who nervously crunched on a single tortilla chip.

"Uhh, no, thank you." He flushed and shook his head.

"Are you sure? You didn't even order anything."

"I just, uh… had a big lunch."

Grizzly boomed out a laugh. "Yeah, Burkiss, I'm sure you did." He slapped his partner on the back. "At least you learned your lesson this time."

Clyde's jaw clenched. "You're the one who picked the damn restaurant."

"How was I supposed to know you have the digestive system of a ninety-seven-year-old?"

"Grizzly, enough," Clyde muttered.

"Aw, come on Clyde, it's a great story!" Grizzly grinned, finishing off his strawberry margarita.

"We don't need to tell that story thank you very much." Clyde glowered at him over his glass of water.

"What story?" Coby asked, grinning at Clyde, who was refusing to look at any of them, flushing a darker shade.

"Coby," LJ muttered, obviously not wanting to encourage Grizzly.

"What, we're journalists, we love a good story." Coby grinned, swatting Clyde's arm good-naturedly.

Grizzly leaned back in his chair. "It was 2009. Police Appreciation Dinner. Right here in this very restaurant."

Clyde clapped a hand over his face.

"'*Taquitos Mexicanos*,'" Grizzly announced.

Clyde groaned from behind his hand.

"So the entire police department is here." Grizzly motioned around the tiny restaurant. "As well as half the town."

"Sounds fun," Coby prompted.

"It was *anything* but fun," Clyde mumbled under his breath.

LJ shook her head.

"Speeches were made. Donations were given. By the end of the night, the townsfolk went home and most of the off-duty officers were drunk. Clyde was supposed to be the designated driver." Grizzly grinned at his partner, who didn't even look at him. "But the little pansy ended up on the bathroom floor."

"Too much tequila?" Coby teased.

"Oh no, no." Grizzly shook his head. "Too much Mexican."

Clyde sat up straight. "Can we please change the subject?"

"Shh, no." Grizzly leaned an elbow on the table. "So it's three a.m., and I'm trying to find the DD so that we can all get home alive, and the waiters are trying to close up the damn restaurant, and nobody's seen Clyde. Finally, a bartender – can't speak two words of English – pulls me over to the restroom door and starts jabbering and pointing and getting pretty pissed, and I open the door and there's Officer Burkiss, fast asleep on the floor."

"Whoa now, hold on." Clyde scowled. "'Fast asleep' implies a level of comfort. Let's not forget that I'd spent the previous four hours writhing in agony while the depths of hell burned a hole through my gut."

"You poor thing." Coby reached across the table and squeezed his arm. Clyde flinched, turned red, and tried to hide it by reaching for his water glass.

"Whoa, whoa, careful there, Clyde," Grizzly warned. "Don't you know you're not supposed to drink the water in Mexico?"

Clyde turned a darker shade of red and LJ took mercy on him. "Can we get back to the topic we're all here to discuss?"

"I thought you didn't care about *my* topic, LJ," Coby teased, crunching on a salsa-loaded chip.

"I don't especially," LJ retorted. "But it *is* the reason we're here, keeping the local law enforcement from their duties."

Grizzly held up his empty margarita glass. "We're off duty, and it's our pleasure. Or mine, at least. If Clyde could stop blushing for five seconds he might be able to agree with me."

"So what kinds of cases do you guys work in Cow Town, Wisconsin?" Coby asked as she reached over and tapped LJ's notebook. She ignored the squint LJ sent her, not caring that she was being bossy, even though it obviously unnerved her partner. "Lots of boring stuff?"

Grizzly took a sip of his second, very pink, margarita. "*Lots* of boring stuff. Sometimes it's funny boring stuff – like the Vandenburgs who call in to report each other and bring us out to their domestic dispute at least once a month. Usually they have it cleared up by the time get there." He set down the glass and crossed his arms on the tabletop. "But most of the boring stuff is *really* boring. Like complaints about leaves and grass clippings blowing into people's yards and whiners who like to complain about eyesores and barking dogs." He pointed at Clyde with his thumb. "I make him deal with those situations."

Clyde stared at his untouched drink and narrowed his eyes with a sigh, which earned him a throaty laugh and a clap on the back that nearly sent him across the table.

LJ jotted some notes on her paper. "What about the less boring calls?"

Grizzly shrugged a shoulder. "There are a few noteworthy ones. We had a kid hyped up on PCP who was breaking into houses and doing serious damage. Luckily, most of the homeowners were out of town, but a few people were injured before we caught him. The drunk calls are always interesting, and frequent." He paused, seeming to struggle for more subject matter.

"And there are the missing girls," Clyde piped up, still staring at his margarita. His eyes got wide and he immediately reached for the beverage and tried it.

Something changed in Grizzly, and he lost a touch of enthusiasm for a second before reaching over and thumping Clyde on the back of the head. "That's confidential, Bupkiss."

Margarita sloshed and Clyde choked. "Sorry, I know I shouldn't, I didn't mean –"

Coby cocked her head in interest, and LJ raised an eyebrow at her as her pen scribbled a little faster.

"Don't worry about it." Grizzly shot Clyde a smile but it didn't reach his eyes. He looked back at the girls across the table. "I can't share all the details with you. But I can relay what our newspapers have reported in the past."

"Sounds fair enough." Coby nodded.

"They're not all missing."

Clyde sighed forcefully.

Grizzly scowled, turning away from Clyde, intent to ignore him. "There have been a few bodies."

LJ flinched at how much Coby perked up at the word "bodies."

"Over the last several years, we've lost a few girls."

Coby pulled out her own notebook and leaned forward. "How many?"

Grizzly hesitated. "Twelve gone missing. Found three."

LJ's brow furrowed.

"Details on the girls we found were never released, and I can't give you those. But they were kind of gruesome… Let's talk about something else." Grizzly finished off the second margarita.

Clyde took a deep breath and shook his head.

LJ set down her drink and clicked her pen, jumping on the opportunity to get back to the article. "Perfect. So… what's with the naked lady statue in front of City Hall?"

***

"I can't believe you made me sit in that restaurant for two hours just so you could flirt. I have writing to do." LJ scowled, slamming her purse down on the dresser and shrugging off her jacket. She flopped down on her mattress with a huff.

"What are you talking about?" Coby asked, a bewildered look on her face, kicking off her boots by the door.

"Oh please, you couldn't stop touching him," LJ said, rolling her eyes.

Coby's eyes widened in horror. "We were just talking about serial killers." Her brow furrowed in confusion.

"*Not* you and Officer Teddy –"

"Grizzly."

"Whatever, I meant Burkiss!" LJ said with an eye roll, popping upright and shuffling over to her suitcase, dragging out pajama pants and her laptop.

Coby gaped at her for a moment before shrugging and scoffing. "Oh please, have you ever witnessed me flirting? I was just trying to…I dunno, include him in the conversation. He seemed so uncomfortable, poor thing…

like a lost puppy," she said as she tied back her hair and padded into the bathroom to wash her face.

"You're the one who's been begging for a dog," LJ called over the sound of running water, pursing her lips as she booted up her laptop.

She heard Coby sputter through a handful of water before yelling "Very funny," in a sardonic tone. She stepped halfway out of the bathroom, drying her face off on a hand towel and threw it at LJ. "I got some great stuff for this prison piece, you got tons about the local law enforcement, and Grizzly seems more than happy to help us if we need it."

LJ frowned, picking the damp towel off of her laptop and looking up at Coby with a weary expression. "Why are you so hell-bent on this prison story? I mean, it's not like the entire piece is going to be about the prison; we have tons of other things to research."

Coby blinked at her and seemed to deflate a little bit. "Yeah... I know," she said with a shrug, stepping back into the bathroom to change.

LJ narrowed her eyes and craned her neck a little bit, looking towards the bathroom.

"Have you seen my glasses?" Coby called from the bathroom.

LJ leaned over and snagged them off the bedside table. "Here," she called, as she held them above her head.

Coby poked her head out of the bathroom again and shuffled over to LJ. She snatched the glasses and put them on before she flopped onto her bed. "Sleep."

LJ glanced up at her. "Sorry, I gotta jot some of these things down before I forget them."

"You mean you got something out of our 'pointless flirt meeting'?" Coby teased as she rubbed at her eyes under her glasses.

LJ made a face at her. "Yes, because I was there for business, not officers," she shot back at her.

Coby scoffed. "Yeah, yeah, yeah." She tossed a pillow at LJ's head.

***

It was late. All the lights were off. But he didn't need them on. Didn't need people wondering. Most people didn't sit down in their basements past midnight, he realized. So the lights would stay off.

He couldn't sleep. There was a story gnawing at the corner of his brain. Not leaving him alone. He pulled forward his typewriter and started. He liked typewriters. The sound was nice and he didn't trust his stories to computers. Computers were too easily hacked and searched and nothing was ever actually deleted.

Taptaptap

Two girls. Going town to town. Only a matter of time before something happened to them. Only a matter of time.

But *what* would happen? He wet his lips and drummed his fingers on the counter. This was what he loved. A million plot points flooded into his mind as his pulse quickened, all loud and colorful, clamoring for his attention. But he pushed them back. No. No, not yet.

He would savor every one of them, explore each scenario and linger on every detail. It had been too long since his last story and he would have to make this one linger… last…

It would be his finest work. He would make sure of it.

Chapter Fourteen

"I'm just saying, we have the Memorial Day Parade to worry about. We can't go out drinking with strange women all hours of the night."

Grizzly let out a loud laugh. "Clyde, that parade lasts ten minutes, if we're lucky. It's a bunch of people and a handful of horses that sit in the church parking lot. And strange? I think you mean *fine*." He waggled his eyebrows.

Clyde frowned, sitting down on his chair and shuffling through some papers. "Well Grizzly, if you want to spend your time flirting with those journalists –" he sputtered, looking flustered.

"Hey, hey, what's your problem?" Grizzly asked him, raising his eyebrows. "You didn't say three words to them. I mean, sure that LJ chick seemed a little uptight, but Coby was nice."

Clyde cleared his throat and stared intently at the month-old McDonald's receipt he had in his hand, avoiding Grizzly's gaze as he waited for an answer.

"Oh," Grizzly said, realization hitting him. "OH."

Clyde's ears turned pink but he still refused to acknowledge his partner.

"Oh, come on, Bupkiss," Grizzly groaned. "I don't know what they teach you down south, but when a man like you likes a girl you have to talk to her. Or at least, you know, acknowledge her existence."

Clyde looked up at him quickly, shooting him an irritated look. "I don't… she isn't – you don't know what you're talking about Grizzly," he garbled out, mindlessly shifting papers around.

"You're an appealing guy!"

Clyde narrowed his eyes.

"I mean… you're a *law officer.* That's *sexy.*"

Clyde sputtered. "What?!"

"Sure, you have a weird tea obsession, but your hair does that thing when it's wet…" he smoothed back his own hair, which was getting dangerously close to passing the point of acceptable for an officer.

Clyde turned red as he stared at him like he was insane.

Grizzly gave him a slow, knowing smirk and chuckled. "She's pretty isn't she? Just all smiles and plaid and waiting for some southern jackass to, I don't know, *speak* to her," he said, stepping forward whapping the back of Clyde's head.

Clyde winced and glared up at him, the flush on his neck and ears fading away a bit. "Look, I don't know her at all, and she's here for her job, not a date."

Grizzly grinned and shook his head. "Ain't nothing wrong with getting to know someone on a date Buttkiss. You should try it sometime."

"I have, thank you very much, and the only thing I've learned is that I don't know how to get to know women," Clyde said shortly.

Grizzly shook his head at the small man before him. "Don't be a quitter Burkiss. If you like the girl, ask her out. If she says no, she'll be leaving soon, no harm done." He spread his arms and shrugged at him.

"Is that why you kept staring at LJ's ass?" Clyde asked him, a scolding expression on his face.

Grizzly's bemused smile slammed down into a scowl. "Don't make me sound like a pervert Clyde, I wasn't staring, I was just… noticing."

"Of course, silly me."

"Hey, you seem a little on the irritable side right now. Why don't I make you some tea? I'll put in extra sugar, sourpuss."

Grizzly saw a muscle twitch in Clyde's jaw as he turned and walked away. "Just… don't over-steep it this time," Clyde's voice called after him.

Grizzly rolled his eyes and chuckled. He threw a mug of water into the microwave, which he knew Clyde hated, and dug out two packets of sugar and a bag of earl grey. Once the microwave beeped, he tossed the sugar and tea bag into the water, swirling the mug to stir it. He closed the microwave and he pulled out his cell phone, dialing the number Coby left him.

He trudged back to Clyde's desk, handing Clyde the mug of tea as the call went to Coby's voicemail.

Clyde accepted the mug, trying to keep a grimace off his face as Grizzly sighed and scratched his beard. "Hello Coby, this is Police Chief Grizz – Gregory Adams of the Waupun Police Department. I'm calling you back about our conversation last night." From the corner of his eye he saw Clyde snap his head up, spill tea on his lap, and curse.

Grizzly bit back a chuckle. "Uh, yeah so, Officer Burkiss said he'd be happy to give you some more information about the cases and that you should call him to set up a date, uh, I mean, a time."

Clyde launched himself around his desk. "Grizzly," he snarled, looking both livid and horrified.

Grizzly danced a few steps away from him, holding his phone securely to his ear. "His number is 920-324-0047. He'll be awaiting your call. You ladies have a nice day. Bye now," Grizzly said before hanging up and giving Clyde a satisfied smirk.

Clyde pursed his lips together, jaw twitching again and shook his head, hands planted on his hips. "Great, Grizzly. Just great. Information? I don't even think that's *legal* much less –"

"A simple thank you would suffice, Clyde."

Chapter Fifteen

Night was falling and any traffic Waupun saw at rush hour was long gone. An occasional evening straggler floated by the front window of the laundromat, and more often headlights would flash by. After weeks without a washing machine, Coby and LJ were long overdue for clean clothes. The laundromat was empty except for the two of them, which they both appreciated since they'd spent the day interviewing multiple people.

"I called the prison and asked if we could get a tour, even just of the grounds or the visiting area or something, but they weren't exactly super negotiable on the phone." Coby shrugged as she settled a collapsible hamper full of socks on top of a folding table. "I mean it won't be hard to write without getting a tour, it just would have been nice to see the place."

LJ let out a hum that made her sound more irritated than interested, which she was.

"But at least we've gotten a few good stories from the places we've visited already. And we've set up more interviews… and we can always talk to Officer Clyde and Chief Grizzly some more. Especially about those unsolved murder cases," Coby said, voice lifting with excitement.

"We need to talk about this, you know," LJ said, digging her damp clothes out of the washing machine.

She could see Coby clam up a bit out of the corner of her eye. "About what?"

"This." LJ waved her hand between them. "You wanting to leave me to write about serial killers and sasquatches –"

Coby's shoulders drooped a bit and she turned away from her pile of socks to look at LJ. "I don't want to *leave you*."

"You said you didn't want to do *this* forever. What's that about? Am I that terrible to work with?"

"*This* being traveling around the USA, never settling down, never getting close to anyone, not *this* us being best friends and writing together… it's not about us, LJ," Coby said with a small frown, folding her arms, and looking genuinely hurt.

LJ scoffed, slamming the lid of the dryer. "Well, obviously not," she muttered.

"That's not what I meant. I just… I want to settle down at some point, you know… get married, have kids… and I'd like to have a bit of a writing portfolio by then… try some new things," Coby said softly, eyes on the ground. "We've talked about that. You can't honestly picture living out of a car with me, working for the magazine forever." Coby looked up at her, green eyes searching hers.

To her horror LJ felt a hard lump wedge in her throat and her eyes start to water. "It's enough for me," she said, willing her voice not to break.

Coby looked up at her. "I don't think so. I think ever since you broke up with Colin, you've just poured yourself into work."

LJ felt her entire body tense. That subject struck a nerve and she didn't want to talk about it. At all. "I've always loved my work," she said, voice shaking.

"Yeah but not like this LJ. You don't do anything anymore. We used to do all sorts of fun stuff. We used to *enjoy* the towns we visited and now all you want to do is get back to your laptop and beat the deadlines," Coby said with a sigh, looking sorry to have to say it at all. "And that's fine, I knew you needed to tuck yourself away. He was a jerk and he hurt you. But that was a while ago, and not everyone's like Colin."

LJ felt hurt but also a little bit angry. And very defensive. "What, your solution is for me to start going on random dates?" she asked sharply.

"No. But LJ you keep acting like it's *me* who's not enjoying this job anymore, and that's not true. I basically had to force you to go interview the guys because it might actually be fun. Every time Grizzly as much as looked at you, you treated him like he was Colin –"

"That's *not* true," LJ interrupted, desperately wanting the conversation to be over but unsure how to stop it from picking up momentum.

"LJ. You don't have to worry about me leaving you, okay? I'm not Colin either, I would never do that, even if I do end up leaving the magazine or getting married someday, we're still going to be best friends, okay? Our relationship doesn't have to end because change happens. I'm never going to leave you," Coby said and her voice caught a little bit, LJ saw her blink away tears.

Silence filled the void between them, and the only sounds were the appliances. Once again, LJ was glad there was no one else in the laundromat. She finally felt the tension leave, gut clenching with shame. "I… I know you're not. I didn't mean –" she faltered.

Coby rubbed the sleeve of her shirt across her nose quickly and looked up at LJ, attempting to give her a grin. "And seriously, like I'm anywhere near getting married or anything, this is not something we have to worry about right now," she said, nudging her laundry bag with the toe of her boot.

LJ swallowed, glancing down. "Yeah," she said, unsure what else to say.

Coby's phone beeped and she took it out of her pocket to glance at the screen. "It's just a voicemail from the station. I'll call them back later. Are we okay?" Coby asked, looking up at LJ.

LJ stared at the phone and nodded before looking up at her. "Yeah… always."

Coby smiled, a real smile, and stepped forward, holding her arms open. "You know what's happening now."

"Oh gosh, please no."

"Don't try to fight it."

"Don't touch me."

"Shush."

LJ hadn't hugged Coby that tight since the break-up, and she was pretty sure they both knew it.

***

Grizzly groped around for his coffee mug, refusing to look up from the case file he was reading. He found the ceramic handle and brought the cup to his lips, twitching and grimacing at the chilled liquid that filled his mouth. He put the mug down and straightened, eyes finally leaving the small print and squinting up at the clock on the wall. He'd been at it for hours, and it would be hours before he quit.

He cracked his neck and rolled his chair back, looking at the mess he'd made of his desk. Papers spilled off one end, making an abused pile on the floor. The wastebasket was overflowing with crumpled sheets of stupid, useless theories. His map on the wall was littered with pushpins and post-it notes.

The crime scene photos nagged him the most. Every time he pulled out the files, he meticulously laid out every shot, sometimes going so far as to tape them next to the map in straight, chronological lines. Forcing himself to look at the pictures and have the pictures looking back at him kept him focused, kept him driven.

Grizzly got to his feet with a groan, heading for the water cooler in the next room. The coffee pot had long ago been turned off, and caffeine wouldn't do him any good at this point. Neither would the water, but he drank a cupful anyway. Only one thing would settle his nerves when he got this strung out.

The late spring air was nippy, but refreshing and tolerable in just a long-sleeved Henley. Grizzly shut the back door of the station and leaned against the brick wall, gazing up at the stars as he pulled a cigarette and a lighter from an old Marlboro pack.

Smoke hit his lungs like an old friend clapping him on the back. He exhaled slowly, watching the haze lift against the streetlight across the back lot. The buzz in the back of his head lessened, and his anxiety lowered a few notches.

"*Gregory.*"

Grizzly flinched so hard he nearly flung the cigarette to the pavement. He dropped his hand at his side and turned to look at the small frame standing in the doorway. He hadn't even heard the door open.

"Jules, hey. What are you doing here so late?"

"I left something on my desk." Julia stepped outside and crossed her arms, staring up at Grizzly accusingly. "What are *you* doing?"

Grizzly waved his other hand in the air, brushing off the oddness of working so late, but mostly trying to clear the air of smoke. "You know. Just going over some files."

Julia shook her head slowly, all but tsking her tongue at him. "You put that out."

Grizzly scowled. "I don't even smoke anymore."

She pointed at the glowing cigarette in the hand he was practically hiding behind his back. "Oh really?"

"This is *one.*"

"Put it out."

"I'm allowed to have one damn cigarette."

"Gregory –"

"I am the *chief of police* –"

"–*Stephen* –"

"Fine!" Grizzly huffed and dropped the Marlboro to the asphalt and crushed it with his toe. "Dammit."

Chapter Sixteen

LJ rubbed her eyes and stared at her phone screen, trying to make out the time through bleary, early-morning vision. Sunlight peeked over the eastern horizon, but LJ wasn't really buying it. It didn't feel like morning; it felt like hell.

She sniffed, fighting off morning allergies that threatened to make her lie down right there in the Chevelle and go back to sleep. The chill in the air wasn't helping anything.

LJ hauled her laptop out from behind the seat and shoved the keys into the pocket of her jeans. Her cowboy boots sounded ridiculously loud on the pavement of the empty parking lot; the creak of the old car's door echoed off the houses across the street. LJ eyed the neon sign in the window claiming the place was open, even at the ungodly hour she decided to pry herself out of bed.

The bell on the door jingled as she crashed through it, laptop bag heavy and limbs tired and uncoordinated.

End of the Trail Candy Shoppe had a back entrance that opened up into a miniature gift store, with everything from stuffed animals to touching sentimental presents to plaques boasting "man cave." LJ walked blindly past it all, fumbling up the few steps into the coffee shop.

"Good morning!" A petite, dark-haired girl who didn't look old enough to drive sang from behind the counter. LJ bared her teeth in what was supposed to be a smile and tried to focus on the menu. She quickly gave up and scanned the labeled coffee pots against the back wall.

"Strongest brew you've got. Large." LJ shoved money toward the girl, who didn't attempt further conversation and simply obeyed the grunting.

LJ took her coffee and turned toward the tables in the café. She picked the one in the corner and hunkered down there, breathing in the steam from the coffee before sliding her laptop out of the bag and opening the screen.

Coby was still curled up in the motel room, undoubtedly having some elaborate dream off in the wonderful world of sleep, where she would remain until well after nine o'clock. LJ scowled to herself as she powered up her machine to get started on work. Her resentment was entirely self-imposed – no one forced her to get up early and work. In fact, that was one of the beautiful perks of working on a personalized schedule with a once-a-week deadline – she could do whatever she wanted as long as the article was sent in on time.

And yet, for whatever reason, LJ liked to sentence herself to this punishment at least once a week, getting up at the crack of dawn and trying to make a dent in their workload. It made her feel accomplished and usually ended up being a smart move that put them a step ahead.

But it was never worth the effort until after ten.

"Kita, darlin', how are you this fine morning?"

LJ flinched and peered over her laptop. Of all the voices to hear before the sun was fully up, Police Chief Grizzly Adams' was the last one she wanted invading her space.

"I'm doing pretty good, Chief. How about yourself?" The girl beamed up from behind the cash register, hands folded on the countertop.

Grizzly grinned back through the unruly beard that LJ found as irritating as the man himself. "Oh, you know, can't complain too much."

"You heading in or out?"

LJ couldn't see his expression from her position in the corner, but from the giggling that erupted from the girl she assumed it was amusing. "What do you think, hon?"

"Decaf then, if you're going home to sleep?"

He waved her off. "I can sleep when I'm dead. Get me the strongest brew you've got. Large."

LJ looked down at the large coffee in her hands, hoping desperately that he'd just pass her by. The tall, broad-shouldered movement beyond her laptop screen caused her gaze to dart back up.

"Well, damn. This really is a small town, isn't it?"

LJ squinted at him as he snatched his coffee off the counter and winked at Kita before turning back toward the corner table and ambling over. LJ stiffened as he pulled out a chair and promptly made himself at home in her domain, completely taking over her space. He rested his elbows on the table top and cocked his head at her as she continued to glare overtop her computer screen. "Just what are you doing out at this hour besides leaving an icy trail in your wake?"

LJ bristled, seriously considering dropping her hot coffee in his lap before storming back to the motel, laptop and research be damned. "Did your cop school teach you how to harass civilians, or do you just come by that naturally?"

Adams sipped his coffee but the cup didn't hide the grin on his face. "I've been told it's all natural."

LJ glowered at her laptop screen. She decided to ignore him, opening up the document she needed and resolving to do exactly what she came to do.

"Where's your cohort?" It seemed he refused to be ignored.

"Where's your boyfriend?" she shot back.

"Left him back at the station. Gotta have my independence once in a while."

LJ refused to look at him. She focused on the article and skimmed the outline she'd written the day before. Her usual skeleton consisted of five parts, and Coby had jotted her own notes and ideas between LJ's paragraphs. Something about wanting to express the different cultures intertwined in the community, and possibly a humorous bit about the noon whistle that still sounded every day but Sunday, as well as…

LJ looked up at the imposing form before her, exasperated. Adams leaned toward her, watching her intently, amusement as evident as the tattoos peeking out from the collar and sleeves of his rumpled uniform. "Can I help you, Chief?"

"I was about to ask you the same thing, since you seem to be stalking me and all."

LJ straightened. "Oh, this should be good."

Adams removed the lid from his coffee. "First you literally run into my cruiser –"

"I didn't run into anything. Coby was driving."

"And now you're waiting for me at the best coffee joint in town," he finished, looking pleased with himself.

She narrowed her eyes. "It's the only coffee joint in town. It's also the only place open this early that has Wi-Fi."

"Excuses, excuses." Adams took another swig of coffee, eyes crinkled with the constant enjoyment her discomfort seemed to bring him. "We both know it's my animal magnetism."

"Sorry to disappoint you. I wouldn't waste my time on a man already so obviously spoken for."

"Come on now. It's the twenty-first century. A man can't have a boyfriend and a female paramour?"

LJ sighed. He seemed impossible to unnerve. "Do you mind? I'm trying to get some work done."

"Not at all. Go for it," Grizzly prompted, sitting back comfortably and taking a swig of his coffee.

LJ shut her eyes and mentally counted to ten.

***

Coby yawned and rubbed her eyes, as she stood in the motel room doorway and stared at the empty parking space she was pretty sure had held the Chevelle the night before. Sometimes she wondered if LJ lived her life trying to find ways to get Coby riled. It wouldn't work. Coby was stubborn in few ways, but refusing to get upset when people tried to get her upset was what kept her going.

The sun was out, the skies clear. There was a chill in the May air, but it held a promise of a beautiful day regardless. Coby leaned back into the room and pulled on her jacket before snatching her bag and heading out.

The police station wasn't far. She was pretty sure it was easily within walking distance of the motel, provided she could figure out which way down Main Street she needed to go. Coby paused on the sidewalk to look both ways, not sure just which way that was. She started west – she was pretty sure it was west – but after ten minutes she turned around and headed back.

The building was cut in half, with one end housing the fire department and the other used by the Waupun police. Coby approached the doors and eyed the hours painted on the glass. She pulled out her phone to check the time, then smiled to herself at her dumb luck and opened the freshly unlocked door.

***

"What is this supposed to be?"

Clyde stared at the HP logo on his desktop. He focused hard on it, feeling his eyebrows furrow together intensely, trying to ignore the question.

"Is this your report on the Vander Slunt incident? Is that actually what you think this is?"

The computer logo was blue. Clyde wasn't sure he'd noticed that before. He tried to find it fascinating.

"I guess I can't really be surprised. Maybe this passes as good police work back in Hazzard County with Roscoe and Boss Hogg, but here in the real world, this, this is laughable."

Clyde heard a grinding noise and realized it was his teeth. "Would you like me to go over it again, Officer Pritchard?"

Shaun Pritchard dropped the file onto Clyde's desk and straightened his uniform tie. "I don't know why I expect anything else, being teacher's pet."

There was a faint pounding sound in the back of Clyde's head as he squinted up at Pritchard. "What is that supposed to mean?"

Pritchard rolled his eyes and sauntered toward his desk. "Just reminding you that we all read those reports, Burkiss. Not just your beloved police chief bestie."

Clyde sighed and thought about leaping out of his chair and wrapping his hands around Pritchard's throat. Pritchard had been with police department longer than either Clyde or Grizzly, and had always assumed he would become chief of police. He resented Grizzly for taking the title from him, and Clyde for being promoted to first officer. But Pritchard wasn't the amazing cop he thought he was; he was arrogant and had an unhealthy sense of entitlement. Which was proven by his constant questioning of every judgement call Clyde or Grizzly made.

Strangling Pritchard was something Clyde debated every day, but rational thinking always won out, and it did so again. He glanced at the file Pritchard had tossed at him and reached to open it.

Silence. At last. He had just started to relax when he heard Julia laughing from the front desk, and a frustrated sigh crawled out of his throat. He wondered if Grizzly was back already. Clyde had told him to go home. The man had worked through the night and on no sleep he would just be a bear, no pun intended.

Footsteps started down the hall towards him and he braced himself for a fight with the man while shuffling some evidence bags off his desk, not even bothering to look up. "Grizzly, I thought I told you to go home, you look like hell warmed over, you stubborn idiot."

"Well you don't look so hot yourself," a feminine voice shot back at him from the doorway.

Glancing up, Clyde inadvertently launched backwards, sending his wheeled chair rolling across the linoleum. "Co– Miss, uh, Miss Anderson?"

The blonde smiled a ray of sunshine at him and he could feel his tongue swelling. "Good morning!" she said. "I just wanted to follow up with our meeting the other night, if you're not too busy, of course."

Horror flooded through him. Heat creeped up his neck. Somewhere in the back of his mind he wondered if his skin could turn a darker shade of scarlet than his usual hue. Grizzly would be so disappointed he'd missed it. "Uhh…"

"What was the other night, Officer Burkiss?" Pritchard piped up from his desk.

"Just… just a business meeting." Clyde all but scrambled to his feet in a delayed reaction to Coby's entrance. "Miss Anderson, I'm not - sorry… I mean, I'm not not sorry, I mean I'm sorry I'm not busy." He squeezed his eyes shut and wished his desk were closer to the wall so he could smash his forehead against the drywall. "I'm sorry. No, I'm not busy. Of course I can follow you up." He forced up a cough to clear his throat, hoping she didn't notice how weird his last line sounded.

Coby's smile never wavered. "Great! So you mentioned the missing girls… I completely understand if there are confidentiality issues. Like, I don't expect to see the files or anything. I just hoped you could take a look at them and let me know if there's any information you're allowed to share." She set her bag on his desk and dug through it until she came up with a notepad. "I also have some more questions, if you have time to answer them."

Clyde twitched as she pulled up a chair and plopped down in it, staring up at him eagerly. He cleared his throat again and moved to sit down, very nearly spilling onto the floor when he almost missed his chair. "I, uh, I can't really give out information on the files."

"Sure, of course. What did you tell the press?"

He smoothed his uniform and tried to sit up straight. "I don't really talk to the press." He forced his gaze to his computer screen when she seemed to be fighting off a laugh.

"Of course, that makes sense, they'd want to talk to the chief," she said, smile warm. "So what did Grizzly tell them?" she prompted, crossing her legs and shifting forward.

Clyde glanced up at her again and diverted his eyes to her pen and paper, frowning and clearing his throat. "We found a little girl named Kacey Schelling on one of the playgrounds two months ago. She had been dead for three months already." Coby had started to scribble on the notepad, nodding her head in acknowledgement. She was wearing dark blue jeans, and a grey sweater that hung loose on her. It looked too soft to be actual clothes. Her hand had stopped moving.

"Gun shot?" she asked him and he startled out of his reverie.

Clyde hesitated, wincing, unsure of what he could tell her. "No, she —"

"What are you doing?" A harsh voice floated from Pritchard's desk.

Clyde closed his eyes and willed himself not to shoot the man.

"That is an open investigation, all evidence is confidential! You can't tell her anything, Burkiss." The scathing voice stomped closer to him.

Clyde slowly opened his eyes to see Coby watching him intently with a small crease between her eyebrows before she turned to look at Shaun as he strode towards them.

"I'm not telling her anything confidential, Pritchard," Clyde drawled slowly at the man as irritation filled him.

"Oh, did you get that out of the way 'the other night'?" Pritchard drawled back at him, mocking his accent.

Coby squinted at Pritchard as he leered at them, before standing up promptly and setting her notepad down on Clyde's desk. Clyde twitched, starting to rise out of his seat and tell her she didn't have to go, but he was cut off.

"Shaun!" Coby said, a wide smile was plastered on her face, but it lacked its usual warmth. "Do you have business to take care of with Officer Burkiss?"

Pritchard looked at the short woman under his nose. "No..."

Coby grinned, looking more and more like she was baring her teeth at him. "Oh, well if you don't mind, I'm trying to interview him. He is the first officer, correct?" She closed her mouth in a tight smile.

Pritchard stepped back with a frown.

"I'm sorry if this is distracting for you all, I'll be out of his hair soon. Thanks!" Coby said, turning away from Pritchard and sitting down, taking the notepad back into her hands.

Clyde's eyes widened at the woman before him. What was happening?

Pritchard crossed his arms. "Listen, little lady, this is a police investigation –"

"Officer Pritchard, we'll be done soon," Clyde said sharply to the man.

Pritchard turned purple with anger and walked away. "Julia! I needed those files *yesterday*!"

Coby clicked her pen again and scooted closer to the desk, smiling at Clyde. "Sorry if this is a pain, I can leave…"

"No! I– no," Clyde stammered quickly. "No you're fine, I mean, it's fine."

***

Grizzly took another sip of his coffee as he watched LJ save the document and click her laptop shut. She leaned back in her chair and lifted her coffee to her lips. "If you're going to be a dick about this, you might as well answer some questions," she stated flatly.

Grizzly looked back at her and gave her a sleepy grin. "My name is Gregory Stephen Adams. I'm thirty-six. I'm the Waupun police chief. I like long walks on the beach, romantic movies, and –"

"Let me just stop you there." LJ held up a hand and then placed it on the tabletop. "If you wanna talk, we can talk about police work in a small town. About how nice and safe your little Dutch community is." She narrowed her eyes at him as she dug around in her laptop case and pulled out a notepad, slapping it down on the table between them and clicking her pen open. "Unless of course, you'd rather talk about the disappearances you mentioned," she threw at him, voice a challenge.

Grizzly felt his smile fall along with his stomach and good spirits. He took a deep breath in and looked down at his coffee. "What do you want to know?" he asked, feeling the weariness hit him like a train once again.

LJ cocked an eyebrow. "Whatever you're allowed to tell me," she said. He knew she didn't really care about the missing girls; that wasn't what a travel magazine would want. But it seemed if he was going give her crap, she was going to dish it right back.

He sighed, taking another sip of his coffee as he pondered. "I'm not allowed to tell you anything, darlin'," he said honestly, even though bitter feelings were piling at the back of his throat.

"LJ," she corrected. "And are you sure? Because then that sounds like this conversation isn't going anywhere. Also, you look like you could really use a nap. You kind of look like shit," she said brightly, giving him a triumphant, pursed-lipped smile.

Grizzly rubbed a hand over his face. Her words didn't upset him but they did ring true. "I kind of feel like shit," he admitted and sighed again. There was a long pause between them as he fought with what to say. He saw LJ shift forward, like she was about to excuse herself and Grizzly suddenly found himself speaking. "Twelve years old. Twelve. Except she didn't even look that, you know? Little thing. She looked about eight."

LJ froze, a frown on her face as she listened. She slowly settled back against her seat. He knew he shouldn't be talking about this but what harm was it doing? Most of the people in this town knew all of these details. What good was he doing by holding it inside of himself?

Words kept spilling out of him. "Someone called it in. Spring, the snow was melting, things were thawing... she was thawing out. They smelled her before they saw her." Grizzly shook his head at the memory, feeling the horror of it all over again. "I've seen…" he paused, tasting his words. "I had a bad past, and I've seen a lot of shit, but that… that little girl. She was decomposing, still part frozen…" He grimaced, feeling both sad and disgusted. "Her heart was cut out. Bastard took her heart."

LJ's face mirrored his feelings as she slowly set her pen down next to the note pad. She looked like she didn't know what to say. He knew he should feel bad, maybe guilty for putting all that on her, but all he could feel was relief.

Grizzly looked away from her quickly and swirled the coffee in his cup, shifting his large form awkwardly on the small chair, and sniffing. "I knew there had been some disappearances before I was the chief… I knew how much they weighed on Walter, but…" He cleared his throat. "I can't help but think that finding them like *that* is even worse."

LJ reached forward and placed a hand over his.

Grizzly paused, his words dying on his lips before quickly shaking his head and looking up at her. "Never thought it would feel this bad," he finished, before gathering himself. He gave her a big smile and patted her hand. "Sorry. I shouldn't have told you that. Any of that."

LJ shook her head, withdrawing her hand quickly. "Don't worry about it. It's all off the record." She smiled a small smile back at him.

They talked for a bit longer, and then Grizzly left her at the coffee shop. He still felt exhausted, and melancholy, but also like a weight had been lifted.

He smiled to himself, recalling LJ's expression when he had pulled up a chair. That girl looked like she

could have dumped her coffee right in his lap and yet…
he could have sworn she looked disappointed when he
got up to leave.

Maybe he just needed some sleep. He glanced
down at his empty cup and snorted.

He was going fishing.

Chapter Seventeen

Coby looked out of the passenger window of the police cruiser, munching on a french fry. They had ended up talking for a long time at the Police Department, which she apologized for. Clyde told her not to worry about it, that he would just take his lunch break. She hadn't had breakfast that morning, and so here they were, finishing their conversation with a McDonald's bag between them. She glanced back at Clyde and smiled. "This is fun, thanks for lunch!"

He flushed, not looking at her. "Don't mention it."

She glanced around at all the gadgets in the car curiously. "So, can we pull someone over?" she asked, grinning at him impishly.

"That's not nearly as fun as you may think." Clyde glanced at her out of the corner of his eye, a slight smile playing on his mouth.

"But you get the siren going, everyone's gotta red sea it for you to take down the guy hopped up on speed…"

"Except for the Guy Hopped Up On Speed is sometimes a single mom trying to get to her second job after dropping her kid off at daycare, and she breaks down sobbing when you ask her for her license and proof of insurance."

Coby blinked and chewed on another fry. "On second thought, let's never pull people over. There are more important things, you know. Stupid cops."

She got a chuckle out of him for that one. She felt a rush at the fact that he seemed to be loosening up a bit around her. "Well, now I know all about Trevor, the good-for-nothing father of her child who hasn't paid his child support for the last six months." He smiled wryly.

Coby shook her head. "I hope you tracked him down and beat him up for her."

"Not exactly. But she was going to get herself a lawyer, last I heard. Which she should, because if little Elton is as talented in dance as she thinks, she really should be able to afford to get him lessons." He shrugged, and then winked at her.

She laughed. "So… did you uphold the law at all costs and give her a ticket?" she asked him, eyebrows raised.

He cleared his throat. "Uh, no."

"You are a decent person, Clyde Burkiss."

***

Clyde was trying very hard not to sweat through his shirt.

They had arrived back at the police department and Coby was leaning against the cruiser laughing at something he said. He couldn't even remember what it was anymore, but he was sure glad he said it.

"Well, I should let you go. LJ is probably wondering what happened to me." She chuckled, glancing at her phone. "Thanks for everything." She smiled at him and he desperately hoped she couldn't hear his pulse hammering away.

"Anytime." He smiled back at her as she straightened and started down the sidewalk, giving him a wave. He watched her go and took a deep breath, so very glad Grizzly had taken the rest of the day off.

Chapter Eighteen

The motel room smelled like mildew and greasy fast food sacks. LJ sat at the flimsy desk, staring at her computer with bleary eyes. She forced herself to focus on the clock, then leaned back in her seat when she realized how long she'd been sitting there.

She twisted to look toward the only window in their room, wishing yet again that it wasn't stuck shut. Just a breath of fresh air might help with the staleness.

Her eyes drifted to Coby, who leaned against the scuffed headboard of her bed, eyes closed. Her sheets bunched around her, and the floral print bedspread from 1972 was crumpled on the floor.

"You want to go for a walk?" LJ stretched her arms above her head. "I can't see straight anymore."

Coby's eyes popped open and she turned toward the window. The day was just beginning to wane, shadows stretching across the parking lot. "Yeah, sure! I bet I could get some nice shots with this lighting." She sat up and reached across the bed for her camera case.

LJ stood, pocketing her phone as she followed Coby out the door. They filed out of the lot, heading down Main Street toward the center of town. Coby took pictures of everything, pausing occasionally to check the shots and decide whether to keep them or scrap them. They trailed all through town, stopping at the End of the Trail statue just as the sun began to dip behind it – which Coby couldn't stop going on about. They took a boardwalk trail through a wildlife area and snapped pictures of some ducks they spotted on the water, before working their way back toward Main. They talked about their interviews and the places they had researched.

"Officer Burkiss was saying we could go on a ride along with him and the chief some evening if we wanted to. That might be cool, getting a look into the life of a small town officer," Coby said, leaning over and snapping a picture of some wildflowers growing along the sidewalk.

LJ rolled her eyes as they crossed the road. "What, so you and the police chief can frolic off through the blood and gore together and I can get stuck awkwardly shuffling around town with the one who doesn't speak?"

Coby rolled her eyes right back at LJ. "No. *I'll* go with Clyde, gosh."

LJ raised an eyebrow. "Clyde?"

"*Officer Burkiss*," Coby corrected herself, scowling at LJ through the growing darkness as they walked down the sidewalk in the dying semi-light. "And I will go –"

"How much have you been talking to 'Clyde', hmm?" LJ interrupted.

"*Clyde* is his actual name, thank you very much, and– what's that?" Coby stopped abruptly on the bridge and peered down at the water of the small river that ran through the town.

"Don't try to change the subject, Coby Anderson," LJ said, plowing onward, wanting to get back to the motel before it was pitch black out. "I'm trying to get this article written and I would very much appreciate a little bit of help from my *writing partner*."

"LJ, no, I think that… that's a person–" Something in Coby's voice was off and she launched off the sidewalk and started down towards the river.

LJ turned quickly. "Coby," she said, eyes widening as she hurried after her friend. "Coby!"

"Look, LJ, *look*– call 911!" Coby gasped, scrambling towards the river, pointing towards the water and coming to a halt at the edge of the riverbank. She looked around before crouching down and placing a foot in the water. LJ came to a stop beside her, grabbing her shoulder and hauling her back.

"Stop. I don't think 911 is going to be able to help," LJ said, face pale. A gray, bloated body of a female bobbed in and out of the water, caught along the weeds under the bridge, naked. Both legs were sewn together with a thick, black thread. "We better call Grizzly."

***

"So I'm gonna build the porch back here. Then I've got a spot for sunrises *and* sunsets. And I might screen this in since I'll be out here at night and the damn mosquitos are taking over the state." Grizzly turned from the open back doorway of his cabin to see if Clyde was even listening. "You could use a shotgun on those things."

Clyde was digging through the kitchen cabinets.

"I live here, you know. I probably know where whatever you're looking for is."

"The teapot." Clyde straightened and moved to the cupboard above the refrigerator.

"Oh, naturally." Grizzly chortled. "I don't have one."

"I gave you one for Christmas." Clyde didn't stop looking.

"You... did?" Grizzly wrinkled his brow, trying to remember. "I remember when you got me that 'kiss the cook' apron..."

"That's because you wear it every day." Clyde let a cabinet door swing shut with a bang. "That was a joke. I got you a teapot because it's actually a useful thing and tea is good for you."

Grizzly pointed above the stove. "I've got a microwave. It does the same thing in half the time." He smirked when he earned the pointed glare he'd been trying for. "Quit messing around – we're gonna miss the start of the game."

Another pointed glare.

"You moved to Wisconsin seven years ago, Clyde. It's time to embrace the Brewers as your own." Grizzly moved to the fridge and pulled out a couple of beers.

Clyde reached for the bag of tortilla chips he'd left on the counter. "Over my dead body."

"You realize the Braves were from Milwaukee originally?"

He huffed. "That means nothing."

"And what the hell is with that shirt? The Falcons? Take it off right now, I will give you one of my Packers jerseys if you must dress for the fall."

"I'm not stripping for you Grizz, sorry."

"Come on! It's un-American –"

"The Atlanta Falcons are *in* America, Grizz." Clyde crunched a chip. "Besides, you're from Arizona. What's your obsession with the Packers?"

"Once you go Pack, you never go back." Grizzly opened the beers and handed one to Clyde as he headed for the living room.

He settled in the giant green recliner that took up forty percent of the room, snagging the bag of chips as Clyde passed him. The flat screen mounted on the wall cut from a commercial to Miller Park at the same time Grizzly's phone buzzed in his pocket. He nearly groaned until he fished it out and looked at the number on the screen.

"LJ?"

Clyde glanced over.

LJ's voice was rattled through the phone. "Hi, uh, listen… sorry to bother you out of the blue… and maybe we should have just called 911…"

Grizzly straightened. "What's wrong? Are you okay?"

"No, no, we're fine." She sighed heavily. "We were walking through town and…" Another deep breath. "We found a body."

Grizzly stood and set his beer on the end table. "Where are you?"

"On Brandon Street… near the windmill. She, uh… she's in the river."

"We're on our way. I'm sure it goes without saying but…"

"We won't be touching anything. Don't worry."

Grizzly hung up the phone, scowling hard. He moved for the front door and reached for his boots.

"Grizz? What happened?"

It. It had happened. Again. Another one. Grizzly mentally paged through faces of the missing persons reports he looked at daily.

"*Adams.* What's wrong with you?" Clyde scrambled for the remote and turned off the television before trailing after Grizzly. "LJ called?"

Grizzly was out the front door already. "They found one."

Clyde paused, cowboy boot in hand. "Found one… what?"

Grizzly stood on the running board of his truck and glared over the roof. "What do you *think?*"

Clyde paused for a beat, then scrambled after him, trying to cross the driveway and put his boots on at the same time. "Where?"

"Just get in the truck."

Chapter Nineteen

Red and blue lights from the cop cars cut through the darkness, surrounding the white glow of the flood light aimed at the bank of the river. LJ rubbed her temples and hoped their boss would give them an extension if they promised a larger spread.

Police tape was everywhere, roping off the bank. Only the medical examiner and Grizzly were inside the circle, but a small crowd was beginning to gather outside of it. A man with a press ID around his neck was jotting notes off to the side, and a Madison news van was parked across the street. LJ had overheard Grizzly asking if the girl could be April Marsden, and the ME seemed fairly certain. Someone had already snapped a bunch of pictures but LJ suspected Coby's might be better.

Coby had been banished to stay by the cop cars a few minutes ago but she was already lingering halfway towards the bank, furtively trying to peer around Clyde who stood outside the circle of tape taking notes as he listened to Grizzly and the examiner talk.

LJ looked down at her phone and debated whether or not it was too late to call her boss and attempt to explain the situation that was going to cause their article to be late. How would she even have that conversation? *Sorry, but Coby's wildest dreams came true and now we're in a Nancy Drew novel.*

Before she could make up her mind, Grizzly stood up, lifted the police tape and headed for them, causing Coby to stumble backwards towards LJ and attempt to look innocent.

"Well ladies, last but not least, we're going to need a report from you two," Grizzly said with a sigh, brushing his hair back. He looked tired and about ten years older. LJ felt her annoyance with her own work situation fade, replaced with guilt as she looked at the man. She did not envy him.

Coby's eyes were wide and she nodded, fingers drumming on the edge of her camera as she looked up at Grizzly and Clyde with rapt attention. LJ wondered just how much adrenaline was coursing through Coby's system right now.

Grizzly shot a weary glance over at her before turning his gaze to Clyde. "You get Coby, I'll get LJ," he said, grabbing a piece of paper and a pen from the officer.

LJ thought she saw Clyde blush through the darkness, but fought the urge to watch them like a hawk as he and Coby walked away a few steps. She turned her attention to Grizzly.

"All right darlin', just tell me what happened," Grizzly said, clicking the pen and looking up at her.

LJ folded her arms against the cool night air, letting the "darlin'" comment go. "Coby and I were out for a walk. She was taking pictures for the magazine, we were talking…" Grizzly nodded as he scratched quickly on the paper. "And then she saw something down in the river as we were crossing the bridge. I didn't see it but she ran down there and I followed her…" she trailed off, rubbing her arms. It had been too warm for a jacket earlier. "She was going to hop in there and get her I think, but I stopped Coby when I saw the girl was dead." She shrugged slightly. "Then we called you guys," she said, glancing back over at Coby and Clyde.

Grizzly nodded again and kept scratching away at the paper for a little bit before looking up. "Great. Did you notice anything that I should take note of? Details?"

LJ shook her head. "No, not really… Coby took a million pictures before you got here, but I'm sure she'll tell Clyde that."

Grizzly passed a hand over his beard and gave her a tired smile. "Good… good. Thanks. We'll drive you girls back to the hotel."

LJ nodded, not about to protest. She prided herself in being independent, but walking around in the dark, in a strange town after they had just stumbled across a murder victim wasn't appealing. "Thanks."

Grizzly bumped her elbow gently. "You okay?"

LJ nodded quickly. "Yeah… yeah."

Grizzly looked at her for a moment longer before nodding back and motioning toward Clyde and Coby. "Let's see where they're at."

LJ trailed after him, sighing heavily as they approached Clyde and the very pale, blonde woman.

"And I just… her legs are stitched together." Coby stared off into space for a long moment before looking up at Burkiss. "It's straight out of a horror movie."

He reached out and touched her arm, opening his mouth to say something, but then closing it again.

"Are you good to go?" Grizzly asked Clyde, but watched Coby carefully.

Clyde nodded somberly. "They're gonna need a ride back."

Grizzly was already reaching for the cruiser door.

***

Clyde sat in the passenger side of the cruiser and gripped the door handle tightly, grinding his teeth. He was angry about everything. He was angry that there was another dead girl. He was angry that she'd been murdered and they hadn't seen it coming. He was angry at the killer, or killers. He was angry the murder happened at all. He was really angry that Coby had found the girl. But most of all, he was really angry that both Coby and LJ had been out walking around town after dark.

"What were you *thinking*?" He almost jumped at the sound of his own voice. He hadn't realized he was ready to speak aloud.

Grizzly said "What?" at the same time LJ said "I'm sorry?"

"Two young women, walking around an unfamiliar town well into the evening? You really thought that was a good idea?" Clyde twisted in his seat to look at Coby. LJ, too, but mostly Coby. "How do you think people end up like that girl in the river?"

LJ glowered at him. Coby stared at her hands in her lap.

"Do you *know* the statistics of women who disappear –"

"Burkiss, settle down," Grizzly interrupted. "They didn't do anything wrong."

Clyde faced forward and tried to calm himself.

"Where are you staying?" Grizzly asked, looking up at the rearview.

"The motel. Off of Main Street. Right up here," LJ replied.

Grizzly slowed the car. "You've gotta be kidding."

Clyde stared at the flashing Van Camp Inn sign with a new level of rage. "Boarders is right up the road."

"The magazine pays for room and board." LJ sounded like she was rolling her eyes. "We don't get anything above two stars."

Grizzly stopped in the small, shady parking lot, hesitating. "You two can't stay here."

"We already are." LJ stated firmly.

Grizzly held up a hand. "Now hang on a second, you guys are... crime scene… witnesses. Maybe we can–"

"No." LJ frowned, folding her arms. "We're fine," she said, voice steely but not unkind. Until she leaned forward to look at Clyde. "And just for your information *Officer Burkiss*," she shot at him. "We travel the entire country by ourselves. At night, too."

Clyde scowled back at her, not in the mood for this at all.

Grizzly climbed out of the cruiser and opened the back door to let LJ out.

Coby looked up quickly, snapping out of her thoughts as LJ rounded the car to get Coby's door. "LJ, cut it out," she said as she stepped out, then looked down at Clyde. He felt a tiny bit of shame creeping up his throat at having scolded Coby, but she gave him a tired, reassuring smile. "Thanks for the ride. I'll go through the pictures and drop them off tomorrow." He flinched as she leaned down to see past him, looking at Grizzly as he slid back into the driver's seat. "Good luck guys." She smiled at Grizzly and touched Clyde's shoulder before following after LJ who was already storming past her, into the motel room.

Grizzly didn't drive away as the poorly painted door with the number four on it closed and locked behind Coby. He looked over at Clyde. "You okay?" he asked.

Clyde could hear a croak in his partner's voice, his own weariness reflected back at him. He tried not to feel defeated, but it wasn't working. Clyde shook his head. "Nothing about this is okay."

"I know," Grizzly said softly. "I know." He started the car, pulled away from the curb and headed towards the police department.

Chapter Twenty

Light barely managed to pierce through the quilt-thick curtains when Coby started dressing the next morning. She rolled down the sleeves of her red flannel shirt and swiped her hair into a ponytail without brushing it, deciding that a layer of quickly applied lipstick would make up for the hairdo.

"What time is it?" LJ asked hoarsely from a pile of bedding on the other side of the room.

"I don't know." Coby slipped her phone out of her pocket and glanced at it. "Eight-thirty."

"Where are you going?"

"I want to go over my pictures for the articles. And I've got some other things to go through." She shrugged. "I'll probably hit the library."

LJ sat up, elbows resting against her knees, and rubbed her eyes. "You didn't sleep either, did you?"

Coby shook her head and reached for her camera bag. She double-checked the memory card, then the battery out of habit. "Doesn't matter. You think that girl's parents slept last night?"

LJ gazed blankly at the wall.

"I'm taking the car. Call me if you need anything." She slung her laptop bag over her shoulder and clutched her keys in the same hand as the camera bag. The cloudy morning felt dark and cold to Coby, despite the spring air and rising temperature.

The Chevelle was the first car to arrive in the parking lot, and it wasn't until Coby killed the engine that she realized the library probably wasn't open yet.

She leaned her head back against the headrest and sighed. She needed coffee. And sleep. And an Advil. Her stomach turned over for the millionth time since the previous night and she forced her eyes open, reaching for her laptop for a distraction.

As soon as the screen lit up, she knew the attempt was futile. This "distraction" was literally what happened the night before.

The pictures loaded faster than she wanted them to. She took her time, scanning through the ones she'd taken their first few days in Waupun. Sculptures, City Hall, the police station. A picture of Grizzly standing in the doorway to his office, and one of Clyde turning a particularly interesting shade of red that she'd forgotten she'd taken.

A car slid into the space next to her, and she jumped and looked over. She recognized Neal Murphy, the librarian, as he pulled his keys from the ignition and saluted her, with a confused expression on his face. Coby closed the laptop and slid it back into the bag.

"You're not supposed to be here," Neal stated as she got out of the car.

"What?"

"Getting here before the librarian. It makes said librarian look bad."

"Oh. Sorry." Coby shrugged, then realized Neal was kidding when he started to chuckle. "I didn't really think about what time it was."

"Not a problem." Neal led the way toward the front door.

Coby went straight for the table she'd used last time, spread out her things and opened the computer back up. She stared at the welcome screen for a minute before taking a deep breath, rolling her shoulders, and going back to the pictures.

This time she skipped ahead until she found the pictures taken on the boardwalk. Then she slowly clicked through a few shots of the neighborhood, stopping on the first distance shot of the windmill.

Dread built in her gut as she shuffled through each picture, getting closer to the ones of the girl. Both the inadvertent and intentional ones. Coby took one more deep breath, squeezed her eyes shut, then opened them and forced herself to look. Closely.

The first shot was innocent. The bridge railing, the river, the fresh leaves on the newly bloomed trees. The body wasn't even visible until the second picture, where a pale hand could be seen against the bank.

Coby shuddered but refused to look away, studying every detail of the few angles she had. She hadn't gotten close – for a lot of reasons – and as much as she wished she could see better, she was glad she stopped when she had. The job of getting close-ups of the bloated corpse that had once been a young woman luckily belonged to the criminal investigators that worked for the state.

The pictures looped back to the beginning of the album and Coby went backwards until she found the best shot she'd taken. It was as close as she and LJ had dared to get, and it was a full body shot. In the moment, Coby hadn't been sure of what she was doing, whether it was sick and morbid, or even legal, or if she was actually going to be a help to the police. She'd put the camera away shortly after, deciding it didn't matter and she didn't want to photograph the dead ever again.

She stared at the picture. The body hardly looked human; it had been in the water far too long. Coby could practically smell the stench through the computer screen and she warded off another shudder. Her gaze refused to leave the black thread, still holding the flesh of the legs together despite the decomposition. What had obviously been perfect stitches at the time of application were still strongly bound from groin to toe.

Coby sat back and scowled. It was like a fin. A tail. A mermaid tail.

She tapped her fingers on the laptop. She shook her head, then looked through the pictures again. After five minutes of inspection, she still hadn't changed her mind. She thought back to LJ telling her about the case Grizzly had relayed to her. The little girl with the missing heart.

"That can't be a coincidence," Coby muttered under her breath.

The computer was snapped shut. The memory card ejected. Coby scrambled everything together and blundered for the stairs, nearly bowling Neal's cart of books over as she went.

"Whoa, what's the hurry?" Neal steadied her, then stooped to pick up a stray book.

"Uh, well, I need to get some pictures printed." Coby kept going, then backtracked to hand him another fallen book. "Sorry about that. I gotta go."

"Drive safe."

Coby barely heard him as she tore down the stairs and back to the car.

***

Clyde jumped as a figure suddenly appeared at his desk and slammed an envelope down in front of him. "I need you to look at this."

He gazed up at Coby, not sure where she'd come from or what she was talking about or why her lipstick looked so striking this morning. "Huh?"

Coby pulled up a chair and sat beside him, opening the envelope and leaning closer to him. She smelled like lilacs. "I took pictures yesterday, I told you that. You said I'd need to bring them in, so I was planning to look them over and find the shots where you can actually see the body, and these are it, but while I was looking at them it suddenly dawned on me." She pulled out a standard sized photo envelope and set it aside, then slid three eight-by-ten photographs onto the desk.

Clyde, still a little lost, looked at the photos, which really just looked like glorified crime scene photos, except without evidence markers and with much more artistic angles. "These are good. Thanks."

"*No.*" Coby pointed at the body, sliding her fingers down the length of the legs, which were sewn together. "What does that *look* like?"

Clyde opened his mouth, trying to come up with the right answer, but just ended up shrugging. "A horror movie, honestly."

"It's a mermaid tail. He turned her into the little mermaid."

Clyde looked at the picture again and felt his stomach clench.

Coby stared at him intently. "And I know about the little girl whose heart was cut out. You know what that's from, right?"

Clyde faced her, mouth dropping open. "*How* do you know about that?"

"LJ told me."

"How did LJ know about that?"

"Grizzly told her."

"What? Why?"

"Because he likes her, obviously." Coby tapped the envelope of smaller prints. "Here are the rest of the photos, but I really don't think they'll give you anything you don't already have." She shook her head and twisted in her chair so she was facing him. "They don't even matter. It's the story that matters."

Clyde squinted at her. "Story? What are you talking about?"

"I think the killer might be rewriting the stories."

Clyde's lost expression must have been enough.

"Okay." She slumped back in the chair. "When I was a kid I had this book – I mean, who didn't, it's pretty standard for a kid to have a book of fairy tales – but it wasn't just Cinderella and the singing mice. It was all those legitimate, original fairy tales that Disney turned into kid's movies. Like how Snow White was supposed to be lured into the woods by the Huntsman because the Queen wanted her heart, but at the last minute he chickened out and let her go, then brought the Queen an animal heart instead."

Clyde scowled. "What are you saying?"

"I think the Huntsman did his job," Coby pointed back to the prints on the desk. "And I think he also did this."

"I'm not following."

Coby leveled her gaze at him. "I think he's rewriting these fairy tales. He's making them end how he wants them to – with Snow White's heart brought to the Queen like it was supposed to be." Her knee bounced with intensity. "Are any of your other cases based off of fairy tales?"

Clyde pondered the question for a minute, then realized what he was doing. "I can't share that information with you –"

"Clyde, we could actually be on to something. Something that might find some of those missing girls. Maybe bring the families closure, and *stop a killer from killing again.*"

He stared at her intense eyes, searching his, begging him to believe her and to let her help. "I… don't actually know…"

"That's what I thought." She bit her lip. "Do you think I could look through the reports? If there's a pattern, I'll find it."

He clenched his teeth together and held onto the feeling that she was seeing something he'd never considered before, pushing aside the way her wide eyes made his pulse race and palms sweat. He turned toward his computer, pulled up the private files, and put in the password without bothering to inform her that she was not only convincing him, but that he was wrapped around her finger.

Chapter Twenty-One

LJ had gotten up not long after Coby left. Lying in bed wasn't going to help her sleep, closing her eyes only made her replay the lights reflecting on the bloated corpse of the girl. Which was just great. Her salary was NOT going to cover the cost of a therapist.

She fixed her hair, dragged on jeans and a purple long sleeve shirt, and threw some eye make up on. Not that that was going to cover the dark circles. She sighed, pulling on her boots and jacket, and threw on a pair of sunglasses. It was a day she wished was already over but there was nothing to do but tough it out.

LJ stepped out of her room, closing and locking the door behind her, and shivered slightly against the cool breeze. She needed coffee and figured she had enough information to get started on one of these articles. She headed to the local Kwik Trip and got a 24 ounce cup of black coffee, determined to head to the library, thinking vaguely that Coby would probably end up there if she wasn't already.

However as her feet hit the sidewalk, she paused, her fingers tapping on the shoulder strap of her laptop case. Then she started walking back toward the bridge, toward last night's horrible scene. What was propelling her? Morbid curiosity? She shook her head, unwilling to deal with that. That's what the psychiatrist was for, the one she couldn't afford.

She strode toward the bridge, needing to see the place in the daylight. See what had happened with everything. Maybe the police cleaned it all up. Maybe she wouldn't spend tonight picturing the dead girl in the water.

There was a truck parked on the side of the road but there were no other signs of the media or police or even civilians.

LJ walked forward, slowly looking around. She frowned and came to a stop on the sidewalk.

Grizzly was standing on the river bank, in jeans, a flannel shirt and a black beanie, rolling up police tape.

LJ frowned, confused, and walked forward. "What are you doing?" she asked, eyes darting around, not seeing his police cruiser anywhere.

"Just cleaning this up. I made them come back down here and get every scrap of evidence they possibly could. We don't need people coming here and gawking at everything," he said, walking around and ripping out some flag markers.

"Oh," she said, unsure what to say. She settled for taking a sip of coffee. The place looked so normal and non-threatening in the daylight with no bloated corpses.

Grizzly made his way up the river bank, arms full of the last traces of last night. "Could you do me a favor and open the door?" he asked, nodding toward the door of the truck parked on the road.

"Oh, sure, of course," LJ said, starting forward and fumbling with her coffee slightly before opening the back door.

"Thanks," Grizzly said with a smile after he shoved his armful of stuff in the back. He closed the door and stepped back, looking at her, and shoving his hands in his pockets. "Coming to do some investigating?" he asked, with a grin.

"No, I… I was just..." LJ blinked. What *was* she doing? "I was just taking a walk… clearing my head."

"Well that sounds like a good idea," Grizzly said, taking a deep breath and rolling his neck. He looked like he was running on little to no sleep again, LJ noticed. There were dark circles under his eyes despite the smile on his face. "You know what's good for clearing your head?" he asked abruptly.

LJ jumped slightly. "What?"

"Yard work," Grizzly said simply.

"Okay… I wouldn't know," LJ said with a short laugh and a shrug. "Coby and I live in an apartment complex when we're not driving around together. And when I was little I always lived in the city."

Grizzly stared at her. "You've never done yardwork?"

LJ shrugged and spread her hands. "No, not really."

Grizzly shook his head and opened the passenger door to his truck. "Tragic. Just tragic. Hop on in. I'm going to show you what you've been missing."

LJ raised an eyebrow at him. "You want me to come do your yard work for you?"

"No," he said walking around to his side of the truck. "I'm going to show you the light. There's no better way of clearing your mind than engaging in some physical labor. Plus I don't really care to be alone with my thoughts all afternoon so you're a good distraction." He grinned at her and she was reminded once again what he must be going through.

She hesitated but Coby's comment the other night floated to the front of her mind. "*Not everyone's like Colin.*" Before she could even think of the twenty-five reasons why this wasn't a good idea or a good use of her time, she was climbing into the passenger seat of Grizzly Adams' pickup truck.

She shut the door and awkwardly held her coffee and laptop case in her lap. "So… where do you live?" she asked, realizing getting into a truck with a man was a stupid idea. What with potential serial killers and all. But then again, she had seen Grizzly several times already and he was the police chief so that had to count for something.

She realized he hadn't started the engine yet, and was just staring at her.

"What?" she asked.

He shook his head. "Nothing," he said with a grin, turning the key and pulling away from the curb. He looked surprised, probably shocked that she had actually gotten in the truck.

She was shocked too.

"I don't live too far from here… got a little place out in the country." He spoke up after a little while and it took her a second to realize he was answering her question.

She nodded. "Big yard?"

He laughed, the sound so loud it filled up the cab of the truck. "Don't sound so excited."

"I'm not– I mean– I am… excited… just – fine," LJ garbled and threw him a scowl, taking a sip of her coffee.

"You're gonna love it. Trust me," Grizzly said, his smirk making him look far too pleased with himself.

"Yeah, sure. Trust the man who is gloating over his new-found slave labor," LJ said, eyes narrowed at him.

"Oh come on now… I'll make you coffee," Grizzly bribed.

LJ held up her Styrofoam cup. "I already have coffee."

Grizzly laughed again. "Okay, okay… I'll… make you a steak."

LJ perked up, coffee sloshing. "Deal."

It didn't take long for them to reach Grizzly's house. It was a nice little place, tucked away in a wooded area. LJ was surprised at how well taken care of it was. Of course this was the man who thought yard work was fun, so maybe she shouldn't be.

They got out of the truck, Grizzly whistling. "You can bring your stuff inside," he said, nodding towards the door of his house.

LJ followed him looking around curiously. The house was simple but nice. There wasn't much decor but it had a slight cabin-y feeling. And it was clean. She awkwardly set her now empty coffee cup and laptop bag on the table in the kitchen. "Well, I'm impressed," she said, folding her arms and looking around. "You even have a tea kettle."

"Uh yeah, that's from Clyde."

LJ raised an eyebrow at him. "Remind me again how you two *aren't* married?"

Grizzly placed a hand to his chest. "Only in our hearts," he teased. "Can I get you something to drink?"

"I'm good, let's get to the slave labor," LJ replied, pretending to crack her knuckles.

"Well, yard work really isn't yard work without a beer," Grizzly said with a grin, pulling two out of the fridge.

LJ smiled. "Okay, okay. Just because we're going for an authentic experience here," she said, taking the beer from him.

"Damn straight. You're gonna end up writing an article about this just you wait." He winked at her before heading outside.

Grizzly seemed to decide it was his mission in life to educate her on everything one needed to know about having a yard. First, it was gathering sticks, and then it was raking. After that, they had to dig up some unwanted tree-like plants that had started to spring up. Then he moved her on to operating the lawn mower and trimming.

LJ didn't mind. She was even enjoying herself too, not that she would ever admit that to him. It seemed to be keeping them both from thinking about what happened last night. She hadn't seen Grizzly get that serious and weary expression on his face since they started.

That was until LJ had to go get the gas can for the mower. She was chuckling to herself as she made her way back from the garage, until she turned the corner and saw him standing there, leaning on the rake, zoned out, that expression on his face again.

She hesitated for a second, but then approached him, tucking her hair behind her ear. "What's the matter Chief, you need a nap?" she asked, smiling at him.

He snapped out of it and looked at her, giving her a tiny smile. "Just thinking…" he trailed off and the smile vanished. "I used to run with these kinds of people." He shrugged, like he was admitting defeat. Like last night had caught up with him, despite their yardwork denial. "I was in a bad crowd when I was younger. Deadbeat dad, bipolar mom… I joined up with a biker gang. I think what I wanted was a family, but it got me into a world of trouble." He looked over at her, gauging her expression as he spoke. Like he expected to see judgement or fear. LJ held his gaze. "I was in southern Arizona and we carted drugs across the border. I knew it was wrong but I didn't care at the time. We weren't hurting anyone directly. At least I wasn't." He sighed and rubbed a hand over his face, shaking his head. "But, I knew things were happening. Rape, murder… And I never did a damn thing to try to stop them." He planted his hands on his waist and squinted down at her. "And now it's my *job* to stop them and I just– I can't. I can't figure out how." He broke eye contact with her and looked at the ground. "It just kinda feels like now I'm paying for my mistakes."

LJ swallowed back the lump in her throat and stepped forward. "Hey, that's not what's happening. This isn't on you," she said with a frown, bumping his arm with her elbow. It was hard to see someone like him looking so broken.

Grizzly nodded. "I know. Just feels like it," he said, looking up at the trees and not at her. LJ bit her lip and shoved her hands in her pockets. They stood there like that for a while, not speaking.

LJ let out a sigh and surveyed the ground. "So! What now? Are we planting a garden next?"

Grizzly scoffed at her. "Oh please, I'm not Burkiss."

"I didn't realize gardening was a Burkiss thing."

"Oh yes. He has a tea garden." Grizzly snatched up the gas can LJ had retrieved and headed toward the shed in the backyard.

LJ trailed after him. "Really? Wow. Now that's something I could write an article about." She followed him to the generously-sized shed and stopped in the doorway, flinching at the sight of a motorcycle parked inside. "Whoa… so you didn't leave this behind in your life of crime. Do you still ride?"

"Not as much as I used to." Grizzly chuckled. "But whenever I can. Why, is *that* worth writing about?"

LJ approached it, looking it over wistfully. "My dad had one when I was a kid." She reached out and touched the leather of the seat. "He never let me ride with him."

Grizzly's mouth dropped open in an exaggerated look of horror. "You've never been on a Harley?"

She snapped her hand back and shrugged. "No. I mean, it's not a big deal."

"Ohh, babe. If you haven't ridden, you haven't *lived*." He set down the gas can and stalked back to the doorway and pushed both doors open wide. "I'm taking you out. Right now."

LJ thought she might throw up. "What?"

"What do you mean, 'what'? Do you need to be somewhere?" He reached up and pulled a helmet off the shelf.

"No... I just..." She looked back at the bike. "It's really not that big of a deal. You don't have to –"

"Nonsense." He shoved the helmet at her. "I'm doing this for you."

LJ took the helmet, fumbling and nearly dropping it. "I–I don't –"

Grizzly swung a leg over the bike and rolled it outside. "I don't mind, darlin'. I love this thing."

LJ inhaled sharply.

"Are you scared?"

LJ hugged the helmet to her chest, attempting to cross her arms defiantly. "No."

"Sure you are."

LJ gritted her teeth and prepared to defend herself.

"I'm a very experienced motorcyclist. Been riding since I was a teenager – haven't had an accident since I was twenty-two." He flipped out the kickstand and let the bike rest. "And I'm chief of police. You couldn't be safer."

She scowled, stomach churning, and looked the Harley Davidson over again. She mumbled.

"What's that?"

"Fine. Let's go before I change my mind."

Chapter Twenty-Two

Shaun Pritchard stared at the blinking cursor on his computer screen, desperately trying to focus on the email that needed to be written. But the memory of Coby Anderson leaning over Clyde Burkiss's shoulder earlier that day plagued his mind.

She had no reason to be there. And Burkiss was certainly not authorized to show her anything at his work desk with no one around. Burkiss had been sweating nervously and mentioned more than once that he "wouldn't want anyone to find out about this."

Shaun leaned back in his chair and allowed himself to look over at the desktop that seemed to be whispering seductively from across the room. It wasn't like he *tried* to check up on Burkiss. The little man was just always doing something that required being checked up *on*. No, Shaun didn't need to come into work early that day, but he had seen Coby's Chevelle drive by and he'd gotten curious, especially when he'd followed her straight to the station.

It wasn't his fault that he lived on Main Street and happened to spend a lot of time watching things out his front window. And he was a cop – he was supposed to keep an eye out for strange, out-of-town vehicles. Particularly those that belonged to beautiful women.

Beautiful women who were somehow drawn to Adams and Burkiss like flies to honey. If honey were disgusting, loathsome assholes who got their jobs handed to them, and flies were hot, sexy, independent women.

It always seemed to work like that.

Shaun closed his eyes and felt his lids twitch. Burkiss had been showing her confidential files. Shaun was absolutely sure of it, and that bothered him even more than the hand she'd had on Clyde's shoulder during most of their conversation.

He got to his feet. The office lights were dim, as the second shifters were out on patrol. Shaun reached for the desk lamp as he sat himself in Burkiss's chair. The desk was clear, perfectly organized with its stapler, keyboard, mouse, and jar of matching ballpoint pens. Shaun glanced around the room as he pulled open the top drawer and started rifling through it.

If Clyde Burkiss had one thing to learn about being secretive, it was to never leave incriminating evidence in your desk where anyone could find it.

Shaun flipped through the top file. Ellie Miller, age eight. Found mauled to death in the woods. Shaun recalled the incident from quite a while back, but he couldn't figure out why they were looking at it.

The second file in the drawer was McKenna Douglas. Age 17. Drugged and found dead from an overdose in a cemetery. Shaun closed both files and drummed his fingertips on the arm of the chair, opposite hand stroking his upper lip as he thought it over. Why was Burkiss going over these with her? Were they dragging up old files together? Either way, it had to be stopped.

Burkiss was directly disobeying regulations by showing that woman confidential case files. Shaun was supposed – no, it was his duty, really – to inform the police chief of such violations. Burkiss was a risk to everyone on the force if he was willing to give classified information to a civilian just because she had a nice rack and big eyes.

Shaun replaced the files gingerly and glanced around the room again, though there was no one to pay him any mind. He flipped the switch on the lamp and moved back to his own desk, mind reeling with ways to take Burkiss down, and get him out of his way for good.

***

It was late. Coby sat on her bed with nine different volumes on fairy tales, mythology and folklore piled up around her. She had spent a good chunk of the day at the police station going over old case files with Clyde. He had been nervous talking about it at the station where people might overhear, so they went to lunch again and she picked his memory some more. When they were done, he went out on patrol and she went straight back to the library, grabbed every book she thought might be helpful and started researching on the internet.

LJ had texted her in the afternoon wondering where she was. Coby told her she was working at the library. Which was actually one hundred percent not a lie. She wasn't going to hide this from LJ, in fact she was kind of excited to tell her, but she figured it would be better done face to face and not over text. Especially with LJ being so touchy about the prison piece.

Coby thumbed through an old beat up copy of Hans Christian Andersen fairy tales. She chuckled to herself as she came across Thumbelina. It was the only fairy tale Clyde really remembered. Apparently it stuck out because he recalled being horrified at the thought of marrying a mole. She shook her head. It was a nice lunch. She liked talking to him and he seemed to be getting more comfortable around her.

Her eyes drooped as she scanned the fairy tale. She felt more and more the effect of her restless night. The only thing that was keeping her from sleeping was her growling stomach. That and the fact that LJ should be back soon. Lunch had been a long time ago, and she selfishly hoped LJ would come through the door balancing a pizza.

She jolted awake at the sound of the door closing, her book falling to the floor. She looked up to see LJ, then quickly glanced at the clock. She was relieved to see she hadn't dozed off for more than a few minutes. "Oh hey!" Coby mumbled. "Aw, you didn't bring me food."

"Um, you took the car. I wasn't about to carry groceries around town," LJ said, closing the door behind her as she took a bite of an ice cream sundae. LJ paused and narrowed her eyes at Coby's book nest. "Reverting to childhood? You're really procrastinating on writing your articles, aren't you?"

Coby rubbed her eyes and sat up. "No. But guess what," she said in an excited rush. LJ's eyes widened at her as if she was worried Coby was going insane. She gave her that look a lot and it didn't faze Coby in the slightest. "I was looking over my pictures so I could bring the ones of the crime scene to Clyde and it just hit me… you know how her legs were stitched together?"

LJ's eyes were still bugging at her. "Yeah?"

"It was like a mermaid! That's all I could think of, and you know how you told me about that little girl with her heart cut out?" Coby waited expectantly.

LJ raised her eyebrows and shrugged. "Yeah?"

"*Snow White*," she said. "So I brought the pictures in, told Clyde what I thought and I convinced him to show me some of the old case files and so many of them matched that pattern! So many were like *fairy tales*. I mean, I haven't figured out the story behind all of them, but that's why I got all these books out." Coby motioned to her books, excited. "I think it could be a serial killer."

"Wait… just…hang on. Was that what you were doing all day?" LJ asked with a frown, tossing the empty ice cream container in the trash.

"Well yeah, pretty much. It ended up taking a while and then we went to lunch and talked about the cases, and then I went to the library."

LJ pinched the bridge of her nose and planted her other hand on her hip. "And… *Clyde* just… *showed* you the confidential case files?"

Coby nodded, hesitating. "Well yeah, eventually, he wasn't really supposed to, but –"

LJ frowned. "Oh, okay. I'm… I'm really tired, I'm going to hit the hay," she said with a sigh, walking into the bathroom and closing the door firmly behind her.

Coby blinked at the door and sank back against her pillows. Disappointed at LJ's lack of enthusiasm, she sighed, piled her books on the floor, shut off her light and closed her eyes.

Chapter Twenty-Three

Clyde watched the dark-haired woman burst through the station doors in a huff. She crossed the room, gripping the sleeves of her shirt in clenched fists as her boot heels stomped forcefully on the floor. Julia looked up from her desk as LJ approached it, greeting her with a bright smile and wary eyes. "Hello again, dear!"

"I need to speak to Officer Burkiss," LJ clipped. She followed Julia's gaze halfway across the room and spun toward Clyde. "I understand you've been speaking with Coby."

Clyde felt his throat close up and he started sweating involuntarily. "I, uh…"

"She told me about some… paperwork… you discussed with her." LJ narrowed her eyes at him, pointedly.

Clyde's eyelids fluttered, his gut landing somewhere between defeat and sheepishness. He glanced at Julia, who was pretending very hard to ignore them. "She… I didn't mean…"

"I'd appreciate it if you'd go over that paperwork with me." LJ crossed her arms. "I'd like to be on the same page as my writing partner."

Clyde nodded and got to his feet. He glanced at his watch. Grizzly wouldn't be back for a while. "Uhh… sure." He motioned toward Grizzly's office. "If you'll come with me…"

He led the way down the hall, smoothing his unruly hair back and trying to calm the sweat. Grizzly's office was a mess, as usual, and the sight of it did nothing to settle Clyde's nerves. He closed the door behind LJ and turned on her, eyes wide. "Are you trying to get me fired?"

"I was trying to be subtle." She ran her hands over her ponytail and sighed. "Listen, I'm sorry. It's not your fault Coby left me out of the loop on this." Her lips pursed and she shook her head in disbelief. "Sometimes I just…"

Clyde's level of discomfort was making him squirm. He moved toward the filing cabinet, boot toes dragging on the rug. "I'm not supposed to show you anything. I shouldn't have shown her."

"I think we're a little past that, Officer."

Clyde clenched his jaw and pulled open the top drawer. He glanced over his shoulder at the door before pulling out several folders and turning toward the desk. He opened the first one reluctantly and tried to figure out where to start with his explanation.

"I just can't believe she went behind my back." LJ was staring out the window, not even glancing at the files. "I knew she had ideas for another project – a book or something – but this whole thing is becoming insane. I thought it was crazy when she wanted to research the high security prisons, and now she's investigating ongoing murder cases?" She whirled on Clyde. "And you're *helping* her?"

Clyde opened his mouth to respond, but she continued and he was relieved because he had no idea what to respond *with*.

"That could get dangerous!" LJ strode back toward the door. "She's not a cop. She's not even an investigative journalist. She's just a magazine writer and photographer. Is this really a serial killer you're hunting down? You can't involve civilians with that!"

Clyde leaned his palms on the desk and watched her turn and walk back to the window.

"And this whole 'wanting to settle down' thing... it just doesn't even make sense." LJ crossed her arms. "I mean, who is she going to 'settle down' *with*? She'd probably end up with some overprotective worry wart who wouldn't even let her go out after dark." She paused in her pacing. "Someone like *you,* no offense, and has she even thought about that? *No.*"

Clyde straightened up and closed the file.

"I just don't get it. She can try other things. She can build up a portfolio. Why does she have to ditch me?" LJ shook her head.

Clyde squinted, desperately wanting to be anywhere else. But escaping wasn't an option, even if he could get past the lost look on LJ's face. "I, um... I don't know what it's worth, coming from me, but... she talks about you all the time. I don't think she wants to ditch you."

LJ flinched, turning to focus on him. "What?"

The sweating gained momentum. "She talks about your work and how she admires everything you put into your writing... she doesn't want to quit working with you. She called you her best friend."

LJ's brow furrowed.

"As for the files, you're right. I shouldn't have shown her anything confidential. That's on me." He spread his hands. "And that ends here. But you can't think she wants a future without you in it." He rubbed the back of his neck and hoped he didn't look as nervous as he thought he did. "Coby's smart. She's got ideas, and they're good. She wants to branch out, but that doesn't mean she wants to get rid of you. She loves you."

LJ stared at him for a long time. Clyde squirmed under her gaze. He waited for her to scoff or yell or flip him off and storm out, or beat him up. It took him a moment to realize her eyes were wet and she was trying to keep tears from falling. She finally sniffed and looked down, brushing her lashes rapidly and clearing her throat. "Well, I guess… I, uh…"

Footsteps boomed outside the door and Clyde flinched, body tensing and heart racing as the door flew open. "What are you doing–" Grizzly stopped in the doorway, surprise lighting his face as he spotted LJ and his gaze went back to Clyde. "What are you *doing?*"

Clyde tried to remember.

Grizzly looked at LJ still wiping at her eyes and something boiled in his expression. "Clyde, what the hell?"

"I didn't, she just came in to –"

"Did he say something to you?" Grizzly stepped closer to LJ, sending a warning look at Clyde.

LJ sniffed hard and forced a laugh. "Who, him? He could barely get anything past the foot in his mouth." She waved a dismissing hand at them both. "I'm fine. I should go." She stepped around Grizzly and headed for the door, then paused and looked to Clyde. "Hey, um… thanks."

He nodded, mouth twitching into a half smile.

LJ nodded back and left.

Clyde stared after her for a second, then made the mistake of looking at Grizzly.

"Dude?"

Clyde's eyes widened. "I didn't – she wasn't – she just was talking about –"

"Did you make her *cry?*"

"*No*! I just–"

"You *broke* her."

"I didn't break her, she was just upset about the case files." Clyde motioned at the folders and realized he'd made another mistake.

"You showed her confidential case files?" Any trace of possible humor dropped from Grizzly's tone.

"No. Actually I did not show her anything at all." Clyde's hand landed on his heart.

Grizzly squinted. "But you showed someone." He cocked his head. "It was Coby, wasn't it?"

Clyde tried to keep a straight face, but his left eyelid betrayed him.

"*Burkiss…*"

"Grizz, I'm sorry, I know I shouldn't have, but she brought in the crime scene photos, and… she noticed things."

Grizzly's frustration paused. "What kinds of things?"

"Stuff we haven't seen before." Clyde began piling the folders he'd taken out of the cabinet. "I let that slip, and then I figured, what the hell. She's a new set of eyes and she was helpful."

"Set of pretty eyes," Grizzly muttered, grabbing the case files from off the desk and throwing them back into the filing cabinet with force.

Clyde frowned. "Like LJ's?"

"What?" Grizzly snapped at him, confused.

"I know you told LJ about Kacey," Clyde said, folding his arms, and suddenly feeling like he had a bit of standing in this conversation. "That was confidential, too."

Grizzly blinked, and looked down at the ground, hands on his waist, clearing his throat. "That was different. It just… I just had to get something off my chest and it slipped out."

"Well, Coby actually came to me with information. And I think she might *actually* be able to help us," Clyde stated.

Grizzly sighed, and looked up at him. "Okay, Clyde. Tell me what she found."

Clyde pursed his lips at him, yanked the file drawer open and took the files back out. "She brought in these pictures she took of April," he said and laid out the pictures of the young woman. "And she said all she could think of was that she was a mermaid. That our killer turned this woman into the little mermaid."

"Like, 'Part of Your World', 'Daddy, I Love Him', little mermaid?" Grizzly asked, eyebrows raised as he picked up the picture.

"More or less. But that's not all, LJ told her about Kacey… that her heart was cut out in the woods," Clyde said. "And that reminded Coby of Snow White. Then she asked me… she asked if any of the other cases were based off of fairy tales."

"And?" Grizzly asked.

"And I had no idea, so… I showed her," Clyde said, glancing awkwardly away from Grizzly and back toward the case files, pulling a few out. He pointed to a picture. "McKenna Douglas. Found dead from an overdose in the cemetery? Shot up through her index finger? Sixteen years old?"

A look of dawning realization appeared on Grizzly's face. "Sleeping Beauty."

"Yeah," Clyde said, looking up at him. He could see confusion forming on the man's face. McKenna wasn't even on their radar as an unsolved case. She ran with a bad crowd sometimes, had a reputation. They always assumed it was just an accidental overdose or possibly suicide.

"And Ellie Miller? Age eight, throat chewed up, we thought she was killed by a coyote?" Clyde pulled out the evidence photo and pointed to the little girl's hoodie. "Little Red Riding Hood."

Grizzly frowned. "We found DNA evidence of a rabid coyote."

Clyde shrugged, straightening back up. "I showed her a few others and she wasn't sure about all of them, but she was going to look up a few things."

Grizzly lowered himself onto the edge of his desk slowly, looking a bit dazed. He thought for a few moments in silence. "It's not enough to go on. No real evidence… it's all speculation. Hell, half of these aren't even murder cases."

Clyde sighed. "But you have got to admit it's *something*, Grizz. If this is all one person, one sick bastard, then who knows what else he's gotten away with?"

"Maybe. Maybe it's something." Grizzly looked up at him. "I'm not saying she's wrong Clyde, but we sure as hell don't know she's right. I want to know if she finds anything else. And you're responsible for making sure she doesn't blab this stuff anywhere," he said, pointing at Clyde.

"She just wants to help, Grizz," Clyde said.

"I know. And I just want to make sure you keep your job."

Chapter Twenty-Four

LJ walked toward the motel with a little bit of spring in her step. It was sunny, she had gotten the paper, some muffins and two cups of coffee from the Kwik Trip down the road. It would have been a good day for yardwork, and that thought made her smirk. The Chevelle was parked outside their room which probably meant Coby was still there. She smiled, shuffling her purchases around as she fumbled to pull out her room key. As she reached the door, she jumped at the sight of a bouquet of flowers placed on the doormat, nearly spilling her coffee as she tried to avoid crushing them.

She unlocked the door, stepped over the flowers, and stumbled inside. She placed the food on the small table and looked at Coby who was sitting on her bed, typing away at her computer.

"Good morning, sunshine," LJ said, striding over and handing her a cup of coffee before throwing the curtains open.

"You're an angel," Coby said, taking a sip of the coffee and then shielding her eyes from the onslaught of light. "Ugh, it burns."

LJ snorted and pulled the muffins out of their bag. "It's a gorgeous day out there, you're going to turn into one of those cave trolls you keep reading about."

"Excuse me, I was just finishing up a lovely little piece on Dutch heritage, thank you very much. Boom!" Coby said, triumphantly, turning her laptop towards LJ with a flourish.

LJ's eyebrows raised. "I am impressed," she said, tossing Coby a muffin and leaning forward, snatching her laptop. "Also, your boyfriend left you flowers," she said casually.

Coby's eyes narrowed at her. "What?"

"Go see for yourself," LJ said, motioning towards the door.

Coby shuffled over, opened the door and peered down at the flowers. "Huh," she said, picking them up and bringing them inside. "Maybe our caring host left them for us," she said, with a confused chuckle.

"If Van Camp wanted to leave us things, he could make us breakfast. Roses are a bit too romantic for my taste," LJ said, scanning over Coby's writing.

Coby chuckled. "Van Camp's a smooth operator."

"Maybe they're from Clyde. It's kind of standard issue to send flowers after a date, isn't it?" LJ smirked, enjoying bugging Coby.

"It was a business lunch, thank you," Coby scolded. "Maybe they're from Grizzly... Dear LJ: Dat Butt Though..." Coby poked her, then examined the bouquet for a note.

LJ rolled her eyes heavily. "Maybe they're not actually for us and we should put them back so the doofus realizes his mistake."

Coby laughed. "Okay. Well, there's no note. If they're still here in the evening I say we claim them as ours by common law marriage," she said, placing the vase of roses back outside the door.

"Oh, that's how that works, huh?"

"Yup." Coby rolled her shoulders. "So, where are we off to today?" she asked, and walked to her suitcase so she could dress for the day.

Chapter Twenty-Five

LJ hit the "save" button and chewed on her lip in frustration. "It's just... not done." She exhaled, reaching into her pocket. She pulled out her phone and texted Ron, their editor, to inform him that she was almost finished. He would love that. "Almost" finished was a big waste of Ron's time. LJ shifted her laptop toward Coby. "Take a look."

Sitting across from her, Coby didn't look up. She had seven different fairy tale volumes spread over her half of the table, and she seemed to pore over each one simultaneously. Her laptop was shoved to the edge of her space, teetering on the edge of the table. She adjusted her glasses, noticed LJ giving her a pointed stare, and straightened. "What?"

"Remember, way back, like… two or three days ago… when we were journalists for a travel magazine and we didn't find bodies in rivers?" LJ tapped the screen. "I'm as done as I can be. Your pictures are in there, and I covered pretty much everything we discussed for the feature. It just feels like it needs something else. Maybe another interview?"

Coby removed her glasses and rubbed the bridge of her nose. "Yeah, sure." She jumped when one of her thick books toppled off the table and crashed to the floor. "I'll look at it."

LJ crossed her arms on the tabletop, fingers drumming on the rolled sleeves of her shirt. "How's your project going?"

Coby tucked her hair behind her ears and sighed. "I don't know. I feel like there's something right in front of my face that I'm just not seeing."

"What are you trying to do?"

"Just make connections." Coby reached for the bag on the chair beside her. "A couple of these cases seem to line up with fairy tales. But there is less information in the missing persons files."

LJ just watched her.

"They're connected. Don't look at me like that."

Shrugging a shoulder, LJ straightened up in her chair and arched her back to stretch. "I didn't say anything. I just think you should prepare yourself for the fact that you *could* be mistaken on this."

Coby's brow was stuck in a scowl of concentration. "I'm not."

LJ nodded. She wanted to believe her, but doubt and concern for her friend loomed in the back of her mind. "Then keep it up. You'll find something." LJ stood and stretched again. She looked sideways at Coby, hoping her voice wasn't giving away the doubt. "I'll be right back."

Coby didn't respond.

The Waupun Public Library was impressive for a town of eleven thousand. Two stories and countless places to get lost in a book – or a magazine article, for that matter. LJ wandered through the stacks in the general direction of the restroom, trying to recall if she'd seen a drinking fountain there. She glanced across the open center of the second floor, toward the floor-to-ceiling windows that framed the correctional facility right across the street. LJ shook her head. In reality, the prison had been what brought them to Waupun. If it hadn't been for Coby's interest, they could have easily bypassed the place for another small Midwest town. If it hadn't been for that damn prison, they might never have come here, they might never have found that body, they might never have met Clyde and Grizzly…

LJ turned the corner and ran into a shelving cart, her boot catching the wheel and knocking a set of hardcovers onto the floor. "Oh, wow, I'm sorry." She stooped to grab the books and replace them. "Daydreaming, I guess."

Neal, the librarian, stared at her unblinkingly. He continued to watch her as he delicately placed the book in his hand on the shelf and slowly turned to face her completely. With a glare, he reached for the cart and moved away from her without saying a word.

LJ cocked an eyebrow as he rolled the cart away, disappearing between the bookshelves. She brushed it off and continued her quest for the water fountain.

By the time she made it back to Coby, LJ's empty half of the table had been overtaken by more books, most shoved over to make room for the laptop Coby had decided to utilize. LJ plopped into her seat and reached for her own laptop. "Did you read it?"

"What?" Coby squinted at her. "Oh. That. Yeah. I like it, it's fine. I mean, it seems like it might be missing something… there are not as many comments from locals as we usually have."

LJ felt annoyance flare inside of her. She didn't usually feel bothered by Coby's criticism, but Coby had been about zero help on this article so far. "Then we better go get some more, Coby." She tried to keep her cool. She knew this fairy tale stuff was important to Coby and she was trying to be more understanding about it.

"Mm-hmm, okay," Coby mumbled as she jotted something down.

"*Soon*, we need to get this emailed in! I'm going to look up where else we can go." LJ frowned as she tried to keep her cool with her friend and access a new browser window. After about a minute she snorted in frustration. "Is the internet working for you?"

Coby didn't look away from her computer, but actually heard her speak this time. "Yeah, it's fine."

LJ sighed, adjusted the laptop's position, and tried to reconnect. "Well, it's being obnoxious for me."

"Just ask Neal about it. Sometimes the password needs to be re-entered. He can get it for you." She continued scrolling.

LJ groaned under her breath and turned to look back toward where she'd last seen Neal. She flinched when he was standing at the end of a row, watching her from behind his shelving cart. "Excuse me, the internet connection isn't working."

"It's working fine for Coby." Neal reached for a book.

LJ scowled. "Well, I need it to work for me, too. Could I get the password again, please?"

"It'll have to wait. I'm working." He moved down the aisle out of sight.

LJ looked at Coby incredulously. "Does he have a problem with me?" she whispered.

Coby tore her gaze away and scowled. "What are you talking about?"

"That guy is a total prick." LJ shook her head and tried to connect her laptop again.

"Neal? He's nice!" Coby scoffed. She reached into her bag and pulled out another copy of a case file. "I'm really striking out on 'The Elves and The Shoemaker'."

The page finally connected and LJ relaxed as her search loaded. She scrolled through the links, trying to find something new. She sighed loudly. Coby didn't notice and flipped through her file, leaning on her elbow and tapping her forehead with her fingers.

The shelving cart wheels squeaked from across the empty library, and LJ scowled to herself. "Coby, I could use some help here, can you please look up some place we could go for an interview?" she implored, frustration rising in her voice.

Coby glanced up at her sharply, a touch of annoyance on her face. "I don't– let's… let's just talk to Van Camp tomorrow."

LJ raised an eyebrow. "Van Camp?"

"He's a business owner in Waupun. He probably sees a lot of people coming and going. It would be a good perspective. Call him, would you?" she asked, turning back to her books. "I just gotta…" she trailed off and LJ sighed.

"Yeah, okay. I'll call him."

Chapter Twenty-Six

Grizzly's eyes were burning.

Burkiss had left. Hopefully, anyway, since Grizzly had told him hours before that he needed to go home and get some sleep. The man was getting obsessive over Coby's insane theories, and Grizzly was getting concerned with their… involvement. On several levels.

He groaned as he looked down at Ellie Miller's file. Clyde insisted on him taking another look at it, and quite frankly, it wasn't helping anything. It was just making him depressed.

The little girl was murdered. Clyde wasn't wrong about that. But it hadn't been a person, it had been an animal. Forensic evidence said a rabid coyote. It was tragic, and the crime scene photos were horrific, but it was a closed case. One he didn't have to worry about.

A knock sounded at the door. Grizzly looked up at the clock on the wall. If Clyde was still working, Grizzly was going to kick his ass. "Come in." Officer Shaun Pritchard poked his head inside. Grizzly hadn't realized he was still at the station, and he raised an eyebrow at the man. "Something you need, Pritchard?"

"Yeah, if you've got a minute." He stepped inside and closed the door behind him without waiting for a response.

"Of course." Grizzly turned off his desk light and reached for his coffee, taking a sip before realizing the cup hadn't been fresh for hours. He grimaced and set it down. "What do you –"

"I just want to make sure we're clear on something." Pritchard placed his hands on his hips. He raised his gaze and squinted at Grizzly. "I never agreed with DeJager on his decision to name you chief."

Grizzly leaned back in his chair, brow furrowing. "I'm sorry?"

"You're a poor choice; I think we can both agree on that, Greg." Pritchard looked toward the office window. "You've got a lot of flaws but being egotistical isn't one of them."

Grizzly's eyelid twitched. He'd been up for too long and he'd been looking at the files of too many dead girls. He thought about ripping that smug look off of Pritchard's face, but decided he should probably find out why it was there in the first place. "What the hell are you getting at?"

"What I *absolutely* can*not* stand, is favoritism in the workplace." Pritchard narrowed his eyes at Grizzly. "Being teacher's pet is one thing, but when teacher's pet decides to make his best bud first officer, I get a little… irritated."

Grizzly ground his teeth together.

"And beyond that? Forrest Gump is dragging in civilians and showing them confidential files." Pritchard shook his head. "I won't sit back and watch that."

Grizzly waited.

"Now I don't know what kind of agreement she's got with him, but it's inappropriate behavior. And I will be reporting it to the mayor if it's not handled." Pritchard shrugged. "But I know you'll deal with this, Chief."

He had the nerve to leave the door open when he strode out of the room. Grizzly sucked his teeth and leaned his elbows on the desk, resting his head in his hands. He should have seen something like this coming. Pritchard was being a dick, but he wasn't wrong.

Clyde was no longer toeing the line, he was tap dancing a mile on the other side. Bending over backwards to show Coby the files was bad enough, but now he was jumping down the rabbit hole with her. Even if he believed her, he couldn't just go along with the theories of a serial-killer enthusiast writer.

Even if she was pretty and nice to him.

***

Coby wore a turquoise pendant shaped like a feather. The tip of the feather disappeared beneath her tank top now and again. Van Camp had a hard time keeping his eyes off of it.

"How long have you owned the motel?"

He forced himself to look over at the brunette, whose plaid shirt was buttoned one too many to keep his attention. "Uhh, going on fifteen years."

"Do you get a lot of customers in such a small town?"

Van Camp scratched his wiry gray head. "Depends. No pattern to it, really. Sometimes it gets busy."

LJ stared at him like she expected him to go on. He shrugged. She sighed. "What can you tell us about Waupun?"

He shrugged again, then leaned back on his stool and crossed his arms, tapping his fingers on his scrubby chin. "It's a nice place, I guess. Got some decent fishing spots and good beer on tap."

LJ blinked, then jotted something down on her notepad. "Mmm-kay… what about –"

"Anything newsworthy going on?" Coby interjected, tapping her own notepad with the eraser on her pencil. "Things only local townspeople would know about?"

LJ twisted in her seat to look at Coby, who stood a few feet behind her. The blonde raised her eyebrows and shrugged. LJ rolled her eyes as she turned back to Van Camp. "Sure. Anything like that?"

Van Camp jerked his gaze away from Coby's neckline, which wasn't actually anywhere close to her neck. "What's that now?"

"Small towns have a rumor mill. I'm sure Waupun is no exception." Coby stepped forward and pulled up a chair. "We've heard some rumors already."

"Oh, yeah? Like the couple getting busy right out on Main Street?" He chuckled. "Lots of people named names but that was actually my cousin and his –"

"No. Like missing people," Coby stated, adjusting her glasses. LJ shot her a look, but Coby didn't look away from Van Camp. "We've heard about some girls that have disappeared."

Van Camp straightened up in his seat. "Well, sure. A couple. A couple of bodies found nearby, too."

"Really?" Coby asked, leaning forward and looking interested. "What do you know about all that?"

"Okay," LJ interjected. "I'm not sure we should really talk about that in our article."

"Wait, wait." Van Camp shifted in his seat, waving a hand dismissively at LJ who in turn looked highly affronted. "I know some of those girls' families. Raised a big to do about it. Tons of fund raisers, signs everywhere, like we didn't all know what they looked like already." He scoffed. "Nothing ever came of it though," he said, leaning back. "No one ever came forward with information." He shrugged with a slight smile. "I've always said I was willing to bet it was the truckers that pass through here all the time."

"Truckers that stayed here?" Coby asked sharply.

"Coby!" LJ snapped.

"Nah, they sleep in their trucks most of the time if they stop here." He shrugged. "People treat Waupun like it's the 70s still… teenagers and kids are always out walking around alone, all hours, bike riding and such. How easy would it be to just snatch a pretty one?" he asked with a shrug.

"Or one who's eight years old?" The blonde asked flatly, nostrils flared and looking a lot less pretty.

"Y-yeah." Van Camp shrugged, leaning back away from her.

"Coby. This is an interview not an interrogation," the brunette hissed.

"Well, if that's all ladies…" Van Camp said awkwardly, slapping his hands on his knees and pushing his chair back.

"Wait, sir, if we could just ask you a few more questions," LJ said quickly, rising. The blonde still scowled.

"I got some rooms to clean," he muttered, waving at them before walking quickly out of the room.

Chapter Twenty-Seven

Grizzly watched the coffee splash into his insulated mug with little interest. It had been sitting in the pot all morning and it was down to the last bit. Hardly worth drinking, but he didn't really care.

His phone buzzed. He headed back to his office and looked at the screen, spirits lifting just a touch as he recognized LJ's number. He hadn't heard from her since he'd made her rake his yard. Inhaling, he put the phone to his ear and opened his mouth to greet her with the words "Mornin', darlin'," but she was talking before he got a chance to speak.

"I'm calling to give you a heads up."

"What?"

A breathy sigh scratched through the speaker. "Coby has a theory." There was another voice, muffled, on the other end. "I'm *not* negating you – I just don't think you should be *this* certain –" LJ sighed again. "We're pulling into the parking lot. I just wanted to warn you so this wasn't coming at you from left field."

The line went dead and Grizzly paused in the hallway, scowling at the phone. Within seconds, the station door opened, and he heard the muffled argument from the other side of the building.

"It'll be there."

"You need to calm the hell down."

"But I know it's there. Everything points to this."

Grizzly turned around and headed for the front. LJ was the first thing he saw when he entered the waiting area. Her hair was down and the blue in her shirt was doing something fantastic to her eyes, even though he had spent their last outing together noting her eyes were dark brown. She was looking at Coby with concern.

Coby's eyes were wild. Her ponytail was unkempt and she carried a map in one hand, loose pages in the other.

"Ladies," Grizzly greeted them, still holding his phone.

LJ was giving him an apologetic look, but Coby's eyes darted right past him. "Hey," she said breathlessly, her face lifting in a quick smile before slamming back down in focus. "Where's Clyde?" she asked, moving to see around him but Grizzly shifted so he was standing between her and her path back to the desks.

"Busy," Grizzly said, not needing this right now, especially with Pritchard here. "What do you need, Coby?"

Coby paused finally, her eyes searched his for a brief second. She frowned, waving a hand at LJ as if lumping them together. "You're not going to listen to me."

Grizzly folded his arms and looked down at the small woman. "Why don't you try me?"

Coby held up her fist full of papers. "Maria Wells. Missing person. She was pregnant. With her first child," she prompted.

"That's all in the report." Grizzly nodded.

"Yes," Coby said. "And she was the great-granddaughter of the man who owned the Rock River Hemp Mill."

Grizzly frowned and narrowed his eyes. "Okay?"

Coby nodded. "*Okay*. It's Rumpelstiltskin. That's the fairy tale. We need to go to the mill. I know we're going to find her there. Probably… without her baby."

She shook the map in her other hand.

Grizzly tried really hard not to sigh deeply. He managed, but Coby scowled at him anyway.

"See? I told you you weren't going to listen."

"It's not impossible… I guess. I don't think it's a crazy theory… exactly…"

LJ filled in the rest of his train of thought. "It's just a little out there, Coby."

Coby threw her hands in the air with an eyeroll. "You're not listening to me, you're just hearing the far-fetchedness. It's only crazy if you don't see the pattern, and you guys haven't been looking at all the stuff I've been looking at and researching. If you stop scoffing and let me show you, you'll see."

Grizzly bristled. "What have you been looking at?"

"Files, Chief. It's not a secret." She gave him a pointed look. "What are you going to do about it, arrest me?"

He scowled.

"Now where's Clyde?" Coby took his moment of distraction to slip past him and book it down the hallway toward the desk area.

"He's *working* –"

"*This* is what he should be working on." Coby threw over her shoulder at him as he trailed after her, trying to decide if he should physically pick her up and remove her from the premises. She burst into the room and made a beeline for Clyde's desk. Other officers looked up at the commotion and watched. Clyde lit up when he first spotted her, then caught sight of Grizzly and didn't look as thrilled.

"Coby, hey, what's going –"

"I found Maria Wells."

"She didn't *find* her." LJ gave up the act and sighed audibly. "She *thinks* –"

"Clyde will get it!" Coby yelled over LJ and glared at her. She threw the map onto Clyde's desk and spread out the papers she'd carried in. She looked at Clyde. "Rumpelstiltskin."

Grizzly grew more irritated with Clyde as realization spread across the little man's face. One word – one *ridiculous* word – shouldn't have put him on Coby's side.

"What's happening?" Pritchard leaned over Clyde's desk and looked at the papers. "Is that the missing persons report on Maria Wells? She shouldn't have that."

"This doesn't concern you, Officer Pritchard," Grizzly spat out at him. He reached over Coby and snatched up everything she'd set on the desk. "Anderson, I'd like to speak with you in private."

"Grizz, we have to check it out." Clyde's statement silenced the group. Grizzly clenched his jaw and gave his partner a hard look. Pritchard was looking back and forth between the two of them, and Grizzly could feel his judgement. "I'm not saying she's right. I'm saying she could be, and it's our duty as law enforcement officers – as decent human beings – to go and see if this missing girl has been lying dead at the mill for the last three years."

Everyone in the room was staring at Grizzly. He refused to acknowledge it and just continued to glare at Clyde, who managed to hold his gaze with confidence. He finally broke the stare and glanced at Coby, who crossed her arms, and LJ, who just stared up at him, wide-eyed. She seemed to be the only person who wasn't holding him accountable.

He deflated. "Okay. We'll check it out." Pritchard's mouth opened, but Grizzly silenced him with a glare. "It's a lead."

Clyde was already leading the way out back to where their cruiser was parked.

***

Coby leaned forward in her seat behind Grizzly, squinting through the wire caging that separated her and LJ from the officers in the front seat. "It's a left up here."

"Since when do you know how to get *anywhere?*" LJ scowled.

"Since I memorized the layout of Fond du Lac County," Coby snapped back.

"I was just teasing."

"Well, why don't you stop? We're about to find another dead person, Laverne."

LJ lifted her chin and clamped her mouth shut.

"I know where the damn mill is, Anderson," Grizzly growled from behind the wheel. He was angry with her, but she didn't care in the slightest. "We're not spending the rest of the day here, I hope you know. And I'm not calling out CSU."

"We'll see." Coby sat back.

Clyde stayed silent in the passenger seat.

They pulled into the overgrown gravel driveway of the abandoned mill. Grizzly creeped up to the old structure and put the cruiser into park.

Clyde opened the back door and Coby bolted out. "Coby, slow down."

"Clyde, it's fine. We just have to figure out where he put her."

Clyde snagged her sleeve. "This place is falling apart. You can't go in there; there could be rats, and –"

"We have to *look*. We're going to find her." Coby screeched at him and tore away, storming inside the dilapidated building.

Grizzly frowned and slammed his car door. "Son of a –" he trailed off with a growl, stomping after them.

Coby slowed when she entered the crumbling old mill, nose assaulted with the smell of rotting wood and moss. She looked around wildly, taking a deep breath. She had to focus. Clyde followed her inside, wincing at the general filth of the place.

Coby crept forward, looking around slowly, trying to take everything in.

Grizzly and LJ stepped into the building, LJ looking tentatively at the floor, testing every step, fingers splayed like she was afraid Grizzly was going to make it collapse beneath their feet. Grizzly let out a sigh, his boots echoing in the abandoned old place. "So, where's this body?" he asked.

Coby frowned. "Shh," she murmured, looking around, replaying all her research in her mind. Panic started buzzing in the base of her brain and she shoved it away. The girl had to be here. She knew she was here. She slammed her eyes shut, going over every detail.

"Coby?" Clyde asked, reaching forward and touching her elbow.

"Shh!"

If she was wrong about this, this was the end. There was no way they would let her keep the files, and they'd never listen to another thing she said. She had to find this body. She had to! There had to be a clue in the fairy tale… where he would put the body...

"'The devil has told you that...'" she recited. "'...he plunged his right foot so deep into the earth… he tore himself in two.'" Her eyes flew open and she looked down at the rotting floorboards. "The floor, she's in the floor! She's got to be!"

Clyde looked over at Grizzly, who deflated slightly. "Burkiss," he protested.

"Come on," Clyde said, walking into the middle of the floor, bending down, gripping the rotten board and looking up at Grizzly, waiting for him to join him. Coby swallowed, feeling a surge of affection for him infusing with the adrenaline pumping through her system.

Grizzly let out another sigh and stepped forward, kneeling down by the floorboard, and yanking. Nothing.

LJ was looking at her now, concern and sympathy on her face.

Coby ignored her as Clyde moved a few paces to the right and tugged on another, Grizzly following and helping as well.

Another.

Another.

Grizzly grunted as they yanked on another piece of flooring. "Burkiss, I'm not tearing up this whole –"

A weird mixture of horror and triumph flooded through Coby. She let out a yell at the same time as Clyde, who stumbled backwards and dropped the floor board he had pried loose. Grizzly swore and LJ's hands flew over her mouth.

A ripped in half, decomposing body lay face up beneath the floor, and the smell of decaying flesh permeated the room.

Chapter Twenty-Eight

Clyde crouched near the ripped up floorboards. Far enough that he wasn't in the way of the techs, but close enough that he could stare into what was left of Maria's face.

She had been there, right there, under their noses for three years. She'd gone missing, Clyde and Grizzly and everyone on the force had looked for her, and slowly the search had dwindled down to nothing. It was one of the first cases they'd worked with Grizzly as chief, and not finding her had added to his stress. As much as either of them would hate to admit it, they'd forgotten about her as time wore on.

But here she was. Torn in half, straight up her body, the split stopping at the throat to leave her head intact. Clyde's eyes kept trailing down to her middle despite his best efforts to look away. Even decomposition couldn't hide the fact that someone had cut her unborn child from her belly, but no one had had the stomach to mention the elephant in the room yet.

"Just when I think this nightmare can't get any worse," Grizzly spoke from behind him. Clyde stood slowly, knees popping from being in one position for too long. Adams looked exhausted, but he wasn't staring at the body. He watched Clyde carefully. "They say anything yet?"

Clyde shook his head. "Still looking everything over." He ran his hands through his hair, noting how greasy it was. "You take the girls back to the motel?"

"No, they're outside." Grizzly crossed his arms. "Couldn't get them to leave. Coby keeps throwing out more ideas about other cases. Her brain is going to melt if she keeps this up without any sleep."

Clyde nodded absently.

"We're going to need to question her," Grizzly muttered, under his breath and looking sideways at Clyde.

Clyde focused, eyes narrowing at his partner. "What?"

Grizzly sighed. "This is going to come out in the open, and people are going to be wondering why in the hell some girl from out of town nailed the location of a missing person without so much as batting an eye. We're going to have to get alibis."

Clyde's hands shot out and shoved all two hundred and twenty pounds of Greg Adams two steps backward. "You think she was involved in this?"

Grizzly looked more surprised by his balance being offset than Clyde's actual anger. "*I'm* not saying that. I'm saying other people are going to think that."

Clyde stood there and seethed. "Coby's not a psychopathic murderer. Just because she's found a girl you've been trying to find for *years* does not mean she's some freak looking for fame. It just means she's better at your job than you are."

Grizzly's glare didn't falter, but he also didn't look as wounded as Clyde wanted him to. "I never said she wasn't being helpful, Burkiss." He shook his head and glanced down at the body, then turned and headed outside.

"Officer Burkiss?" a timid voice spoke from behind him. Clyde stared after Grizzly, pulse still pounding in his ears, then turned to look at the tiny, female CSU tech. "We, uh, we've got some information on the body."

"Right. I'm listening." Clyde pushed down the anger and gave the woman his full attention.

"As far as we can tell, she was dead when she was split in two, so she was dead when she was buried here." The woman looked down at her clipboard, Canon hanging from the strap around her neck. "However, the file states that she was pregnant at the time of her disappearance, and lacerations to her midsection indicate that the fetus was surgically removed."

Clyde blinked. "Is that… what killed her?"

She tapped a pen on her clipboard. "It's likely."

He swallowed a mouthful of bile. "Good work."

She nodded and awkwardly glanced between him and the doorway Grizzly had walked out of before going back to work.

Clyde sighed and ran a hand back through his hair. He needed air. And sleep. And… he shook his head and walked out of mill.

The media had arrived. A reporter for FOX 47 News was speaking to one of the officers, no doubt wanting an interview with the police chief, but Grizzly was talking to some officers and ignoring the cameraman beyond the tape.

Coby was standing next to a pale looking LJ, talking animatedly to her. Coby noticed Clyde coming out of the mill and walked towards him quickly. Clyde swallowed and bit back the anger he was feeling towards Grizzly. Serial killer? Coby Anderson? Right.

"Update?" She looked stressed, and Clyde wished she didn't.

"Uhh… yeah. I gotta tell Grizz." He rubbed the back of his neck. He wanted to go home. He wanted a drink. He wanted to do anything that didn't involve talking to Grizzly, if he was being honest.

Grizzly didn't see Clyde approach. He dismissed the other officers with a nod and aimed for LJ, who still stood against his cruiser. He touched her arm and ducked to look her in the eyes, and Clyde wondered if he should wait and leave them alone. Pushing the thought aside, he cleared his throat loudly, probably turning scarlet when they both looked up at him. "They're thinking she bled to death when her killer removed the baby via cesarean. She was cut in half and buried under the floor after she was dead."

LJ's face took on a greenish tint. Grizzly was angry. Coby didn't look the slightest bit surprised. "I wonder if he still has it," she whispered, looking a little more startled by her own thought, then sickened by it. "The freak."

Grizzly shook his head, a growl sounding in his chest. "Well you've been right about everything else." He glanced up at Coby. "All this research you've been doing? I'm gonna need you to show me –"

Pritchard was suddenly there, cutting Grizzly off. "Ms. Anderson, we're going to need you to come down to the police department," he demanded, grabbing her arm and taking a stride towards the cruiser.

"What the hell?" LJ demanded with a scowl, stepping forward.

"Wait. What?" Coby asked, looking genuinely alarmed, attempting to pull away from him, more out of confusion than anything. Pritchard's grip tightened on

Coby's arm. Clyde saw Pritchard's other hand stray towards his cuffs and something inside of Clyde snapped.

He didn't remember punching Pritchard, but he did remember Coby shouting his name and Grizzly practically picking him up and setting him down on the other side of himself. He blinked as his best friend's face was suddenly in his. "Clyde, calm down!" Grizzly growled at him, his dark eyes searching his, as Pritchard scrambled to his feet, nose dripping blood.

Grizzly turned to Coby who looked more scared than Clyde had ever seen her. "Coby, you're not being arrested, we just have to ask you for an alibi," Grizzly began gently as Clyde tried to catch his breath and see through the haze of anger.

"She was with me!" LJ stated angrily, though her rage was directed at Pritchard who was trying to wipe the blood from his face. "She's always with me and everything we've done for the last five years has been documented."

"You show that girl confidential files, and now you're assaulting an officer? I'll see you lose your badge for this, Burkiss," Pritchard spat at him.

Grizzly turned toward Pritchard, drawing himself up to his full height and pointing at him. "Go home, Pritchard! I don't want to see your face at this crime scene again!" he bellowed at him.

Pritchard ground his teeth and looked like he was contemplating arguing but then turned and strode away quickly. Grizzly took a deep breath and let it out before turning to Coby.

Her eyes were big and for the first time that day she was silent. "I'll tell you whatever you want to know," she whispered. Clyde wanted to follow Pritchard and tear him limb from limb.

Grizzly shook his head. "I don't think you did it, sweetheart. Don't worry." He gave Clyde a pointed look before turning back to Coby. "I'll have you write a report so people like Pritchard don't make trouble for us."

Coby and LJ both nodded in agreement.

"And you're going to have to bring me up to speed with all this fairy tale stuff."

Coby nodded and there was silence before she looked up at him. "Well," Coby sighed. "It's pretty Grimm."

They all turned to look at her.

"...What?"

***

"This is bullshit," LJ muttered, arms crossed, staring through the glass window with tired eyes.

Clyde stood next to her, one hand on his belt, the other scraping through the stubble on his face. "Yeah, it is."

They watched Coby in the next room, leaning back in a chair, hands folded on top of the table, thumbs twiddling. Her eyes were wide, searching the interrogation room uncertainly.

"How long is he going to make her wait?" LJ snapped, turning to Clyde as if the whole situation were his fault, when she knew it wasn't. It probably wasn't even Grizzly's fault, even though he was in charge. It was probably just one of those things that had to be done. But it felt personal.

Clyde didn't answer, but she heard his teeth grinding.

The door opened and Grizzly paused in the doorway, looking exhausted. LJ had the urge to punch him in the chest, but she refrained and barked at him instead. "What are you doing in *here*? She's been sitting in there for half an hour like some kind of criminal –"

Grizzly held up a hand. "I know, I know. And I'm sorry. There's just a lot of channels to go through, and letting you stay back here isn't actually allowed."

"Don't give me that. You're the chief of police," LJ scoffed. She pointed toward Coby, on the other side of the glass. "You can't keep her here without cause."

"I realize that, thank you. All of it," Grizzly growled at her and then looked at Clyde. "I'm taking the reins on this. I just came in here to see if you have anything to add."

Clyde continued to watch Coby and only acknowledged Grizzly with a shake of his head. Grizzly sighed and left the room, giving LJ one last glance before shutting the door.

LJ seethed, fighting the thought in the back of her mind that was saying he looked like a forlorn puppy who needed a hug and a long nap. That didn't matter. He was keeping her friend hostage in an interrogation room like a convict, and she wasn't okay with that.

Grizzly reappeared on the other side of the glass, and Coby jumped at the opening door. Grizzly flashed a tired smile at her and sat down at the table. His demeanor was apologetic, even as he turned his back to the glass, and LJ tried not to let that assuage her anger. "I'm sorry about this, Miss Anderson. It's standard procedure."

Coby nodded, a touch of irritation on her face.

"Now, I've got some people checking on your alibis for the dates that these women went missing. LJ's... Miss Reed's as well."

Coby nodded again, looking tired but still stubborn. "We're not lying."

Grizzly hesitated and nodded. "Good. Just a few more questions then." He cleared his throat and sat back in his chair. If LJ were in a better mood, she would have been amused at the differences of height between the two.

"How did you know that the body was in the mill?" Grizzly asked.

"I was following a hunch. Doing a lot of research on some cases and trying to match them to my theory. Maria is a descendant of the man who originally built and owned the mill. She was pregnant. It was all lining up with the fairy tale Rumpelstiltskin," she said calmly. "Want me to break that down for you?"

Grizzly shook his head. "Not yet." LJ could see his shoulders sag a little more. "How did you get the information on Maria Wells?"

LJ felt Clyde tense beside her and she saw Coby hesitate, looking conflicted.

"You gotta tell me the truth, Coby," Grizzly said gently, a knowing tone to his voice.

"Officer Burkiss," Coby said quietly. "Because I told him about the theory based on the pictures I took at the crime scene of April –" she rushed and Grizzly held up a hand to stop her.

Clyde sighed audibly. LJ looked over at him. "Is that going to come back to haunt you?"

"It already has."

"When did you first hear of these missing persons cases?" Grizzly leaned his elbows on the table.

"Sometime after LJ and I got to Waupun." Coby shrugged a shoulder. "It's not exactly a secret. There have been a lot of them."

LJ closed her eyes and shuddered. She had been forcing herself not to think about Maria Wells or April Marsden. Or the fact that Coby, crazy Coby with her nutty fairy tale theory, had been right and led them all straight to a dead body. LJ still couldn't believe this was happening.

She felt Clyde's eyes on her, but refused to look at him. She didn't want to acknowledge just what they had gotten themselves into. Or that she felt like she was dangerously close to some kind of mental and emotional breakdown. She didn't want to do anything other than get Coby out of there, go back to the motel room, lock all the doors and go to bed.

Grizzly sighed and ran a hand over his face before standing and offering Coby a hand. "All right. I think that's enough for tonight. Thanks, Coby," he said. "For everything," he added.

She looked at him before taking his hand, letting him pull her to her feet. She nodded. "Thanks for listening."

Grizzly shook his head. "Don't thank me. That was all Clyde." He patted her on the shoulder as they both moved towards the door. "But I'll be listening now. I can promise you that."

LJ and Clyde moved around towards the door. "He's not going to get in trouble is he?" LJ heard Coby's muffled voice through the door.

"Don't you worry about that," Grizzly reassured as they stepped through the door and came to a stop at the sight of them.

LJ was struck with just how exhausted Coby looked, like she was going to fall over and sleep right there on the floor. Clyde must have noticed too because he reached forward and placed a hand on her arm, steadying her. "You should get some sleep."

LJ nodded. "Yeah, Coby, let's get back to the motel."

Grizzly held the door open for them. "Clyde will drive you."

"But there's so much more to go through." Coby stayed where she was. "This was just one. I have more ideas, and there are a few case files I haven't looked at really closely yet."

LJ snagged her by the sleeve and pushed past Grizzly. "Coby, you don't actually work for the police department. We're leaving."

"But," Coby protested, stumbling after her.

"LJ, hang on, let Clyde –"

"I can drive, Grizzly," LJ said shortly. Not really angry with him, just upset in general and needing to take her best friend and leave.

"Get some sleep, Coby. I'll call you tomorrow and we'll talk about it," Clyde called after them as LJ marched with Coby out to the car.

Coby didn't protest again and she seemed to doze off during the short drive back to the motel. LJ fought off exhaustion and adrenaline at the same time, wishing she'd never heard of Waupun or its inhabitants, dead or alive. Never in her life did she think writing for a travel magazine would have thrown her into a fray of gruesome murders. She glanced sideways at Coby as they pulled up to the motel, then shoved her awake and headed for the room. She snatched the roses off the stoop in frustration, threw the door open, and tossed the flowers into the trash.

Part of her couldn't understand Coby's obsession with the situation. That same part wanted to pick up and hightail it back to the road, where things weren't always predictable, but always home.

Another, very small but annoying piece of her wondered what else Coby might find.

***

Grizzly turned to Clyde as the girls left the building. "I still don't like them staying at that creepy little motel," he muttered and then sighed when Clyde didn't make any sign of response. "Look, I'm sorry, okay? I'm sorry I'm a shit chief, I'm sorry I didn't listen to Coby and I'm sorry I had to interrogate her, okay?" He planted his hands on his hips. "I'm sorry I doubted you, and I'm sorry you punched Pritchard – actually I'm not sorry about that. That was freaking awesome."

Clyde turned and looked at him. He sighed as well. "You're not a shit chief. But you're right, you should have listened to Coby," he added. "What are we going to do now, Grizz?" He rubbed his other hand over his bruised knuckles.

"You're going to go get some sleep. Then tomorrow we're going to call up your little fairy tale Indiana Jones and… I dunno. Make her official. A… private detective or consultant or something. We can do that, right? They do that in the TV shows." He thought out loud as he grabbed his keys and his coat.

"I'll look into it," Clyde said with a nod. "Where are you going?"

"I get to go tell a young man that we found his missing wife, but not his unborn child," Grizzly said, giving him a sad smile. "Go home, Burkiss. I can't have you hitting anyone tomorrow." He winked at him before heading out the door.

"Grizzly, wait." Clyde stopped him, grabbing his jacket. "I'm coming with you."

Grizzly swallowed and nodded as his first officer fell into step behind him.

***

He heard. The whispers. News traveled fast in small towns.

Did you hear?
They found her!
Maria Wells! Murdered!

Maria Wells had been gone for years. Most people didn't think twice about her anymore. Except perhaps the husband she left behind. Missing persons were cruel things… there was no closure with them, as there was with murder. But that wasn't his fault.

He had given up on the cops finding that one. He had simply filed it away in his mind… a story that would never be appreciated by anyone. Fine. They always missed the points of his stories anyway. No one understood his craft. No one understood his stories.

But Maria Wells. This one they found. He couldn't believe it. A win for the local law enforcement. They needed a win, considering all the losses.

Maria Wells… he sighed and closed his eyes, replaying the story in his head. She hadn't gone without a fight, that was for sure. But women have always fought to protect their children.

He wondered what they thought when discovering Maria. She had been so beautiful. She was even beautiful in death.

Years buried under the mill. Two girls, out-of-towners, had figured it out. He overheard some people at Helen's Kitchen speculating that the girls had stumbled upon the body and then called the police.

He knew differently.

Chapter Twenty-Nine

LJ's eyes flew open at six the next morning, bloodshot and dry. She turned to look at the clock on the bedside table, then reached for her phone next to it. Her vision blurred when the screen lit up her side of the room, and she squinted as she threw back the covers and tapped through the contacts.

"What are you doing?" Coby garbled from the other bed. She made no movement to find a lamp.

"Did I wake you up?" LJ peered through the darkness.

"I was already awake." Coby shuffled until she was sitting against the headboard, covers still up to her chin. "You?"

"I just realized that Ron probably thinks we're headed to Minnesota by now." LJ sighed and held up the phone. "He called me twice yesterday and I missed it both times. I should probably call him and explain the situation."

"He's not gonna be happy."

"Yeah, well, there's not a whole lot we can do about that, is there?" LJ sat on the edge of the bed, elbows on her knees, tangled tresses hiding her face. "It's not like we can just pick up and leave."

There was a rustling sound and LJ assumed it was Coby nodding against the headboard. "So I guess you're on board with this fairy tale theory."

"I think we're all on board with your fairy tale theory, Coby." LJ got to her feet. "It's seven in Michigan, right? That's not too early to call Ron."

"He'll be thrilled to hear we're not sleeping in on his dime." Coby yawned and flipped on the light as LJ reached for her jeans and a sweatshirt.

She stepped out into the early darkness after tugging on a pair of boots. She shivered and zipped up her sweatshirt as she let the phone dial Ron's office number.

"Reed, I was supposed to hear from you forty eight hours ago. What the hell is going on?"

LJ sat on the bumper of the Chevelle and gazed across the parking lot, hearing Ron's face turn red. "Some things came up."

"Are you in Albert Lea?"

"...No."

"*Reed* –"

"I *know*." LJ squeezed her eyes shut. "We're kind of tied up in an investigation right now. It's a long story."

"'Investigation'? Like a police investigation? Did one of you get arrested?"

"No, Ron, slow down. *We're* not under investigation." LJ hesitated, then decided to leave the details of Coby's interrogation the night before out of the conversation. "We're going to be in Waupun for the rest of the week, and probably into next week too. But I'm going to make it work, I promise."

"Oh, do tell, I'm dying to hear."

LJ rolled her eyes. "There's more here. It's a nice little town, but there's more to it than that. The devil's in the details, right? Give us another week, and I promise we'll have a lot more for our feature. And maybe even more than that."

"What are you getting at?"

"Not just *Pure Travel*. Maybe for some of the other titles." LJ knew she was going out on a limb, but if it would buy her time, it was worth it. Besides, she wasn't wrong. Webster House journalists solving crimes would sell magazines and shine light on Webster House Publishing. Provided they were allowed to write the articles and publish them for the public. Grizzly wouldn't like that. "We're sitting on something big here, Ron. I can't get into it yet, but in the meantime, there's enough here for me to write more for next week's deadline." Silence on Ron's end of the line was punctuated by the hum of the connection. LJ waited.

"You'd better come through on this. That's all I have to say."

LJ shook her head and looked at her phone as the call ended. She stood and the Chevelle creaked. Despite getting technicalities out of the way, she didn't feel any more at ease about their current situation. She headed back for the room, then paused outside the door. She frowned at the sight of flowers, once again on the door step. This time it was a bouquet of white roses. Someone was aggressive. Her first thought went to Clyde, though, the word "aggressive" could hardly be applied to him. That being said, how aggressive did you have to be to anonymously leave flowers on someone's door step?

Not aggressive, she supposed. Just obnoxious.

Her mind flashed briefly to Grizzly. He was obnoxious. But no, he hadn't done anything, really, to make it obvious he liked her like that. At least not to the dozen roses level.

Sighing, she snatched them up, examining them for a note. Once again there was none.

She shook her head. Someone was wasting a lot of money on flowers that she was just going to keep throwing away. Maybe it was Van Camp, the creep. Though she was surprised he didn't just let himself in and sprinkle the petals on the pillows himself, and hide in the shower while he was at it. She rolled her eyes. Maybe she should have taken Grizzly up on the offer to upgrade to a nicer place.

LJ glared at the flowers, making up her mind to just ignore them as she set them back down. If she didn't throw them away, more couldn't show up right? Maybe whoever kept coming around would finally get the hint and realize flowers weren't welcome.

She stepped over them with resolve, closing the door firmly behind her.

***

Coby wrung out her dripping hair over the sink, then mopped at it uselessly with a motel towel that was little more than a washcloth. She stifled a yawn and swiped the steam off the mirror, grimacing at her exhausted reflection. "Anderson, you are going off the deep end."

Her phone buzzed loudly from the next room, and she scowled, unsure where she'd even left it or who could possibly be calling her at this hour. She opened the bathroom door and scanned the room. LJ dug through a duffel bag on her bedspread and pointed toward the floor.

Coby found the vibrating phone in the pocket of yesterday's jeans. The screen went dark as soon as the device was in her grasp and she growled in annoyance at it. "Missed it."

"Well, it wasn't Ron. I just hung up with him." LJ lazily folded a sweatshirt and stuffed it in the bottom of the bag.

"I think it was Grizzly," Coby replied.

"Why is Grizzly calling you?" LJ sat on the edge of her unmade bed.

"Jealous?" Coby teased. "I have no idea." She entered her password and held the phone to her ear to listen to the voicemail.

"Hey, Coby, Grizz here… I need to talk to you about working with us. I'm still working out the details, but if you have some time today or tomorrow to come in, I might have a proposition for you."

Coby raised an eyebrow and plopped on her bed, dropping the phone in her lap and looking at LJ. "Huh."

"What?"

"I think your boyfriend is offering me a job."

Chapter Thirty

"You want her to what?" Clyde stood in the doorway of Grizzly's office, voice carrying a lot further than he'd intended.

"Will you shut your face and close the door behind you? You want the whole damn town knowing our business?" Grizzly hissed, rising from his chair and moving for the door himself.

Clyde closed it before he got there and scowled up at the chief. "Are you nuts?"

"*No*, actually, this is probably the brightest idea I've ever had," Grizzly whispered. "If she's working for us, we're legally allowed to share confidential information with her. No red tape."

Clyde shook his head. "No, Grizz, *more* red tape. A consultant? What the hell is she a consultant in? Fairy tales and fables?"

"Well… yes." Grizzly shrugged. "Do *I* look like an expert on the subject? I *need* someone with knowledge on the subject matter if we're going to crack these cases and track down a –" he cut himself off, eyes darting to the door again. "–possible serial killer."

"This could be dangerous for her." Something nagged at the back of Clyde's mind, but he brushed it off. It was perfectly rational for him to be worried about Coby. It was literally his job. "I don't think it's a good idea."

A look of amusement passed over Grizzly's features for a split second before he sobered and leveled his gaze. "I won't let anything happen to her, Clyde. If anything, I think she'd be safer, working in close quarters with us. LJ, too. They work well together. They'll both be useful."

Clyde clenched his jaw and crossed his arms. "Did she agree to it yet?"

"I didn't get a hold of her."

"I guess we'll see what she says."

***

"So… this is really a thing we're allowed to do. This is really a thing that's happening," Coby said carefully, looking at Clyde and then at LJ.

"Yup," Grizzly said, placing his elbows on his desk and leaning forward, looking at them both. "If you ladies would be so kind."

He saw Coby give LJ a serious look. Pleading. Not that she needed to. LJ had been nodding somewhat receptively the whole time, her anger from last night seemingly gone. LJ gave Coby a long look and Grizzly assumed they were communicating telepathically.

They both turned and looked at him. "We're in," Coby said.

"For now," LJ added. "We can't stay too long or we'll lose our jobs." She brushed her long brown hair behind her ear. "But we'll do what we can."

Grizzly slammed his hands on the desk triumphantly. "All right!" He beamed at them and stood up. "Julia's printing out some papers for you guys to sign and we can get this all squared away… legally," he said and headed toward the door.

The girls stood as well and filed after him, Clyde bringing up the rear. Heads turned to look at them as they all made their way out of Grizzly's office and Pritchard stood and stared. Grizzly ground his teeth and closed his eyes, ignoring the man, but Pritchard decided to make himself heard. "Is there something we need to be aware of, Chief?" Typical. Coby took a step toward Clyde, glaring at Pritchard as if she was going to be the one to punch him next.

Grizzly came to a halt so quickly that LJ almost plowed into him. He faced the room and gave Pritchard a stern look. "Yes, actually, I have an announcement to make. Everybody listen up!" he said loudly to the whole room. Pritchard and the handful of other officers fell silent, looking up at him expectantly. Coby and Clyde exchanged glances.

"This is Coby Anderson and LJ Reed. They're coming on for a little while as consultants to help us with a few investigations." Confused looks were exchanged but everyone kept a respectful silence. Pritchard looked like he had swallowed bad milk and he crossed his arms. "As some of you may know, we have Miss Anderson to thank for finding Maria Wells yesterday. We're hoping she and her partner, Miss Reed, can shed some light on a handful of other cases that have similar… circumstances," he said. Now there was muttering.

Grizzly cleared his throat. "So they'll be around for a little while. Thanks." He nodded at the room and motioned to LJ. They walked down the hall to Julia's desk, the hushed whispers following them out of the room.

He could feel Clyde's eyes on the back of his head as he came to a halt at Julia's desk. "Hey darlin', do you have those forms ready for us?"

Julia beamed at the girls and handed them some papers and pens. "You're going to have to sign these.

Clyde dear, you can sign here. And then this one is for Greg."

Coby scanned over them quickly, signing as she went. LJ's brow was furrowed as she read everything meticulously. It took them a solid ten minutes but they got everything signed and sealed so Julia could take it from there.

LJ's phone rang and she stepped outside to take the call. Grizzly looked down at Coby, who was standing next to Clyde. She was always next to Clyde. Grizzly shook his head. "So... after this hassle, I hope you've got some more ideas, Lady Grimm." He winked at her.

She chuckled wryly. "Well, I do. But there's a lot more digging to be done. It's not like whoever's doing this is just sticking to one kind of fairy tale... I'm glad LJ's on board, she'll be a big help."

"*Kind* of fairy tale?" Grizzly asked, confused.

"Well yeah, I mean each culture has its own collection... so there are literally thousands of possibilities. Luckily, so far, nothing's been too obscure. Snow White, Rumpelstiltskin, The Little Mermaid... those are all pretty basic, most people have heard about them," she said.

Clyde nodded. "That makes sense. If it *is* a serial killer, they're usually looking to be noticed," he said.

LJ came back inside, tucking her phone into the pocket of her dark wash jeans, which she was wearing very well. "Mechanic. Said he finally got the parts in, so we should drop the car off." she said to Coby.

Coby nodded. "Okay." They both glanced at Grizzly, unsure if they were done.

Grizzly nodded. "Great, I'll follow you and give you a ride back," he said, heading back to his office to get his keys.

***

Coby pulled out of the station parking lot and LJ leaned back against the headrest with a sigh.

"I kind of forgot about the car," Coby piped up. "Probably because we've been hanging out with the cops instead of getting pulled over by them."

LJ wished she had a cup of coffee. "Or maybe because you've been a little preoccupied finding dead bodies."

"Yeah..." Coby trailed off.

"I'm sorry, by the way."

"For what?" Coby looked over at her.

LJ shrugged. "For not believing you. I didn't exactly think you were nuts or anything, but I wasn't on board right away."

Coby shook her head. "Don't worry about it. If anything, you helped keep me grounded."

"Which you obviously need, because this stuff is insane." LJ ran her hands over her head. "We came here to write an article on the town, and now we're consulting on missing persons cases? How did this happen?"

Coby turned into the mechanic's driveway and brought the car to a stop by the garage door. "I don't know, but I think we're in the right place. We can help. I know these girls are probably all dead... but we're still helping." She killed the engine and climbed out of the car.

LJ nodded to herself and followed suit.

Jimmy stepped out of his office and greeted them with a single nod, eyes on the banged up headlight. "Good morning, ladies. Sorry this took so long."

"That's okay, really. We've been tied up in town longer than we thought anyway." Coby held out the keys. "When can we pick it up?"

LJ glanced over at Grizzly's police cruiser as he pulled into the lot.

Jimmy raised an eyebrow. "I'll give you a call. Should be by the end of the day."

"Awesome." Coby smiled. "I really appreciate all the trouble you've gone to."

"Not a problem."

***

Grizzly approached the girls and the mechanic slowly, looking the Chevelle over for himself, though not for the first time. "Can't be easy getting parts for a classic on short notice."

"No, not really at all," Jimmy said, shoving his hands in his pockets and leaning back. "But I pulled a few strings for these ladies," he said with a grin, his eyes trailing down the neckline of LJ's shirt. He brought them back up to her face and gave her a nod. "That's not something I do for just anyone."

Grizzly squinted at the young man, sizing him up blatantly. Jimmy was roughly five ten, a hundred and sixty pounds, with reddish blonde hair and a touch of a ginger beard. He was probably twenty-five, but could have passed for eighteen without too much effort. LJ was so far out of his league, Grizzly found it hilarious.

"Well, we do appreciate it," LJ replied, voice tired. If she noticed Jimmy's wandering gaze she didn't seem bothered by it.

Coby stepped past Grizzly, heading for the cruiser. Grizzly was headed after her when Jimmy moved toward LJ, and Grizzly paused.

"It's a beautiful car," Jimmy pressed.

LJ smiled and nodded politely. "Yeah."

"You've got good taste," Jimmy stated, as though his stamp of approval meant something.

"It's Coby's car." LJ shrugged.

"Come on," Jimmy scoffed. "You'd look better behind the wheel, I'm just saying." He cleared his throat. "I've got a '65 Mustang Fastback parked behind the garage. Bet you'd look fantastic driving that beast around. Maybe we could go to dinner and you could take it for a spin?"

Grizzly watched LJ's face closely, ready to step in and throw the guy on his ass if she wanted him to, even as he was smirking widely at the little guy's pathetic attempts at flirting. LJ looked too tired to be uncomfortable, and she shook her head and headed for the cruiser. "Thanks, but I won't be in town long. I'm sure it's a great car, but you'll have to drive it yourself."

Grizzly swallowed a laugh as Jimmy's face fell, eyes following her retreating figure, then looking up at Grizzly sharply. Grizzly gave him a friendly farewell nod and turned to the cruiser himself, but not before he recognized a look of swelling resentment on Jimmy's face.

Chapter Thirty-One

Clyde was wrapping up his report on finding Maria Wells as he waited for Grizzly to get back with the girls. He ignored everyone else in the office. They hadn't tried to talk to him, all of them having gone back to work after he sat down at his desk. But he knew they were all abuzz with gossip about what was going on.

He was scanning over what he had written, glancing at his watch, wondering when they would be back, when Pritchard walked over and came to a halt in front of his desk. Clyde tensed, bracing himself for another fight.

"Burkiss." Pritchard placed both hands on Clyde's desk and leaned down to look at him. Clyde couldn't make himself feel sorry for the man's black eyes and broken nose.

"Pritchard," Clyde muttered in reply. If the man was looking for an apology, he wasn't going to find it.

"Is this your idea? Hire your girlfriends so you can't get in trouble? You two are making a mockery of this entire police department," he hissed, looking livid.

Clyde leaned back slowly and leveled his gaze at the man. "Would you like to bring this accusation up to the chief, Pritchard?"

Pritchard let out a snort. "That man is no police chief. I told you you were going to pay Burkiss, and you are. And seeing as your best friend would never kick you out of the job, I talked to someone who's a little less partial and has a little more authority," he said with a sneer.

Clyde clenched his jaw in anger. He could hear his blood pounding in his eardrums. "Why don't you get back to work, Pritchard? Seeing as you're so against civilians coming in and solving more cases in a day than you have in your entire career."

Pritchard straightened quickly, glancing around to see if the other officers were paying attention. "Just wait, Burkiss. I'm going to make sure you lose your job. And then I'm going to make sure your incompetent best friend loses his. And then, you know what? Then I'm gonna bang the blonde."

"Thanks for the ride, Grizzly." Coby's voice sounded from the hallway and stopped Clyde from adding another homicide to their plate. Pritchard walked swiftly back to his desk, obviously not wanting to get chewed out by Grizzly.

Clyde tried to see past his rage, tried to clear it from his face before the girls and Grizzly entered. He had been on an emotional rollercoaster for the last 24 hours, and he was starting to wonder if he was losing it. He probably needed to go home and sleep. But all it took was Coby Anderson entering the room and suddenly he didn't want to go anywhere.

She looked right at him and he smiled at her, trying to shake Pritchard's words from his mind. She smiled back but her eyes studied him. Apparently he didn't shake them soon enough.

"Clyde," Grizzly greeted him. "The girls are going to work here for a while. We need to get Coby some more files to look at."

Clyde nodded as Coby walked over towards him. Grizzly pulled out a chair at an empty desk and looked at LJ. "You can use this computer." He looked over at Clyde as LJ sat. "You ladies figure out what we should be focusing on. I'll be right back."

Clyde pulled open a drawer in his desk, only flinching a little when Grizzly's giant hand landed on his shoulder. "Let's get the files from my office, shall we?"

Coby sat on the edge of Clyde's desk and smiled at him, distracting him from Grizzly, who all but dragged him down the hallway. "Okay, okay. I'm coming with you. What is your problem?"

Grizzly opened his office door and stepped inside. "I don't have a problem. Do *you* have a problem?"

"No. Why do you think I have a problem?"

"Burkiss, you've got a list of problems so long I'm not even getting started on it." Grizzly unlocked his filing cabinet and pulled the top drawer open. "What I'm wondering about right now is why your face is angry red."

"'Angry red'? What does that mean?" Clyde scowled.

"Your face is usually some shade of red, but it's not dark enough to be your normal, embarrassed red." Grizzly tucked a stack of folders under his arm and let the drawer shut as he faced Clyde. "You're mad."

Clyde seethed but tried hard to calm his breathing. "I think Pritchard is going to make problems for us."

"That's nothing new." Grizzly sighed. "I'll handle it, Burkiss. Don't worry about him."

"He's been throwing threats right and left and it's not just me he's going after, Grizzly, it's you too," Clyde said, guilt flooding his gut. If Grizzly lost his job because of him…

Grizzly let out a short laugh. "That little snot has been gunning to throw me out of office since the day I got sworn in." He shook his head. "I need you to focus on these cases and let me worry about Pritchard. Don't let him get in your head. Coby found those bodies, so your hunch was right. That's counts for something, even if you broke the rules," Grizzly said firmly.

Clyde frowned, fidgeting and wondering if his face was still "Angry Red." He chewed on his cheek for a moment. "I don't want him around Coby. Or LJ," He added.

Grizzly looked at him sharply. "Why?" he asked.

Clyde shrugged. "Things he's said."

"What kind of things?" he asked, his voice taking a scary edge.

"Just… inappropriate things," Clyde said, clenching his fists, not wanting to show how angry Pritchard's words made him.

Grizzly studied him. "Okay. I'll put him over time on highway patrol until they're gone. And if he missteps, I'll suspend him."

Clyde looked down at his shoes and nodded.

Grizzly tucked some files under his arm and walked over to him, punching him on the shoulder, lightly, but it still hurt. "And remember, Coby and LJ are tough. I think they could take him," Grizzly added with a smirk.

Clyde glanced up at him and smiled. "Yeah… they could."

"Come on, we better get back out there before Anderson doodles hearts all over your desk," Grizzly said, and then laughed and pointed at Clyde's face.

Clyde frowned at him. "What?"

"That's the red I'm used to."

***

The acidic stench of decaf coffee exploded as the cold mug teetered and then tipped on its side, sending gritty liquid across the desk and down the side, pooling on the floor. Clyde fumbled to clean up the spill, but only succeeded in knocking over a pile of papers and burying Coby beneath them. She sat up abruptly and looked around the room, hair tangled and eyes puffy.

"Sorry, I bumped – and it just… I didn't mean –" Clyde clamped his mouth shut and proceeded to mop up the mess with the nearest cloth he could find.

"That's my shirt," LJ mumbled from the next desk, stretched out and slouching in the chair, eyes at half-mast as she watched him, unconcerned.

Clyde looked at his coffee-soaked rag and realized it was indeed LJ's button-down, which she had shed sometime in the last three hours, claiming the station was a thousand degrees and she couldn't breathe. "Oh. I'm sorry. I just –"

"No biggie." LJ yawned and closed her eyes.

"Where'd I leave off?" Coby got to her feet and stretched. She looked over Clyde's desk with blurry eyes.

"I stopped listening when you said Hansel and Gretel." LJ didn't move.

Clyde hesitated, then finished sopping up the coffee with LJ's shirt. "I think we were on the Michelle Louis file."

Coby shuffled through one of the paper mountains. "Where is it?"

Clyde got to his feet, knees popping. "Umm…"

"Yay, it ran away and we can all go home and go to sleep," LJ murmured.

Grizzly stepped in from the hall to his office, unbuttoning the collar of his uniform and sighing heavily. "Are we getting anywhere?"

"We haven't been getting anywhere since three this afternoon." LJ peeked at the computer on the desk where she sat. "That was four hours ago."

Grizzly rubbed the back of his neck. "Why don't we call it a night?"

"No!" Coby snapped, smoothing her hair into a ponytail and reaching for the papers again. "We just need to organize these and look at them from a different angle."

"It would help if we had more space to work with." Clyde realized he was still holding LJ's shirt and fiddling with it. He started to hand it to her, then wasn't sure if he should, and stood there awkwardly.

"I might be more help if I had food." LJ lifted a boot and crossed it over the other.

Grizzly nodded. "I could order pizza."

Clyde cringed, not only at the thought of Grizzly's choice of pizza, but at the idea of pizza boxes adding to their already littered desks. "What if we took a few files and brought them to my house? Focusing on a smaller amount of cases instead of everything we've ever investigated in the last five years might give us some perspective… and we all need a change of scenery."

"That might be nice." Coby tilted her head and smiled at him.

LJ shrugged. "Is there food there?"

"I have leftovers. And beer."

"And we can still order pizza." Grizzly nodded and fished his phone out of his pocket.

Clyde sighed and set LJ's shirt gingerly on the corner of his desk.

Coby started to rifle through the papers again, but this time with purpose. She pulled out a particularly thick file and tucked it under her arm. "I'm just gonna grab the cases that made me look twice."

"So you mean all of them," LJ droned.

"Very funny. Just a few." Coby grabbed a reasonably sized stack.

"Hey, Tony. It's Grizz," Grizzly boomed into his cell phone as Clyde grabbed his coat and Coby's bag, handing it to her.

LJ perked up, listening to Grizzly's conversation about the pizza. She stood up and snatched her coffee-soaked shirt from Clyde's desk.

Grizzly led the way out of the police department and towards the vehicles.

Chapter Thirty-Two

Clyde lived in a small house a few streets back from the station, parallel to Main Street. LJ looked around as they pulled to a stop in the driveway. It wasn't big or elaborate in any way, but it looked clean, the grass and trees well cared for. She looked over at Grizzly as he killed the engine of his pickup truck and swung his door open, whistling. He was definitely chipper now that they were away from the office and food was on its way.

LJ knew exactly how he felt.

Clyde had parked in the driveway and he and Coby made their way towards them. Coby held the evidence files tightly to her chest as she trotted next to Clyde, looking around at everything.

LJ hopped out of the truck and stretched, her spine giving a small pop. Grizzly slammed his door and headed toward the steps like he owned the place. Clyde was not far behind him, wiping his palms on his uniform. Coby and LJ filed after the guys and went inside.

The entryway opened into the living room, with a short hall on the left leading into the kitchen. The carpet was vacuumed, the plaid couch and matching pillows immaculate. The coffee table had two stacks of three coasters placed on either side of a very straight pile of magazines. Two recliners joined the couch in facing a dust-free flat screen mounted on the opposite wall, framed by an oak entertainment center.

Grizzly unlaced his boots and tossed them off, moving to the couch and reaching for the magazines. LJ looked at Clyde as the stack was moved to the floor carelessly, but only detected the slightest touch of annoyance.

Coby, still holding the files, didn't notice the free space and continued to look around the room. LJ realized she was inspecting the frames on the walls, and she decided to inspect them for herself. Most of them were of large groups of people at what looked like family holiday gatherings, along with a few official police photos, and some not-so-official ones featuring Grizzly.

"Just make yourselves at home." Clyde ran a nervous hand through his hair. "Can I get you anything? Beer? Tea?"

"Pizza will be here shortly." Grizzly looked at his watch, then patted the coffee table. "Let's take a look at those."

Coby tore her gaze away from the wall and met Grizzly's expectant look with a confused one until she looked down at the folders in her arms.

"Oh!" she said moving forward and setting down the files and opening the one on top. "Tammy Ford. Age 15. Found in a local farmer's garden just east of town…" she began.

LJ moved forward, brow creasing. "'Found with…' oh, *gross.*"

Grizzly slid the paper toward him. "'Nose was removed with surgical instrument… not recovered at scene.'"

Clyde took off his jacket and shoes. "Autopsy found 24 black feathers inside of her intestine," he added from memory, before raising his eyebrows and pointing at the girls. "What can I get you?"

"Beer," Grizzly stated from the couch.

LJ sighed and sat beside him. "Same for me."

Coby settled on the floor to have full access to the coffee table and everything on it. "You said you have tea?"

Grizzly leaned back and ran both hands over his face. "Oh boy, here we go."

Coby threw Grizzly a puzzled look before looking back at Clyde.

"Yes, what kind would you like?" Clyde asked.

Coby paused. "Um… what do you have?"

Grizzly looked at LJ. "Maybe we should just go buy some pajamas, we're gonna be here all night," he said scathingly.

"Well, here, why don't I just show you?" Clyde said, motioning towards the kitchen. Coby hauled herself to her feet and followed after him.

LJ frowned and looked at Grizzly. "What's with the tea?"

"Whoa!" she heard Coby exclaim from the kitchen.

Grizzly shook his head. "Just go see for yourself," he said, waving his hand.

Curiosity got the better of her and she stood and followed the murmuring coming from the kitchen. It didn't take more than one step into the room to understand that Clyde had a problem.

The far wall was covered with racks of jars, each jar meticulously labeled with hand written script. Another step closer and LJ discovered that they were alphabetized. She looked at Coby, who was legitimately impressed, and tried not to snicker.

"Holy crap, I've never seen so much tea in one place. I didn't even know there were this many kinds," Coby said eyes bugging. "Are those rosehips?" she asked, striding closer. "Whoa, this is –" Her eye caught something out of the window, and she did a double take. "Do you *grow your own tea*?"

LJ followed Coby's gaze for a split second before looking back at the wall of loose leaf tea, turning sharply on her heel, and striding back to the living room.

Grizzly looked up at her and grinned. "What's going on out there? Is Coby telling him to get his rear in gear?"

LJ shook her head. "Nope, she's geeking out about it," she said with an eye roll, plopping down on the couch and grabbing the file Coby opened.

"She does that a lot?"

"You have no idea." LJ shook her head and smirked. "So... fairy tales."

"Yeah…" Grizzly said, raising an eyebrow at her.

"Maybe it's… Maybe it's… uh…" LJ floundered, trying to drag up faint memories of fairy tales she may have heard in her youth, but she couldn't grasp anything. Her parents had never taken a lot of time to read her bedtime stories. "Oh gosh… who remembers this stuff?" she asked, setting the file back down and rubbing her temples.

Grizzly shrugged. "I dunno. Coby, I guess. Whoever is doing this."

LJ shook her head. "Weirdos."

Clyde entered the room with two beers, Coby following behind him. Apparently they had gotten over their tea geek fest. LJ glanced sideways at Clyde as he moved to the recliner, a faint smile on his face. He reached across her to hand Grizzly a beer, and Grizzly audibly snickered, earning a scowl from Clyde. "What?"

"She liked your tea, huh?"

"Shut up." Clyde turned scarlet and grabbed the nearest paper to bury his nose in.

Coby sat on the other recliner pulling a folder into her lap. "Okay so... theories?" she asked. There was a chorus of sighs, causing her to look up at them quickly and scowl. "*Hey*. Come on, we gotta try. Tammy Ford, go."

"Um, okay… feathers…" LJ began. "Something with angels or birds."

"That's good… that's good…" Grizzly murmured, taking a swig of beer.

"And the nose was cut off… What has noses? Or… doesn't?" LJ asked.

Clyde shrugged, looking totally bewildered.

"OH! OH! WOODEN PUPPET THING," Grizzly shouted, lunging forward, a bit of beer sloshing onto the carpet.

LJ scowled at him and Clyde snatched the beer out of his hand. "You mean Pinocchio?"

"Yeah, I don't think that's the right direction." Coby tapped her chin thoughtfully.

Grizzly shrugged, scowling at his repossessed beer that Clyde set out of reach.

"What about that one big bird?" LJ leaned back against the couch, tugging a throw pillow out from behind her and hugging it with one arm, lifting the beer to her lips.

Coby looked at her from behind the file, eyebrow raised. "...you mean Big Bird?"

"I don't know, maybe."

Coby slapped the file down in her lap. "LJ, by what stretch of the imagination is Big Bird a fairy tale?"

LJ screwed her eyebrows together as Grizzly started laughing. She closed her eyes. "I don't know, okay? It's all a blur of terrifying images from my childhood."

Coby snorted a laugh.

"Why couldn't it be Pinocchio?" Grizzly pouted.

"Well… It *could*, I just have no idea where the feathers come into play then." Coby frowned.

Clyde glanced up at her. "Is there something with the number of feathers? Two dozen seems like a pretty specific amount."

"You're right." Coby straightened up. "Numerology is always significant."

"So what has twenty-four in it?" LJ lifted her socked foot to place on the coffee table, then retracted it when she caught Clyde glaring at her leg.

Coby stared across the room blindly. LJ thought she might pop a brain cell from thinking too hard.

The doorbell rang, and Grizzly went for the door before Clyde even looked up. "We can figure out what has twenty-four feathers after we eat."

"Eat…" Coby muttered softly under her breath.

LJ stood up and shoved Coby's head lightly, messing her hair. "Hey, it's time for a break. Pizza. Stop thinking, you're making my head hurt."

Coby swatted at her before standing and stretching. "Okay, okay," she mumbled as she watched Clyde walk into the kitchen.

LJ stared at the back of Grizzly's head, willing this little interaction with the pizza man to hurry up. Grizzly paid for the food and carried the boxes toward the kitchen. LJ trailed after, then paused and looked back at Coby, reluctantly grabbing her arm and pulling her away from the files. "Come on. They'll still be there when we're done."

        ***

Clyde looked at the clock, his eyes bloodshot. There were empty plates, bottles and cold cups of tea everywhere but he didn't even care. 11:58. They had been at this all day and now, all night.

So much for focusing on one case.

"Maybe we're barking up the wrong tree, maybe this one isn't by the same guy," Grizzly muttered from the recliner where he was lying with his eyes closed.

LJ was lying spread eagle on the floor and staring at the ceiling fan. "If that's the case I will kill all of you losers with my bare hands." She groaned.

"Put her in cuffs, Clyde, confession of intentional homicide," Grizzly demanded lazily.

"It's by the same guy," Coby insisted from the couch next to Clyde. Her legs were curled underneath her and her shoulder was starting to rest heavily against his. She looked like she was going to fall asleep under the pile of files. Clyde didn't move an inch and he couldn't look at her. He was just glad LJ and Grizzly seemed to have lost all interest in tormenting him.

LJ let out a loud groan. "Tweety."

"No," Coby mumbled closing her eyes and flopping her head back against the couch.

"Foghorn Leghorn."

"No."

"The Road Runner."

"These are all from Looney Tunes, you doofus."

LJ chucked a napkin at her but it just ended up hitting Clyde's knee. "Fine. Mary, Mary quite Canary –"

"It's quite *Contrary*, and that's not a fairy tale either. It's more of a nursery –" Coby paused and Clyde felt her tense next to him. "– rhyme."

Grizzly chuckled from the recliner. "Clyde, say something like Foghorn Leghorn, do it."

Clyde frowned. "No."

Coby straightened and looked at Clyde. "Do you have a laptop?"

"Uh, yeah."

"I need to use it."

"Okay…" Clyde reluctantly moved away from her and to his feet. He went around the coffee table and stepped over LJ.

"Did you think of something?" LJ piped up.

Coby stood and started shuffling through papers. "Maybe. I need to google something."

Grizzly moaned and his eyes opened into puffy slits. "Does that mean we can't go to bed?"

Clyde walked back with his laptop and handed it to Coby. She grabbed it and looked up at him. "Thanks," she said plopping back down next to him as he lowered himself to the couch. She had that wild, focused look in her eyes again and her fingers were drumming on the corner of his laptop as she waited for it to start.

She chewed on her cheek and started typing, her eyes running over the screen like they were racing with her hands. "AHHHHHHHH!" she shouted, standing up abruptly, and Clyde lunged forward to catch his laptop before it hit the floor.

Grizzly and LJ jolted upright, eyes wide.

Coby snatched the file back up and let out another shriek. "I got it!" she exclaimed, throwing her arms around Clyde and hugging him tightly before pulling away and hitting him with the file. "OH MY GOSH I HAVE IT."

"Have *what*?" LJ demanded, standing with a groan.

"'Sing a Song of Sixpence'," Coby shouted and Clyde stared at her, dazed.

"Sing a song of *what?*" Grizzly squinted at her, putting the footrest of the recliner down.

Coby snatched the laptop back from Clyde and held it on one palm, scrolling with the other hand. "'Sing a song of sixpence, pocket full of rye... four and twenty blackbirds, baked in a pie'!"

"There was no pie at that crime scene." LJ lay back on the floor.

Coby snorted at her over the laptop. "Twenty-four black feathers." She moved her finger over the screen as she scanned the words. "'Hanging out the clothes...down came a blackbird, and pecked off her nose'!" She set the laptop on the coffee table and lifted both arms in victory. She rounded the coffee table backwards and landed a heel in LJ's side, earning a yelp and nearly toppling herself over.

"Watch it!" LJ sat up and crawled backward, settling closer to Grizzly's chair.

"Sorry," Coby replied, sounding anything but sorry. She bounded back to the couch and landed beside Clyde, reaching for the files spilling off the table. "This is a nursery rhyme, not a fairy tale. That's why I was so stuck."

"What the hell is the difference between a nursery rhyme and a fairy tale?" LJ whined, sighing and flopping back against the recliner, head resting beside Grizzly's knee. She didn't seem to notice, or if she did, didn't care.

Grizzly noticed. Clyde was sure of that.

Coby found the folder she was searching for and made room for it by shoving everything else off the edge of the coffee table. "'Midsection slit open, twenty-four black feathers removed from postmortem wound. Nose cartilage removed prior to death.' *See*?"

Clyde picked up the laptop and settled it on his knees. He skimmed the rhyme, remembering the file's crime scene photos without double-checking, though Coby was pulling them out of the folder and laying them out on the table in front of him anyway. Grizzly leaned over and turned the laptop screen toward himself so he could read it as well. The movement caused him to disturb LJ, who reluctantly got to her feet and leaned over Grizzly to read the nursery rhyme.

"This changes everything." Coby looked over the photos she'd lined up on the table. "If he's going with folklore in general, then we've been going over all of these half-blind."

Clyde passed the laptop to Grizzly and looked over the photos. "You're probably right."

"It could be that some of those unsolved cases are just unexplained deaths, like Martha Vanderkin," Coby said. "She probably did have a stroke and die in her kitchen, even though that was never confirmed because her family opted out of the autopsy."

LJ snickered. "What, you don't think she was the prequel to Little Red Riding Hood?"

Grizzly chuckled.

Coby rolled her eyes. "This helps."

"How does it help, Coby?" LJ sat on the arm of the recliner and looked at Coby. "Deciding that this guy diverts from Grimms and dips his toes in the Mother Goose waters doesn't bring us any closer to figuring out who he is or what he's going to do next."

Clyde bristled at LJ's accusatory tone, but Coby just shrugged. "That's true. But every step counts. The closer we get to understanding him, the closer we get to finding him."

Grizzly was quiet, observing the conversation with a deep scowl as he thought it through. "He's gotta want this. This much effort in recreating these scenes or... stories or whatever. He's been at it for a long time, with no recognition. These cases are years old. It's probably driving him nuts."

The hair raised on the back of Clyde's neck. "You think he's waiting for publicity."

Coby nodded. "It makes sense. He's recreating stories. Retelling them how he thinks they should be told. But no one's ever noticed that."

"And they won't," Grizzly stated adamantly.

"Well..." Coby hesitated. "Maybe they should."

LJ gave her a look. "You're not actually siding with the serial killer, are you?"

"No, of course not. But..." she shrugged and looked at Clyde. "If he realized that someone finally saw his... 'art' for what he thinks it is, maybe he'd show off and mess up."

Clyde glanced at Grizzly, who glowered in his chair. Clyde turned back to Coby. "Theoretically, that might work. But realistically, it's not something we can risk."

Coby nodded. "I know. But it's something to consider, or at least be aware of."

Grizzly shook his head. "He's not getting that satisfaction. Ever."

Clyde raised an eyebrow at him. "That might be exactly what's keeping him going, though."

Grizzly clenched his jaw and closed the laptop.

Coby nodded again. "As long as he's not getting the attention he thinks he deserves, he's going to keep telling his stories." She reached for the laptop and Grizzly handed it to her. "Which is why we're nowhere near done with this tonight."

LJ groaned and slumped against Grizzly's shoulder.

Chapter Thirty-Three

He sat on a park bench and surveyed the children playing on the equipment over the top of his newspaper. It was a bit too cold to be sitting outside reading. But the fresh air would do him good. He spent far too much time bent over his typewriter lately. He curled his fingers around his cup of tea and watched. He had to look ahead to other story ideas. His current story would only take him so long after all, as fun as it may be. And it was. Very fun.

It felt good, writing something new. It was a risk, and he knew it. But things had been getting so boring lately, so meaningless and repetitive. So unfulfilling. And this was exciting. The girls were bright, very smart. They could appreciate his work, and he respected that. They were worthy of being in his story, but it was a game now. He had to write quickly, before they figured it out. He smiled to himself and took a sip of his tea. He wasn't worried. Characters were never a match for their author. They never knew they were in a story. He would bend them to his will.

After all, he was the author.

Two of the children clambered up the steps to the slide, cheeks rosy from the cooling temperatures. They giggled and pushed each other, a little girl and boy, he guessed to be five and three. Their mother scolded them and placed her hands on her hips, looking weary as she watched them with pursed lips.

He wondered if she ever thought about leaving them in the woods.

The woman caught him looking at her and gave him a suspicious frown. He smiled back and turned a page of his paper. She turned back to her children. He wondered how long children actually took to cook through.

***

Coby plopped down at their table in the library and opened her laptop before she set it down. LJ shuffled up behind her and sat in the chair on the other side. Coby looked up at her. LJ's eyes were puffy and bloodshot, a line permanently etched between her brows. They had left the motel at quarter to nine, after getting dropped off there sometime after two a.m. To top that off, their motel was not equipped with complimentary coffee. LJ was suffering without her caffeine fix.

"Did Jimmy call about the car yet?" LJ grumbled.

"No, not yet," Coby replied.

"Well did you check your phone? He said it would be done last night."

Coby nodded, but pulled her cell out of her pocket to check it anyway. "He must have gotten caught up."

LJ scanned the second floor of the library. "This place needs a cappuccino machine. Or at least a pot of coffee."

Coby watched her computer power up, then got to her feet and headed for the shelves, still within sight of LJ's grumpy figure. "You can go get something. I'll just be looking around here."

LJ slumped back in the chair and sighed. "No. I'll just suffer."

Coby snickered and faced the shelf that was eye level, running her finger along the spines of the books on fairy tales that she had already perused twenty times. Her hand landed on a favorite and slid it from its home, the pages falling open to a broken spot in the binding. She looked at the page knowingly, scanning the picture that had become familiar over the last several library trips.

"Do we have the Brittany Ferguson file or is that one still with Clyde?"

LJ shrugged one shoulder and reached for the bag containing the paperwork without moving the rest of her body. "Why would I remember that?" She sat up to dig through the bag.

"I can't let it go." Coby brought the book to the table and laid it out. "The first time I saw her picture I thought of Rapunzel, and it just keeps bothering me."

LJ pulled several folders from the bag and looked them over one by one. "You're in luck." She handed Coby the Brittany Ferguson file. "Is there a body with that one?"

"No. She's been missing for seven years." Coby opened the file and slid her laptop out of the way. "She was a high school senior who disappeared two weeks before graduation." She pulled Brittany's picture from between the pages and inspected it. "She's gotta be Rapunzel."

LJ took the photo from her, looking at the smiling teenager with blonde locks all the way down to her cheerleading skirt. "She looks the part."

Coby turned back to the old book. "I just have to figure out what he did with her. Where we can find her."

"In a tower?" LJ suggested, slowly getting out of her chair and heading for the shelves that held books on local history and locations. She scanned them and pulled out a topographical map of Waupun they had used before. "That's the story, right?"

Coby nodded, still looking through her book. "Pretty much. There are thorn bushes and a forest, too, but that probably doesn't help at all. Are there any towers in Waupun?"

"Prison towers." LJ brought the map to their table and left it open while she reached for her laptop. "But I'm betting she's not in one of those."

Coby sighed. "Probably not."

"Can I just search 'abandoned towers in the middle of nowhere near Waupun, Wisconsin'? Do you think that will give me answers? I'm trying it," LJ mumbled while she typed. "Oh look, haunted house attractions." She gave Coby a bored look.

"You give up too easily." Coby slid the map closer to herself and scanned the outskirts slowly. "It's farm country. He'd have to use whatever was available to him. Towers are few and far between, so he'd have to settle. What about a barn silo?"

"Those are a little too common, Coby." LJ squinted. "If that's what you're going with, you're gonna have to narrow it down."

"I don't suppose just one silo is sitting in the middle of a forest, surrounded by thorns," Coby joked, looking away from the map as LJ's phone buzzed on the tabletop. "Is that Jimmy? If the car is done, tell him I love him."

LJ closed her laptop, looking awake for the first time that morning as she answered her phone. "Hello?"

Coby shoved the map aside and reached for LJ's laptop to run a few searches for herself.

"Perfect. We'll be over shortly." LJ hung up the phone. "He said the car is ready and we can pick it up now."

Coby did a chair dance and then looked for her own phone. "Should I call the guys?"

"Why?" LJ looked at her, confused. "Pretty sure they don't need to be bothered with this information, even though it is spectacular news."

"I meant for a ride."

"Oh." LJ grimaced. "I guess that might be nicer than lugging all this stuff across town."

Coby was already scrolling through her recent calls as LJ piled their books. She settled on Clyde's number and let it dial. "*Much* nicer."

Chapter Thirty-Four

Grizzly sat down at his desk with a heavy sigh. It had been a long night. Not unpleasant, but long. He sipped his coffee and closed his eyes, relaxing. He didn't know how he felt about all this. It was going to be a long road. A long, horrifying road. But they were also so much closer to finding answers. And that felt right. He frowned and stared at his phone, debating whether or not he should inform someone with more authority about this serial killer situation. But then what proof could he bring them? He was fairly convinced Coby was right and that they were onto something. They had found the body of a missing person, but it wasn't enough.

Oh well. They had waited this long for answers, a little longer wasn't going to kill anyone.

Actually, it could. Grizzly frowned, disgusted at his own thoughts. Yet he had faith that Coby was onto something. A surprising amount of faith, actually. Maybe he should tell the mayor what was going on. He would hate for her to find out through the gossip chain that he had hired out-of-state consultants.

He would also hate for the gossip chain to inform her of Clyde punching Pritchard. Or the little detail of Clyde sharing confidential information with Coby.

He flipped open one of the folders from yesterday, glanced through it, and closed it again. It was useless trying to figure this stuff out without the girls. He didn't remember a damn thing about most fairy tales.

His mug was empty. With a groan Grizzly stood up and walked out of his office towards the break room. Maybe he should start with something he was good at. He knew a lot of people in this town. Question was, which one of them might think it was fun to go around killing people. He pondered for a moment before walking out to Julia's desk. "Hey Jules… any chance you could pull up some records for me? I need anyone with a juvie record in the town for the last twenty-five years," he said. Start small. Maybe the killer had slipped up, or showed signs of a disturbed mind at a young age.

Julia blinked at him. "Absolutely, Gregory. Rough night?" she asked, assessing his puffy eyes and messy hair.

"Nah, it was good. Just working late at Clyde's," he replied.

"Anyone else with you?"

"Jules, we're grownups, we don't need a chaperone to be alone together."

She flung a pen at him. "Did you work the cases with those lovely young ladies last night?"

Grizzly winced at her emphasis on the word "young." "Come on Jules… how old do you think we are? Don't make us sound like perverts." He frowned and folded his arms. They weren't that young.

"Well, were you?" she pressed, eyebrows raised.

Grizzly sighed and nodded. "We might have had a breakthrough. It's a little early to tell. I'm just trying to figure out the next step."

"Well, you had a call from the mayor this morning. Why don't you start with that?" Julia said, handing him a note with the mayor's name and number scribbled down on it.

Grizzly tensed slightly. "Did she say what for?" he asked.

Julia shook her head. "No, just that she wanted to speak to you and I told her you weren't in yet. I didn't ask,

I just told her you'd call her back when you got here."
She shrugged.

Grizzly nodded. "Okay, okay. Thanks Jules. I'll… do that," he mumbled staring off into space.

"Gregory, is something wrong?" Julia asked, peering up at him.

"Wha– uh– no." He shook his head vehemently. "Nope, not that I know of!" he added cheerfully. "I better get on this and see what she needs. Thanks Jules!" he called over his shoulder with a wave, as he turned back to his office.

Grizzly closed the door quickly behind him and fought the urge to close the blinds. He didn't have anything to hide. He was just calling the mayor back. It wasn't unusual for the mayor to talk to him about things. Maybe she had a question about the Memorial Day Parade coming up. It probably didn't even have anything to do with Clyde. No way she could respond this quickly if Pritchard had complained, could she? She had important things to do, mayoral things… things that didn't involve checking up on every little weasel-like complaint.

Grizzly planted his hands on his waist, chewing on his lip stubbornly for a few moments before swearing under his breath and striding over to the phone. He muttered to himself as he dialed the number.

It rang three times before the office assistant answered. "Hello, Mayor Newton's office, this is Angela speaking."

"Hey Ang, this is Grizzly, I'm just calling the mayor back."

"Sure thing, Chief Adams, one moment please."

Grizzly tapped his fingers on his desk and sat down on his chair with a huff.

"Hello, this is Sandra." The mayor's voice sounded cheerful through the phone.

Grizzly swallowed, hoping that was a good sign. "Hi Sandra, it's Grizzly."

"Well hi, Chief, how are you doing?" she asked. Sandra had an easy way about her while still seeming professional. She was good like that.

"Oh, I've been better," he said with a short, humorless chuckle.

"I know, I've been meaning to give you a call. First April, and now you find Maria after all these years."

"Yeah well, I didn't actually find Maria, I had a little help on that. On April too, actually," Grizzly started.

"Ah yes, about that," Sandra replied.

Grizzly felt a sickening clench in his stomach at her tone, sensing a shift in the conversation. She was getting to the reason for the call.

"I heard you hired yourself a couple of consultants?"

Grizzly swallowed. "Yes ma'am, two journalists from Michigan. They stumbled upon April and have been helping us out ever since. Seemed only right to go through the official channels."

"Mm-hmm," she said. "I'm going to be up front with you Grizzly, because… well, I like you. You know I'm not one for gossip and beating around the bush. We've always been straight with each other."

"And I appreciate that, Sandra."

"I've just had an official complaint filed against Officer Burkiss. And against you, though on a much smaller level."

"Pritchard," Grizzly hissed.

"Now Grizzly, I'm not at liberty to say who, but is it true that Clyde assaulted a fellow officer?"

Grizzly sighed. "Sandra… if you were there you wouldn't –"

"Grizzly, I need a straight answer."

Grizzly frowned, rolled his eyes and let out a huff. "Well okay, yes, he punched him, but Pritchard was totally asking for it."

"I also heard that Officer Burkiss released confidential information to a civilian he's been, um… well… sleeping with," she said awkwardly.

The rage Grizzly felt building in his chest erupted into slightly deranged laughter. "He's not sleeping with *anyone*," he snorted into the phone.

"And you know that for a fact?"

"Well yeah, I mean, I think so, I would know –" Grizzly sputtered.

"Grizzly, that's really beside the point. Has he shared confidential information with a civilian?" Sandra asked, though not unkindly.

"Well… yes, but he had a hunch and went with it. Coby ended up finding a body, I wouldn't have hired her otherwise."

There was a sigh and Grizzly lapsed into silence.

"What are you going to do about this, Chief?"

"Well I'm not going to fire him." Grizzly bristled despite himself. "He's the best officer we have. He's given everything he's got for this job and this city."

"I know, Grizzly, I know. Officer Burkiss has certainly proven his worth and he's very appreciated by the community. But you know what this looks like. You know I can't allow this to slide," she said calmly.

"I'll… I'll…" Grizzly sighed, rubbing his hand over his eyes. "I'll put him on probation."

"That would be perfect," she said. "I'm sure he'll get through it with flying colors." She sounded upbeat again, relieved that there was a solution.

"I hate this," Grizzly growled under his breath.

"I know. I hope you know it gives me no pleasure. Goodbye, Chief, and good luck," Sandra said and Grizzly knew she was being genuine but it didn't make him feel better.

"Goodbye, Sandra," he said and hung up the phone with more force than he intended. No one knew Clyde like he did. No one knew how perfect his record was, how by-the-book he was. Grizzly sighed. The one time Clyde took a gamble and broke the rules, he'd screwed himself over.

Chapter Thirty-Five

Clyde was impressed with how little he was sweating despite Coby sitting only six inches to his right. He caught a glimpse of LJ in the rearview, gazing out her window. Risking the stability of his adrenal glands, he glanced over at Coby, who caught him and gave him a smile. He flushed and wished he hadn't looked over because he was forgetting how to drive.

"Thanks, by the way. We probably could have just walked to the mechanic, but this is a whole lot easier." Coby reached over and squeezed his arm.

Clyde swallowed and nodded in response. He focused on driving so he wouldn't pass the repair shop and embarrass himself further.

They cruised into the parking lot and Clyde pulled to a stop. The girls climbed out of the car, and Clyde hesitated, unsure if he was supposed to leave, wait, or get out and stand around awkwardly. He sighed, knowing he would settle for the latter.

The Chevelle was parked in front of the garage door. LJ walked over and crouched at the fender to inspect the headlight, and Coby stuck her head inside the office, then disappeared and let the door close behind her. Clyde stood on the walkway with his hands in his pockets. He rocked on his boots and stared after Coby for a second, then ambled over to the car. "How's it look?"

"As good as a sixty-year-old car can look." LJ straightened and gave the hood a pat. "Definitely an improvement from when we crashed into your cruiser." She looked at him. "How is that, by the way?"

Clyde shrugged. "Still in the shop. Probably will be until the snow flies." He nodded toward his current cruiser. "But we're covered, so it's fine."

The office door opened again and Coby stepped out, a small-framed man who appeared to be the mechanic close behind her. The man glanced toward the car, and his posture changed when he spotted LJ. Clyde felt uncomfortable.

"She looks nice, right?" the mechanic asked LJ.

LJ rolled her eyes for Clyde's benefit before turning to the mechanic and putting on a bland tone. "Yeah. Thanks."

The man looked only slightly defeated as he sent a nod toward the Chevelle. "Keys are above the visor."

LJ gave a solitary nod of understanding, and the man gave her a lookover that made Clyde really glad it wasn't Coby he wasn't scouting out. Clyde didn't want to be throwing punches again. He scowled at that thought. He'd never been a confrontational or violent person, but apparently Coby brought out a different side of him.

"Clyde?"

He jumped and looked down at Coby, who was apparently speaking to him. "What?"

"We'll meet up with you later?" She smirked at his obliviousness.

"Oh. Right. Sure. Call me." He headed back toward the cruiser and nearly slammed his face onto the hood. "Call me" didn't exactly give off an aura of maturity, professional or otherwise. "Call me" was more emotionally unstable teenage girl. He sighed and reached for the door handle, vowing to redeem himself next time. Again.

***

LJ slid into the Chevelle, relishing the familiar creak of the old door and inhaling the comforting scent that was more homey than her actual home. Coby plopped into the driver's seat and adjusted it accordingly before reaching for the visor.

"He's so cute," Coby said, voice quiet.

"Who, Jimmy?" LJ smirked.

"*No*," Coby scoffed. "Not *Jimmy*." She pulled the visor down and the keys landed in her lap. "Cl- whoa, ew." Coby brushed her legs off and flung the keys to the floor mat. "What *is* this? Hair? Gross!"

"What's your problem?" LJ looked her over in confusion.

"There's… I don't know… hair… everywhere." Coby picked up a few strands of white and held them up for LJ to see. "Where did this come from? This isn't my hair."

"Well it's definitely not mine. I'm not gray yet." LJ took the strands and inspected them in the light.

Coby shuddered. "Gross." She fished for the keys carefully and looked relieved when they turned up hair-free.

"That's more than gross, Coby." LJ pulled the hairs taut and scowled at them. "That's bizarre."

"It's probably Jimmy or somebody who worked on the car." Coby turned the engine over and backed out of the space. "Did you see Clyde blush when he –"

"Jimmy doesn't have white hair. Who has white hair this long?" LJ rubbed the strands between her thumb and forefinger. "This is really course."

"And you're really gross. Throw it out!" Coby shuddered again.

LJ shook her head and let the hairs drop, despite the nagging confusion and longing to understand. She clasped her hands in her lap and tried to let it go.

"So," Coby began. "What did you and Grizzly do last week anyway?" Coby pulled onto the road. Clyde's cruiser had already disappeared down Main Street.

LJ stiffened. "Just… talked about the cases and… stuff. That's all."

"That is not *all,* Laverne Jeannette." Coby poked her friend in the shoulder. "You've been unusually chipper."

"I am not *chipper.*" LJ wrinkled her nose.

"You were singing in the shower this morning."

"Humming. I was humming."

"You don't hum."

"I hum!"

Coby shot her a pointed look. "You do *not* hum. What did you guys do?"

LJ slumped down in the seat. "I went to his house," she mumbled.

"You did *what?*" Coby shrieked excitedly.

LJ flinched. "He invited me out to his house for a while. It was after we found the body and we both just needed something else to think about."

Coby turned and stared at her openly despite cruising through traffic in the middle of town. "And what exactly did you *do* to take your mind off of your troubles?"

"Yardwork."

"What?"

LJ smirked in satisfaction. "He was a real charmer. Talked me into raking and weeding his lawn."

"Hmm." Coby turned back to driving. "But you came back with ice cream."

"Yeah…"

"Who *bought* the ice cream?"

LJ clenched her teeth.

"Ah-ha." Coby waggled her eyebrows and snickered. "Anything else?"

Shrugging, LJ straightened up as they approached the road for the motel. "He has a motorcycle."

"You were out on a motorcycle with Grizzly?" Coby looked surprised for a beat, then shook her head with a fond smile. "That's so fitting."

LJ threw the door open before Coby finished parking. "Stop smiling."

"And really… romantic."

"Shut up."

Coby climbed out of the car. "I'm just saying."

"What?" LJ paused in the lot and looked at her. "You're just saying *what*?"

Coby smiled, unfazed by LJ's attitude. "You like him."

The scoff left LJ's throat before she even opened her mouth to snap back at Coby. "Oh. Right. I like him."

"You do." Coby was adamant as she breezed by LJ, room key in hand.

"Come on. Why would I like him? I mean he's… he's so…"

Coby leaned back from the doorknob to their room and batted her eyelashes. "Likeable?"

LJ growled. "You are a freaking –" She huffed and pushed into the room. "You and Clyde sure have been… cozy recently."

"We have," Coby affirmed, blowing LJ's comeback up in her face.

"'We *have*'?" LJ stared at her. "You mean you *do* like him?"

"Of course I do." Coby laughed at LJ's dumbfounded face. "He's a good guy. And he's cute and sweet and just… really adorable."

LJ just stood, befuddled, in the motel room. "So, what? You're going to date him now?"

Coby sat on the nearest bed and grabbed a pillow, hugged it to herself, and shrugged. "Maybe. I don't know. Clyde and I haven't had an actual date like you and Grizz."

"That was *not* a *date*." LJ sighed and flopped onto her stomach on the other bed. "You and Clyde have spent way more time together than Grizz and I have."

"Yeah, working. Not doing leisurely outdoor activities and going for motorcycle rides and out for ice cream."

LJ wanted to snap back with a smart remark, but nothing came to mind. She was too distracted by the idea that Coby could possibly be right.

"Okay. Back to the grindstone." Just like that, Coby dropped the subject. She went to her laptop bag and pulled the computer and the case files out.

LJ propped herself on an elbow and watched Coby spread everything out on the bedspread. "It wasn't really a date, was it?"

Coby let the laptop boot up and raised an eyebrow pointedly. "I think he probably thought of it as a date."

"But it's not a date unless you're asked specifically, right?"

"I don't think that's necessarily true."

"So you and Clyde have been 'dating' all week?"

"Psshh, no." Coby pushed her hair over her shoulder. "We've been working all week. But we've definitely gotten to know a lot about each other."

LJ chewed on her lip.

"But the answer to your actual question is yes."

LJ's brow wrinkled and she looked at Coby.

"Yes, Grizzly likes you." Coby smirked and turned back to her work.

LJ went back to chewing her lip. "I'm gonna order a pizza."

Chapter Thirty-Six

Pritchard's eyes followed Grizzly as the man paced around his office, pulling files out of the cabinets, bringing them to his desk and flipping through them, and then repeating. He had been doing that since Pritchard got back from his morning patrol.

Clyde was sitting at his desk, looking more agitated than usual… but with all the murder cases and Coby Anderson around, that was becoming the norm.

It infuriated Pritchard that Burkiss was working the cases with the chief and two gorgeous ladies, while he was stuck in a cruiser with a broken nose, handing out speeding tickets.

Pritchard tossed his pen down on the desk with force. He stood abruptly and stormed up to Grizzly's office. He stopped, composed himself and cleared his throat before knocking sharply on the door.

"Come in," Grizzly called out and Pritchard opened the door.

"Chief." Pritchard nodded.

The big man looked up at him and sighed, deflating back against his chair. "Pritchard. What can I do for you?"

"Just checking in to see if you've talked to the mayor? Because if you haven't, I certainly can. I just want to make sure –"

"Oh, like you haven't already, Pritchard," Grizzly snapped at him. "I don't want to hear about this anymore. It's been dealt with. And if I hear you've been hassling Officer Burkiss while he's on his probation, you'll be right there with him. Have I made myself clear?"

Pritchard blinked, feeling a bit stunned. "Yes, Chief."

"Shouldn't you be starting another patrol?" Grizzly demanded.

"I –"

"Shut the door behind you," Grizzly shot at him before turning back to the file on his desk.

Pritchard turned on his heel and walked out of the office, closing the door behind him before looking over at Clyde.

He had expected to feel satisfied, justified. But here Burkiss was, still working the missing persons cases. Nothing had changed other than a slap on the wrist. He knew Grizzly would never take this seriously. Sure Burkiss was on probation, but under his best friend's authority that meant nothing.

He had to do something else. He had to create a greater punishment. Anything to make them pay.

***

Clyde tapped his pen on his desktop aggressively, knee bouncing, head aching. Grizzly's words from that afternoon were still on repeat in his brain, and no matter how hard Clyde tried to focus on work, or Coby, or anything at all, he couldn't shut them up.

Probation. Clyde had never been in trouble a day in his life. Except for once, in third grade, when he'd accidentally bumped into the teacher's desk and spilled her coffee all over her papers during the Pledge of Allegiance. Mrs. Mulder made him skip recess and sit during the Pledge for a whole week for being careless and "rambunctious." Twenty-five years later, he still thought about that day.

However, this was worse. Hearing it from his best friend, who was also his superior, made it even harder. Grizzly's obvious remorse made Clyde want to jump off a building.

He threw the pen at his computer screen and leaned back, running his hands through his hopeless hair. He went back and forth between what he'd done wrong and why he'd done it and why it wasn't wrong but why it actually wasn't right. It was exhausting. He needed to go home, make tea, read a book, and get out of his own head.

His phone buzzed on the desk and Coby's name lit up in bold. Relief hit him, not enough to ease the tension in his neck, but just enough to make him feel a touch better as he reached for the phone. "Hello?"

"Clyde, hi! …Are you okay?"

He cleared his throat. "Yeah, fine. What's going on?"

"Um, well, I think I have another location." She let out a deep sigh into the phone. "I've been going over this stuff all day, and I have a lot of maps of the surrounding area of Waupun, and this old farm south of here just… makes sense."

Clyde leaned forward. "You found something?"

"Nothing definite. I just have a feeling."

"Which case?"

"Brittany Ferguson." Papers rustled. "She was a senior when she disappeared, and she had really long, really blonde hair. I think she's our killer's Rapunzel."

Clyde picked up his discarded pen and brought the end of it to his lip. "Okay… what's our move?"

"Like I said, there's this abandoned farm about eight miles southeast of Waupun. I think we need to go there."

"What are you thinking? Cadaver dogs? The whole Crime Scene Unit?"

"Whatever we had at the Maria Wells scene. My first thought is that she might be up in the rafters, or whatever, of the silo… but that seems a little ridiculous. So dogs are probably a smarter idea."

Clyde's mouth twitched at the lilt in her voice. "Okay. First thing tomorrow, we'll head out. Do you have an address?"

Coby recited it and Clyde jotted it down. He bit back an overly-affectionate farewell and hung up, then got to his feet and shook off his pity party. It was time to do his job and inform his boss of a new lead.

Chapter Thirty-Seven

He ran a hand over his chin as he sat in the dark, staring at his typewriter. He thought he should turn on a light, but didn't move. He wondered if they had found his gift. Had they noticed it? How long would he have to wait until moving to the next part of his story? He let out a low growl of annoyance. Patience wasn't a virtue he possessed.

He tapped his fingers absentmindedly on the keys of his typewriter, soft enough that it left no mark on the page. He recalled the fairy tale. It was his mother's favorite. He had heard it often, back when his mother would read to him.

Don't read those to the boy, his father would say. *Fill his head with fairies, next thing you know he'll want to be one.*

But he loved the stories, just as he loved his mother. He would have to make sure to tell this one just right. He couldn't mess up her favorite story, after all. She would be so happy that he still loved all the stories. That growing up alone with his father hadn't changed him, that he hadn't forgotten her.

Placing the beard in the car visor was an obvious choice, but he wasn't sure it would be obvious enough to the girls. Perhaps he gave them too much credit. So busy and focused… unable to see what was right in front of their faces.

To keep his game fun, to keep the story moving, he'd have to be more obvious with his next move. Surprise them with something startling.

He grinned slowly at his idea, and started to type with purpose.

His mother would be so proud.

***

"This can't be right," Coby said for what must have been the millionth time, but she couldn't help it. Nothing was making sense.

She was supposed to be here.

"Well Cobes, I don't know what to tell you," Grizzly spoke from behind her. She could hear it in his voice. He was trying to sound upbeat.

Coby closed her eyes and ground the palms of her hands against her forehead, trying to think, trying to come up with another solution. She was letting them down.

This couldn't be happening. She was so sure, *so sure*. She bit back the urge to suggest they look over everything again. They already had, three times.

"Coby..." LJ said, stepping forward.

Coby swallowed and turned around and looked at them all. So many officers, dogs, a whole CSU unit, Clyde, Grizzly, LJ...

She felt sick to her stomach. "Okay. Okay. I was wrong about this spot, then. That's all." She took a deep breath, to settle the nausea and clear her head. She turned back to the broken bricks and surveyed the gaping hole in the side of the old barn silo. The CSU team had carefully inspected every crack in the structure, and even had the fire department rig up a pulley system to test the rafters in the roof. Coby was still desperately hoping they would find some trace of DNA from Brittany on those rafters, but she wasn't holding her breath. She turned back to the group. "There was another place that stuck out to me."

Grizzly nodded encouragingly. Coby didn't look at LJ, afraid there might be a touch of doubt in her face, and she couldn't handle that right now. She risked a glance at Clyde, who was still looking around the outside of the silo as though he might find something worthwhile.

"Yeah… yeah… let me just…" She started towards the cruiser she had driven in with Clyde. She ripped out a map on which she had located all the silos in the surrounding area. She spread it out on the hood of the cruiser and pointed to all the red circles. "These are all the possible locations."

Grizzly loomed up behind her and looked down at the map with a frown. "That's a lot of circles there, darlin'."

"I know," Coby said, taking a deep breath and trying to shove the headache away before it took over her whole brain. "I know, but these are all the old farms with silos, or at least the ones that had them around the time of her disappearance," she said earnestly.

LJ and Clyde had joined them by now, looking around her shoulders at the map.

Grizzly sighed and nodded. "All right. We're gonna have to split up or this will take us weeks." He pointed at Clyde. "You take LJ and hit Dodge, Coby and I will take Fond du Lac. We'll send everyone else home until we find something."

Clyde nodded and turned around to pass the news onto the expectant officers.

Coby glanced over at LJ who was staring at her intently, obviously trying to figure out how sure Coby was on this new direction. Coby looked back at Grizzly quickly, trying not to puke. Grizzly gave her pat on the shoulder. "Let's go, Sherlock."

***

LJ felt the familiar ache of hunger starting in the back of her head as she leaned against the cruiser window, watching the cornfields – endless, empty, cornfields – roll by. She could hear Clyde grinding his teeth from the driver's seat, and she turned to look over at him. "How close are we?"

His eyes flitted down to the GPS on the dash. "Two miles."

LJ smoothed her hair back and sighed. "Good."

Clyde mirrored her, running a hand through his already disheveled hair and making it worse. He opened his mouth as though to say something, then closed it again and shook his head.

LJ felt the overwhelming urge to agree with him despite his lack of saying anything.

He turned down a two-track dirt driveway and creeped the cruiser toward a dilapidated white barn. He stopped near the open, empty doorway and LJ climbed out of the car, observing the gaping slats between the boards. She lifted her sunglasses to the top of her head and raised an eyebrow at Clyde. "There's no silo."

He lifted his hands in exasperation and slammed his door, then headed for the lone barn.

LJ trailed after him hesitantly, thinking the barn might collapse on top of them as they walked through the door. She watched Clyde lean back to look up at the rafters. He moved toward the west wall and looked closely at the weeds growing up through the floor. "What are we looking for, exactly?" LJ called.

Clyde stopped and looked at her, defeat evident in his face. "I don't know." He ran a hand over his face. "She was wrong this time, I guess."

LJ set her jaw and stared at the ground, wanting to argue but knowing it was pointless. She looked back up at Clyde, realizing he was just as disappointed and unaccepting of the situation as she was.

"Well, Coby was right last time," LJ said stubbornly, planting her hands on her hips.

"I know," Clyde said, raising an eyebrow and looking at her.

LJ chewed on the side of her cheek and let out a short breath. "We'll just have to do some more research I guess. She can't be that far off," she said, adjusting her pony tail with determination. "She just can't be… we're on a time schedule, we can't stay here forever…"

Clyde frowned and rubbed the back of his neck, looking over the barn once again. "Y'all planning on leaving soon, then?" he asked, not looking at her as they both turned and headed slowly back to the cruiser.

"Well, I mean, we'll have to. Sorry," she said, shoving her hands in her pockets, and glancing away awkwardly. "I know you and Coby have like… a thing," she said waving a hand at him.

Clyde finally stopped trying to look for clues and stared at LJ, face blank. "We… do?"

LJ shrugged. "I guess so, yeah."

His eyebrows raised and he gazed past her, looking at nothing. "Huh."

"That's what I thought, too," LJ muttered, then hoped he hadn't heard her. He seemed lost to the world, so she figured she was safe. "But I told our boss that we'd be here for a while. That's only going to keep him off our backs for so long, though."

Clyde nodded absently. "No, I get it." He sighed, coming back to the present and giving the barn another once-over. "I think we're done. There's nothing here."

LJ watched him trudge past her and moved to follow. "I mean, I'm just saying. We *can't* stay here forever."

"I know. You said that." Clyde reached for the door handle.

"So we'll do what we can here, but then we have to move on." LJ slid her sunglasses back into place and paused outside the cruiser.

Clyde gazed at her. "You have a deadline to get out of town?"

LJ shrugged a shoulder. "No. I'll have to give my boss one soon, though. One more week is what I'm thinking."

"But you could stay longer."

She shook her head. "No, we can't."

He watched her, bracing his hands against the roof of the car and the open door. "Why not?"

A flicker of annoyance and a spark of anger nearly lit a fire in the pit of her stomach, but LJ let out a breath and reached for her door. "Because our job is driving around the country. We literally get paid to leave this town, and a thousand others just like it." She slid into the seat and slammed her door.

Clyde leaned down and looked at her for another second before following suit and reaching for the keys. "So, you're gonna do that forever?"

LJ looked over her shades at him. "Are you serious?" She couldn't believe this was coming from Clyde. Hadn't she just had this conversation? With *Coby*?

"What?"

"Nothing." She crossed her arms and sat back. "Maybe we are going to do that forever. It's none of your business."

He clenched his jaw and started the car. He only let the silence linger for a moment. "You *want* to do that forever?"

She clenched her own teeth together and crossed her arms tighter. Her stomach turned over as Clyde's words made her head pound. What she wanted was not something she was willing to ponder, especially not with Clyde Burkiss. She lifted her chin. "Are we getting out of here or what?"

Clyde sighed, but he let the subject drop and turned the car out of the driveway.

Chapter Thirty-Eight

Grizzly looked over at the woman in the cruiser next to him. Coby was staring out her window, chewing on one of her knuckles, looking fairly strung out.

They only had one more circle left on the map to go and so far they had come up with absolutely nothing.

He was pretty sure she was wrong about Brittany, and that Coby knew it, but he wasn't going to force her to admit it until they had looked into every possibility. He figured he owed her that much.

"So if this doesn't pan out, we'll head back to the station, call Clyde and LJ, and go from there," Grizzly said, giving her a smile.

Coby nodded but didn't say anything.

Grizzly peered out the windshield as he crept up to a long drive off the old country road. "Looks like this is it!" he announced, pulling in and parking the car before getting out and looking around. There were no cars in the driveway, but he went up to the door and knocked just in case.

No one came to the door so he shrugged and turned back to Coby who had gotten out of the car and was glaring at the barn behind the house like she was challenging it.

"Well, no one's home... shall we?" Grizzly asked.

She nodded again and started towards the barn quickly. He trudged after her.

They spent over an hour scouring every inch of the barn, stables, and where the silo used to be before Coby stopped moving. She just stood there, looking at the foundation where the silo had once been, looking small and defeated. Grizzly tentatively walked up next to her and paused before clearing his throat. "Cobes... you know it's... it's okay," he said with a sigh. "We'll hit the books. We'll figure it out. No one's... no one's doubting you, okay?" he said, patting her shoulder.

Coby slowly turned and looked up at him. "I'm so sorry," she said in a hoarse whisper and Grizzly saw her eyes rim with red. "I can't believe this. I was so sure... you guys were counting on me. Clyde's sticking his neck out for me and –"

"You don't have to worry about Clyde. Just because he's on probation, doesn't mean –"

Her eyes widened in horror and Grizzly quickly tried to backpedal. "He's on *probation?*" she squeaked, a storm cloud passing over her face. "Are you *serious?*" she thundered, glaring at him.

"Look, I had to do something. Pritchard's got the mayor breathing down my – never mind," he shook his head, unsure why he was explaining himself to her.

Coby looked like she was going to cry, nostrils flaring as she turned away.

Grizzly mentally kicked himself. "Hey. You can't be right about everything. We're going to figure this out." He placed a hand on her back and gently nudged her toward the cruiser. "And Clyde is going to be fine." He rolled his eyes.

They piled back into the car and Grizzly glanced over at her as he pulled out of the driveway.

"So," he said, attempting to lighten the mood in the car. "How much time do you guys normally spend in one town?"

Coby hesitated, obviously not in the mood for small talk. "The whole process takes about a week."

Grizzly nodded. "Huh. Process? Do you do the same thing every time or do you just wing it?"

"We interview people. Check out the local attractions. Usually find a fun restaurant or two. If it's a new state, or a really fun place, LJ gets a bear." She shrugged. "It's always new things but there's usually a bit of a rhythm to the madness."

He looked over at her. "A bear?"

She smiled, and he was glad he'd gotten one out of her, but he hadn't been trying and now he was curious. "She collects teddy bears. Her room at our apartment is full of them. Sometimes, when we're gone for weeks at a time, she has to mail a box of teddy bears to herself."

Grizzly laughed. It seemed so contrary to LJ's nature. "Teddy bears…" He shook his head. "Did she find one from here yet?"

Coby shook her head and let out a short laugh. "No, we've been a bit busy with, you know, murder."

"Right, sure, sure." Grizzly nodded. He chuckled to himself again, then looked back over at Coby, who had resumed staring out the window and looking lost. "I'm gonna find her one."

Coby looked back at him and laughed for real. "Okay, you do that. And if it's not a grizzly bear I'm going to be disappointed."

Grizzly chuckled. "That won't be too pointed?"

"What do you mean?" Coby asked him, narrowing her eyes at him curiously.

"Like would it say: 'Here LJ, cuddle me'?" He shrugged awkwardly as Coby burst out laughing at him. A little hysterical perhaps, but it was better than crying.

"Is that what you *want* it to say?" she asked him, still chuckling as she wiped at her eyes.

"What? No. Pfft. I just, I don't want it to be weird."

"Uh-huh. I know you brought her to your house and took her out on your motorcycle. Did you think I wouldn't find out about that, young man? What are your intentions with my best friend?" Coby asked, eyebrow raised, obviously teasing him, but he couldn't help but feel like a little kid caught with his hand in the cookie jar.

"I was just – she had never been on a bike!" he said, shrugging his shoulders up to his ears in innocence.

"There's a reason for that. The reason is that LJ isn't a reckless person." She snickered.

"And you think I am?" He put a hand to his chest in mock offense. "Just because I'm an ex-biker-turned-cop? You don't know me at all."

"Oh really? I'm pretty sure I know who you like," Coby said, nose in the air.

"What are you, eight?" Grizzly scowled at her.

"I'm not the one we're talking about right now. Just because you're a police chief, doesn't mean *anything*. I eat police for breakfast." She narrowed her eyes at him.

"Yeah, you run them over with your big ass car."

She chuckled again. "And don't you forget it," she said with a nod. She paused and then glanced over at him. "She's… she was with a real jerk not too long ago. He really broke her down. It's her business but I just figured…" She shrugged.

Grizzly frowned and glanced over at her. "Sounds like an asshole," he muttered.

"Yeah. And I messed him up big time, so just remember that Mr. Ex-Biker Cop Man."

Grizzly glanced over at her tiny form, eyebrows raised. "Oh really? Bruise his ego?"

"Want me to bruise your face?"

***

LJ unfolded herself from the passenger seat with a groan of relief. She stretched her arms above her head and popped her back as Clyde slammed his door and headed for the station entrance. LJ thought she recognized the cruiser Grizzly and Coby had taken earlier parked next to the Chevelle, but she wasn't positive since most of the cruisers looked the same.

The sun was starting to dip toward the western horizon as she followed Clyde into the station. They'd all been out wandering the Wisconsin farmlands for hours, and despite being cranky, tired, and hungry, LJ hoped that Coby wasn't getting too down on herself.

As they stepped into the office space, Coby's boisterous laughter filled the room. She was sitting in Clyde's chair, Grizzly perched on the desk in front of her, apparently telling her some hilarious story. LJ felt a surge of appreciation for the man, getting her friend to laugh instead of letting her kick herself for being wrong with her Rapunzel theory. She observed Grizzly, and Coby's words from the night before came to mind. Her face got warm as she forced the thought away and propelled her feet forward.

"Hey guys," Coby greeted them, face apologetic as her gaze lingered on Clyde. LJ didn't miss the soft smile he gave her. "So, I'm sorry."

LJ scoffed. "Please. That was fun, driving all over the state with the quietest man alive."

Clyde actually shot her a dirty look instead of turning red and looking at the ground. "Like you're such a conversationalist."

"Pfft. If you would have stopped for food, I would have talked more."

Coby snorted and shook her head at LJ with a smile. "Or coffee. You wouldn't have been able to shut her up if you wanted to." She laughed.

Clyde raised his hands in the air. "You didn't say you wanted food!"

"Well I do. Coby, let's get food before I eat Julia. I bet she tastes good." LJ snapped her mouth closed before she made more of a fool of herself. Being hungry brought out a side of her she'd rather not have Grizzly witness. Again.

Coby got to her feet and patted Grizzly on the arm. "Thanks for putting up with me. And again, I'm sorry."

"Don't worry about it, darlin'." Grizzly waved it off. "No harm done."

Clyde looked like he wanted to say something, but he settled for a small wave that Coby returned as the girls headed for the door.

Coby pulled her keys from her purse as LJ caught the door and stepped outside behind her. They got in the car and Coby paused before starting the engine and turned toward LJ. "I'm sorry."

"Coby!" LJ burst out, buckling her seat belt. "Get over it and get me some food!"

Coby snickered and turned the key. "Okay, okay. But *then* I'm going through that paperwork again, and looking at the maps, and the fairy tale, and –"

"Whatever. I'm eating an entire restaurant and going to bed. You can do all the research you want." LJ put her foot up on the dash.

They drove to McDonald's and pulled through the drive-thru. LJ ordered two specials and Coby got a snack wrap that made LJ laugh violently. They went back to the motel with the food, but LJ had balled up her first paper bag before they pulled into a parking spot.

"So it wasn't that bad?" Coby put the car in park and let the engine idle as she looked over at LJ with an eyebrow raised.

"No, it wasn't." LJ swallowed a fry. "It was a little awkward sometimes, but I'm still not convinced Clyde can be *not* awkward."

"But he's very nice and very sweet," Coby stated, pointedly.

LJ rolled her eyes. "Okay whatever. I'm done talking about this." She grabbed her other paper bag of food and got out of the car.

Coby yanked the keys free and followed suit. "Well, my afternoon with Grizzly was… informative."

LJ stared at her over the roof of the car. "What?"

"Nothing," Coby sang and flounced to the motel door.

"No, not nothing. What?" LJ started for the door, eyes dropping to the threadbare welcome mat in front of their room. "What is *that*?"

Coby poked her head back out of the door and looked. "Huh. Dead bird?"

LJ crouched to get a better look.

"Don't *touch* it!"

"I'm not touching it," LJ snapped. The bird was white and plump and laying right in the center of the doormat. LJ peered up at Coby. "How did you miss this? I can't believe you didn't step on it."

Coby shrugged. "We should probably tell Van Camp. He can get it out of here for us."

LJ straightened up and poked the bird with her boot toe. "It's a white dove. Where did it come from?"

"It's just a dead bird, LJ."

"No, it's a dead white dove. *On our doorstep.*" LJ motioned at it.

Coby gave her a raised eyebrow. "I think you're freaking out over nothing."

LJ looked back down at the bird, wondering if Coby was right. "But white doves aren't like… wild birds. They're not pigeons. They aren't just flying around. They're like pets, aren't they?"

Coby stepped over the mat. "I think sometimes pigeons just turn out white. Or maybe some ceremonial birds got loose at a wedding and this one died right here. I'm going to get Van Camp."

LJ scowled at the dead creature, then glanced around the parking lot. They were the only ones who were at the Van Camp Inn for an extended stay. Any other guests they'd encountered had only checked in for a night or two at a time. So, either some kid was pranking them and would be gone tomorrow, or someone was watching them.

LJ looked back at the bird, then stepped into the motel room. Or Coby was right, and having a white dove lying dead on their doorstep wasn't that strange at all.

Chapter Thirty-Nine

Neal Murphy shuffled around his kitchen, making coffee and cracking eggs into a frying pan. It was one of the lovely things about Sunday. Breakfast, reading, quiet time. It was the only day the library was completely closed. He smiled and turned on some music as he surveyed what he had in the cupboards. Maybe he'd make some muffins and attend the potluck at the Lutheran church in town. Several of the patrons attended there regularly, so he'd visited before.

He pondered what kind of muffin he would make and tried to remember what time the potluck started as he turned back to his eggs, adding some onions and peppers.

He was just about to rummage through the fridge for blueberries when his phone went off. He frowned. Who would be calling him at this time? On a Sunday morning? He glanced over the number before answering it. "Hello?"

"Hi Neal, this is Coby Anderson."

A smile broke over his face. "Good morning, Coby. What can I do for you?" he asked, tucking the phone under his chin as he reached over to pour himself a cup of coffee.

"Well, I'm here at the library…" she began.

Neal chuckled. "It's Sunday. The library's closed," he said as he added sugar.

"Yeah, I realized that after I got here, actually." She let out a short laugh. "I've kinda lost track of what day it is."

"Understandable, as you've been basically living between bookshelves." Neal smiled.

"Yes, well… I was wondering if you could do me a huge favor, and I apologize in advance."

Neal turned off the burner of the stove and adjusted his glasses. "You want me to unlock the library," he said.

"You may have heard me bemoaning the internet at our motel."

"I may have."

"And you may have guessed that you have a much better selection of books than the motel."

Neal laughed. "I'll open the library for you."

"Are you serious? Oh my gosh, thank you, thank you so much!"

"I'll be there in twenty minutes."

Neal hung up the phone. He quickly ate his breakfast before pulling on some clothes that were a little bit more suited for meeting women. He fixed his hair quickly while snatching his keys and headed over to the library.

As he pulled up, he saw the Chevelle parked close to the entrance. He slid in next to her and killed the engine. She smiled and waved at him before climbing out of her car. He followed suit and held up the keys with a smile.

"Thank you so much, really, you're a life saver," she said as she trailed after him, her laptop slung across her shoulder. She was wearing dark jeans and a red sweater with matching lipstick, and glasses, her hair piled on top of her head. She looked a little more put together than the previous days he had seen her, though just as determined, and still like she wasn't sleeping very much.

Neal smiled to himself and walked up to the door, unlocking it and holding it open for her. She paused in the doorway. "Thanks again, I'll try not to be too late. Should I just give you a call when I'm going to leave?" she asked.

He blinked at her and shook his head. "I can't let you in here by yourself." He laughed at her.

Coby crumpled slightly. "Oh no. I'm sorry, this is your day off. Don't worry about it. I have other places to go… I'll go to the station, or Clyde's –"

"I thought you said you wanted books, too?" Neal interrupted with an amused shake of his head.

"It's okay, really –"

"Coby. It's fine," Neal said. "Really, I don't mind. I was just going to read at home, anyway. Maybe I can help you with whatever you're researching," he said with a shrug. "I know a lot about the town." He smiled, quite honestly happy to spend his day off with Coby Anderson.

She hesitated. "I promise I won't be long," she whispered before darting into the library.

"Take your time." He chuckled as he stepped in after her.

***

LJ slung her bag over her shoulder and strode to the corner, adjusting her sunglasses as she looked up and down Main Street. She headed toward the four corners, determined to find something worth writing about that would keep Ron happy until they figured out their next move.

Coby had already disappeared with the car, and LJ assumed she'd gone back to the police station to do more research. Why she hadn't dragged LJ along with her was the strange part, but it wasn't all that surprising.

Especially with how focused she'd been, on both the cases and on Clyde.

And LJ couldn't do anything else to help Coby. She'd done plenty of researching and co-theorizing and she'd even been stuck in a car with Clyde for an entire Saturday on a wild goose chase. It was time to get down to business and get some of their actual work done.

LJ reached City Hall and made it halfway up the steps before realizing it was Sunday morning and the offices would be closed. She paused, tapping her fingers on the metal railing as she tried to come up with a Plan B. Diners, coffee shops, and local businesses were all on her mental list and she trotted back down the steps to continue up Main Street, vowing to stop at the first one she came to.

It was a small security business, and it was closed. LJ narrowed her eyes at the door, then continued on her way.

Four closed signs later, she was on the opposite end of town empty handed. She'd bypassed the bars, though she was pretty sure she'd hear some good stories from the frequenters inside. As interesting as that might be, it probably wasn't the best use of her time.

She got her hopes up at a lit sign for a corner diner up ahead, only to have them dashed at the sight of the dark interior and the paper "closed" sign secured to the front door. LJ sighed, tucked her hair behind her ears, and promptly gave up.

She didn't intend to go to the police station, but when she found herself walking past, she headed for the door without much hesitation. The parking lot was lacking Coby's Chevelle.

The waiting area and the front desk were empty. LJ walked down the hall toward the back without a second thought. Coby might be the brains of the operation when it came down to the consultation aspect, but LJ was part of the deal too, and that meant she was allowed to barge on to police property unannounced. She hoped.

The back room was mostly empty too, which was to be expected on a Sunday morning. LJ's eyes darted toward Grizzly's office, but she couldn't see the door from where she stood.

"Looking for me?" LJ jumped and whirled around to where Grizzly was leaning against the break room door, eating an apple. Amusement played on his face as he watched her. "Whoops, sorry, didn't mean to scare you."

LJ scowled. "You didn't."

"Oh, so you leapt for joy at the sound of my voice? That's even better," he teased.

"No." She sighed and rolled her eyes. "I'm sorry if I'm not supposed to be back here."

"Don't worry about it." Grizzly leaned back into the break room to toss the apple core in a garbage can. "What brings you in? I can't believe you got tired of your glamorous motel room."

"I was trying to find some new material for a follow-up article I need to write for the magazine." LJ tucked her sunglasses into her bag. "I mean, we're both supposed to write it, but I kind of figured I'd take the brunt of it since Coby's taking the lead on these cases."

Grizzly nodded. "And how's that going for you on a Sunday in Waupun?"

"Every. Damn. Thing. Is closed," LJ growled.

He laughed. "Welcome to 1952."

She shook her head. "We've been to a hundred small towns across the nation, some of them a quarter of the size of this one. Lots of them have a whistle at noon, some are completely closed on Sundays, and some even have local polka stations, but Waupun is the first I've encountered with all three."

"Waupun has its charms." Grizzly smirked at her expression. "Maybe closing down on Sundays isn't one of them in this case. But hey, if you want it, I can get you an interview with the police chief."

"No, really?"

"Absolutely. He'd be honored."

LJ laughed. "Well thanks. I might just take you up on that."

"I'm free now, if you've still got time," Grizzly offered, giving a pointed nod toward the back of the room. "We can go to my office."

LJ's palms began to sweat immediately. Her pulse sped up at the idea of asking Grizzly personal questions for an article, and she pushed back the anxiety forcibly. She wasn't Barbara Walters. There was no reason to pull out the deep questions. Even if she did want to know if Grizzly had ever been married, or if he'd ever consider having children. She glanced back toward Clyde's desk, even though she knew it was empty. "I should probably check in with Coby first. How long ago did she leave?"

Grizzly wrinkled his brow. "She hasn't been here today."

LJ mirrored him in confusion. "What? She left this morning. I figured she came here – better internet for researching." She dug into her bag for her phone. "I'd better call her." She tried not to be conscious of Grizzly watching her as she listened to the line ring.

"Hello?"

"Coby? Where are you?"

"I'm at the library. I haven't actually come up with anything new yet, but I'm looking at –"

"The library? It's open?" LJ frowned.

"Oh, I just called Neal and he opened it for me. This is a police investigation, after all." Coby chuckled at her self-appointed authority. "Do you need me for something?"

LJ hesitated. "No… I just… never mind. Just wondered where you were, that's all. You heading back soon?"

"Uh, yeah, probably. I'll call you when I'm leaving. Maybe we can get dinner and I'll have something new to go over with you."

"Okay. Bye." LJ ended the call, feeling more than seeing Grizzly's raised eyebrow.

"Something wrong?"

LJ sighed and shook her head. "No, it's… it's nothing."

"You look worried."

She looked up at him reluctantly. "There's just been… I'm probably being paranoid. It's all these murder files and missing people and... bodies." She shuddered.

Grizzly lifted his chin. "Being paranoid is vastly underrated. What's going on?"

"No, really. We found a dead bird on our door mat." LJ shrugged. "That's not worth worrying about. I'm just tired and…" She scowled, remembering the roses. "Did Clyde send Coby flowers?"

Grizzly's face split into a grin. "What?"

"There were flowers, outside our room. Twice, actually." LJ shook her head. "I didn't think Clyde had it in him."

"Neither did I." Grizzly ran a hand over his beard and nodded approvingly. "Well. Attaboy."

LJ resisted the urge to argue about all the things that were wrong with that entire situation and wiped her palms on her jeans. "So. About that interview... it would actually be extremely helpful."

Grizzly motioned her ahead of him toward the office. "I aim to please. After you, darlin'."

***

After hours of pouring over her laptop, books and case files trying to figure out where she went wrong, Coby growled in frustration, taking her glasses off and setting them roughly on the table.

Neal looked up over the top of his book at her from across the table, eyebrows raised. "You okay over there?" he asked her.

"Yeah. No. Ugh," she said, picking up the copies of case files, scanning them and then slapping them down in frustration.

"What's up?" he asked, closing his book and leaning closer.

Coby tensed, realizing she really shouldn't let Neal see the files. She reached and turned them over awkwardly. "Just... researching stuff, and I'm not getting anywhere."

"The missing people?" Neal asked with a small frown.

"I – How do you –" Coby back-pedaled quickly. The last thing she needed to do was spread information she shouldn't even have in the first place.

"Coby, come on, the entire town knows you and LJ are here helping the police department find bodies," Neal said with a shrug. "You don't have to tell me anything. I'm not going to pry," he said, adjusting his glasses before reaching forward. "But what's with all the fairy tales?" he asked, grabbing one of the many books she had spread out in front of her.

Coby raised an eyebrow at him. "This is you not prying?" she asked, but gave him a smile. He was just trying to be helpful. He always was. She really owed him for letting her come in on his day off.

"Okay, okay… fair enough," he said, putting the book down and sliding back in his seat, hands in the air. "I just wish I could help you." He shrugged, running a hand back through his hair.

"Me too," she said in frustration, rubbing her eyes before realizing she was probably smearing her makeup everywhere. She snatched up her glasses and put them back on before letting out a frustrated snort and closing her laptop. "So if you had to find a 'tower' in Waupun, what would it be?" she asked.

"Ummm..." Neal raised his eyebrows. "I don't know. The *water* tower?"

Coby felt her jaw drop and her eyes bug. "I am such an idiot." She gaped, a feeling of relief rushed through her along with humiliation. She stood up quickly gathered her laptop and files together. "You're a life saver. Thank you so much. I could kiss you."

Neal blinked in confusion and shrugged. "Okay then." He grinned, stood up and helped her with all the books she had spread across the table.

Coby hoisted her computer bag over her shoulder and sighed, feeling ten times more focused and energized than she had a few moments ago. "I'm ready. Thanks again, seriously, you may have just helped me figure something out."

"Okay!" He shrugged still looking confused. "Glad to help." He nudged her with his shoulder, his arms full of her books, and smiled down at her. "Ready to go?"

"Yup!" Coby announced. She was itching to take a look at the water tower.

Chapter Forty

Coby burst through the door of Cuco's Mexican Restaurant. She grinned as she locked eyes with LJ and strode towards her. LJ blinked at her as she plopped down in the booth and grabbed the menu with a flourish. "Hey!"

"Hey," LJ said, examining her best friend.

"Did you order already?" Coby asked, scanning the menu but LJ could tell she wasn't reading it.

"Nope, still looking," LJ said.

"I'm just going to get the burrito," Coby said in a rush, closing her menu and drumming her fingers on the table top.

"There's like seven different bur–"

"Well, I'll just take the cheapest one then," Coby said, waving her hand quickly. "Ooh, chips!" she said, reaching for the basket.

LJ furrowed her brow. "So, how was your time at the library?"

"It was great! I mean, it wasn't. It was pretty awful and I was getting super frustrated, but I think I got a lead!" she announced.

"That's awesome!" LJ said, closing her menu. "What is it?"

"I'll show you when we're done eating." Coby smiled. "What did you do today?"

LJ shrugged, feeling defensive. "Well, you were just gone, so I got up and walked around town. I thought I'd get some interviews for work, but *everything was closed.* So I went to the station. I thought you'd be there."

"And?" Coby asked, eyebrows raised.

"And you weren't," LJ said.

"No, I wasn't. Was anybody else?"

LJ took a drink of water. "Grizzly was there," she mumbled.

"OOOOOoooh."

"Shut up. So I called you, and then thought I might as well interview him while I was there so I could work on the article," LJ said in a rush, ignoring Coby's toothy, foxlike grin.

"What did you ask him about?" Coby pried.

"Just interview stuff. Work stuff. Normal stuff, Coby." LJ glared at her.

"Has he been the chief for a long time?"

"What? No. Not that long," LJ sputtered, flustered.

"Was he born in Wisconsin?"

"No, he –"

"Does he want kids?"

"Yes –"

"You asked him if he wants *kids*?" Coby looked absolutely beside herself with glee.

LJ mentally kicked herself. "Shut. Up. Coby." She glowered at her.

"So, did you guys have, like, private wine –"

"What the hell is private wine?"

"You know what I mean."

"I know you are a butt."

The waiter approached before Coby could make any more comments or LJ could bean her in the face with the basket of chips.

***

It was getting late by the time Grizzly finally climbed into his truck. LJ had stayed for the entire afternoon, and as he pulled onto the street, he realized he kind of wished she was still with him.

He pulled his phone out and hit Clyde's number, never mind he was a block away and would probably be in the driveway by the time Clyde answered. He had apparently overstayed his welcome at his first officer's house, as Clyde had demanded a heads up before Grizzly barged onto the property, but Grizzly didn't let it bother him. "Dude. I'm almost to your house."

"Okay…"

"Scratch that, I'm here. You told me not to surprise you anymore."

"This is hardly giving me notice, Grizzly."

"Well I'm here and you'd better let me in this time."

"That was once. One time, and I wasn't even home."

Grizzly smirked as he hung up and killed the engine and went for Clyde's front door. It opened instantly and Grizzly stepped inside without waiting for the invitation. "So, how was your day?"

Clyde blinked at him, tea mug in hand. "I spent most of it going over our case files, just like we have been for the last week. Why? What's wrong with you?"

"I had a fabulous day, thanks for asking." Grizzly painstakingly unlaced his boots and then straightened, hands on his hips, looking toward the kitchen. "Beer?"

Clyde motioned toward the doorway. Grizzly led the way.

Grizzly opened the fridge and found a bottle of Heineken in the back. "Aren't you going to ask me what I did?"

Clyde took a sip of tea. "You're going to tell me whether I ask you or not."

"You're absolutely right." Grizzly popped the top on the edge of Clyde's counter, ignoring the protesting look he received. "LJ stopped by the station today."

Clyde closed his mouth and raised his eyebrows. "She did?"

"Don't look so surprised." He took a swig of beer. "She interviewed me."

"For their magazine?" Clyde asked, nodding slowly. "That's probably a good idea. If we don't get anywhere with these cases she's going to have to come up with something else before they –"

Grizzly held up a hand. "First off, we're gonna solve these cases. All of them. Coby's onto something. Just because she had an off day does not mean we're failing and won't nail this guy." He leaned against the countertop. "Second of all, they might not leave."

Clyde raised his eyebrows.

"Let's not even go there." Grizzly cleared his throat. "You're raining on my parade here, partner."

Clyde shrugged and moved to the kitchen table, setting his tea down and pulling out a chair. "So LJ interviewed you. Or did you interview her?"

"I don't appreciate that tone. I'll have you know I was a perfect interviewee."

"I doubt that."

Grizzly scowled. "Listen, it was her idea."

"Really?"

"Well, basically her idea. I mean, I offered, but…" Grizzly muttered as he lumbered over to the table and sat down next to Clyde.

Clyde took another drink of his tea and looked over at Grizzly. "Don't you think you're being a bit… I don't know… a bit optimistic about LJ?" he asked, a small smirk on his face.

Grizzly gave him an offended look. "Excuse me. I'm not the one sending love bouquets, *Clyde*."

Clyde blinked up at him, looking completely confused. "Wait. What?"

"Don't you play innocent with me, I know you've been sending Coby flowers."

"I have *not*." Clyde looked horrified, a flush creeping up his neck.

Grizzly frowned, placing his beer down on the table. "So you've been sending *LJ* flowers?"

"I haven't been sending anyone flowers, Grizz. Come on."

Grizzly passed a hand over his face thoughtfully. "Dammit Burkiss, I was so proud."

"Does *Coby* think I'm sending her flowers?" He looked even more mortified and Grizzly had to bite back a laugh.

"I dunno. LJ's the one who mentioned them." Grizzly shrugged. He frowned, suddenly, realization hitting him like a truck. "That means somebody *else* is sending them flowers." He growled. "I bet it's that little mechanic punk, Jimmy."

Clyde frowned, looking down into his tea. "I don't even know if Coby would like flowers."

"I tell you, small towns. A pretty girl shows up and suddenly it's like we're in the Wild West again," Grizzy muttered under his breath, not listening to Clyde.

"I can't believe LJ thought I sent them to Coby. I really think she hates me, Grizz."

"We don't send our cruisers to Jimmy's shop, do we? If we do, we're finding someone else."

"She thinks Coby's going to leave her and she thinks I'm trying to take her away."

"Like LJ would *ever* go for such a scrawny little..."

"Grizz."

"Yeah?" Grizzly asked, pausing his rant and looking over at Clyde.

"LJ told me they were leaving in a week."

Grizzly felt the fight leave him. "…Yeah."

Chapter Forty-One

"What is happening? Why are we here? I feel like a hooligan," LJ said as she picked her way around some shrubs, following Coby towards the water tower. "We're going to get arrested."

"Good thing the police chief gives you 'private audiences'." Coby said in a low lusty voice and snickered as she shone a flashlight at the base of the water tower.

"Shut up. It was just an interview for our job that I'm trying to keep. You're the one who has pictures of Clyde on your computer." LJ snorted as she came to a stop behind her. She frowned at the flashlight. "What is this, Scooby Doo? Shouldn't we call the guys?"

"I am *not* calling the guys on a hunch from the librarian, no way. They can wait until we have a body in possession," Coby muttered as she set off, shining the light around the base.

LJ tiptoed after her, somewhat afraid she was accidentally going to step on the body. "I can't believe this. This is dumb."

"I have pictures of Grizzly too, by the way, if you want them." Coby grinned back at her, shining her flashlight in her face.

LJ scowled and shoved her hand away. "Geesh, you're chipper. What's wrong with you?"

Coby shrugged and kept walking. "This is kind of fun."

"What?"

"You know, you and me… the two of us... looking for clues…"

LJ raised her eyebrows incredulously. "What did they put in your burrito?" They walked around the entire water tower, three times, before LJ threw her hands up in the air. "Coby, I hate to tell you this because I still feel kind of guilty about all the doubting, but I don't think she's here."

Coby was frowning, but thoughtfully. "I think she is, actually," she murmured, walking a little further and pointing to a bush about ten feet away. "I think she's right there."

LJ scowled. "And why is that?"

"Thorns," Coby said, before turning and scampering back to the car.

LJ blinked at the bush before taking a few steps after Coby. "Thorns? What does that *mean*?"

"It means there were thorns at the base of Rapunzel's tower that the prince fell on. His eyes were scratched out by them," Coby said, rummaging around in the trunk.

LJ made a face. "Mmm… pleasant fellows, those Grimm brothers."

Coby closed the trunk of the car and returned, holding out two shovels with a wide grin on her face. "Borrowed these from Neal just in case."

LJ's eyes bugged out of her head, holding out her hands in protest. "Whoa, no. We are definitely calling the guys."

"If I'm right, you can absolutely call your boyfriend, LJ." Coby rolled her eyes.

"Coby! This is grave robbing!"

"LJ, this is not a cemetery and we're not stealing anything."

LJ's brows slammed down in a scowl. "Fine. But it's destruction of public property and I will not be party to it."

"Then I guess you'll just have to look pretty and whistle while I work." Coby gave her a snotty smile before tromping over to the water tower, setting down the second shovel and surveying the thorny bush with determination.

"You… are a brat," LJ said.

"Uh huh…" Coby said, slamming the shovel into the ground and stepping on it.

"I'm going to go to Clyde and tattle on you."

"You do that."

"And I'm going to tell him about your ninja turtle pajamas."

"I am not ashamed of those pajamas."

LJ watched her for a solid five minutes before she walked over to a large decorative rock and sat down on the edge, crossing her legs. "Hurry up, you're going to get us in trouble."

Coby straightened and glared at her. "Laverne Jeanette, if you want this to go faster you can pick up that shovel."

"You know how long it's going to take you to dig a 6 foot hole?"

"I'm really hoping the killer skimped on the whole depth thing."

LJ let out an annoyed growl before jumping to her feet and picking up the shovel.

"That's my girl." Coby grinned at her.

***

Hours. It felt like they dug for hours. Her whole hand was a blister. LJ couldn't feel the pain in her back anymore, but she wasn't sure she'd ever be able to stand upright again. She had been completely on edge, jumping at every sound. She cursed Coby under her breath, as she drove the shovel down with force. It hit the ground with a weird thud and LJ was sure she had hit another rock.

That's when she saw the arm.

"Oh my– Oh my GOSH– AHHH, UGH!" LJ screeched, abandoning her shovel and clawing her way frantically out of the hole, shuddering violently. She heard Coby talking at her but paid her no mind, trying to keep herself from puking or rolling around on the grass as an impromptu shower.

"We did it!" Coby gasped in awe, tossing the shovels out and clambering out of the grave after her. "We found her, LJ!"

"Don't talk to me. I can't *believe* you talked me into this!" LJ shakily tugged at her clothes before Coby threw her arms around her in a massive hug. LJ clawed her way out of the embrace. "*Don't* touch me with your slimy, gross, corpse hands!"

Coby snorted at her and grabbed LJ's cell phone from off the ground, dialing Grizzly's number.

It rang four times before he answered it, sounding groggy. "Hey, LJ."

"Hey Grizz, it's Coby." She paused, still sounding out of breath, and pushed a button. "You're on speaker. LJ and I are at the water tower –"

"Is everything all right?" Grizzly asked, suddenly sounding much more awake.

"Well, we're fine, but y'all need to get out here –" Coby said, brushing her arm across her sweaty forehead.

LJ paused in fixing her ponytail and gave Coby a horrified look, cutting her off. "Did you just say 'y'all'?"

Grizzly let out a laugh. "Coby, I think you've been spending a little too much time with your Southern Belle."

LJ thought she saw Coby blush but it was hard to tell in the dark. "Listen, *you all* need to get down here right now!" she sputtered. "I think we found our Rapunzel."

***

Clyde filled up two mugs of hot water and placed the tea bags inside. He walked back to his desk where LJ, Coby and Grizzly had all been talking. The girls were in the bathroom, washing the dirt off, so he set the mugs on his desk, slid his hands in his pockets and looked over at Grizzly. "Do you want me to make the call?"

Grizzly ran a hand over his exhausted face and shook his head. "I'll take care of it, and we're not worrying about that until morning anyway."

Clyde glanced at his watch and decided it was probably better not to mention the fact that it was almost six a.m. He pushed a mug toward Grizzly.

LJ returned from the restroom, hair freshly brushed into a ponytail, face free of dirt streaks. She inspected her hands as she reached Clyde's desk, and Clyde grimaced for her at the sight of the blisters on her palms. "Shoveling is kind of a bitch."

Grizzly leaned back in Clyde's desk chair and took one of her hands in his to look at it. "Hey Burkiss, where's that first aid kit you're always nagging me about?"

Clyde narrowed his eyes but moved to the bottom drawer of his desk and pulled out the white box. Grizzly took it and proceeded to doctor LJ's right hand.

Coby reappeared, and Clyde felt his stomach flip flop. He swallowed and told himself it was an improvement from the cold sweat and impending panic attack he'd felt every time he saw her the week before. "Okay. What else?" he asked.

Grizzly didn't look up from squeezing antibiotic ointment out of a tube. "That's about it. We've filed the reports and sent everything to the lab. Autopsy's scheduled for eight a.m. We can't really move forward until we have more information."

Coby nodded and rubbed her eyes. "But I can keep going with the other cases."

LJ twisted to look at Coby but still let Grizzly work on her hand. "Maybe *not* tonight?"

Coby shrugged. "Well, I guess maybe after we get some sleep."

"And after we discuss the laws you broke?" Grizzly looked up at her.

Clyde joined him, eyes narrowing at Coby.

"Well…" Coby looked sheepish. "I mean, we're consultants, right? That's got to count for something."

"It doesn't. At all, actually." Grizzly swiped a roll of gauze from the kit but LJ retracted her hand before he could start wrapping it. "That's going to get infected."

"We're fifteen years into the 21st century, Chief. I know how to use soap." LJ pulled up another chair.

"But we found a missing body." Coby pointed out.

"By trespassing and destructing public property."

"That's not really the point."

"Illegal activity aside," Clyde piped up, surprising everyone, including himself, with his tone. "That move was careless, and it could have been dangerous. Yes, you found a body. That just confirms our suspicions on this killer and his patterns. But we don't know enough about him. He could be watching. He could have been *there.* You shouldn't have gone alone."

"I wasn't alone!" Coby said, holding her hands out pointedly at LJ.

"O... kay... no offense –" Grizzly said slowly as he gave LJ a skeptical look.

LJ hit him on the shoulder with her other hand. "Watch it."

"LJ doesn't count. You were both way out of line," Clyde stated, frustrated with the situation.

Coby chewed on her lip and looked up at Clyde. "Hey, can I talk to you for a second?" she asked, grabbing his hand without waiting for an answer, and walking towards the other side of the room.

Clyde felt the bottom of his stomach drop and his ears burn as he followed after her. He caught Grizzly and LJ sharing a look and heard the chief mutter "I don't like it when mom and dad fight."

"What's up with you?" Coby asked once they were away from the other two, looking up at him. He was expecting a fight from her, but she just looked concerned. It made him feel worse. It made him want to kiss her.

"Coby," he said somewhat desperately, trying to formulate his thoughts into words. "You're dealing with a murderer here... a *serial killer.* And you're being reckless about it! You should have called me."

Coby sighed and glanced away. "I'm sorry, I just... I couldn't handle being wrong again. And I know, I know that's my pride, but I couldn't risk failing again, especially with you on probation, and –"

Clyde felt blindsided. A sudden wave of anger rushed over him. How did she even know about that? "That – that's my business – that is *not* for you to worry about, okay?" he sputtered, sure he was getting "Angry Red."

Coby frowned, a small crease forming between her eyebrows. "Says the man who's been worrying about me being outside at night."

"That– that's different!" He said, feeling flustered.

"How is that different?"

"That's my *job*!" Clyde said in frustration, trying to keep his voice even.

Coby blinked. "Oh." She looked like he had just slapped her.

Clyde instantly felt sick. "Coby, wait, I didn't mean –"

"It's okay," she said, flashing a smile that wasn't real. "I'll just… I mean… LJ and I should get back to the motel." She gave a firm nod and turned to head back toward LJ.

Clyde's heart sank. He thought he might throw up. He wanted to grab her arm and make her understand that he didn't want her going after murderers in the dark by herself because he was worried about her getting hurt, and the last thing he wanted was for her to turn up like Brittany or Maria, and *not* just because he was a cop and it was his job, but…

"I'm heading to the car," Coby said to LJ, then turned her gaze to Grizzly. "Sorry this took all night, again, but at least we're on the right track."

Grizzly nodded and gave her a salute as she went for the door. He turned to look at Clyde. Clyde ignored him as he stared after Coby.

LJ waved her antibiotic covered hand at Grizzly. "Thanks, I guess. See you tomorrow... or, today, I guess?"

"Sure thing." Grizzly smiled at her as she trailed after Coby. He looked at Clyde and raised an eyebrow. "Dude? What the hell?"

Clyde turned, kicked the corner of his desk and walked out the back door.

Chapter Forty-Two

He walked towards the Chevelle. The sun was coming up, and everything was bathed in a pinkish kind of light. He wasn't concerned though, everyone was asleep, the girls had had a long night. He always liked this time of day anyway.

The Chevelle was unlocked, as luck would have it. He opened the door and climbed in, inhaling the scent. He flipped down the visor and smiled. Good, they had found it.

He pulled out a handful of nightshade berries, sprinkling them on the dashboard and seats, before crushing some in his gloved hand and smearing them on the inside of the windshield.

It was a more aggressive move, but it was time. Couldn't have anyone getting bored, and the girls had seemed highly unconcerned about his previous gifts, if they had even noticed them as such.

He wasn't sure they were as bright as he originally hoped, but then again, if they were, that would only force him to rush his story.

Couldn't have that.

The more time he had to tell his story the more fun he could have.

And he was having lots of fun.

***

"We can stop for breakfast, don't worry."

LJ rubbed the towel over her damp hair, then surveyed her reflection in the mirror. "Good."

Coby was rustling around the beds, packing up her files, loose pages, and laptop. LJ waited for her to start humming, as she did every second of every waking moment, and once in a while during sleeping moments as well, but she never started. LJ glanced at the motel hair dryer, then began tying her wet hair back in a braid instead.

Coby sat on the edge of her bed, scrolling through something on her phone. She'd been quiet since the night before. LJ hadn't thought much of it. They'd gotten in as the sun came up. There was really no reason for making conversation, but as they'd gotten ready for the day, it wasn't just the humming that was absent. Coby was lacking a spring in her step.

LJ pulled on a sweatshirt and started gathering her own things. "Are you okay?"

Coby looked up and shifted to put her phone in her pocket. "Yep. You ready?"

LJ scanned the room and nodded. "Let's go."

They stepped outside, and Coby turned to make sure the door was locked. LJ went for the passenger door of the Chevelle and balked.

"Holy shit."

The windows were smeared with red. LJ's first thought was paint, but the second thought that creeped into her mind and gave her chills was that it resembled dried blood. Coby scowled at the car and moved to unlock the door, only to realize that it was already unlocked. "What happened?"

LJ pulled open the passenger door and looked at the interior, which was also covered in the drying slime. "Someone is really screwing with us, Coby."

"What the heck *is* this?' Coby asked, leaning into the car and looking around. She reached up on the dash and scooped up a handful of berries. "Huh."

"I think we need to call the guys," LJ said, looking up at Coby.

Coby raised an eyebrow. "It's just berries."

"Coby! Someone broke into our car and messed it up!" LJ said, eyes wide. "This is not okay!"

"But we left our car unlocked. It was probably just some punk kids," Coby replied, giving the windshield an annoyed look.

"Why would punk kids try to terrorize us?" LJ asked incredulously. "Punk kids would have at least stolen the music."

"LJ, people know what we're doing here. They probably *were* trying to freak us out."

LJ chewed on her lip nervously. "I don't like this Coby. This feels like a pattern."

"Well, can you help me clean the pattern up? Then we'll go get some food in our systems before we freak out about this. We'll report it to the guys when we see them," she stated, going back to the room to get some tissues.

***

"Are we even allowed to bring food in here?" LJ hissed as Coby pushed through the second set of library doors with McDonald's bags in hand.

"Neal won't mind. Especially if we explain about last night."

LJ screwed her brows together and jutted her chin toward Coby. "Shhhh! You know you're not allowed to talk about that!"

Coby sighed dramatically. "You're such a worry wart."

"You're a freaking loudmouth."

"Calm down."

"Don't *tell* me to *calm down*."

"You ladies back for more Grimms? Or are you feeling a little more Andersen this afternoon?" Neal spoke from behind the circulation desk, wearing a blue polo and his library ID on a lanyard. He leaned against the edge of the desk, a stack of returns in front of him.

"Both." Coby lifted her laptop bag onto the desk to get the weight off her shoulder strap. "What do you know about fairy tales?"

Neal raised his eyebrows, then crossed his arms and tapped a finger on his chin in thought. "398.2 in the Dewey Decimal System. Though you already know that."

Coby rolled her eyes. "It's only my most visited section, as you've apparently noticed."

Neal shrugged. "I might be more help if I knew what you were looking for exactly."

LJ adjusted her own computer bag, feeling extra conspicuous knowing that the confidential police files were right there at her fingertips. "We're not at liberty to give you that information, but honestly, we don't actually know ourselves."

Coby was tapping her foot. LJ knew she was itching to yank out the first file she could reach, but before she could worry about that actually happening, Coby let out a sigh and brushed her hair behind her ear. "It's true. I guess at this point, I'm just ready to hear something new. We've gone over every fairy tale I've ever heard of, and I've heard a lot. So I either need to be surprised, or get a new perspective." She stepped back from the counter. "I'm open to suggestions, if you've got any."

Neal shrugged. "I might have a few things in storage, or on the racks for the summer book sale."

"That would be great! Thank you," Coby gushed as he disappeared into the back office. She looked back at LJ. "Shall we?"

LJ mocked surprise. "Oh, are you talking to me? I thought you were ignoring me because I was getting in the way of your flirting."

"That was *not* flirting."

"That was a ridiculous nerdfest over fairy tales, that's what that was."

"I wasn't flirting with him," Coby said sharply.

"Okay." LJ blinked at her tone. Coby turned away and headed up the stairs to grab a table. LJ shrugged and followed after her, wondering if she should ask about last night or not. They had both gone straight to bed, too exhausted to talk about anything. LJ honestly hadn't thought much about it, everyone had been so overtired at that point, but it wasn't like Coby to be snippy or to let LJ's teasing get to her.

When LJ rounded the top of the stairs, Coby was already booting up her laptop and pulling out library books. "I hope Neal finds something to focus on because I can only re-read this stuff so many times before it stops making any sense."

LJ nodded and held up her hands. "Hey, it already makes no sense to me."

Coby chuckled and held out a hand. "Files, please."

Chapter Forty-Three

Grizzly killed the engine and closed his eyes, leaning against the headrest with a sigh. Informing the Ferguson's that DNA evidence proved the body found buried near the water tower was their daughter's remains was not how he'd wanted to start his day.

He groaned as he climbed out of the cruiser, determined to reach the coffee pot before anyone inside saw he was back.

Julia looked up as he walked through the front door of the station, opened her mouth, then a look of understanding passed over her face and she gave a solitary nod before going back to her paperwork. Grizzly returned the nod and made a beeline for the coffee pot in the break room.

He caught a glimpse of Clyde out of the corner of his eye, and paused in the doorway. He stared at the coffee, a mere three feet away from him, and sighed. He abandoned his quest for caffeine and went for Clyde's desk.

Clyde didn't bother looking at him as he approached. "What do you want?"

Grizzly leaned forward, placing his hands on the edge of the desk. "How about you and me grab a couple beers tonight and watch whoever's playing over at the Goose Shot?"

Clyde kept typing, but rolled his eyes enough to look at Grizz. "Are you asking me out?"

"Do I have to bring you flowers first?"

Clyde refocused on his computer screen. "I'm sure Coby will have more leads by tonight. We'll probably be working late."

"Everybody has to take a break sometime, Buttkiss."

Clyde leaned back in his chair and ran both hands through his hair. Grizzly was surprised the man hadn't started losing it after the past two weeks. "I'm fine, Chief."

Grizzly pursed his lips and surveyed Clyde.

"Really," Clyde said. "You don't have to coddle me because you had to put me on probation."

"I'm not coddling you."

"And just because I blew it with…" Clyde trailed off, set his jaw, and moved back to the keyboard. "I'm good."

Grizzly straightened, still watching his first officer, reading him like a book. "You wanna talk about it?"

"No, Grizz, I said I'm good."

Grizzly nodded, more to himself than to Clyde. He wasn't sure what had gone down with Coby, but he'd observed enough to know she'd left in a huff and Clyde had been kicking himself ever since. It bothered him. He liked Coby and he liked what she did for Clyde's confidence. Some part of him was still rooting for them, despite reality having everything against that outcome. LJ and Coby, after all, would be leaving town before long, as LJ regularly liked to point out.

Grizzly shoved his hands in his pockets and started for the break room again, trying not to think about it.

***

Neal came up the stairs, holding out a book with a triumphant smile. "'One Thousand and One Nights' or 'Arabian Nights', as it's more commonly known here," he said, holding it up. "It's pretty beat up, so I had it in the free pile," he said, handing it to Coby. "It's now yours."

"Thanks!" she said, grinning and taking the book from him. "This is great. I've just been searching them online, haven't made it through very many. I've been so focused on Grimm's, because that's what we've had the most luck –"

LJ kicked Coby's foot, and shook her head.

"–with," Coby said, frowning at LJ and kicking her back.

"Well there are some pretty popular tales there… maybe not as popular as Grimm's. But most people know about Aladdin, Sinbad, Ali Baba," he said, shoving his hands in his pockets and leaning against the shelf.

Coby nodded. "Thanks, I'll take a look at those first," she said. LJ frowned at her.

"Okay well, I better, get back to it." Neal clapped his hands and smiled at them before turning and heading back down the stairs.

"Coby!" LJ hissed at her.

Coby raised her eyebrows. "What?" she asked, looking confused.

"You can't just let Neal join the club!" LJ hit her arm with one of the case files.

"What are you talking about?"

"This is confidential stuff Coby, and you need to use a little… discretion," LJ reminded her.

Coby rolled her eyes. "I didn't tell him anything, plus I'm sure the whole town already knows what we're doing here. I don't think it's a secret. He's just trying to help and he already *has* helped," Coby said, giving her a shrug.

"Just be careful. You're going to get in trouble if you're not careful with this stuff."

Coby let out a huff. "I don't need *another* lecture, thanks," she said, turning a few pages in the book. "Let's take a look at good old Ali Baba."

LJ sighed, before turning back to her laptop.

***

Pritchard walked into the station, stiff. He looked distractedly at his desk before making his way into the break room and grabbing a cup of coffee.

Days of patrol.

He hated it. He hated them. He hated being sentenced to pulling over seventeen-year-olds in pickup trucks while Burkiss was working on the cases.

He had hoped the mayor would strike some fear into them. That she would bring some order to this madness. Strike the fear of God in the chief. But she hadn't. There was no justice in this town. It was time for Grizzly to be taken care of. As much as Pritchard personally hated Clyde, he knew the chief was the bigger problem here. Pritchard wasn't going to leave it with the mayor. He didn't need her.

He placed the coffee pot back on the burner and growled inwardly, rage building. He would find a way to take care of this. Take care of both of them. He knew their weaknesses. He knew when they misstepped.

A drawer slammed from the next room. Pritchard felt his blood boil, knowing Burkiss was sitting at his desk, doing the job Pritchard deserved to be doing. He gripped his coffee mug tighter and left the break room. Sure enough, Burkiss was dutifully at it, leaning over a stack of papers like the little kiss-ass he was. "Burkiss."

Clyde looked up, head propped on his fist. "Officer Pritchard."

Pritchard gritted his teeth. "Sucking up to your boyfriend again?"

"Pardon?" Burkiss straightened up in his chair, head tilted as he squinted at Pritchard.

"Must be nice, doing whatever the hell you want, never getting any flak for it." Pritchard set his cup on the desk and crossed his arms. "All you got was a little reprimand and you're still allowed to work these cases? What the hell do you bring to the table?"

Burkiss glared, jaw clenching. His boot toe tapped under the desk. "A hell of a right hook, or so they tell me."

Pritchard's jaw popped as he ground his teeth together. He lunged forward, reaching across the desk to grip Clyde around the throat. The coffee cup teetered and sloshed dark liquid over the case files. "You listen to me, Burkiss. This is going to bite you in the ass. Take my word for it."

Clyde grabbed the man's hands and pried them off of him as he stood. "Get out of my face, Shaun," he growled, eyes flashing a cold kind of hate.

"*Officer Burkiss.*" Chief Adams approached, and Pritchard turned his glare on the big man, who was glaring right back. "You've already assaulted the guy once, Officer Burkiss. You want to get suspended?" He spoke to Burkiss but continued to stare Pritchard down.

Pritchard was up for the challenge. In fact, he was considering how much force it would take to put Adams on the ground. He clenched and unclenched his fists, trying to get a grip on himself before he did something that landed him in a jail cell. He'd come this far. He couldn't afford to screw up now.

Adams broke the glare first, looking over at Burkiss with what Pritchard could only interpret as concern. Pritchard wanted to puke.

"Walk it off." Adams nodded at Burkiss. Pritchard slid his gaze over to the first officer, who refused to look back at him as he stormed out of the room.

Pritchard swallowed the bile rising at the back of his throat and brought his pulse down a notch. He noticed Adams watching him intently, and his anger surged again. "What?" he spat.

Adams was biting back something that would have thrown Pritchard into a blind rage, he was certain. The chief shook his head, turned, and headed back for his office wordlessly.

Pritchard seethed for the millionth time and grabbed the half empty cup. It was time to focus. They would both get what was coming to them.

Chapter Forty-Four

Coby laid her forehead on her hands, nose pressed against the tabletop. "I need a shot of whiskey." She groaned dramatically.

LJ rubbed her eyes. "I think you just need a nap." She looked at her phone. "It's getting late."

Coby looked at her laptop clock. "It's seven p.m."

"Twelve hours ago we were literally just going to sleep."

Coby shrugged. LJ wasn't wrong. Sleeping for five hours after pulling an all-nighter was probably not the healthiest thing a person could do. But neither was obsessing over what she thought was a potential romantic relationship, and she had been lapsing into those thoughts since they'd left the station. Clyde snapping at her that his only concern for her came from a place of professionalism had been a sobering reality check. At this point, a shot of whiskey would be a step up.

Part of her wanted to talk to LJ about it, get her perspective, but Coby couldn't even formulate her feelings on the matter much less put them into words. She also wasn't ready to hear LJ bash Clyde or say that it didn't matter because they were leaving, so she pushed it aside. She'd deal with it later.

"So you're leaning toward this 'Ali Baba' story?" LJ tapped the ripped page of the book Neal had left for Coby.

She nodded. "Yup. I think it's our best bet. These missing girls?" She spread out four files. "They were friends. Kate McCurry lived in Waupun. They all have records for shoplifting. Busted at the same time in the

Fond du Lac Mall like a little gang of thieves. I bet you anything they're in barrels somewhere."

LJ made a face. "Coby. Morbid."

Coby shrugged. "Sorry, but I'm like 85 percent convinced. I got a list of potential places," she said, pulling out a sheet of paper.

LJ nodded. "Okay... so we should call the guys."

Coby hesitated, before nodding as well. "Tomorrow. I'm thinking you can go with the guys in the morning and scout out the locations. I really want to focus and work on these other leads some more."

LJ frowned at her quickly, eyebrows pinching together. "What?"

Coby waved a hand at her notepad where she had been scratching notes. "These fairy tales that stuck out to me... 'The Princess and the Pea', 'Snow White and Rose Red', 'The Wolf and the Seven Little Kids'."

"Since when don't you want to go find a body?" LJ asked incredulously.

"I really think I'm onto something, and I want to keep going."

"Coby, you have to come, I don't know what to tell them. These are all your ideas!" LJ sputtered, raising her hands helplessly.

"We have been over all my ideas together about six times. You can call me if you hit a wall and I'll give you all my notes." Coby said with an eye roll, closing her notepad and shuffling her books together.

"Coby, is this about Clyde?"

Coby paused for a moment and went quiet. "I just really want to follow these leads. I'm on a roll."

LJ watched her for a few moments before shrugging. "Okay, fine. Let's just go get some sleep. And food. Food first."

Coby glanced up and gave her a half smile. "Okay," she said, and closed her laptop with force, stuffing it in its bag and throwing it over her shoulder. She was beginning to realize how much she had been looking forward to seeing Clyde the last few days. And she kind of hated that she liked him so much. It made her feel like a stupid girl with a head full of fairy tales. Which, she guessed, she kind of was. Not that they were exactly the romantic kind, but still.

LJ scooped up her own laptop and the case files before raising her eyebrows at Coby. "Shall we?" she asked, starting towards the stairs.

Coby followed after her, running her thumb over the tattered edges of "Arabian Nights." She could have sworn Clyde Burkiss liked her back. In fact, there was a part of her that was still convinced. She snorted. It was sad really, she understood the mind of a serial killer better than she understood most men.

***

Coby rolled over and turned off the alarm as it sounded angrily at seven the next morning.

LJ let out a groan from the bed, before sitting up and looking around the room with puffy eyes. "What day is it?"

Coby rubbed her eyes and flopped back against the pillow. "It's seven."

"That's great. I asked what *day* it was."

"Oh. It's Tuesday. I think. Yeah. I'm pretty sure."

LJ squinted at her. "Wasn't it Tuesday yesterday?"

Coby let out a groan and grabbed her phone to check the date. "Well if it was, then today's Tuesday, too."

LJ let out a sigh. "I can't believe you're making me do this."

Coby hoisted herself up into a sitting position and looked over at her with a confused face. "Do what?"

"Go with the guys by myself."

"Oh, pfft." Coby flopped back on the bed again.

"Don't you pfft *me*, you jerk." LJ threw one of her pillows at Coby's face.

"Uhhh," Coby complained as the pillow collided with her head. "I'm getting dressed," she said with resolve, launching out of bed and stumbling over to her suitcase, ripping out a new shirt and some jeans before padding over to the bathroom.

LJ glared at the door before letting out a huffy breath and laying out her own clothes.

"You can take the car," Coby said from the bathroom. "'I'll just walk if I need to go somewhere."

LJ shook her head. "No, I'm just going to walk. I'm sure I'll ride with the guys once I get there anyway."

"Okay!" Coby called from the bathroom and the shower turned on.

LJ chewed on her lip, wishing there was a coffee pot in the room. This was going to be a long day.

Chapter Forty-Five

LJ sat in the back of the police cruiser stiffly, hoping her annoyance was hidden behind her aviators but guessing it wasn't due to the amusement literally twinkling in Grizzly's eye in the rear view mirror. This was why she'd wanted Coby to come along. If Coby was there it only made sense to split up into two cruisers and have empty backseats. But Coby, of course wanted to continue the research side of this gig while she made LJ do the fieldwork.

Because forcing LJ into situations where she had to sit in the back of a cop car and put up with Grizzly's obvious glee and Clyde's awkward tension brought Coby's dark soul joy.

LJ stared out at the passing countryside. She had a sneaking suspicion that the real reason Coby had opted out of body hunting had everything to do with Clyde, but she wasn't going to press the matter.

"You okay back there? Too hot? Too cold?" Grizzly was much too chipper.

"I'm good, thanks." LJ stared at him in the mirror, hoping her sunglasses made it unclear where she was looking. She reached into her computer bag and pulled out the list of places Coby had given her. It was organized by location, starting with the nearest ones that Coby thought were the most likely. LJ had been adamant that they get the sewage plant out of the way before anything else, and they'd come up empty handed.

Waupun Waste Water Treatment Facility was next on their list. LJ had no idea how close it was. It was likely down the block, but sitting in the back of a cop car made it feel like the drive would never end.

She pulled out her phone and opened a new message to Coby. *I'm riding around like a criminal. I hope you're happy.*

"This is it, Sunshine," Grizzly boomed as they pulled into the driveway. "We're going to let you out now."

LJ refused to react and confirm his sarcasm. She adjusted her sunglasses and waited for the car to come to a stop so Grizzly could let her out.

Clyde got out next to her and squinted at the building before them. He was quiet. Well, who was she kidding, he was always quiet, but it seemed like more than usual. Grizzly stretched and meandered towards the back of the car. "Well, I suppose. Here's hoping Coby's on the right track."

"I'm sure she is," LJ said, more because she was annoyed with them than because she was actually confident in Coby's theory.

As Grizzly took the lead, LJ and Clyde filed in after him.

The entryway held little more than a doormat and an unoccupied metal receptionist desk. Papers and an ancient telephone cluttered the desktop. Pools of water samples were spread throughout the small room, and a door opposite the hallway was labeled "caution" with a biohazard symbol.

Grizzly leaned down the hall. "Hello? Waupun Police Department… we called…"

LJ looked at Clyde. "We did?"

Clyde shrugged.

"Yeah, yeah, I'm coming," a voice filtered from somewhere down the hall. A man in a navy blue polo appeared, carrying a clipboard and wearing a disgruntled expression. "Now what in the hell – Greg?" The man's face split into a grin. "Holy shit, man!"

"Hey, Nick." Grizzly grasped the man's hand and clapped him on the shoulder. "How've you been?"

"Pretty good! Yourself?" Nick set his clipboard on the desk and crossed his arms. "What can I do for you?"

"Well, we're working a possible angle for a case. It'd be great if we could take a look around."

Nick scowled. "Whoa, wait. What? You going after one of my guys?"

"No! Well, I mean… we're following a lead." Grizzly shrugged. "I can't give a lot of details, but as of right now we don't suspect any of your employees."

Nick looked over at Clyde and LJ, then back to Grizzly. "She a detective? You got the Feds in on this or something?"

LJ suppressed a smirk and kept a straight face.

Grizzly sighed and shook his head. "Not yet. Nick, we just need to look around a bit."

Nick hesitated, but then motioned down the hall. "'Course. I don't know what you think you're gonna find…"

Grizzly followed him, Clyde close behind him and LJ taking up the rear. "Not gonna lie to you, Nick. I don't know either."

***

Coby drummed her fingers against the back of the book cover she was reading and glanced over at her cell phone as it lit up with a text from LJ. Coby read it but didn't bother to respond. LJ would call if she needed something important. Coby needed to stop thinking about what everyone else was doing and focus on the fairy tales she was supposed to be studying.

She let out a breath, tucked her hair behind her ear and turned her attention back to the stories. She wasn't getting anywhere just re-reading. It was time to start listing facts and details from the stories and start thinking like a murderer. Such a lovely way to spend the day.

She pushed the books to the side, grabbed her notebook and flipped it open to a new page. She froze.

There on the page, written in a black, tight, cursive script. *"What once gets into their hands, and in their caves, does not easily see daylight again."*

It wasn't her handwriting. It wasn't LJ's handwriting. She felt her stomach drop and bile crawl up the back of her throat as something clicked into place and fear gripped her. She reached for her phone, fumbling with it as she tried to bring up LJ's number.

***

The silence was the most frustrating thing.

LJ wouldn't have even cared about not finding anything if one of them had just had enough nerve to voice the opinion that Coby could have been wrong again.

She sighed, propping a hand on her hip as she stared into another empty water barrel. She shouldn't be discouraged already. They were only at the second location on Coby's list.

"So… why are you looking through empty barrels?" Nick piped up from the doorway. He'd let them be for a good hour, checking in on them once in a while but never interrupting.

"It's a case we're working on." Grizzly stacked a barrel on top of another empty one. "And the *why* doesn't concern you."

Clyde knocked on the lid of one, looking bored at the echo it produced. "Did we look through all the storage areas?"

Nick scratched his head. "There are two more down in the basement, and we've got the waste management spaces, too."

LJ grimaced and sincerely hoped they either lost interest or found bodies before they got to that part of the building.

"Well, I think that does it for this one," Grizzly stated and looked at Nick. "Where to?"

Nick showed them to the next room, quickly making an exit with a shake of his head. LJ glared after him enviously.

Clyde took the lead this time, coming up with a system and actually bossing Grizzly and LJ around. All three of them each got a section to work through, and LJ immediately felt the difference. They made progress in half the time it had taken them to go through the previous storage room. LJ's head was starting to hurt from all the noise they were making, knocking on the facility's endless supply of blue barrels.

She reached the last corner, and a sense of excitement at the prospect of being finished took over as she counted eight barrels left to check. Two barrels in, the hollow echo she was expecting came as a dull thunk instead.

"Whoa, that was different." Grizzly was crossing the room in an instant.

LJ stared at the barrel with wide eyes, confused and suddenly terrified of what might be inside.

"You got something?" Clyde sounded hopeful, but wary.

Grizzly knocked on the barrel for himself. The same sound, short and dim, came again. "We just might." He started to pry the lid off.

LJ backed away, fighting the urge to cover her eyes as memories of digging in the dark of night flashed to mind.

The lid clattered to the floor and an undeniable stench filled the room.

All four of them were there. Kate McCurry and her three partners in crime.

Forensics couldn't confirm identities on scene, but LJ had little doubt. The CSU team identified four young female bodies, completely submerged and mostly decomposed in some kind of oil. Cause of death was yet to be determined.

LJ knew. The fairy tale said the thieves had died when boiling oil was poured on them. Coby had been right again.

She pulled out her phone, hitting Coby's icon and watching the call connect. She listened to the voicemail message and waited for the beep. "Hey, me again. You should probably call me back. We've definitely got something big here, Coby." She hung up and shook her head. Typical, that Coby would have her phone off at a time like this.

"Get a hold of her yet?" Grizzly was suddenly behind her.

She flinched and turned to look at him. "No." She exhaled. "She's probably got the phone on silent while she's reading or she's just ignoring me because –" LJ cut herself off and slid the phone in her pocket. The last thing she wanted to do was try to explain Coby's situation with Clyde.

"Because of Clyde." Grizzly crossed his arms and nodded.

LJ looked at him. If anyone was going to be able to give her a new perspective on this dilemma, it was Grizzly. But he was also the person she wanted to discuss it with least. She refused to think about why.

"Are we finished here?" LJ nodded toward where the forensics team was securing the last barrel on a cart to be wheeled outside to their van.

That familiar look of exhaustion washed over Grizzly's face. "Yeah. We've got some reports to fill out, then I'll give you a ride back to your motel." He whistled to get Clyde's attention, then waved toward the door.

Clyde was stressed, but not too stressed to give Grizzly an annoyed look before heading to them.

LJ got into the back of the cruiser without so much as a huff this time, though she was still grumbling in the back of her mind. Mostly about Coby leaving the grunt work to her, while she sat around reading stories.

Chapter Forty-Six

Thump, Thump, Thump.

Her head hit against his chest with each step.

He'd have to change his shirt.

He walked down the steps with her, into the back room, and laid her down on the concrete floor, the side of her head bleeding, but not terribly. He had made sure to only render her unconscious. He stepped away and examined the blood she had left on his fingertips before licking them off.

She looked so much smaller down here in the dark, asleep on the floor, red mixing into her blonde hair.

He smiled. He'd come back for her soon. Turning on his heel, he ran back up the stairs, locking the door at the top behind him.

He pulled off his shirt and tossed it into the tub as he passed the bathroom. He'd bleach that later.

He tugged on another shirt and buttoned it quickly as he tracked down his keys and headed back out to his car. It was getting later and he had to be careful. He ran a hand through his hair and glanced at the house in his rearview mirror.

She'd be there when he got back. And he had to keep working on the story.

He pulled up on the street that ran by the motel and got out, twirling the key he had taken from her around his finger. He walked up to their room with an easy confidence and rapped on the door, pausing and listening for LJ. Then he unlocked the door and entered the room. He looked around and felt a strong sense of calm fill him.

He closed his eyes and inhaled as inspiration and clarity hit him. It was all coming together just as he hoped. He was almost disappointed by how easy it was.

He reached into his shirt pocket, pulled out the typed note, then looked around the room again. He walked gingerly over to one of the beds, passing a hand over the pillow before reconsidering and walking into the bathroom. He spent some time in there, thinking... trying to visualize her night time routine. He shook his head and walked back out by the beds, grabbed a couple of books and flipped through them before putting them back exactly as he had found them.

He frowned, frustrated, until his eyes settled on a laptop case. It was LJ's. Quickly striding towards it, he opened it up and slid the laptop out. He examined it and smiled. He opened it and slid the note inside, then closed it and slid it back into the bag, careful to reposition the strap as it had been before.

He looked around the room one more time and nodded to himself before exiting and heading back to his car. He had to get back. She was waiting for him.

***

Grizzly sighed and tapped his pen on his desk. He could always tell when he'd been awake for too long. Aside from the pounding in his head and the tugging at his eyelids, there was an extra level of paranoia. Even when he was alone in his own home he jumped at shadows and checked under the bed.

Dealing with dark cases always added to both the paranoia and fatigue. But factoring LJ into the equation somehow made everything worse.

He bounced his knee the entire time he wrote his report of the crime scene. He was unable to think of anything but dropping LJ off at her creepy motel room later. He kept shooting glances her way as he tried to come up with an idea that would convince her and Coby to move to a better hotel. An idea that would make him sound like a concerned police officer and not an overprotective mother.

Twenty minutes later, he still came up empty, and now he was halfway to the motel with LJ in the passenger seat.

"Are you sure you don't want me to put you guys up in the Boarders Inn?" Grizzly finally said, a touch of weight lifting off his shoulders just for saying the words.

It was dimly lit in the car, but he spotted her wrinkling her nose. "No. We're fine at this place, really."

"We could split the difference in price."

"No, Chief, it's okay." She yawned. "It's not as bad as it looks, I promise."

Unease settled back in his gut as he pulled into the motel parking lot. He parked next to the Chevelle, leaning forward to inspect the motel room window. "Is Coby here?"

LJ grabbed her bag and reached for the door handle. "Ha, no. Coby would have every light on in the place if she was here, even if she was asleep. She's probably..." She looked at the clock on the dashboard. "Maybe at the coffee shop, if they're still open. Anywhere where the WiFi is better than this place."

Grizzly climbed out of the car even though LJ only had to walk five feet to get inside the room. "Hey... you've got me on speed dial, right?"

LJ slammed the passenger door and raised an eyebrow at him over the roof of the car. "Speed dial? What is this, 2001?"

"You know what I mean." He rolled his eyes.

She smirked and pulled her phone out of her pocket. The screen lit up her face as she squinted down at it, then turned it around to show him. "Recent calls, top of the list. Two taps and I'm calling you. Satisfied?"

Not even close. "Yeah. You guys need anything, don't hesitate."

LJ nodded, eyes tired but smile genuine. "Have a good night, Grizzly."

"Sweet dreams." He grinned. He waited until she closed the motel room door and he heard the deadbolt slide into place before he got back in his cruiser, knowing his own dreams would be anything but sweet.

Chapter Forty-Seven

Coby's eyes fluttered open and the pounding headache was quickly shoved to the side as the confusion flooded in. What had happened? Where was she?

She struggled to sit up, but was having trouble finding her center of gravity. Her head swam and she strained her eyes, trying to see through the darkness. She touched her scalp and winced at the pain it caused and the wetness now on her hand. She was bleeding. Bracing herself and closing her eyes, she tried to calm her breathing and heartbeat, pushing back against the panic and anxiety rising in her.

How did she get here? She tried to remember, pushing through the fog that felt like a lot heavier than what a simple bump on the head would cause. Had she been drugged? What was the last thing that happened to her? She had been reading, researching the stories... the note. She had tried to call LJ, and that was the last thing she remembered.

Coby's eyes snapped open and she looked around the dark room once again, trying to shuffle to her feet without falling over or making too much noise. She felt like she was going to throw up. She stumbled backwards until her back hit a cement wall. She leaned against it and tried to catch her breath.

She vowed this was one fairy tale he wasn't going to rewrite. She knew something all the other girls didn't. She knew what she was dealing with. True, she didn't know where she was, but she was going to find out and then she was going to *get* out. She just needed the room to stop spinning first.

When she was confident she wasn't going to pass out, she took a step forward and then another, aiming for the metal shelf she made out alongside the other wall. She frowned as she approached it, squinting at the dusty jars and boxes on it. She reached for a jar and wiped the dust off of it with the corner of her sleeve. She launched herself backwards, smothering a yell as it tried to claw its way out of her throat. The jar held an unborn baby, suspended in a yellowish liquid. Her vision swam and she tripped over her own feet and hit the ground. Darkness crept at the corners as she fought to stay awake.

Then she heard the car pull up.

***

LJ rolled over and flailed a hand at her phone alarm until it quieted. Rain sounded on the roof. Light filtered its way through the threadbare curtains across the room, and LJ threw the ancient comforter off her legs with a groan. She stretched and turned to look over at Coby's bed.

LJ sat up and squinted through the dim light. She hoped the lingering sleepiness was playing tricks on her eyes.

Coby's bed was empty. It was still made from the day before.

Nervousness rose in LJ's stomach. She flitted around the motel room and grabbed her shower bag, clean clothes and the belt off of yesterday's jeans before tearing into the bathroom. Skipping the shower, she dressed in a rush and tore a brush through her hair. She debated about brushing her teeth, but one moment spent analyzing the taste in her mouth and she reached for the toothpaste.

She went back to the nightstand for her phone while she brushed. The screen boldly stated that she had zero new messages and no missed calls. She called Coby's number as she went back to the sink to spit, but the call went to voicemail.

"Coby. Call me."

LJ gave her reflection an eye roll before giving up and grabbing things she needed in her bag. Maybe Coby had ended up at the police station and worked all night with Clyde. Maybe that's what they needed to get past their differences from the other day. Maybe Coby had gotten up super early and made her bed again and gone back at it before LJ woke up. Maybe LJ was nervous for no reason and she'd drive up to the station to find Grizzly passing out doughnuts and Coby going on about some new fairy tale.

LJ reached for her laptop bag and slid one of her interview notebooks inside. A piece of paper poked out of her computer. She pulled it free, and scanned the typewritten note.

"What once gets into their hands, and in their caves, does not easily see daylight again."

LJ's stomach flipped over. She gripped the page with sweaty hands and snatched at her keys, leaving everything else she'd needed strewn across the bed.

***

LJ's hands shook. She tried to scroll through her phone to try Coby again, but her fingers wouldn't work.

She dropped it in her lap and accelerated onto Main Street without checking for traffic.

She careened into the police department parking lot, sloshing through the rain on the pavement. She ripped the keys out of the ignition and ran for the door, drenched by the downpour despite her quick pace.

"Grizz? Grizzly!" She thundered through the station, feet squelching in her shoes. Random uniformed officers glanced at her confusedly as she passed them. One of them stood and grabbed her by the arm, and she nearly knocked him over backwards trying to get away.

"LJ, what's wrong?"

Panic made her take a minute to recognize him. "Clyde. She's gone." Her voice wavered and she nearly stomped her foot in frustration.

"What?"

"I need to talk to Grizzly. Where is he?" LJ turned toward Grizzly's office.

Clyde grabbed her again. "Coby? Coby's missing?"

"Not just missing, Clyde, she's *gone.* He *took* her." She wiped rainwater from her forehead. "I should have known. I got back to the motel and I didn't even realize. She was gone all night. Maybe all of yesterday, and I didn't even know." She threw open Grizzly's office door with Clyde hot on her heels.

"LJ?" Grizzly pushed his chair back from his desk and stood.

"He's got her," LJ choked on the words, pressing her hands against her head with desperation. "She's gone – she never came back last night. I found this this morning." LJ groped at her back pocket and pulled out the paper she'd found in her laptop, shoving it at Grizzly.

"I was making excuses for her, assuming she got up early or stayed here… who knows how long she's actually been gone. She could be dead already." She gasped and bent at the waist, palms landing on her knees with a clap.

"Whoa, okay, okay." Grizzly rounded the desk and put a hand on her shoulder. "Sit down." He motioned at Clyde, who was already pulling up the extra chair from against the wall. He settled her in the chair and crouched in front of her, inspecting the note.

LJ took a deep breath. "I didn't talk to her all day yesterday. I don't even know where she went." Her eyes welled up. Water dripped down the back of her shirt from her sopping ponytail. She reached out and grasped Grizzly's hand without thinking twice.

Grizzly looked back at her with somber eyes and squeezed her fingers. He reached up and handed the note to Clyde. "We don't know what this means –"

"It *means* we got too close to these cases and he *knows*," LJ's voice quivered.

"You tried her cell?"

"Straight to voicemail." LJ tried to get a grip and not sound like she was wailing. "Since *yesterday,* Grizzly!"

"Okay, okay, that is not your fault." He got to his feet and looked at Clyde. "Send CSU to the motel. Get somebody tracking the phone. I want security camera feed pronto. LJ," he paused and looked back at her. "Where do you think she went?"

LJ shook her head, following Grizzly's lead and standing. "I guess I figured she'd go to the library. We've been there a lot lately for research. Otherwise we've been here or the motel…" She wracked her brain. "Maybe the coffee shop like I said last night?"

Grizzly nodded and glanced at Clyde. The smaller man had paled considerably and LJ wondered if he was okay to take on any of the orders Grizzly had just given him, but he turned on his heel and strode out of the office with purpose.

"I wanted her to come with us. I didn't want to go without her..." LJ trailed off and wiped at her eyes.

"Hey, it's not your fault," Grizzly repeated. He pulled her into a hug without hesitation. "We'll figure out what happened. We'll get her back."

LJ fought to keep herself together with her face pressed into Grizzly's massive shoulder. His badge dug into her cheek but she didn't care. She swallowed hard as he released her and looked her over before moving away. "I'm coming with you," she blurted out. She stared at him, wondering if she was allowed to go with him, even if he did want her tagging along.

"Of course." He grabbed his keys off his desk and moved for the door. LJ followed.

***

Grizzly placed a hand on LJ's shoulder before striding over and pointing at an officer who had just entered the room. "I need a trace on this number right now," he shot at him, slapping a post it note with Coby's number on his desk.

He glanced back at LJ who sat in one of the chairs, looking like she was fighting hyperventilation. His heart twisted and rage filled him. Coby and LJ were their girls, and this had gotten far more personal than he had ever expected.

He glanced back at the officer as he walked towards LJ. "Make it happen," he demanded before crouching down in front of LJ again. "Okay darlin', we're going to need you to help us. What was Coby working on yesterday? Do you know where she was planning on going?"

"No!" LJ said, frustrated. "I only know what I said before, that she was going to do some more research – that she had a few new fairy tales she wanted to look into."

Grizzly frowned and nodded. "Well, then let's start at the library and go from there. Clyde's at the motel right now, and they'll go over everything."

LJ swallowed and nodded, standing shakily. "Let's go."

Grizzly drove to the library in silence. LJ looked like she was going to puke at any second, her color ashen and her face stony. He wanted to comfort her but he didn't know what to say. The only thing he could do right now was find her best friend.

They pulled into the parking lot. LJ jumped out of the car and stormed toward the door before Grizzly could pull the keys out of the ignition. He swore under his breath and launched himself after her.

"*Neal*!" LJ bellowed as she stomped towards the empty desk.

The librarian popped up from behind the desk, looking confused. "May I help you?" he asked LJ, looking put off by her attitude.

Grizzly cleared his throat and stepped up next to LJ. He wanted to get control of the situation before LJ decapitated someone. "Neal, this is important. I need to ask you some questions."

"What's wrong, Chief?" Neal asked, looking mildly concerned at their expressions.

"Coby Anderson. Has she been in here today?"

A look of horror passed over Neal's face. "Did something happen to Coby?"

Grizzly's face slammed into a frown. "What do you know about this, Neal?"

"The same as everyone else – that she's been researching the murders. She comes in here and reads over fairy tales all the time. What happened?" Neal asked.

"Nothing, we hope. We just need to get ahold of her with some information." Grizzly said calmly. He could see LJ watching him out of the corner of his eye. "You let us know if you see her or hear from her at all, okay?" Grizzly asked.

Neal nodded. "Of course," he said still frowning. "And hey, let me know if you find her okay?"

Grizzly nodded. "Absolutely," he said as he put an arm around LJ's shoulder. She looked like she was going to cry. "It's okay, darlin'," he murmured. His phone rang and he dug it out of his pocket. "What did you find?"

"Chief, we got a location on the cell phone..." the voice said, sounding wary.

"That's great, where is it?" Grizzly asked, frustrated with the hesitation on the other end of the line.

"Well –"

Chapter Forty-Eight

Clyde wanted LJ to be wrong.

He wanted to get to the motel to find Coby in the room, books spread out on every flat surface, scowling behind her glasses as she studied her computer screen. He wanted her to look up in irritated confusion when he threw the door open, and he wanted to stutter through an apology that made him flush and sweat.

But the motel room was empty. Clyde dug through the cruiser for latex gloves as he dialed Coby's number and held the phone to his ear with his shoulder. She didn't answer.

"Damn it." He hung up and tossed the phone into the passenger seat, then climbed back in for it in case she tried to get a hold of him.

The forensics team was thirty minutes out, and Clyde wasn't going to wait for them. He started on what he presumed to be Coby's side of the room – the bed was made, but everything else was in disarray. LJ's side was the opposite – the covers were thrown back, but there wasn't anything cluttering the bed, nightstand, or floor, aside from a duffel bag at the foot of the bed.

He stared at the piles of library books and stacks of case files, not knowing where to begin. He strode towards the nightstand, looking for a cell phone, a notepad, anything that might give him a clue of her thoughts or where she was headed.

"That's my job!"

His last words to Coby played like a skipping record in his mind. The look on her face when she stepped back and walked away from him was impossible to stop thinking about. He threw a spiral bound notebook onto the bedspread and ran both hands over his face. One look around the room would tell anyone that Coby hadn't been taken from here. That realization brought him further frustration.

A knock sounded at the door, and Clyde flinched, confused for a split second before the door swung open and the Crime Scene Unit began to file through. The team leader gave him a nod. "Officer."

Clyde sighed, letting go of the brief flicker of hope that it could have been Coby coming back to the motel. "Not sure if we have anything here. She wasn't taken from here, that's obvious. Estimated time of disappearance is… twenty to twenty four hours ago." He motioned hopelessly around the room. "Anything you come up with could be helpful."

"We'll do what we can." The man joined the other team members and reached for the nearest stack of books.

Clyde felt uncomfortable with them going through Coby's things, even though he knew it was necessary. He waited around for a couple of minutes, but couldn't stand it any longer and stepped outside. His phone buzzed in his pocket and he scrambled for it, disappointed when he recognized the number as Grizzly's. "Got anything?"

"Maybe, maybe not." Grizzly sounded guarded. "Meet us at your place."

Clyde scowled. "My house? Why?"

"Just do it, Burkiss." Grizzly hung up.

Clyde stared at the phone screen as it went black. The scowl deepened as he reached for his car door.

***

He got in his car and drove quickly back to his place. The drugs should be wearing off by now, he only hoped her head injury had kept her out. Not that he was that concerned. She had no way of escape, no way of calling for help.

She could just wait for him to finish dealing with everyone. She'd probably have fun looking around all his treasure. It was what she liked to do best, after all. This strange girl knew him better than anyone. It was flattering. He never had anyone appreciate his work before. She understood him. She understood everything about him.

He chewed on his lip and drummed his fingers on the wheel in anticipation. He could still smell her on himself. He couldn't wait to get back to writing.

**

Shaun Pritchard pulled up to Burkiss's address, unsure of what to expect. Adams had said little besides "All available units to 498 Woodland Drive." Pritchard drove there accordingly, recognizing it as Clyde's house. Grizzly's cruiser was parked closest to the garage, and Pritchard wondered if that meant Burkiss was there too.

He parked on the street and headed for the front door, but the driver door of Grizzly's car opened and he stepped out. "Officer Pritchard, we're waiting for Burkiss."

"What are we doing here, Chief?" Pritchard asked, though he felt he already knew.

Grizzly clamped his mouth shut and crossed his arms, leaning back against his car. Pritchard caught movement inside the car and realized LJ was in the passenger seat. "Coby Anderson is missing."

"And you think she's here?"

Grizzly didn't answer.

Another cruiser pulled up behind Grizzly's and Clyde climbed out. LJ climbed out of Grizzly's car.

Clyde glanced over at Pritchard as he approached the group, eyes landing on Grizzly. "What's going on?"

Pritchard looked to Grizzly as well, hoping his answer would be what Pritchard was waiting for.

"We tracked Coby's phone."

Clyde's brow furrowed and he continued to stare at Grizzly, waiting for an actual explanation.

"Here. We tracked her phone here."

Surprise washed over Clyde's face. "What? Is she here?" He took a step toward the door.

LJ was suddenly in front of him. "What did you do?"

Clyde looked down at her, confused. "What?"

"Don't 'what' me." She shoved him in the chest. "Where is she? What did you *do?*" Clyde took a step backwards, confusion evident as he turned to the chief. Pritchard watched in wonder. It was better than he could have even planned.

Grizzly stepped forward and caught LJ firmly by the elbow, pulling her away from Clyde. "LJ," the large man murmured.

Clyde was gaping at her. "You think – you think, *I* kidnapped Coby?" he asked, voice hoarse. "You think I'd hurt her? That I'm a *serial killer?*" The look he gave the chief was too hurt to be angry.

"Clyde, of course we don't –" Grizzly began quickly but LJ interrupted him.

"Her phone is *here* Burkiss, at your *house*, how do you explain that?" Panic and hatred were evident on LJ's face as she shook her head and tried to pull away from Grizzly. "She trusted you, she *liked* you –"

"I did *not* take Coby! Search the house, search everything, I don't care, but we're wasting time! We need to *find* her!" Clyde shouted back at her.

Pritchard moved forward and grabbed his wrist. "Hands behind your back, Officer Burkiss."

"Pritchard, stand down," Grizzly growled as more units arrived, officers stepping out of their cars and surveying the scene in front of them cautiously.

Pritchard stared at him wide-eyed. "You're actually going to let your favoritism get in the way of a time-sensitive missing persons case? You can't –"

"Shaun, we don't have any actual evidence and you know that." Grizzly leveled his gaze at him, voice low. "We search the house first. We find anything questionable, you can slap the cuffs on him. We don't, and you calm the hell down." He cocked an eyebrow. "Got it?"

Pritchard clenched his teeth and forced himself to let go of Burkiss. Clyde stepped away from the trio and went for his front door.

"Search everything. If she was here, I'd want to find her." Clyde tripped on the front step as he fumbled with his house keys.

Grizzly was close behind him. LJ seemed to be attached to the chief's hip. Pritchard seethed as he watched a few other officers file inside, and he heard Grizzly begin to inform them of the situation. He wanted to strangle Clyde. No, he wanted to strangle Grizzly with Clyde's body.

Pritchard took a deep breath. It was fine. He still got to look forward to tearing through Burkiss's home, and that was happening whether they found incriminating evidence or not.

Which they would find. Pritchard was sure.

Chapter Forty-Nine

It was like a roller coaster. One second, LJ was livid. The next, she was scared. Then she turned around and was hopelessly optimistic. It was so exhausting that she'd started to think of exhaustion as an emotion all in itself.

The officers searched Clyde's house, but Clyde and LJ weren't allowed to participate. They sat in the living room with upturned couch cushions and displaced magazines in tense silence. LJ wanted to scream at him some more, but as time went on she became more and more certain that Coby wasn't tied up in his basement.

Grizzly appeared after what seemed like days. LJ checked her phone – no missed calls – and saw that it had only been about an hour since he'd told them both to stay put.

Clyde launched to his feet. "Anything?"

Grizzly shook his head. "We got the phone, that's all. Not that I thought we were gonna find anything, Burkiss. I didn't expect that for a second."

"I don't give a damn about –"

"We found the phone in the backyard," Grizzly interrupted. He clapped Clyde on the shoulder. "I know you don't give a damn, but you'rc off the hook. It wasn't inside the house. They found it on the back deck, where anybody could have put it."

LJ's stomach sank. If she'd been thinking rationally, she probably never would have suspected Clyde. But if Coby wasn't in the house, then that meant she was still missing. LJ blinked back the tears that pricked at her eyes.

"Get it analyzed for prints. Check the GPS on it, see where it was before someone brought it here," Clyde ordered.

Grizzly squeezed Clyde's shoulder. "We're on it." He looked at LJ. "How you doing, darlin'?"

LJ dropped her gaze and clenched her teeth so hard her ears popped, but she kept herself from bursting into tears. "What's next?"

Grizzly took a deep breath and straightened. "Well I guess we should go get some food... maybe grab what you need from the motel?"

Clyde looked over at her sharply. "You're not staying there," he said before taking a few steps away.

LJ blinked at him, annoyed that he told her what to do but also weirdly touched. No way was she staying there anyway. She got to her feet. "But what's next for finding Coby?"

Grizzly sighed. "What Clyde said. And I'm sure CSU will be bringing her stuff back to the police department. We should probably go through what she was reading, see if we can find out where she might have been last." He pointed at her. "We're going to need your help with that."

LJ nodded. "Right. She mentioned... 'The Princess and the Pea', I think. And some other ones, but I don't remember."

"That's fine. We'll figure it out once we get her notes." Grizzly's tone was pacifying. It bordered on condescending.

LJ's temper flared. "Don't patronize me. We can't take our time with this."

Grizzly frowned gently. "LJ, I want to find her. We will go as fast as we can. I'm on your side." He watched her carefully.

LJ almost felt bad for snapping at him, but frustration was all she could feel.

"LJ, I need you to think of everyone you've interacted with since you came to Waupun." Clyde turned to her, eyes intense and determined. "Anyone who could have seen her, talked to her, known where she would be. Anyone who could have been watching."

LJ's mind went blank. She tried to remember interviews with locals, but couldn't remember anything prior to that morning. "Um… you guys…"

"Auto mechanic," Grizzly mentioned. Clyde whipped a notepad out of his pocket and started writing.

"Um, the guy who owns the motel… I interviewed some restaurant owners with Coby… There was that pastor of the church outside of town… Farnell, I think his name was?" LJ heard the words she was speaking but wasn't entirely sure where they were coming from. "Neal, of course. And the only other person I can think of right now is the mechanic, like Grizzly said."

Grizzly raised an eyebrow at Clyde, looking like he was about to say something, but Clyde beat him to it. "I'll track these people down, feel them out, see if any of them have anything helpful." He rubbed the back of his head. "If it's a dead end, I'll track her movements."

Grizzly nodded. "We'll go back to the station and go through her notes. I'll call you if we find anything, or if LJ remembers something new." Clyde gave them a short nod of dismissal and started for the door, but Grizzly grabbed his arm. "Dude, keep your nose clean.

The shit's already hit the fan, let's try to keep from swimming in the stuff."

LJ screwed her eyebrows together. They were already swimming in it. She led the way out of Clyde's house. They didn't have time for worrying about Clyde or analyzing their next moves. They just needed to get in gear and find Coby.

      ***

The door closed.

Footsteps.

Coby leapt backwards away from the shelving unit. She positioned herself in the middle of the room and squared her shoulders, lifting her chin. She took deep breaths and tried not to panic.

The door at the top of the stairs opened and she could hear him descending, the soft padding of feet on carpet as he approached the room. Coby forced herself not to give in to the urge to make a run for it.

The lights flickered on, illuminating the space she had been occupying. She squinted, willing her eyes to adjust quickly. More footsteps.

She felt her heart hammering in every inch of her body, adrenaline coursing through her.

The door creaked open and his body filled the frame as he slowed to a stop and he locked eyes with her. She felt like she was going to puke.

Of course. *Of course*. Stupid, stupid, stupid.

Coby swallowed, shock and disgust filling her core as she tried to find something to say. "Y-you –" she stuttered.

"Hello darling." He smiled at her, his eyes taking in the blood on her forehead before trailing over her body. She winced, wondering how many times he had looked at her that way before.

He stepped down the last few steps and she watched him, ready to run, kick, claw, bite or whatever she could should he get too close.

"How's your head?" he asked, raising a hand and she launched herself away, eyeing him warily. He blinked at her and then gave her a condescending look. "Now, now, come on, Coby. You know I won't hurt you."

Coby tried to calm the panic and rage that were battling inside of her and find her voice again. "No, not yet. The story isn't finished," she said, watching his reaction closely.

His eyes lit up, delighted. "That's right," he said.

Coby swallowed and raised her chin at him. "What makes you think you'll be able to?"

He raised an eyebrow at her, folding his arms. "To what?"

"Finish the story." Coby narrowed her eyes at him.

He chuckled. "Oh Coby… you know as well as I do, I haven't failed yet."

"You never had anyone onto you before," she said flatly.

"This is true, but here you are darling. Do you really think those idiots will be able to stop me by themselves? They don't understand me like you do." He circled halfway around her, going over to the shelf and examining the contents of it fondly, before turning back to her.

"LJ knew. She knew what you were doing before I did," Coby shot back at him, feeling her lip curling in a snarl. "She'll figure it out."

"Oh, I do hope so." He grinned and Coby felt her stomach sink.

Chapter Fifty

Clyde stared at the motel room door. It was literally just a couple of days before that he'd seen Coby disappear safely inside, and now it seemed to have swallowed her whole.

He scanned the building, looking for security cameras. There was no reason to believe she'd been taken from the motel, but it was as good a place to start as any.

"Slow down, Burkiss," Pritchard said from the cruiser. He'd insisted, for whatever reason, on tagging along. Clyde glared at him, wishing he would go away. Pritchard had one foot on the ground, but the rest of him was still in the passenger seat, hovering over the computer on the dashboard. "This guy doesn't have a record."

"That doesn't mean shit," Clyde snapped. He stalked toward the door labeled "office," refusing to wait around while Pritchard tried to do a background check. Robert Van Camp was first on Clyde's list, and he hoped that if he interrogated the man he would point him in Coby's direction.

The bell on the door jingled when Clyde stepped inside, and he was immediately met with the smell of stale beer and a disgruntled expression, both exuding from the man behind the counter. "Is there something I can *help* you with, Officer?"

Clyde inspected the man. He looked like he'd have trouble lifting a newspaper and remembering his own name, and Clyde had a sinking feeling that Van Camp would not be the lead he'd hoped for. "Robert Van Camp?"

"What's it to you?"

"I'm Officer Burkiss. I'm investigating the disappearance of this woman." Clyde pulled up a picture of Coby on his phone, gut twisting at the sight of her. He handed it to Van Camp. "I'm sure you remember that she was staying here."

Van Camp squinted at the phone, then looked back at Clyde suspiciously. "You think I had something to do with it?"

Clyde snatched the phone back. "When was the last time you saw her?"

"How the hell should I know? You think I just sit around here all day, waitin' for pretty girls to check in so I can watch 'em, all Norman Bates-like?" Van Camp crossed his arms.

"You're not being accused of anything, Mr. Van Camp. But refusing to answer my questions would be highly suspicious and, I'm gonna be honest with you, sir, it's testing my patience and right now I'm running on a short fuse." Clyde gripped his belt. "Do you want to help me out, or do you want me to report that you're obstructing this investigation?"

Van Camp's jaw twitched. "How long are your guys gonna be tearing my place apart? I got a business to run."

"It'll take as long as it takes." Clyde stared him down.

"I saw her yesterday."

Clyde's heart sped up and he pulled the notepad out just in case. "Was she alone?"

Van Camp tapped his chin for a moment, then shrugged. "I guess. That dark-haired one left first."

"Where did she go?"

"Which one?"

Clyde grit his teeth. "*Coby*. The blonde one."

Another shrug. "I don't know. There's one way out of the parking lot, Officer. I didn't follow her to see where she went once she was off the property."

It felt like he got the wind knocked out of him. Clyde let out a tight breath he hadn't realized he'd been holding and shoved the notepad back in his pocket. "You think of anything else, you call me. Immediately. Day or night." He tossed a card onto the counter in front of Van Camp, then turned and stormed back outside.

Pritchard leaned against the fender, arms crossed, looking down his nose at Clyde. "What'd he say?"

Clyde didn't bother answering him. "Get in the car. Mechanic's next."

***

Grizzly came back from the break room, two coffees in hand. He set one down next to LJ and took a sip out of his own. There were books, and papers spread out everywhere, along with case files and both Coby and LJ's laptops. It was an overwhelming amount of information when he had no idea where to start. LJ picked up the coffee and glanced at him. "Thanks," she said quietly, opening Coby's laptop.

"I've been going through records, reading up on juvenile delinquents right before these things started happening. They say there are often signs… dead animals, stalker behavior, peeping toms, etc.…." he said over his shoulder as he walked into his office and brought out a pile of folders. "It's a lot to go through, but not impossible. I'm not sure it will get us anywhere but I figured it couldn't hurt." He shrugged and pulled out a chair across from her.

LJ nodded. "I'm going to go through anything dated recently in here and then start on the bookmarked portions of the books and her notebooks." She sighed and logged into Coby's laptop, looking like she was trying to steel herself for the hundredth time.

Grizzly flipped open a folder and browsed over it quickly. He knew he should probably be combing through them carefully but time was too much of the essence. He kept repeating the things he was looking for in his mind. Sexual based crimes, animal cruelty – animal... He looked up at LJ sharply. "You told me you found a dead bird?"

LJ glanced at him. "Yes!" she said. "There was other weird stuff too... these berries? There were berries all over our car. Coby thought it was just some weird kids pulling a prank."

Grizzly clenched his teeth, wishing the girls had informed him of this sooner. It might have been helpful. He watched LJ's face, watching his, and refused to make her feel worse than she already did by making mention of it. "And there were the flowers, right? More than once?"

"Well yeah," LJ said, looking confused. "But I thought Clyde –"

Grizzly shook his head quickly. "Clyde didn't send them."

LJ's eyes widened. "Did you?"

"No, we're both dumbasses." He smirked, then sobered again. "Is that stuff all in a fairy tale?"

"Well, I'm sure... but the problem is what fairy tale are they *not* in?" she asked helplessly, motioning at all the books. "Berries, flowers, animals... that's like the first five minutes of every Disney movie, right?"

Grizzly frowned, setting aside his folder and picking at the corner of one of Coby's books. "Was there anything else weird?"

LJ's forehead wrinkled in frustration and she raked her hands through her hair. "Uh, well, yes! Yes, the hair! There was this weird clump of hair in the car... up in the visor, after we got it back from the mechanic."

Grizzly straightened in his chair. "That's on Clyde's list. He'll be going there."

LJ nodded. "Good, good." She opened the most recent files on Coby's computer. She started flipping through pictures of the boardwalk, the windmill, the station, him and Clyde. Grizzly glanced away and down at his hands, guilt and responsibility flooding him. She was working for him, tracking a serial killer. He should have been more careful, protected her. He ran a hand over his face. His failures loomed, and he tried not to let them be all consuming. Not only had he been able to get nowhere on these cases, but the one advantage he had, the one person who helped him had been ripped right out from under his nose. He shook his head and reached for the next folder. Regret wasn't getting him any closer to finding her.

***

Pritchard watched Burkiss out of the corner of his eye. The man was a mess, and Pritchard was eating it up.

The whole thing was working out perfectly. As long as Burkiss kept up his psychotic burning at both ends, it would only be a matter of time before he had a complete meltdown. He'd probably take Adams down with him, or at least throw enough shade his way to cause a demotion, and Pritchard was going to make sure he was around to enjoy the show.

They got to the auto repair shop, and Clyde was out of the car before the engine was completely dead. Pritchard trailed him to the door this time. "You know, Burkiss, this guy doesn't have any priors either."

"You know, Pritchard, I'm getting real tired of your shit." Burkiss threw the door open. A bell jingled, and a muffled holler came from another room. Burkiss's phone sounded as Pritchard glanced around, and Clyde scrambled to answer the call. "Yeah."

A young, scruffy looking man opened the back door behind the office desk and stepped inside. "Hey, sorry, I – whoa. Did I do something wrong?"

"You Jimmy Washburn?" Pritchard raised a brow.
"Yeah..."

"We're looking for this woman." Pritchard pulled out his own phone as Burkiss turned back the way they'd come to focus on his call. "We understand you worked on her vehicle."

The man frowned at the picture on the screen. "Look, if this is some kind of lawsuit –"

"She's missing. When did you see her last?" Pritchard inspected the cluttered bulletin board behind the desk.

Jimmy shrugged, eyes wide and brow furrowed. "When she and the hot one picked up the Chevelle. Whenever that was."

Burkiss strode across the room and placed both palms on the desktop and leaned toward Jimmy. "We need to search the premises."

Pritchard raised an eyebrow and grabbed Clyde's arm. "Hey, you need a warrant for that."

"Whoa, whoa, whoa." Jimmy held both hands out in front of him. "You guys can look anywhere you want. I don't know what you think you're gonna find, but I've got nothing to hide." He reached for the back door and opened it, letting it swing wide into his shop.

Clyde moved to round the desk, but Pritchard caught him again. "What the hell?"

Jimmy stepped into the shop, but Pritchard didn't let Clyde follow. Burkiss threw Pritchard's hand off his shoulder and glared at him. "That was Grizzly on the phone. When the girls picked up the car, they found something planted in it. It could have been this guy, or it could have been someone else working here. We need to look around. Find out if he has security cameras."

Pritchard bristled. "You need to calm down."

"I need to find her," Clyde snapped. He glared for a second longer, then strode through the door to the shop.

Pritchard squinted after him, shaking his head. At this rate, Pritchard would be leading the force before the day was over.

Chapter Fifty-One

Bringing his typewriter down by her had been a good idea. He typed away fervently. He had to finish this. Every second counted now. He paused and took a sip of scotch, looking over at her, his lovely inspiration.

She was sitting in the middle of the floor, arms wrapped around her knees, watching him. On high alert, and ready to bolt at a moment's notice. He smiled and leaned back in his chair. "You don't have to act like you're locked up. Come and see," he said, motioning to the typewriter.

Coby narrowed her eyes and didn't move. "I am locked up. And I know the story," she said. Her voice was cold.

"Not the ending, the real ending." He grinned at her, eyes gliding over her red lipstick. "You're very good at understanding my stories, but I doubt even you could predict where this is going, darling."

Coby's nose wrinkled and her eyes carried a glint of loathing. "I know exactly where it's going, and I know what you're writing is wrong."

"Oh really?" he asked, eyebrows raised. He grabbed his glass and took a sip, enjoying her defiance. She was his favorite.

"You seem to forget that we have a bear too. And he has a gun." So much confidence in her tone. It was almost like she believed that the police department could function without her.

He sighed. "Oh, how odious you are. Come, see what my plans are for your dear friend," he commanded, almost hoping she'd defy him. He would so like an excuse to take a break and touch her.

She glared at him and slowly rose to her feet, walking towards him at a painfully slow pace, as if she was measuring every step.

He rolled his eyes as she peered over his shoulder, just out of reach. He pushed his chair back quickly and caught her by the elbow, dragging her forward, ignoring her muffled scream of surprise and resistance. "Read it out loud to me," he said, pulling the page he had just finished out of the typewriter. He handed it to her and leaned back.

She shook as she held onto the piece of paper and stared at him with wide eyes. She glanced down at the paper and swallowed. "'After he covered her in her red, he went to find the other stupid girl who had stumbled upon his treasure'."

He closed his eyes, hands cupped behind his head and smiled. "Skip down to the bottom," he murmured.

She hesitated and he could almost feel her trying to quickly read. "'He took the bleach and scrubbed the next layer of skin, for her name was a lie and' –" Coby's voice shook and she seemed to be choking on words.

"And?" he prompted.

"And then Rosy-Red grabbed a glass and beat him dead," she spat and he opened his eyes just in time to see his glass of scotch slam into the side of his face. He let out a yell as glass shards dug dangerously close to his eye, and he lurched forwards, pawing at the side of his face. He felt her hands snatch at his pocket. Keys. She was going for the keys. He swiped for her but she was already unlocking the door and sprinting away from him toward the stairs.

He let out a roar and grabbed for the only thing in front of him, chucking his typewriter as hard as he could at her retreating form. He heard a thunk followed by the sound of her falling as he stumbled blindly forward, wiping at the sting of glass and alcohol.

She was sprawled on the floor, struggling to get to her knees as he groped for her. He caught her waist but she screamed and he got a foot to the face. He saw stars but he lunged on top of her, pinning her flailing limbs to the ground. He blinked through the blood and scotch. "You helpless, clumsy creature," he growled, getting a hold on her wrists in one hand, while tangling a handful of her hair in his other and smacking her head against the cement floor. She went limp and he sat up straight, breathing heavily.

He needed to clean the glass out of his head. And finish writing. After he gave her another sedative.

***

Clyde dropped Pritchard off at the station and let out a sigh. He knew that Pritchard was right. Ten at night was far too late to be calling on people. The businesses were all closed, most of them had been for hours. And showing up on people's doorsteps this late wasn't okay. It should be, but it wasn't.

He had told Pritchard he was going home to get some things, but that was a lie. He wasn't going home. He was going to the water tower. And the mill. And everywhere Coby may have been or talked about that wasn't locked down for the night.

He wasn't sure when he had eaten last, though he couldn't care less. He wasn't hungry. He wasn't tired. At this moment, he wasn't even angry. He just felt strung out. A hollow pit somewhere in his gut was drilling up through his heart, aching with worry.

He sighed and hit the steering wheel with both hands before pulling away from the station. He would call Grizzly in a while to see if they found anything. He had no interest in going into the office to have the chief tell him to go home and get sleep. There was no way that was going to happen.

It was going to be a long night. But he wanted to chase every second of it.

***

He finished it. On paper, at least. He walked up the steps, legs stiff from sitting too long. She was out, with enough in her system to keep her that way while slept. Then he would start on the next leg of the story.

He turned around and locked the door, sliding the key back into his pocket and sighing. His head was throbbing, despite the medication. He was fairly sure he had managed to get all the glass out. His mother had taught him how to sew. No need to go to the hospital.

Red had surprised him, he had to give her credit for that. It was refreshing really, always interesting when your story takes a turn you weren't anticipating.

He still wasn't sure how he was going to explain the injury when people noticed. Maybe that he had fallen down the stairs and into some… dishes. A glass coffee table. A liquor cabinet.

Ah well, he'd think of something. He'd sleep on it. He couldn't wait until he had them both.

Chapter Fifty-Two

LJ awoke with a start. She tried to get her bearings, uncertain where she was. Faint morning light filtered through the blinds, striping across the desk in front of her. She was still in Grizzly's office, where she'd apparently been sleeping in his chair, and her neck protested as she straightened and scanned the room. Coby's notes were spread out on the desk. LJ flinched at the realization that she'd fallen asleep before finding her best friend.

"Good morning, Sunshine." The cheerful voice entered through the open doorway before Grizzly appeared. His cheerfulness was out of place, and LJ didn't appreciate it. "I picked up doughnuts. And coffee. And also some disgusted looks, but I won't dwell on that."

LJ yawned violently and tried to smooth her undoubtedly horrid bedhead. "How long was I sleeping?"

Grizzly shrugged a shoulder and set the doughnut box on a stack of papers. "Last thing we talked about was 'The Princess and the Pea', around four." He looked at his watch. "It's seven now."

LJ rubbed her eyes. Her last conversation with Coby had been at seven a.m. Forty eight hours ago. "You should have woken me up."

Grizzly dug a cinnamon twist out of the box and held it out to her. "I *should* have given you a pillow and a blanket. You can't run on empty."

"But I can run on sugar and caffeine?" She took the doughnut and set it on a crumpled fast food napkin from the night before.

"It's been working for me for thirty-six years." Grizzly passed her a coffee.

She popped the lid off and held the paper cup with both hands, letting the steam warm her face. "Anything new?" She stared down at the black liquid, refusing to look at Grizzly.

He sighed. "No. I haven't heard from Clyde recently. I'm sure he hasn't slept, but I have no idea where he is. Or what he's doing."

The coffee was scalding hot, but it tasted like sanity. LJ stretched and reached for Coby's notebook. She flipped through the too-familiar pages for what felt like the millionth time, stopping at the last page that contained Coby's scrawl. She set down the coffee cup and rested her elbows on the desktop, running both hands over her face. The helplessness was unbearable. She was frustrated that she'd fallen asleep, but she was more frustrated at the fact that it didn't even matter. She could sleep the rest of the day and it wouldn't make any difference; she was useless.

She caught Grizzly watching her and expected another reassuring comment, but instead he pulled out his phone. "I'm calling Burkiss for an update."

Hollow words of comfort would have been preferred. LJ looked down at the crinkled paper under her elbows and tried to ignore the twist in her stomach.

She squinted at the blank page to her right. It was rumpled, and she didn't remember it from the night before. She straightened and flipped a few more pages, then jumped at the sight of strange, looping and yet somehow blocky script.

"What once gets into their hands, and in their caves, does not easily see daylight again."

Her eyes widened and she reached for one of the large Grimm volumes, sloshing coffee dangerously close to the lip of the cup.

Grizzly raised his eyebrows. "Burkiss, hey. You get anything?"

LJ didn't bother waiting to find out. She pointed manically at the handwritten note and flung the notebook at Grizzly.

"No, us either, but – LJ, what the hell?" Grizzly leaned down to swipe the notebook off the floor. "Just checking in. I'll call you back and we can –"

"It's this one!" LJ shrieked, launching to her feet and slamming the book open with both hands.

"I said I'll call you back." Grizzly hung up and leaned forward. "What?"

LJ's heart hammered. "'Snow White and Rose Red'. I skimmed it last night, because it was one of the last stories Coby mentioned to me. But I missed the note. Coby didn't write this; it's not her handwriting."

"This?" Grizzly inspected the page. "Dammit. I wonder if they checked all of her books for prints."

LJ barely heard him. She shoved the book across the desk toward him. "There's the line. 'What once gets into their hands, and in their caves, does not easily see daylight again.' That's what was typed on the note I found at the motel. And the story – the flowers, doves, berries, the dwarf has his beard cut off. Those are all things he left for us to find." She shuddered but kept going. "And there's the two girls and there's a bear." She stared at him. The soaring rush of hope suddenly dwindled. "But that doesn't actually help us find her."

"No, it might. It's a step closer than we were ten minutes ago, that's for sure."

Her legs wobbled and she plopped back in the chair. She fought off another wave of tears and swiped her hair away from her face. Grizzly set the notebook on the edge of the desk and she reached out to slide it closer. Staring hard, she tried to find something that wasn't on the page.

"Seriously, LJ. This is good."

She refused to look at him. "This isn't *your* handwriting, right? And it's not Clyde's?"

Grizzly shook his head. "I promise." He paused. "LJ, it might be time to call the FBI."

"We don't have time to stop right now, Grizzly." LJ chewed the inside of her cheek and peered at the paper. "I've seen this handwriting before." She squeezed her eyes shut and tried to remember where, or if she was just making things up and wanting it to be familiar.

Grizzly slid the notebook back to his side of the desk, looked at it for a second, then nodded at the stack of library books, folders, notepads, and loose pages to LJ's right. "There's a good chance you saw it somewhere in that pile."

LJ let out a sigh and stared at the daunting, endless pile of information that she'd already gone through with a fine-toothed comb. If she'd looked closer at the back of the notebook the day before, she might have already made a connection that could have helped them find Coby.

"So we'd better get started." Grizzly didn't give her time to wallow. He pulled the top book off the pile and tossed it in her lap, then took a stack of papers and another book for himself. LJ began to flip through the pages, knowing there was no use in kicking herself, but continuing to do so anyway. She forced herself to focus, to think about everything Coby had talked about the last few days, hoping something would shine some light on the situation and help her find her friend.

***

Grizzly bit back a sigh and blinked his bloodshot eyes as he leafed through another book. He glanced at every page, looking for any scrawled notes in the margins. Maybe this wasn't the way to go about it. It kind of felt like they were barking up the wrong tree. Maybe LJ had seen the handwriting a different day when she and Coby were out. Maybe LJ hadn't actually seen it before. Maybe the handwriting didn't even matter. He mentally slapped himself. That was no way to think. They needed to finish this. Follow every lead through to completion. Even the most obscure detail could break the case.

Grizzly cleared his throat, annoyed with himself, and grabbed for another book, snatching an old, worn out paperback. He opened the inside cover and frowned at the scrawl inside. *Property of Neal B. Murphy.* His eyes lingered on the slant of the letters, the flourish of the "L." He hesitated for a second before sliding it forward. "LJ... look," he said, pointing to the name.

LJ glanced up at him, snatched it quickly, and looked it over before placing it next to Coby's notebook on the table, comparing the two. He saw the wave of shock pass over her face. "It's Neal." She breathed, and he thought she might puke. "Neal, that *bastard.*"

He held up his hands to calm her before she started to fashion a noose. "It's Neal who wrote that note, but LJ... that doesn't mean he took Coby. He might have just been helping her research."

"This is the closest thing we've had to a lead, Grizzly," LJ snapped at him, eyebrows scrunched together.

Grizzly frowned and nodded. "I know, okay? I know. Hang on." He stood up and walked over to one of his filing cabinets and rummaged through it.

"What are you doing?" LJ asked, impatient.

Grizzly selected a file and hesitated. He looked it over before bringing it to the table. "It looks like he has a record."

LJ scooted her chair closer to his as he sat back down and flipped the file open. "Of course he does," she said through gritted teeth.

Grizzly glanced at her before laying it open before them. "Trespassing on private property, looking into ladies windows... there was an account of stealing lingerie off a wash line... don't know who in their right mind dries lingerie on the line," he muttered.

LJ was scanning the documents frantically. "Ah! *Look!* Accused of theft from local farmer. He was probably skinning little animals alive for fun," she snarled.

Grizzly let a slow breath through his teeth. "This might be our guy."

"Why are we just sitting here? Let's go arrest this freak." LJ stood, almost knocking over her chair in her haste.

Grizzly felt his heart sink for her. "It's not enough," he said with a sigh, waving his hand at the folder.

"Are you kidding me? It's *obviously* him," LJ said, looking horrified. "Coby could be there. He could have her *right now.*"

"I know," Grizzly said.

LJ raised her hands in defeat. "So what are we going to do?" LJ asked. He could see tears of frustration pricking at the corners of her eyes.

"We're going to go talk to him and see if we can find something that will convict him," Grizzly said firmly. He stood and grabbed his jacket.

Chapter Fifty-Three

Neal wiped the steam off the bathroom mirror and examined the damage she had left. He winced as he prodded at the cuts and bruises. The swelling had gone down, but the dark color was starting to set in.

He frowned, wondering if he should attempt to downplay it with makeup or if that would be more suspicious when the cops came back to the library. And he was sure they would come.

He let out a sigh and adjusted the towel around his waist before walking back to his bedroom and pulling out clothes for the day. He should really give Coby another dose before work. It wouldn't do to have her trying to break out while he was busy shelving books. But he was probably worrying over nothing; she was fine for the time being.

He got dressed, combed his hair and headed down to the kitchen. He dug in the back of the fridge for the bag of syringes and froze when he heard a knock on the front door. Neal slowly stood upright and closed the refrigerator. He hesitated for half a beat before striding towards the front door. He opened it.

"Chief Adams!" he said, looking bewildered. "What are you doing here?" he asked, looking up at the large, bear of a man who filled the doorframe.

The chief frowned, and cleared his throat, shifting awkwardly on the doorstep. "I need a favor from you, Neal."

"Well come on inside. Does this have something to do with Coby? Did you find her?" he asked, voice full of concern and hope.

Grizzly lumbered inside and glanced around before his eyes landed on Neal. "What happened to your face?" Grizzly asked.

Neal blinked in confusion before touching his face. "Oh, I fell down the stairs. Landed on the dishes I was bringing to the sink." He rolled his eyes and shook his head. "You know, one of these days, Chief, you're going to have to carry me out of here." He shrugged before getting serious again. "Did you find something?"

Grizzly let out a sigh and placed his hands on his hips, looking down at Neal. "We need you to open up the library early. We have a team and they need to give the place the official once-over."

Neal frowned and nodded quickly. "Of course." He glanced down at his bare feet before looking back up at him. "Let me get my keys and some socks," he said, heading for the stairs. "Help yourself to some coffee. Mugs are in the top right cupboard," he said, before heading up to his room.

***

Grizzly watched as the man disappeared up the stairs and started immediately towards the kitchen. He looked around frantically as he did so. Nothing seemed wrong. The house was a little too clean but hey, if that was a crime he'd have to lock up his best friend.

He could hear Neal upstairs, opening and shutting dresser drawers.

Turning on his heel, Grizzly combed the rest of the main floor. He stepped into the bathroom, looked behind the shower curtain, and opened the medicine cabinet, but found nothing. He gave up and quickly left to snoop around the living room. There really wasn't much to discover there either, not even a pile of mail or stack of finances.

He grumbled to himself as he stepped back towards the kitchen. He could hear the jangle of keys being picked up as he quickly poured himself a cup of coffee. He began to silently open the cupboards as he did so. His eyes fell on the two doors which he assumed led to the garage and basement but before he could so much as take a step towards them, Neal rounded the bannister and smiled at him. He was fixing his hair, his glasses on his face, shoes on his feet. "All right Chief, I'm set," he said, twirling his keys around his finger before catching them. "Shall we?"

Grizzly nodded and pretended to take a large swig of the coffee before setting it down on the counter. "Let's go," he said, waiting for the librarian to head out to his car before following after him.

"See you there," Neal said, hopping in his car and starting it up as Grizzly headed towards the cruiser parked on the road. LJ sat in the passenger seat, watching him like a hawk as he approached.

"Well?" she asked, when he slid into the seat next to her and started up the cruiser.

"I didn't find anything. And I mean anything, the guy's more of a neat freak than Bupkiss," he muttered as he pulled away from the curb and followed after Neal's car. "But he did have a messed up face. Cuts and bruises… He said he fell down the stairs onto some dishes." He glanced over at LJ who looked absolutely livid.

"Coby... too bad she didn't claw his eyes out. He's got her, Grizz," she said, her voice rising in anger and hysteria.

"Well if that's the case, we're onto him. He's with us now and he's not hurting her."

LJ chewed on her lips, eyes murdering the car ahead of them.

"We're going to find her, LJ," Grizzly said. He reached over and placed a hand on her knee. She nodded and didn't say anything else as they pulled into the library parking lot.

Clyde was already there, standing next to a cruiser, his arms crossed. A forensic unit of four people stood behind him, fidgeting around.

Neal got out of his car, nodded to them, and headed towards the front door. He unlocked it and propped it open for them.

Grizzly walked up to Clyde and grabbed his shoulder. "Hey."

"Hey," Clyde said back, voice hoarse. The man looked like he hadn't slept in a week. "Did you search the house?" he asked shortly.

"Not... officially..." Grizzly said.

"*What?*" Clyde demanded.

"Clyde, we have no actual evidence yet. I can't just barge in there without a warrant, and what am I supposed to arrest him for?" Grizzly asked, finding it hard to believe *he* was the one instructing *Clyde* in protocol.

Neal waved them in and Grizzly raised a hand back, starting for the front door. "We're going to find a lead okay? What we have to do right now is search the premises."

Clyde and LJ exchanged a look that made Grizzly wonder just when they decided to team up against him as they strode into the library. Neal closed the door behind them and looked at them all. "Just let me know if you need anything at all."

Grizzly saw Clyde's eyes fall on Neal's face for the first time and watched as his entire posture changed. "What happened to your face?" Clyde demanded.

Neal turned to look at him, surprised by his tone. "I– I fell down the stairs –" he stuttered.

"No you didn't." Clyde's face twisted into a look of disgust.

Neal took a step backwards. "I was carrying the dishes–"

"Shut up," Clyde snapped, and Grizzly's hand shot out and grabbed Clyde by the elbow, dragging him backwards before he could move towards Neal.

"Hey," Grizzly cautioned, not wanting a repeat of the Pritchard episode.

"Son of a bitch," Clyde snarled under his breath, trying to rip his arm away.

Grizzly shoved him firmly in the chest towards the door. "Outside."

"But *Greg* –"

"*Now.*" Grizzly followed him, feeling LJ's eyes on him as he walked out.

Clyde marched out into the parking lot, fuming before spinning around and glaring at him. "He has her, Grizz. He *has* her. I'm going to beat the shit –"

"Clyde!" Grizzly stepped forward and grabbed the man's arms, forcing him to stop and look at him. "I am doing everything I can right now. And we aren't going to be able to help Coby if you assault him and mess everything up!" he implored and gave him a shake before letting go. He took a breath and ran a hand over his face. "You need to go home, Clyde. I'll call you when we're done here, okay? I'll call you with what we find, the moment we find it, but I can't have you in there. Go home and get some rest."

Clyde stared at him, jaw twitching, before turning on his heel. He yanked the door of his cruiser open and slammed it shut behind him.

Grizzly watched as he started the car and tore out of the parking lot.

Chapter Fifty-Four

"What do you mean 'nothing'?"

"I'm sorry, darlin'."

"*No,* this isn't happening. We *know* he has her, Grizzly." LJ felt her throat closing up for what had to be the hundredth time since this whole ordeal started.

"We don't have enough, LJ." Grizzly sounded completely strung out. "I believe you, darlin'. I think you're right and I'm going to keep coming at him, but right now we may be spinning our wheels while Coby's in trouble."

"I can't believe you're telling me they found *nothing* in that *entire* library!" LJ was yelling at him but she couldn't stop. She knew it wasn't his fault. She *knew* that. But it didn't matter. She'd follow Neal back to his house by herself if she had to.

"We are going to find her, LJ. But I need you, okay? I need you to help me!" Grizzly said and he looked so desperate she bit back her protests and focused.

"Okay. Let's go," she whispered.

Grizzly nodded and turned towards the forensics team to give them instructions. LJ took the moment and pulled her phone out of her pocket, dialing Clyde. "Hey. I need your help."

***

Neal left at five fifteen, waiting in case they had someone watching the library. He walked straight to his car, fighting the urge to look around and see if anyone was watching.

Trying to look casual, he climbed into his car, head pounding. As he backed out of the parking lot he scanned his rear view mirror closely, looking for anyone following him back to his place. He had to get her out of here. The next stage would be more difficult if LJ was with the chief the entire time. But he'd find a way. He had to. The first step was to move Coby. It was only a matter of time before they searched the house, as they obviously suspected him.

He was surprised they had caught onto him already. Not that it really mattered, it just... accelerated things. LJ was brighter than he had originally thought. But that was good. It would make this all the more satisfying.

No one seemed to be following. That was good, too. He still thought they might have someone watching his house but he'd cross that bridge when he came to it. After a few minutes, he pulled onto his street, looking for any suspicious cars or activity. He pulled into the garage and peered out at the windows across the street, looking for movement. Nothing. He closed the garage door behind him and walked into the house.

Coby might be awake by now. But he'd get to her later. He needed to set a few other things in motion, pack, clean up, leave a present for his Snow White... They knew it was him. He was fairly confident about that. No use in hiding it once he and Coby were away. He snatched a kitchen knife off the counter and tucked it in his belt before going to his room and throwing some clothes into a suitcase. He paused to admire his newly completed book of fairy tales – written the way they should have been in the first place – and then placed it into the suitcase with his mother's book of Grimm's. They were the only items he truly cared about.

He hesitated, thinking of all of his keepsakes downstairs… They'd take them. He shrugged and closed his suitcase. His book had all the stories, that's all he really needed. He was relieved he had finished writing his latest installment last night. He wouldn't have to bring his typewriter.

He frowned and walked over to the bathroom, grabbing some razors and his toothbrush. He tried to think of anything he may need to finish his story. He reached under the counter and pulled out the bleach before flicking off the light and going to get the wire grill brush.

***

Clyde killed the lights and pulled up behind a silver Impala parked at the curb. He settled the gearshift into park. The other cars on the one way street belonged to the prison guards working the graveyard shift. His personal vehicle wouldn't be suspicious for hours.

And this wasn't going to take hours.

Clyde stepped outside, streetlights throwing his shadow across the pavement like it was daylight. He almost wished it was – at least he wouldn't look like a hoodlum. But it didn't matter. No one was watching. And if *he* was watching… Clyde hoped he was watching. He hoped Neal knew he was coming and was laughing about it. Clyde knew exactly what kind of impression he gave, and "stuttering, bumbling Podunk police officer" was one of the better descriptions he'd heard. This was the first time he was grateful for his pathetic reputation. It meant Neal had no idea what Clyde was capable of.

Clyde moved up the sidewalk with a new level of focus. He was determined and adrenaline flooded his veins. The library parking lot was empty, but Clyde didn't let that phase him. Just because Neal's car wasn't there didn't mean he wasn't. He was keeping up appearances, after all. He could have driven home and gone about his nightly routine like a normal citizen, waited for his neighbor's lights to dim, and slipped back to the library through the shadows. Not unlike Clyde, actually. Grizzly had no idea Clyde wasn't at home, wringing his hands and "getting some rest" and waiting for a phone call informing him of some new found evidence.

Screw sitting on his ass and waiting around. Coby was here. Her life was in danger and Clyde was going to find her.

He approached the back door, next to the drop boxes, and swiftly lifted a boot to the glass beside the knob. The noise was shocking in the tranquility of the night, and Clyde paused to listen for a security alarm. When nothing followed the last sounds of shards hitting the concrete, he unlocked the door and stepped inside.

It was dark in the back offices, but he followed the light out toward the front entryway, then made his way to where he'd seen the door labeled "basement, staff only." He pulled his gun free with one hand, flashlight in the other, and pushed the door open.

His flashlight beam moved chaotically across the steps as he descended them, pulse pounding in his ears. Something hummed, something else gave off an occasional beep, and there was an actual dripping noise. Clyde aimed the beam at chest level, ready for anything.

Automatic lights kicked in, flooding the space with light that blinded Clyde so suddenly he ducked, shielding his eyes with his arm. Tears stung as he tried to force his eyelids open so he could take in his surroundings.

He let his gun arm drop and he clicked off his flashlight, still shielding his dilated pupils from the ceiling lights.

The room was spacious, open and rather empty aside from storage containers stacked against the walls and a dehumidifier humming in the corner. An alarming layer of dust coated the floor, and Clyde glanced back toward the stairwell, noting that while there were evident footprints besides his own, his were the only fresh ones. His heart sank, but he headed for the other basement rooms anyway. They were just as empty.

Anger was making him sweat. He swiped at the back of his neck and stormed back up to the main level, making his exit twice as quickly as he'd entered. It was a dead end. Clyde fired up his car and tore down the street, tires squealing. He flipped on the interior light and fumbled through the papers he'd lifted from Grizzly's desk, careening dangerously on the road. Neal's address wasn't listed on the file he'd grabbed, and Clyde let out a strangled growl of frustration. He slammed on the brakes, idling in the middle of the empty street. His phone sat in the cup holder on the dashboard, and he stared at it.

He knew LJ didn't give a shit about protocol. Not when her best friend was being held by a serial killer. And LJ was the only person in that station who would sneak into Grizzly's office and find Neal's home address.

He snatched the phone and hit her number on the screen.

Chapter Fifty-Five

LJ's hands shook so hard she could hardly weed through the mess. Grizzly's desk was an absolute nightmare – between the files, books, notes, pizza crust-layered paper plates and crumpled up napkins, it was amazing they hadn't lost a phone or something even more important in the disarray.

Grizzly had kept Neal's file on him like it was gold. The chance of finding it tossed on the desktop was a long shot, but LJ had to try.

She sat in the chair so forcefully it nearly toppled her to the floor. She stared at the computer, which required a login name and password to get past the security lock screen. Even if she thought searching the internet would get her Neal's home address, she couldn't access a browser.

She pulled her phone out of her sweatshirt pocket and called Clyde back. "It's not here."

"Well *find it*, LJ!"

"Grizzly still has the file on him. I don't know where else to find the address, Clyde!" LJ hissed, tears pricking her eyes.

"Okay, okay." He sighed loudly into the phone. "Go to his computer. The juvie records should all be in there. Hopefully his childhood home is listed."

"You think that's –"

"Unless you want to come out here and backtrack to his house, it's all we've got."

LJ chewed on her lip. She'd already considered that, but common sense had set her straight. She couldn't remember how they'd gotten to Neal's house – Grizzly had driven and she couldn't separate one end of suburbia

from the other. "Okay. I'll look. Just… hold on." Clyde
gave her the login information and she typed it in, then
carefully followed his instructions to access the juvenile
records. The page took a while to load, and LJ's pulse
pounded in her ears while she waited. There were three
files labeled "Murphy," but only one with the first name
Neal. "I think I found it."

"The address?"

"Just hang on. I got the file. Let me see… right
here!" She nearly shrieked, choking back excitement.
"439 E. Franklin Street."

The phone line went dead.

***

Coby winced as she heard him upstairs, closing
doors and traipsing through the house. He had been
storming around up there for hours. There was an
urgency to his footsteps and she wondered just how long
he had planned for her to be alive. She tried to think of
what she could use as a weapon but she was having
trouble even lifting her head off the ground. After a while
she managed to drag herself into an upright sitting
position and her vision swam as she held still, trying not
to black out.

She wasn't going to die in Neal Murphy's
basement. She wasn't going to just lie here and let him
win, let him kill LJ. She couldn't do that. She couldn't do
that to LJ, Grizzly or Clyde. She was going to get out of
here and write a book with LJ about how they threw his
ass in jail, about how he'd never be able to hurt any more
women.

She looked once again at the shelving unit that held everything... all of his trophies, his mementos. Maybe the jar with the... she shuddered. Maybe she could break it and use the glass as a knife. She wouldn't, however, be able to do anything if she couldn't even stand up. Her limbs felt heavy, and even turning her head required effort.

She didn't know what he had given her but it wasn't going to happen again. She placed her hands against the cement wall behind her and tried to push herself upright. She got about halfway up the wall when she heard the basement door open. She felt her blood turn cold and she scrambled to stand upright, trying to reach the shelving unit. Darkness crept at the corners of her vision and she silently prayed she'd stay conscious for this.

His footsteps thundered down the stairs and she heard his hand on the door knob of the storage room. He opened the door and stopped, surprised to see her standing. "Hello, my dear," he said and it wasn't until then that Coby realized he had a butcher knife in his hand. Scenes from *Psycho* flashed through her brain and she stumbled backwards until her back hit against the shelving unit. She quickly grabbed for the glass jar that contained the baby, but Neal was already there, grabbing her wrist in his free hand and pulling her towards him.

"Hold still," he murmured into her ear, twisting her around and holding her back to his chest, locking her tightly to him while prying one of her arms out. Coby felt panic rising in her chest as she struggled to get away but couldn't make her limbs cooperate for her. He slid the knife into her arm and she gasped as blood bubbled out of it quickly. Was this his plan? To let her bleed out all over his basement? She guessed that would fit the "Red" part of her namesake.

Neal stepped back and slid the knife into his belt before sliding his fingertips along the inside of her arm, covering them with the blood that was dripping onto the floor. He dumped her unceremoniously on the ground and Coby clumsily clamped her hand over her arm, trying to stop the blood from gushing everywhere.

Neal walked over to the wall by the shelf and started writing something on the wall with her blood. He came back to her a few more times, dipping his fingers in the puddle that was starting to form under her. She fought to stop the bleeding, but that was proving difficult as she could barely keep her eyes open.

Chapter Fifty-Six

There were no lights on inside the house. Clyde parked on the opposite side of the street, hands shaking on the steering wheel as he stared at 439 E. Franklin. The garage door was closed, and all the shades were drawn on the windows. It looked exactly like every other house on the block.

Clyde got out of his car and took out his phone. He checked for the fourth time to make sure the ringer was off, then put it back in his pocket. The street was quiet, and Clyde didn't waste any time looking for nosy neighbors or late night pedestrians. He'd screwed around long enough.

He circled the house, feet quiet on the perfectly manicured lawn. He inspected some of the windows, trying to catch a glimpse of light or even an outline of something inside, but everything was sealed tightly. Stepping lightly, he tried the back door first, hoping he'd find a stroke of luck. The sliding door was locked securely into the frame.

Clyde glanced over his shoulder, checking for neighbors who shared the backyard. It wouldn't surprise him in the slightest for someone to be letting the dog out and call the cops because they spotted a creep sneaking around behind Neal Murphy's house.

If it was actually his house. Clyde swallowed the bile that rose in his throat at that possibility. And if Coby wasn't here, he was going to lose it. Shaking his head, he went back around the front. Neal was a sociopathic serial killer – Clyde was confident that the man still lived in his childhood home. And even if he didn't, Clyde couldn't just knock on the door and ask.

He went straight for the front door, pulling a lock pick set out of his jacket and feeling the sweat bead on his forehead immediately. Picking locks wasn't something he had mastered – every test he'd been put through had resulted in a lot of fumbling and sweating and embarrassment. He had passed, but it had been a struggle. And those tests were against a stopwatch and his peers, not an actual life and death situation involving the woman he…

Clyde swiped at his forehead and dug into his pocket for his flashlight. Clenching the light in his teeth, he crouched in front of the doorknob, tools in hand. He tweaked the knob, just in case it was open, then set to work to unlock it.

It took a total of three minutes, but Clyde aged six years. The door creaked open, loud enough to wake the dead. His teeth ached from clamping down on the metal flashlight, and he didn't move until the door stopped. Slowly, he got to his feet and snatched the flashlight, turning it off and slipping inside the house. He gave the street a final scan before he shut the door quietly behind him.

The entryway was pitch black. Clyde blinked rapidly, willing his eyes to adjust to the darkness. He was nervous that they wouldn't be able to and he'd have to resort to using the flashlight. Objects started to take shape, and Clyde moved forward.

The digital clock on the stove in the kitchen was bright enough to illuminate the entire room, and Clyde tiptoed through, pausing in front of the refrigerator. It was empty of photos, cards, ads, and recipes. There wasn't even a magnet. Clyde squinted, trying to get a feel for the rest of the kitchen in the blackness. He still wasn't certain he had the right house, and he wanted to find out before he got caught and arrested. Explaining his nonexistent plan to Grizzly in an interrogation room was not on his agenda.

The linoleum creaked as Clyde inched across it, praying there were no shoes or dog toys strewn throughout the room for him to trip over.

A crashing sound came from some distance away, and Clyde froze. Silence took over, and Clyde replayed the sound over and over in his mind, trying to both identify and pinpoint it. He could faintly make out an open doorway to his right, and he crept toward it.

***

Neal painted quickly, words that he had long ago memorized flowed from his fingertips onto the wall.

She was laying on the ground, her breathing shallow and panicked as she fought to stay awake. She had obviously fought against fear the entire time he had her here... but it was undeniable now as she lay on the floor, her blood pooling around her, the smell of iron was tantalizing and intoxicating.

The story was finally becoming real.

***

It was a black hole, and Clyde's fingers twitched toward where a light switch would most likely be on the wall inside the frame. He inched his right foot inside the doorway, and the floor fell away, just as he'd suspected. It was the door to the basement stairs, and a new layer of sweat broke out across his neck as he fumbled around for a railing before attempting to descend the steps completely blind. He wasn't good at stairs in broad daylight; trying them in the dark when his knees were shaking and his heart was pounding would most likely result in a lot of noise.

Clyde crept down at a painfully slow pace, gripping the invisible railing for dear life. The further he got, the more clearly he could see a line of light at the base of the stairs. When he finally reached the bottom, he stopped, staring down at the faint light. He reached out carefully, fingers landing on a doorknob, just as he'd expected. He could hear his pulse throbbing in his ears, and his breathing was uneven. He drew his gun and opened the door silently.

***

Coby felt herself slipping away. She couldn't stop the blood from bubbling out of her arm. Neal seemed completely unconcerned about it.

Funny. She figured he would have a more dramatic end for her than this.

After what felt like an eternity, Neal stepped back and surveyed his work with a sigh before turning and looking at her. Coby had an irrational surge of hope that he would stop the bleeding, but it was replaced by panic when she saw him pull another syringe out of his pocket. "Time to go on a little trip," he said.

***

Clyde had expected a torture chamber, but the room was a nicely decorated den, with a flat screen TV and coasters on the coffee table. Clyde looked down the hall, where the light was coming from.

The crashing noise came again, this time closer, and it was followed by a high shriek. Clyde was at the door at the end of the hallway before he knew what happened. The knob didn't move, and Clyde backed up half a step before throwing himself into the door. The frame cracked, and the door flew open.

The light was greenish. The room smelled dank. The walls were concrete, and words were smeared across the far one, written in fresh blood.

"Dear Mr. Bear, spare me, I will give you all my treasures."

Beside the message was a shelving unit containing glass jars filled with questionable specimens.

"Clyde!" The shout came from the right. Neal held Coby by the throat, one knee pressing into her ribs and one pinning her left arm to the floor. Neal looked over at Clyde, surprise evident on his face, then moved the syringe in his hand forcefully into Coby's neck.

***

An officer. Here. Not just any officer either. Clyde Burkiss, how heroic.

He took half a moment to process this turn in events.

The man needed to die.

Before Neal could stand, Clyde hit him like a train and they rolled across the concrete floor. As they struggled to get the upper hand, Clyde grabbed his collar and belted him across the face. Neal saw stars as he threw his arm out to catch himself before he slammed into the wall, and retaliated.

Before Clyde could respond, Neal hit him in the windpipe, watching as the officer choked and gasped for air as he hit the ground. Neal felt excitement flare in the pit of his stomach, as the bloodlust pounded in his ears, and launched at him again. Clyde scrambled backwards, trying to catch his breath, looking around frantically for his gun.

Neal grinned, and slid his knife from his belt. Foolish man. Neal would be leaving more than just a message for the chief of police.

Clyde got to his feet unsteadily, blinking and shaking his head. In a moment so fast it surprised Neal, Clyde charged him, grabbing his wrist and twisting while throwing his other fist towards his face.

Neal dodged the hit and got in one of his own, nearly taking the officer down again with the handle of his knife, but he felt Clyde latch onto his other wrist and knee him in the gut.

Neal doubled over in pain and nausea as he heard his knife clatter away. Before he could lift his head, Clyde had him by the collar again and threw him against the wall. The man's fist collided twice with his face and Neal felt his nose shatter before he managed to shove him back.

He felt it go then. The consciousness unhinge in his mind as the hot blood gushed down his face, pain echoing through his head. Precious time was being wasted. He would finish this story.

Neal dove into Clyde, punching him once on the face, followed by another slug to the stomach, driving him backwards. Then in one smooth motion Neal swiped the knife out of Coby's blood on the floor and lunged, stabbing Clyde in the abdomen.

***

Clyde didn't feel it. Rage boiled in his veins, and he threw another punch, then tried to knock the knife away again. He spotted his gun near the open door and went for it. Neal tripped him and Clyde landed on his chest, wind whooshing out of his lungs. He crawled away wildly and grabbed his gun, rolling over and cocking the hammer back.

Neal was looming above him, Clyde's blood still dripping from the blade in his hand. Clyde didn't wait for Neal to attack, and he didn't shout a warning. He fired three rounds, landing each one in the center of Neal's chest.

Neal dropped the knife, stutter-stepped back, then dropped to his knees with a confused expression. He slumped sideways and stopped moving, eyes staring blankly at Clyde.

Clyde waited for a beat, then holstered his gun and scrambled over to Coby's side. "Coby? Sweetheart?"

Dried blood was crusted in her hair. Her eyelids fluttered, and Clyde wondered what had been in the syringe, which was on the floor near her head. Fortunately, it appeared only half empty, so she had only received half a dose of whatever it was.

His eyes landed on her arm, which was lying limply in a puddle of her own blood. He wrapped his hand around it to staunch the bleeding while he gently pressed his fingers to her neck to check her pulse. "Coby, open your eyes for me, hon." Clyde tried to remember what he'd been trained to do in situations like this, but his hands were shaking and his stomach was rolling and he didn't know if he was going to throw up or pass out.

Her eyelids flicked open and stared up at the ceiling dully for a moment, then she blinked and looked at him. "Clyde?" she whimpered, free hand reaching out to him.

He clutched it and pressed it to his lips without thinking, then smoothed her hair back from her face. "It's okay. You're okay." He fumbled in his pocket for his phone and managed to dial 911 with a shaky and bloody hand. "I'm getting you out of here."

Chapter Fifty-Seven

The ambulance had beat them there. Along with three other cop cars, one of them apparently containing Pritchard, who was bossing around some people carrying a body –

A body. LJ felt darkness cloud the corners of her vision and she gripped the car door handle, willing Grizzly to park the car so she could run. She knew it would be faster.

The car careened to a stop and LJ flung the door open, tripping over her feet as she scrambled out of it. Her heart hammered in her chest. Where was Coby? She couldn't be in that bag. LJ's stomach lurched as she watched the officers lift the body bag onto a stretcher, and was horrified to find herself moving that direction. But she had to know.

Frantic tears built as she went for the stretcher. Grizzly was calling something to her but she couldn't hear him. *Coby, Coby, Coby.* She pushed past one of the officers who tried to stop her on her way toward the stretcher, but something caught her eye and she froze.

There she was. Coby was sitting on the edge of the ambulance, battered and bloody, but clearly alive. Clyde was next to her with his arm around her as he talked earnestly to an officer. Coby was holding onto his belt like a lifeline as a paramedic checked her eyes with a light.

LJ wasn't sure how she got over there but suddenly she was shoving the medic away, sobbing hysterically as she pulled Coby into a hug. "You're alive! You're alive!" she choked out as she felt Coby wrap her arms around her. LJ snuffled, smearing Coby's shirt with the tears of relief that were flowing freely down her face. She felt like she was going to fall over, knees shaking from relief and adrenaline as Coby hiccupped into her shoulder.

After a little while, she pulled away and touched Coby's bleeding head. "Ouch." She let out a watery laugh as she wiped at her eyes.

Coby wiped her nose on her sleeve and hiccupped a few more times. "Thanks for finding me," she managed to say, lip still trembling as she smiled at her.

LJ caught a glimpse of Clyde out of the corner of her eye as his hand found its place on Coby's back again. Maybe it hadn't left. She turned to him. His shirt was open and there was a bandage taped across his abdomen. LJ frowned and gripped his arm. "Thank you," she said, feeling tears slide down her face again despite herself. He smiled but before he could answer, there was a thunderous shout of joy from behind LJ. Grizzly barreled forward, making them all jump, almost plowing LJ over as he gathered them into a massive hug.

"I can't believe – don't you ever do that to me again, Burkiss! No *back up?* You could have died! I should fire you right here, right now. Oh Coby, darlin', I'm so glad you're all right. I knew it though. I knew we'd find you – *Clyde*. Did you get *shot*? I can't believe this!" he ranted as Clyde tried to pacify him before they were interrupted by the paramedic sheepishly clearing his throat.

"Um, excuse me, but we really need to finish making sure Miss Anderson is okay."

"Well, what are you waiting for?" Grizzly boomed and the medic pursed his lips as he moved forward with antiseptic for Coby's head.

Grizzly stepped back but kept his hands on LJ's shoulders and let out a sigh. She could practically feel him relax into a puddle behind her. She knew exactly how he felt. She placed a hand over one of his.

"Clyde," Grizzly commanded. "Once you two get checked over at the hospital, take the girls to your place. I'll meet up with you guys there. I've got to talk to the FBI and wrap things up here." Clyde nodded. LJ noticed Coby was holding onto the corner of his shirt as the medic cleaned her cuts.

LJ frowned as Grizzly stepped away. She stepped forward and hugged Coby tightly. "I'm so glad you're okay. You guys go ahead, I'll follow with Grizzly." She turned and hurried after Grizzly. "Wait!" she called after him before he entered the house. "I… I need to see," she said.

Grizzly paused and looked at her with a raised eyebrow. "Are you sure?"

LJ swallowed and nodded. Part of her wanted to reach for his hand and be led inside like a little child, but she set her jaw and stepped through the open doorway first.

The house was alarmingly normal. It looked exactly as it should, aside from the yellow police tape and the officers and agents roaming around inside. In fact, the only thing striking about the inside of Neal's home was the level of neatness. He had even surpassed Clyde on the OCD scale.

"Clyde found her downstairs," Grizzly said as he stepped away from one of the first responding officers and touched LJ's arm.

LJ followed him to the stairs, then all the way to the back room in the basement. Grizzly stepped inside, and she let him disappear so she could get her bearings. She took a deep breath, wiped her dry but still red eyes, and stepped inside.

The concrete room was small. Fifteen by twenty-five, and completely empty aside from a writing desk, chair, and a wire shelving unit that was filled with items LJ couldn't even process. She stared at the blood on the floor, confused at the amount and wondered how much of it was Coby's. The wall across from the doorway caught her eye, and she jumped when she realized she was looking at more blood.

Grizzly stared at the words, brow wrinkled and jaw set. "He left that for me." He glanced at LJ. "That's from the fairy tale, right?"

LJ shuddered. She couldn't look away from the words, eyes stuck on where the "M" had dripped halfway to the floor. "He wrote that with Coby's blood." She continued to shake.

"Hey, she's okay. We got her back." Grizzly pulled her into a hug, and she held onto him when her knees gave out. "Neal Murphy is dead. He can't hurt anybody anymore."

LJ tried to hold back a fresh wave of tears, but they came full force and she was sobbing in a matter of seconds. She gripped the front of Grizzly's uniform with both hands and cried, dredging up pity somewhere in the back of her mind as Grizzly just rubbed her back and tried to calm her down. She couldn't believe how close she'd come to losing her best friend. Coby had been right in this very room, bleeding, scared to death, staring down a psychopath. He'd had every intention of killing her and finding LJ and doing the same.

"How about we get out of here?" Grizzly brushed his hand over her hair. "I've got to tie up a few things first, and then we can sort it out after we both get some sleep."

LJ took a shaky breath and nodded against his chest. Grizzly kept an arm around her shoulders as they left the hell hole behind.

***

Grizzly took out his key and stepped into the house. LJ followed, looking like she was going to fall asleep on the doorstep.

"You have a key to Clyde's place?" she murmured.

Grizzly pushed the door open further for her. "We don't have family in the area... we're all we've got," he said with a shrug.

LJ nodded. "I get it," she whispered and Grizzly was afraid she was going to cry again.

He cleared his throat quickly. "Uh, hello? Clyde?" he asked, a little worried that the man would pull a gun on them if they surprised him. He stepped further into the house, turning lights on as he went. LJ followed after him. The fan was on in the bathroom but no one was in there.

"Cl–" Grizzly began again until he realized there was a light on in the bedroom. He walked down the hallway and pushed the door open. Coby was curled up in a ball, sleeping under the covers of the bed. Her hair was wet with no trace of blood, and it looked like she was wrapped up in a bathrobe. Clyde was next to her, above the covers, back pressed against the headboard, eyes closed.

Grizzly felt himself smile, glad to see the gun on the side table. He moved it away before shaking Clyde's shoulder. "Hey there, partner."

Clyde jolted upright. He looked panicked and a little dazed as he blinked at the chief. Coby didn't move an inch. "H-hey," Clyde mumbled, raking a hand back through his unruly hair as he tried to get his bearings. Grizzly wondered when Clyde had last slept.

"LJ's here now... Why don't we take the living room." He smiled and patted him on the back. Clyde ran a hand over his face and looked down at Coby. He seemed to hesitate, but Grizzly tightened his hand on his shoulder and Clyde slowly got to his feet.

LJ walked numbly into the room. She pulled off her boots as she went and flopped down on the bed, curling up next to Coby.

As Grizzly turned to go, he saw her reach out and squeeze one of Coby's hands. He smiled to himself before he turned off the light and closed the door. "Night, darlin'."

Chapter Fifty-Eight

Coby sat up with a gasp, hands at her throat, eyes wide, and heart pounding. She looked around the room wildly, unable to place where she was. Daylight spilled through the window. She was sitting on a bed she'd never seen before, and the last thing she remembered was Neal coming at her with another syringe.

A familiar sigh came from behind her, and Coby twisted around in a panic. Her entire body relaxed at the sight of LJ curled up next to her. She was still dressed in yesterday's rumpled clothes, remnants of makeup smeared under her eyes.

Coby breathed easier as the rest of the previous day came back to her in a jumble of exhaustion and relief and strung out nerves. She buried her face in her hands and squeezed her eyes shut, then took a deep breath and stood.

She was still wearing Clyde's t-shirt, striped pajama pants, and bathrobe. She blundered down the hallway toward where she thought she remembered the bathroom being. It didn't matter that her hair was still damp from the night before. She needed to wash off every speck of Neal before she started the day.

Flashes of Neal's basement played in the back of her mind as the water ran down her face. She forced them away, focusing on washing her hair and inspecting Clyde's choice of shampoo and conditioner. She gingerly scrubbed around the scratches, cuts, stitches, and bandages, then shut off the water and redressed in her borrowed clothes.

Her stomach growled as she walked down the hall toward the living room. She paused at the sight of

Grizzly, sprawled on the floor, tangled haphazardly in a blanket, with a tiny throw pillow next to him as though he'd fallen asleep on it and slid off in the middle of the night. He was snoring.

Coby smothered a laugh with her hand, then turned toward the kitchen at the sound of pans clattering. She stepped onto the linoleum and watched Clyde as he poured a bowlful of raw scrambled eggs into a frying pan. He was fresh shaven with wet hair, wearing a t-shirt and jeans. He moved carefully, holding himself upright as though he hurt, but seemed otherwise functional. Everything that Coby could remember was hazy, but it was hard to believe that the man before her was the same man who had broken down the door and saved her life twelve hours ago.

He looked up and smiled at her. "Hey. Mornin'. How's the arm?"

She dropped her gaze to the bandage on her arm and touched it distractedly. "Oh. It's fine." She'd forgotten about it, but now that she was looking at it she felt the stitches tug. She turned her eyes on him, remembering his bloody clothes from the night before. "What about you?"

Clyde shrugged stiffly. "I'll live." He pulled a spatula out of a drawer and stirred the eggs. "Are you hungry? There's coffee and tea."

Coby smiled as she picked out a tea bag and poured herself a mug of hot water. "Smells good."

"Well, it's not a Grizzly spread, but it should hit the spot." Clyde set a bag of bagels next to the toaster and turned off the stove. He put the lid on the pan of eggs and moved it from the hot burner. "I figured I better cook since it's my house."

"What exactly does a Grizzly spread consist of?" Coby leaned against the countertop and held the tea close to her face. She realized for the first time that her glasses were missing when they didn't steam up from the heat.

"Half a cow covered in bacon and hash browns, I swear." Clyde shook his head. "You sleep okay?"

She nodded, still staring at the tea. Her throat got thick, and she tried to ward off tears by grinning. "Yep! Great." The words came out too loud and too happy. She dipped the tea bag in the water and tried to focus on it as she took it out and set it on the counter, but everything got blurry. She cleared her throat and took a sip of the blazing water. "Hey, uh, thank you." Her voice quavered.

Clyde watched her and nodded slowly. "Don't mention it."

Coby looked up at him and tried to smile, but tears spilled down her cheeks. "No, I absolutely will mention it, Officer Burkiss, and you're going to let me." She set down the mug and wiped at her face. "You saved my life. You broke into a serial killer's house and shot him and carried me out of his lair, for crying out loud. I don't care if it's corny because it's literally true – you're my hero, Clyde. So… thanks." She stepped up to him and hugged him, resting her cheek against his chest. He hugged her back, and she could have sworn he kissed the top of her head, which was enough of a distraction to keep her from bursting into sobs.

"Oh, whoops, sorry. You should have put a sock on the doorknob. How was I supposed to know this room is occupied?"

Coby took a step back and wiped her eyes, snickering at Grizzly. He stood by the door, uniform shirt untucked and unbuttoned at the throat, hair standing on end. "There isn't even a door."

"Guess you should have put a little more thought into this, darlin'," he teased, crossing the room for the coffeepot. "How ya doing?"

She sniffled and reached for her tea again. "I'll be okay." She caught Clyde looking at her with a concerned expression and she nodded to reaffirm her statement.

"Damn, Burkiss, did you cook?" Grizzly crowded them at the stove to peer at the food. "Is there bacon?"

Clyde rolled his eyes. "You'll survive."

"I guess. Let's eat." Grizzly moved to a cupboard to get plates.

Coby hesitated. "I'll go get LJ."

Grizzly set the plates on the table and shook his head. "Let her sleep. We've got a lot of crap to sort through today, but this is the first time we're not on a timeclock." He went for the silverware drawer next. "We finally get to take our damn time. And we earned it." He clapped Clyde on the back, then winked at Coby. "We'll wake Sleeping Beauty after breakfast."

Coby laughed, and a touch of weight lifted off her shoulders. "I'm not sure which is worse –waking Sleeping Beauty, or waiting until the food's gone before we do it."

Chapter Fifty-Nine

Grizzly watched as Coby walked back out of the station. She spoke emphatically to Clyde as she pointed out things in Neal's book.

The team had found it, packed away in a duffle bag. His own little sick collection. It was a gold mine of information. Coby had told them they wouldn't leave until she had helped go through the entire book, as long as Grizzly gave the girls everything they needed to write the story of the year. Something he was more than happy to do. Especially when it meant more interviews with LJ.

They had been at it for a few days but with Coby on the case, a fairy tale road map, and basement full of DNA evidence, it had been fairly easy to connect the dots. They had just gone through the last of Neal's fairy tales and brought Eloise Travers's body back to her parents after ten years.

LJ followed Coby and Clyde out of the station, sun catching in her long hair as she threw it back into a ponytail. Grizzly felt a tight ache in his chest and sighed. They only had a few things left to go over and then she would leave. He glanced over at Clyde and smiled down at Coby's excited mannerisms. He knew his best friend wasn't happy about this either, but Grizzly could hardly imagine Coby would stay away from him for long. Not with the way she looked at him.

LJ on the other hand… He didn't figure LJ was the type to come back. Ever. With all the time he had spent with her the only person LJ seemed committed to was Coby. And their job. And he couldn't shake the feeling that the closer he and LJ became, the more likely she would leave and not come back. That she would always choose leaving over staying.

Grizzly ran a hand over his beard and looked down at the handful of case files he was carrying. He couldn't believe these cases were getting solved, that everything was clicking into place. Cases that haunted him, Chief DeJager, the entire town, for years were finally being solved.

He should be ecstatic, and in a sense he was. He just didn't know how to enjoy this while he was losing the girl that had kept him going these past few weeks.

He glanced up as the three of them came to a stop in front of him. He grinned. "Well, what a day. Drinks on me?"

"Sounds great." Coby smiled and Clyde nodded.

LJ hesitated but nodded as well. "Sure! We have to submit our column tonight, but we can do that after."

Coby grabbed Clyde and LJ's arms and led them towards the cars. "Let's go!"

Grizzly smiled and fell into step behind them.

They were going to celebrate and he had to snap out of it. This wasn't the movies and plenty of things had happy endings without getting the girl.

***

The computer screen went blank and Coby closed the laptop. She set it on the bedspread beside her and looked up at LJ, who sat at the hotel room desk, scrolling through a document on her own laptop. Their new hotel room was like The Ritz compared to the Van Camp Inn. "What did Ron think of the article?"

LJ leaned back in the chair, clicked to save the document, and twisted to look at Coby. "He was really happy with it. He said he's getting calls around the clock – people want to interview us… actually, literally. *People Magazine* was one of the phone calls."

Coby raised her eyebrows. "Really? Wow!"

"You're kind of famous, Anderson." LJ smirked. She nodded toward Coby's discarded laptop. "How's your project coming along?"

"Fantastic." Coby leaned over and swiped her notebook off the nightstand. "I've got basic chapter outlines for the entire book, and I've already written sixty pages." She flipped through the notes she'd taken over the last few days. Originally, she'd hoped to leave Waupun with photographs and facts on the serial killers that had stayed in the local prisons, touching on the other penitentiaries nearby. She'd imagined a book filled with artistic images of the old buildings and paragraphs of information about Jeffrey Dahmer and Ed Gein. But after nearly losing her life to a serial killer herself, she couldn't leave the story alone. She was sure it was a coping mechanism, but it was exactly the challenge she'd been looking for. And not only was it *fun*, it was another kick in the face to Neal's unavoidable legacy.

LJ nodded. "Good. How are *you*?"

Coby fiddled with the worn cover on the notebook and chewed on her lip. "I'm okay, I think." LJ's chair creaked as she leaned forward, and Coby waved off her friend's concern with a shrug. "Really, though. It's always gonna be there. I'll probably always have bad dreams. It's not something I want to think about a lot. But I'm okay. I'm alive, he's not. It's good."

LJ watched her carefully. "You sure?"

"Yes." Coby nodded. She got to her feet and stretched, then pulled her phone from her sweatshirt pocket and checked her messages, hoping there was something from Clyde. "Hey, did you find another town for us?"

LJ didn't respond right away. She crossed her arms and sat back in the chair, staring at her computer aimlessly. "Yeah, I think so. Dover, Minnesota is about an hour from La Crosse. We can be there before noon tomorrow, if you want."

Coby squinted at her friend. "If *I* want?"

"If *we* want to, we can get there before noon." LJ shrugged. She sat up and focused back on her work.

Coby sat back down on the edge of the bed, gazing toward the window thoughtfully. She had a sneaking suspicion that LJ's newfound reluctance to leave Waupun had something to do with a certain police chief.

"Here's the cover of our latest issue." LJ pulled up an image on her screen.

Coby stepped over to inspect it. "Nice. Did he send that to me, too?"

"Looks like it."

Coby pulled out her phone again and checked for herself. "I want to show Clyde."

LJ tapped her fingernails on the desk, then squinted at the clock by the bed across the room. "What time *do* you want to head out tomorrow?"

Coby shrugged, setting her phone aside and looking up. "We should see if the guys have time to meet us somewhere first. So maybe we could leave by ten or so?" She watched LJ carefully.

LJ pursed her lips and nodded slowly. She got to her feet, closed her computer, and snatched a pair of sweatpants and a t-shirt from her duffel. "I'm getting ready for bed."

Coby chewed a fingernail. She wondered if LJ had considered that she didn't have to say goodbye forever to Grizzly. The only person she'd ever been close to was Coby, and everyone else she had more or less kept at a distance or shut the door on entirely. Coby hoped that LJ would come back to Waupun with her when she returned to visit Clyde, or at least keep texting Grizzly. The man brought out a side of LJ that Coby knew was good for her friend.

***

Clyde sat on the leather recliner, closed his eyes, and sighed. Despite it being practically June, a fire blazed in the fireplace. A baseball game played on the TV above it. Clyde gazed at it, completely unaware of who was winning, or even who was playing. Grizzly stepped out of the kitchen and handed Clyde a beer, then moved to the other recliner. Clyde expected him to make small talk about the game, but he sat down without a word. It took Clyde a solid two minutes to realize the TV was on mute and they were staring at the screen while listening to the fire.

"They're heading out tomorrow." Grizzly broke the stillness.

Clyde looked over at him, then went back to staring at the flames. "Yep."

Grizzly took a swig of his beer.

Clyde inspected the label on his own bottle, picking at the corner of it distractedly. Part of him really wanted to drive to the hotel right at that moment and ask

Coby if there was any possible way she could stay. Forever, preferably, but even just for an extra night where he could take her out to dinner, just the two of them.

His phone buzzed with a text message and he leaned forward to swipe it off the coffee table. She seemed to know he was thinking about her. *Congratulations, Officer Burkiss, you're officially a cover story.* She'd sent him a link, and it opened to a picture of the new issue of their magazine, with a headline that read "Small-Town Cops Save One of Our Own." Clyde smiled to himself, and sent a reply. *When can I buy a copy?*

You're at the top of the mailing list. See you tomorrow?

Of course.

Goodnight!

Grizzly sighed audibly, then reached for the remote and flipped the channel but kept the sound off. Clyde set his phone back on the coffee table and took a sip of beer. He glanced at Grizzly, bothered by the scowl etched on his friend's face. Grizzly was happy ninety-eight percent of the time, the other two percent reserved for cases like the ones they'd just solved. Under normal circumstances, Grizzly would have been relieved and elated that they had closure on all of the cases, but these weren't normal circumstances.

Grizzly didn't want LJ to leave, and Clyde didn't want her to leave for Grizzly's sake. He was pretty sure he would keep talking to Coby, but he wasn't sure if Grizzly would ever see LJ again, and that troubled him. Grizzly was happy and independent, but he'd never been happier than when he was with LJ.

Clyde sat back in his chair and lifted the bottle to his lips. He wished there was something to say.

Chapter Sixty

The next morning was gray as Coby and LJ rolled into the McDonald's parking lot at the edge of town. LJ had forced Coby to stop at End of the Trail first so she could get a real cup of coffee. They pulled in next to the parked police cruiser. Coby killed the engine and hopped out as LJ slid off her sunglasses and followed suit. She stretched and surveyed the scene before her.

Coby was laughing. She got set back down on the pavement after a bear hug from the police chief. She hit him good naturedly on the shoulder before turning to Clyde and slipping her arms around him.

LJ felt like she was imposing by watching. So she made straight for Grizzly, face feeling warm as she came to a stop before him. He was wearing a red flannel shirt and a black beanie. He looked like Paul Bunyan but... somehow he made it work. Not that anyone would judge his clothes when he was smiling like that. "Hey, darlin'," he said, all trace of weariness, and fearful focus gone. His eyes twinkled at her, filled with warmth. Grizzly was the warmest person she had ever known.

"Hey," she said, unable to refrain from grinning like a dork.

"So where are you girls off to?" he asked, hands in the pockets of his blue jeans.

"Minnesota," LJ said. "Dover, maybe. We're aiming for something without serial killers this time... mix it up a bit."

Grizzly laughed. "Good idea. Our jurisdiction doesn't quite extend to Minnesota."

LJ laughed and shifted her purse a bit, unsure of what to say. She was starting to realize she sucked at goodbyes.

"Oh!" He snapped his fingers in memory. "Hang on, I got something for you." He grinned, stepping back over to the door of the police cruiser.

"For me?" LJ smiled and tried to peer after him.

"A little bird told me you collected these… seems only right you have one from here," Grizzly said with a smirk. He reached into the cruiser and pulled out a fuzzy brown bear. It wore a small jacket with a W stitched on the front.

LJ felt her throat constrict tightly as she took the bear from him. "…Oh. Thank… thank you," she said, looking down at the soft fuzzy creature in her hands. She felt the tip of her nose start to sting. She quickly looked up, blinked rapidly and smiled at him. "For everything," she whispered.

The large man smiled at her, his broad, beaming smile. "Nah, darlin', thank you. You ladies are the reason we were able to solve these cases," he said. He placed a hand on her shoulder and before it fully registered what she was doing, she stepped forward and hugged him tightly, the stuffed bear squished between them.

He wrapped his large arms around her and rested his chin on the top of her head for a moment. "Don't you go forgetting us now," Grizzly murmured, before she pulled away. LJ swiped at her eyes quickly and composed herself.

"Well," she said, clearing her throat and turning to Clyde and Coby, who were talking quietly and holding hands. "I suppose," she said pointedly to Coby.

Coby leaned up on her tiptoes and kissed Clyde on the cheek. His grip tightened on her hands before she pulled away with a smile. She turned and walked to the car, slipped in and started up the engine.

LJ watched her before she stepped forward and held out a hand to Clyde who was still looking at Coby. "Thank you." She smiled softly as he turned his attention to her and shook her hand with a small smile on his face. She had no idea how to communicate her thankfulness for saving her best friend's life… but she knew she didn't have to.

Clyde looked her in the eye and LJ noticed for the first time he didn't seem nervous. "Come back sometime."

LJ smiled and nodded before adjusting her bag on her shoulder. She walked over to the car, got into the passenger side and buckled her seatbelt. She took a breath and looked down at the bear still clutched in her hands as they pulled away.

Coby glanced over at the stuffed animal in her lap and smiled. "Oh hey! He found one! Aw look, it's a *grizzly* bear, that's so cute."

LJ looked in the rearview mirror to see Grizzly and Clyde waving and the lump rose back in her throat. She forced her eyes to the bear in her lap, willing the water levels to stop rising in her eyes.

She hugged the bear to her chest and closed her eyes. She tried to ignore the string wrapped around her heart, pulling tighter as they drove away from the small town. Away from the police chief as big as a bear who's heart was bigger. Away from the officer whose love-struck expression made her feel guilty, while at the same time reflected exactly what she was feeling. She tried to think of something, anything else. To focus on the new town, on the work that lay before them. But she couldn't. A tear slipped past her lashes, then another, and another and then against all her efforts, a sob escaped.

Coby looked over at her, horrified. "What's the matter? It's a bear LJ, that's supposed to make you *happy*, not –"

"Coby, just…" She hiccupped. "Stop the car."

Acknowledgements:

We would like to send out huge thank yous to the wonderful people who helped make this book possible.

Ashley's parents, who shared a very sad, first-draft manuscript and somehow managed to make sense of it.

Lydia's parents, who *scowled* over it in multiple forms, multiple times.

Our dear editor Mevia... Lydia's cousin... who fervently marked up her copy with a red pen and doodles, while watching Spongebob and lounging on the beach in Hawaii.

All the siblings, roommates, friends, extended family, co-workers and acquaintances who gave encouragement, expressed interest, and were kind enough to pester us about keeping our noses to the grindstone.

This book would not be here without your support, the grace of God, and Andrew Lincoln.

And last but not least, thank you to everyone who has picked this book up and read it. You are bringing life to the characters we love so much, and we are so excited to share them with you.

Made in the USA
Monee, IL
20 November 2024

69637554R00233